MARION ZIMMER BRADLEY'S
SWORD AND SORCERESS XXIV

Edited by Elisabeth Waters

Cover Painting:
"Captain of the Guard," Copyright © 2009 by Ahyicodae.

Cover Design Copyright © 2009 by Vera Nazarian

ISBN-13: 978-1-60762-048-8
ISBN-10: 1-60762-048-0

FIRST EDITION
Trade Paperback Edition

November 15, 2009

A Publication of
Norilana Books
P. O. Box 2188
Winnetka, CA 91396
www.norilana.com

Printed in the United States of America

Original Anthologies from Norilana Books

Clockwork Phoenix

Clockwork Phoenix 2

Lace and Blade

Lace and Blade 2

Marion Zimmer Bradley's Sword and Sorceress XXII

Marion Zimmer Bradley's Sword and Sorceress XXIII

Warrior Wisewoman

Warrior Wisewoman 2

Under the Rose

Sky Whales and Other Wonders *(forthcoming)*

Clothesline World *(forthcoming)*

Scheherazade's Facade *(forthcoming)*

The Ladies of Trade Town *(forthcoming)*

Marion Zimmer Bradley's Sword and Sorceress XXIV

Norilana Books

Fantasy

www.norilana.com

Marion Zimmer Bradley's

Sword
and
Sorceress

XXIV

Edited by

Elisabeth Waters

CONTENTS

INTRODUCTION

by Elisabeth Waters

In 1983, Marion Zimmer Bradley wrote in the introduction to the first Sword and Sorceress anthology:

"Valor has neither race nor color—nor does it have gender. . . . That I have chosen stories about both men and women, and written by both men and women, is, I hope, a sign of the times, and a hopeful outlook for the future of heroic fiction. And, since life always imitates art, it may be a heroic sign for the future of both women and men. Anyone can write male sexist fiction . . ."

It has now been 25 years since the first volume of SWORD & SORCERESS was published. The slush pile still demonstrates that anyone can write male sexist fiction—I rejected quite a bit of it this year. I can frequently tell the author's gender without looking at the byline simply by noting how the first female character is described. If the emphasis is on the length or shape of her legs, her long flowing hair, or the size of her breasts—or, worse yet, a totally unrealistic idea of how her breasts hold up a strapless gown (in normal gravity, they don't)—the author is probably male. There are female writers who objectify men the same way, so perhaps we've progressed from "anyone can write male sexist fiction" to "anyone can write sexist fiction." One could call this progress, but I'm not certain that I do.

As for life imitating art, progress is mixed there as well. As I write this, it is June 2009. Next month confirmation hearings will begin for a Federal judge who has been nominated to fill a vacancy on the Supreme Court. Despite Marion's saying in 1985 that she didn't want any more stories of the "you can't be a <insert profession here> because you're a girl" type, there are *still* talk-show hosts who are making tasteless remarks about Judge Sotomayor's gender and biology. Most people are ignoring them, but I have yet to hear anyone say that these men are totally out of line or that their comments are unacceptable. Meanwhile sex has become so pervasive on television that the only shows I've seen lately without commercials for 'male enhancement' products are on the Disney Channel.

It is quite true that valor has no gender. Female members of the armed forces are earning combat medals, despite the fact that they are not supposed to be in combat. Nuns go to places that are both politically unstable and naturally dangerous. Here's an example from a blog posted earlier this year: "After Mass we visited the cemetery within the grounds to pay our respects to the first 3 Mercy sisters who died in Kenya. As an added treat I got to see the grave of the sister who died from a hunting spider bite 18 months ago."

Heroism is not confined to men, and I suspect that it never was. We just need to remind the world of this, and I hope that this volume of SWORD & SORCERESS will do just that.

THE CASKET OF BRASS

by Deborah J. Ross

In Shakespeare's tragedy, Hamlet's dilemma hinges on whether the Ghost is telling the truth, whether dreams are more real than duty. Here, Deborah J. Ross takes inspiration from both HAMLET and THE PRISONER OF ZENDA, and spins them into a tale set in a world richly evocative of the Arabian Nights.

Deborah J. Ross began her writing career as Deborah Wheeler, with stories in the SWORD & SORCERESS series and the Darkover anthologies. Her story "Imperatrix," in the first SWORD & SORCERESS, was her first professional sale, making her one of "MZB's writers." As Deborah Wheeler, she also sold two science-fiction novels: JAYDIUM and NORTHLIGHT, as well as short stories to *Marion Zimmer Bradley's Fantasy Magazine, Asimov's, Fantasy & Science Fiction, Realms Of Fantasy*, SISTERS OF THE NIGHT, and STAR WARS: TALES FROM JABBA'S PALACE. Deborah was the person Marion chose to continue the Darkover series; she's written five novels so far, THE FALL OF NESKAYA, ZANDRU'S FORGE, A FLAME IN HALI, THE ALTON GIFT, and HASTUR LORD (based on a partial manuscript begun by Marion and forthcoming in 2010 from DAW). She is the editor of the acclaimed fantasy series, LACE AND BLADE. Deborah lives in a redwood forest with her husband, writer Dave Trowbridge, three cats, and a German Shepherd Dog. In between writing, she has worked as a medical assistant to a cardiologist, lived in France, studied Hebrew and piano, and revived an elementary school library. She has been active in the women's martial arts network and has spent over 25 years studying kung fu san soo. In her spare time, she knits for "afghans for Afghans" and the Mother Bear Project (teddy bears for children in Africa orphaned by AIDS).

A breathless spring twilight crept across the palace on the hill. Even the twin rivers that nourished Kharazand, City of a Thousand Gardens, flowed gently, imbued with an eerie, somber calm. The twin domes of the royal palace glimmered in shades of pearl and silver.

Hoofbeats fractured the approaching night. Iron sparked on paving stones. Five riders raced from the city gates toward the palace. The leading horse shone like marble, its tail a river of cloud. Its rider was small and wiry beneath a flowing hooded cloak. Four stouter animals followed. They pounded up the tree-lined avenue beside the long, slender mirrored pools. Guards barred their path, scimitars drawn. At the sight of the lead rider, they bowed and stepped back.

The riders clattered to a halt before the formal entrance to the palace, spiral columns framing marble stairs. The lead rider jumped lightly to the ground. Grooms and servants, a dozen at least, rushed forward. The rider shoved back the hood of the cloak, revealing a woman's delicate features, tilted eyes beneath sweeping brows set in honey-gold skin. Her blue-black hair had been twisted into a simple knot, and over her riding trousers, she wore a scholar's robe of thick undyed cotton. Her sole weapon was a dagger at her belt.

She handed the reins of the gray horse to the head groom. "Give the horses a little water now, but only a few sips." Her voice was throaty with the strain of a long, exhausting ride. "Then walk them until they're dry."

The young woman rushed up the stairs, her escort at her heels. Her riding boots rang on the smooth stone of the stairs. She burst through the elaborately-carved double doors before the attendants could open them for her. The senior steward rushed forward, trailing a handful of assistants. She remembered him, an honest man of merit and industry. In the years of her absence, his beard had gone white and wispy, and the body beneath the modestly ornamented robe was gaunt with age.

"Lady—"

"My grandmother?" she cut him off, not slacking her pace.

The steward raised his hands in reassurance. "Still alive, by the grace of the Infinite. Her physician tends her even now. Your uncle, the Most Wise Regent, has been apprized of your return and has bidden me to—"

His voice faltered as she glared at him.

"—to bring you to him," the steward finished uncertainly. "If it is your pleasure."

"It is my pleasure," she repeated the phrase, but without any malice, for the steward could not be blamed for the situation or her own temper, "to see my grandmother while I still can."

The steward's reply was cut short by the arrival of a second young woman, this one dressed in a sleeveless vest encrusted with pearls and rubies, and loose trousers of crimson silk gathered around her delicate ankles. Strings of tiny silver bells chimed from her wrists and earlobes. Veils fluttered from the elaborate curls on top of her head. She glided along the carpeted hall, and half a dozen ladies, dressed in more subdued colors, followed a pace behind.

"Maridah!" the young woman exclaimed. "You've returned! So suddenly! And without sending word so that a proper reception might be prepared for you!"

Maridah forced herself to stand still long enough to greet her cousin. They bowed and kissed each another's palms, according to custom.

"Hadidjah, I am pleased to see you," Maridah said, "but I cannot linger. Grandmother—"

Hadidjah's eyes, a beautiful hazel that contrasted with her golden skin, betrayed no alarm. "She is not well, but her health has never been good since you left us for Samarkhand.

You need not have interrupted your studies to rush home so precipitously."

She touched Maridah's cheek with one hand, her fingertips scented with rosewater and cloves. "I cannot say I am sorry. How I have missed you! Come now, you must bathe and put on something decent. Then I will take you to my father so that he may set your mind at rest. Tomorrow, we will feast in your honor."

Maridah wavered on her feet. Her muscles ached and her stomach had long since hardened into a knot of hunger. She saw herself reflected in her cousin's eyes, unkempt and filthy. Doubtless, she smelled of horse and sweat. She could not possibly appear in court with her hair in such disarray, wearing the same shapeless robe of the most lowly student.

She shook her head to clear her senses. Had her years of study, in a community where ideas meant more than titles or wealth, meant so little that she would throw all away at a word? She would remain as she was, dirty boots and all.

"*You* may not be concerned about Grandmother's health," she said with more harshness than she intended, "but *I* will not rest until I see her for myself." Freeing herself from her cousin's grasp, she pivoted to go.

"But—but my father—" Hadidjah stammered. "He expects to see you without delay!"

A sudden glint of mischief caught Maridah. Unfastening the clasp of her riding cloak, she tossed it to her cousin. "My uncle will have to be satisfied with *that*."

She did not stay to see Hadidjah's reaction.

◌ଔଏଊ

As Maridah hurried toward the long wing of royal family apartments, the pearly radiance of the twilight thickened into shadow. An archway brought her to an interior corridor, carpeted in arabesques of intertwined vines. Her escort, who had been her mother's sworn men before they became her own, followed her like sight-hounds. Palace attendants bowed low as they passed.

Grandmother's chambers were the oldest in the wing. In entering them, Maridah always had the sense of moving from one world to another, penetrating into the heart of a mystery. The outer room was ordinary enough, with low benches for outdoor shoes. The act of removing her boots, with all the dirt of the trail, and pulling on the slippers of soft leather stitched in designs of phoenixes locked in combat with winged serpents, was part of the process of leaving the outer world behind and entering into an enchanted realm.

The inner wall had been painted as a forest, a profusion of branches and greenery. Birds nested in the leafy clusters beside other creatures, some of them very strange. The artist had rendered the mural so beautifully, the tiny blue *djinni* were as lifelike as the hunting falcon or the cowering hare.

Beyond the forest wall, through the door of carved ebony, the noises of the rest of the palace fell away. The sitting room resembled a garden, with rows of flowering jasmine and a fountain of pink marble, carved with winged fishes and river *peris* plucking their harps. In the day, light streamed through the teardrop-shaped windows. Now, the room was filled with the same fading, silvery-pearl luminescence as the outer grounds.

From the garden room, doors led to either side, presenting a choice between the scented darkness of Grandmother's personal chambers or the even more enchanting realm of her workroom.

Entering Grandmother's bedroom was like plunging into a cavern. Once Maridah had asked Grandmother why there were no windows, and the old woman had laughed and said there was more than enough light in the garden room.

Maridah paused as the door closed behind her. Candles had been lit, a row of flickering brilliance. The royal physician, an elderly Persian who had always been kind to Maridah, hovered over the bed.

Drawing in a breath, Maridah caught a riot of odors, the smells of medicines and herbs, the smoky tinge of candle wax, the sandalwood that always clung to her grandmother's clothing. And underneath, the metallic scent she always associated with her grandmother's magic.

Light fell across the physician's face as he came forward to kiss Maridah's palm. The wispy hairs of his beard tickled her skin. He lifted his eyes, bright with age and unspilled grief. "By the grace of the Infinite, you have come in time."

In time. Maridah dared to breathe. "How does she?"

"Leave us," the voice coming from the bed was almost a croak. Maridah hardly recognized it.

"Only for a moment," the physician warned.

Grandmother's face gleamed like old, cracked ivory in the light of the candles. The room seemed unnaturally still. Then Maridah realized there was no music. Her grandmother always had at least one musician about her, as she loved the soft sounds of *oud* and flute.

"My friend." Grandmother reached out her hand, spidery in the flickering light. The physician grasped it. "There is nothing more you can do . . . for me."

The old man bent his head, kissed her palm, and departed. Maridah knelt at the bedside and took her grandmother's hand. The skin felt cool and brittle; the nails had never seemed so hard. Maridah's breath caught in her throat.

"And you," the old woman whispered, "you I will miss most of all."

"No! You must use your enchantments to save your life!"

Grandmother turned on her pillow so that the light filled all the hollows of her skull. "I have." Pause, breath.

Maridah's stomach turned cold. In the back of her mind, a thought curled like a wisp of poisoned smoke. *When she dies, I must take the throne as Princess of Kharazand.*

"Remember. Everything."

"I will."

She would never forget the long sunlit afternoons, playing in the workroom, handling the things that even then she knew were not toys: the wonderful carved horses that would, at the turn of a peg near the saddle, rise into the air, carrying their soldier riders, the balls that gave off colored lights as they spun, the bird of silver, the dagger that would cry out if anyone but Grandmother touched its jeweled sheath. . . .

"In the stronghold. A casket. Of brass."

Maridah nodded. She had glimpsed it, as long as a child's forearm and half again as wide, the worn patterns glimmering in the shadows. Something about the box had drawn her, a message hidden in the calligraphy of the intertwining arabesques.

"Shall I bring it to you?" she asked.

"Safe. Guard."

Maridah felt a new expectancy in the air, an alteration in the quality of the light. Grandmother was asking her to do something more than simply keep the old box in a safe place. An almost holy stillness hung in the room, like the temple on the morning her mother, who was to have been the next Princess, had died. Maridah had been up all night, fasting and praying, willing to bargain away everything she owned if only her mother might recover. She'd been at the very extremity of hope, for Grandmother had not returned from a long trip East and the court physicians had said there was nothing more to be done.

And the air had shifted, even as it shifted now, with a welling pressure, an imminence. . . .

"It will be kept safe." Maridah did not know exactly what she was promising, but she spoke the words like a vow.

"Ah." Thin fingers brushed the back of Maridah's hands. A sigh like a whisper: "Then I have taught you well."

Maridah opened her mouth to ask what it was that Grandmother had taught her, but the air shifted once more, a lightening of that immense weight. The candle light wavered.

Voices broke in upon the stillness, men arguing at the outer door. Maridah recognized the old physician and her own escort, their voices in protest.

"Stand aside!" another man shouted.

Then came her uncle's voice, lower in pitch, calm. She could not make out the words.

"Mari—" Grandmother roused. Brittle fire flared behind her words. "Leave the box. Take what lies within. It must not fall into any hands but yours. Do you understand?"

"You mean, the contents are for the Princess alone."

A mute gesture of denial. "What lies within . . . *makes* the Princess. Yussuf searched . . . when your mother died. He will . . . search again."

My uncle wants the throne? Maridah could not think straight. How could he aspire to such power? Even if he were not a man, he had no royal lineage; his only claim was his marriage to Maridah's mother's younger sister.

"Not for himself," Grandmother gasped.

Maridah could not breathe. Hadidjah, who could claim rightful lineage by blood. Hadidjah, who had always done her father's bidding.

"Go. Quickly—through the door behind the ironwood screen."

The shouting intensified. Maridah could not hear the clash of steel, but she sensed the reek of adrenaline.

Maridah brushed her lips over her grandmother's forehead. The skin was dry, like dusty silk. Then, under the lash of a terror she had never felt before, she raced from the bedchamber.

The workroom was filled with shelves of scrolls, bottles of alchemical reagents, bars of sealing lead, bins of powdered dragon's bone and whale horn, and telescopes and astrolabes in their wooden holders. The stronghold itself was no more than a cavity in the inner wall, covered over with a plain wooden panel. Maridah felt a faint prickle as she touched the panel and her fingertips found the indentation. She held it fast, as Grandmother had taught her. It took no magic to open the panel, only a steady hand. A thief would draw back at the shock and then burst into flames.

The prickling subsided. Maridah pushed the panel aside and reached inside. Her fingers closed around something long and cylindrical, then another. She took out two scrolls wrapped in heavy silk. Next came a small carved cube, apparently a solid piece of rosy quartz. This, too, she laid aside.

The brass casket was about two hands'-span long and half again as wide, its edges sealed with a ribbon of lead. On one side, the lead widened into a circle on which was impressed a seal. The faint coppery tang of Grandmother's enchantments clung to it.

Within the casket, each in a separate velvet-lined compartment, lay the wonderful things she knew so well: the ball of flashing jewels, the top that never stopped spinning until commanded, the horse on wheels that shook its tail.

The horse's wooden body had gone velvety with age. The tail had been made from real horse hairs, black and gray. For some reason, the black hairs had broken off near the base so that only a few long gray ones remained. A rhyme went with the horse, one Grandmother had made Maridah learn by heart:

> *I will carry you*
> *Wherever you truly wish to go,*
> *To master me, you must first master your heart.*

Maridah slipped the horse and the ball into a pocket of her scholar's robe, beside the folded paper for taking notes, a wrapped length of charcoal, two handkerchiefs, and a flint. The other pocket, equally capacious, held a few coins, a single dried fig, and a little folding knife.

Smiling at her scholarly provisions, she turned her attention to the top. It was painted in a harlequin pattern of yellow and blue, and felt warm to her touch, humming slightly as if urging her to pick it up.

Underneath the top, she found a wand of yellowed ivory about twice the length of her hand. Delicate carvings curled like vines around it, but otherwise it looked quite ordinary.

When she reached for the wand, sparks erupted from both ends. Fire lanced up her fingers, sending the muscles of her arm into spasm. Her hand jerked away of its own accord. Sweating and gulping air, she wrapped it in her second-best handkerchief and slid it and the top in the other pocket.

The voices came again, accompanied by crashing sounds. Cursing the impulse that had caused her to linger, Maridah searched for the ironwood screen. She found it, deep in the shadows, leaning against one wall. She tilted it aside to discover a door, even as Grandmother had said, although it looked to be no more than a tracery of fine lines. If she had not been searching, she might not have recognized it.

How was she to get through? She saw neither hinge nor latch.

Something bumped her hip, as if she had put a live hedgehog into her pocket. Puzzled, she drew out the ball. The gems on its surface sparkled with inner fire. Brighter and brighter they flashed, bringing tears to Maridah's eyes. The multi-hued brilliance took on a strange density. The ball grew so heavy, Maridah could barely hold it aloft.

The door creaked open, as if the light from the ball had pushed it ajar. As Maridah slipped through, the ball's radiance diminished but did not go out. The door slid closed behind her.

Holding the ball aloft, Maridah proceeded down the stairs. A delicious sense of adventure filled her. As a child, she'd often evaded her tutors and gone exploring. Her grandmother had secretly encouraged it. Maridah loved exploring the network of corridors, cellars, and dank holes that sent shivers down the back of her neck. Some of these, it was said, were *donjeons* for the keeping of noble prisoners.

The passage twisted, ever descending. At last, she caught sight of a door, its plain wood somehow preserved from the damp. In the chamber beyond, she found a tiny garden, arched over with a dome like frosted glass and filled with pale, diffuse light. She replaced the ball in her pocket.

Heat lay thick and expectant over the dustless benches. Not a fly buzzed, not a leaf of the trellised roses quivered, and not a single fallen twig marred the whiteness of the paving stones.

In the center stood a statue of a young man of transcendent beauty, naked to the hips. His head was tilted to reveal the perfect grace of his neck. His hands hung at his sides, wrought in stone that had the satiny sheen of marble and the warm hue of flesh. The flowing muscles of his torso ended in a block of uncut stone in place of legs.

Maridah, caught by the masterful rendering of the sculpture, came closer. The air shimmered in front of her eyes, like a mirage, so that the statue seemed to quiver and draw a breath.

She sat down on the nearest bench and rubbed her eyes. Heat seeped along her bones, carrying a sweet, heavy lethargy like opium smoke.

She was weary, so weary. She rested her face in her hands and closed her eyes. Her shoulder and neck muscles ached.

Gradually, Maridah became aware of a noise like creaking leather, faint but distinct. She dropped her hands. The statue—surely its arms had been at its sides, fingers loose, wrists curved slightly inward, as if cradling something delicate. Now one of the statue's arms was raised, the bend of the elbow framing its head.

The rose vines quivered, releasing a burst of scent. The statue took a deep, shuddering breath.

Maridah scrambled to her feet.

The statue took another unmistakable breath . . . and groaned. Maridah's alarm vanished at the piteous sound. Moving closer, she saw a tear slip down the statue's cheek.

The statue looked at Maridah. The eyes were creamy, unmarked by any color, not even a pupil. Their blankness gave the statue a quizzical expression, as if it were astonished to find someone else in its private garden.

Maridah opened her mouth, but before she could draw breath, the statue spoke.

"Know, O Princess of a noble race, that I was once as you are. As you will soon become." The statue blinked and two more tears dripped down its face.

This was such an extraordinary way of beginning a conversation, even in the flowery language used at court, and even in a place as full of magic as this garden, that Maridah could only stand and gape. Her mind bubbled with the tales she'd loved as a child, of spells woven and broken, dragons slain, evil *djinni* defeated, sorcerers challenged.

"Are you under an enchantment?" she ventured. "Can I—is there some way you can be freed?"

"Not until the seas run dry and the last dragon falls from the heavens." The statue raised its hands and let them fall, as if hope were too great a burden. "She who is my torment and my delight is as ageless as the sky."

The frosted-glass ceiling darkened, as if a shadow had suddenly swept in front of the invisible light source. The garden turned chill.

The statue glanced upward, its beautiful face distorted with anguish. It flung one arm over its face and cried like a stricken deer.

"What is it?"

"The hour of my punishment—Ah! Not yet!"

The light steadied as the shadow passed.

"For a hundred years," the statue said, regaining its composure, "a great sorceress of old, she who carried me off on my wedding night and imprisoned me in this manner, has visited me daily. She laughs as her scorpions dig out my heart."

"Oh, how terrible!" Maridah exclaimed. "This sorceress must be wicked, indeed! Why would she do such a thing? What does she desire of it, beyond to see you in agony?"

The statue threw his head back. Shudders rippled through his graceful, muscled torso. "Ah! Will I never be free of her?"

Maridah let the question go unanswered, for she began to suspect that if this statue was indeed all that was left of a young bridegroom, he was no longer entirely sane. Tales rose to her memory, poems exalting forbidden liaisons and jealous lovers.

"Perhaps," she said in a calmer tone, "there is something this sorceress wants. She didn't by any chance object to your choice of bride?"

"I've done nothing, I tell you—nothing!" He broke off as the garden shivered as if seized by a sudden gale. "Quickly, you must depart or be trapped here with me! Remember me when you think upon your own fate!"

My own—Was she, too, in danger of some evil enchantment?

The light in the garden dimmed again. A blast of cold air buffeted Maridah, almost knocking her off her feet. She stumbled backward under its impact. Her eyes watered, tears blurred her vision, and her long hair, freed from its scholar's knot, blew across her face.

The next moment, the wind was gone as if it had never existed. The dome overhead brightened slowly and steadily. Around her, the garden lay as eerily still as before. The statue, too, was motionless, frozen in the same attitude in which she had first seen it. Beautiful as it was, it now seemed cold and sterile, all emotion fled along with its semblance of life.

Beyond the statue, in the far wall of the garden, a door opened. Blue and silver light silhouetted the figure that stood there.

One of Maridah's hands went automatically to her dagger. The hilt felt hot, as it did when Grandmother worked her enchantments. She faced the figure squarely. It was unmistakably female, dressed in a loose, gauzy robe that did not disguise the slender waist, strong legs, and full breasts. In one hand, the woman carried a long staff set with crystals.

The woman moved into the garden, bringing with her the scents of sandalwood and copper. As she approached, the overhead light fell upon her features. Clear dark eyes regarded Maridah from a face as unwrinkled and golden as her own. Rose-petal lips curved into a smile.

"Zunayna's grand-daughter! What a pleasure to see you!" The voice was sweet and light, untroubled.

The sorceress, smiling more broadly at Maridah's expression of shock, turned briefly to the statue and gestured with her staff. The statue began writhing, as if in unspeakable agony, but no sounds issued from its mouth.

"Sit by me," the sorceress said, leading the way to a bench. "Tell me how you found my garden."

Maridah followed a pace behind, but would not sit. "Why should I not strike off your head for your evil ways!"

"'Evil ways'?" One slender eyebrow arched upward. The sorceress appeared to be trying not to laugh.

Glaring, Maridah tightened her grip on her dagger. "You compound your own wickedness by mocking the suffering of your victim."

"Which story did he tell you, I wonder? The curse of the three brothers? Or the punishment for disturbing the tomb of the ancient king of the river?"

Suddenly feeling very foolish, Maridah admitted, "He said you carried him off on his wedding night."

The sorceress looked pleased. "He's making good progress. As you see."

The statue was still moving, eyes closed, body twisting and undulating, arms moving as if to music. For a moment, Maridah imagined a smile playing across the stone lips.

"What you see," the sorceress said after a moment, "has all the appearance of a man being turned into stone, but is in fact quite the opposite, as are so many things in the world. This virtuous stone is learning how to be a man, to experience a man's longing and passions, to live a man's history. He undertakes this of his own desire."

Maridah wondered what virtue a stone could have, or why it would want to undergo the transformation into mortality. "So the tale he told me—is not true?"

The sorceress pursed her lips, as if considering the nature of truth. "It is a thing that may come to pass, or not. I cannot tell."

Maridah lowered herself to the bench beside the sorceress. "I do not know what to think. I suspected his tale, but I thought you might be a spurned lover bent on revenge."

Merriment rang out like the sparkling of the tiny crystals in the sorceress's staff. "I should not laugh at you, my dear. It is not your fault if your head has been so filled with such romantic stuff, that you cannot tell one illusion from another."

Maridah felt unreasonably irritated. She ought not to be wasting time in conversation, when her uncle and his men might be hard on her heels.

"You are as safe here as anywhere," the sorceress reassured her. "Zunayna—who was my student, in case you ask—would not have sent you to me otherwise."

"My uncle, the Regent, wants to seize the throne. Or rule through my cousin, which amounts to the same thing."

Again, that arch of eyebrow and fleeting smile. "I suppose it does."

"You say that as if it does not matter!" Maridah made no attempt to rein in her temper. "Why would Grandmother have me safeguard the contents of the brass casket if she did not fear what my uncle would do with them?"

All trace of amusement vanished from the features of the sorceress. "The brass casket? You have taken what lies within?"

Maridah scrambled to her feet, heart pounding. Had she escaped the schemes of her uncle, only to fall into the hands of someone far more ambitious and dangerous? She could not best this slight, young-looking woman, even if she had a dozen spears and scimitars instead of one small dagger. Nor would escape be easy.

Perhaps one of the enchanted toys . . . The horse, to carry her far away . . . back to Samarkhand. To lose herself once again in books and stories . . .

"Beware, my child, for the world is far stranger than anything your professors dreamed of!" With deliberate care, the sorceress laid her staff on the pavement. "I do not expect you to believe me, but I have no desire for what you carry in the pockets of your scholar's robes. I have enough magical troubles without seeking out more. For the sake of your grandmother and the love I will always bear her, I will help you."

Caught between anger and confusion, Maridah forced herself to consider her situation. She could not escape from the garden on her own . . . and the sorceress had known her grandmother's name . . . and the statue was now swaying gently, head tilted back and to one side, a hint of color across his torso and cheeks. He certainly did not look as if he were in pain, quite the opposite.

"I will show them to you, but if you attempt to seize or even touch them, I will use this." Maridah brandished her dagger.

The sorceress managed not to smile.

The ball had gone dark, all its brilliance extinguished, but the top hummed slightly as Maridah placed it on the bench. She set the horse down on its wooden wheels. The wand was still wrapped in her second-best handkerchief.

The sorceress bent over the toys but made no attempt to touch them. "The ball was bespelled to shed its light upon that which is hidden, but I do not think you will be able to use it in that way a second time. This top, when sent spinning, will turn you around to the place to which you least desire to return."

Something in the sorceress's tone, her confidence, her turn of phrase, reminded Maridah so strongly of her grandmother that she no longer doubted the two had known one another.

"This fine little steed, on the other hand, will take you far away, but only if it is your heart's true desire." Dark eyes regarded Maridah levelly, as if cautioning her to use great care in exercising that desire.

"What have we here?" The sorceress pointed to the wrapped bundle.

Being careful not to touch it with her bare fingers, Maridah unwrapped the wand. "I think this is what my uncle is searching for, what my grandmother wanted me to keep safe from him."

"To she who holds it rightly, it grants the power to keep the city safe and prosperous. Certainly, your uncle cannot use it. And it seems you do not wish to."

"I *must* take it up," Maridah said wearily. If she had truly wanted to rule, as her grandmother had, as her mother might have, would the wand have stung her with sparks? Or would the pain have paled as a small price for her heart's desire?

Maridah rewrapped the wand and settled it in her pocket. The ball followed.

"Yes, that seems as good a use for your handkerchief as any," the sorceress replied obliquely. "But the question is, will you then choose the top to spin you back to the palace, or the horse to carry you to Samarkhand?"

Maridah picked up the top and the horse, one in each hand, weighing them.

"I will carry you," the horse sang in her mind,

"Wherever you truly wish to go,

To master me, you must first master your heart."

When she looked up, the sorceress was gone. An empty dais stood where the statue had once been. All about her, rose petals drifted to the ground. Little currents of air carried their sweet, quickly fading scent.

She put one of the objects in her pocket, folded her hands around the other, closed her eyes, and wished . . .

🙰❦🙵

. . . and found herself in the grand audience chamber of the palace, surrounded by courtiers and facing the empty throne. She stood on the intricate mosaic floor, depicting the city, the royal lineage, and the power of the heavens. To her surprise, she noticed a little horse, a ball, and a top, nestled among the heroic figures. Almost immediately, cries of surprise filled the chamber. Someone shouted for order.

"It is Lady Maridah, come back to us!"

For an instant, Maridah saw herself reflected in their astonishment, her hair wild and loose about her shoulders, wearing a scholar's gown, hardly suitable attire for such a place. The courtiers shimmered in their silks and jewels. Some she remembered from her time at court before Samarkhand, but others were strangers. Something was subtly wrong. She saw no trace of mourning, which meant Grandmother must still be alive. Surely the steward who had greeted her upon her return had not been so white of beard, nor so frail.

"My uncle!" she called. "Where is Yussuf the Regent?"

The courtiers and nobles drew back. A man rose from the chair to the left of the throne. At first, Maridah did not recognize him, he seemed so thin and somber, so worn with care. Beneath the robe of gray-figured silk and the heavy gold-link collar, his body seemed to have shrunk. The bones of his skull stood out, and his skin had turned sallow, his eyes red-rimmed.

From the other side of the throne, a woman emerged to stand at his side. She, too, was dressed in silks of muted hue. She wore no jewelry except a coronet bearing a single blue topaz. When her gaze lit upon Maridah, her countenance brightened. She moved forward, smiling.

"Maridah! Returned to us after all these years!" Hadidjah seized Maridah's hands, and kissed them formally. "I never believed you were dead. You look so young, not a hair different from the day you disappeared! Have you freed yourself from an evil enchantment? Is that how you have come back to us?"

"I—I don't understand." Maridah's thoughts whirled. "I have been gone no more than an hour or two. Is Grandmother still among us? Is that why no one is in mourning?"

"Come, my niece," Yussuf said, holding out one hand to her. "Let us speak of these things in private."

"Let us speak of them right now!" Maridah shot back. She had not returned to put herself in his power. "Right here!"

Yussuf and his daughter exchanged glances. Yussuf gestured to a man wearing the sash of a chief vizier. "Clear the chamber!"

Immediately, the guards who stood at the entrance escorted the courtiers from the room. When they were alone, Yussuf said, "It has been five years since Zunayna of the Blessed Memory departed our midst, and five years since you yourself vanished."

Five years! How was that possible? With magic, was anything impossible?

Oh, Grandmother . . .

Maridah shoved aside the pulse of grief. "And you, I suppose, have been ruling in the interim?"

Under the vitriol of her words, Yussuf paled but did not flinch. "I have been serving as Regent—"

"But he has not been ruling," Hadidjah said, her voice edged with steel.

"You? You dared to take my place?"

"Yes, I dared! What else could I have done? When you disappeared, there was no one else. No one to rally our people when raiders came swarming upriver. No one to negotiate trade agreements, to settle disputes and inheritances. No one to—"

"Do you challenge my right to rule?" Maridah faced her uncle.

"No, *I* do!" Hadidjah exclaimed. "My father would be happy to lay down the Regency, if only there were a rightful heir. He's old and sick, even a simpleton can see that! For the past five years, for good or ill, *I* have made those decisions. *I* have exercised that authority. I have made mistakes, and I have learned from them."

She paused, her breast heaving, and went on in a softer tone. "I have always loved you, my cousin, and I rejoice to see you whole, but I have no intention of stepping aside—throwing away everything for which my father and I have labored—for an inexperienced, irresponsible fledgling who has already abandoned this city and its people not once, but twice!"

Maridah glared at her uncle. "This is all your doing! Grandmother warned me of your ambition. If you cannot rule in your own right, you seek to do so through your daughter. I hear your words from her mouth!"

"You hear my own!" Hadidjah cried. "Oh, it is no use reasoning with her, Father. She has made you into a villain and me into your puppet, even as Grandmother did in her final illness."

She faced Maridah, her emotions once more under control. "Yours may be the stronger right by lineage, but I have the advantage of experience. I will not yield to any lesser claim. And when the wand of office is found, I will release my father from his burden."

"Then take it, if you dare!" Maridah reached into her pocket and drew out the wrapped wand. She unfolded the handkerchief, revealing the wand, which gleamed as if moist.

When Hadidjah reached out her hand, her father grabbed her wrist. "Wait, there must be a trick. Why else would Maridah take such care to prevent even a casual touch? See, even now she shields her own skin."

Hadidjah met Maridah's gaze with a troubled expression. "Would you truly seek to poison me? Slay me by treachery? Has your own ambition grown so vast? Have you no memory of the love we once shared? Does power mean more to you than friendship?"

Maridah opened her mouth to protest that they had never been so very dear to one another. Memories swept away her words, of playing together in the palace gardens, braiding each other's hair, giggling over the newest gossip and handsome visitors to court. She had thought Hadidjah lacking in seriousness, too vulnerable to her father's guidance, but never vicious.

More than that, did she herself want to rule? To forsake the world of stories and dreams?

"I touched it once," Maridah admitted, "and it pained me, but caused no lasting harm. Its power answers only to one who truly desires to keep the city safe and prosperous."

Hadidjah's rose-gold complexion paled. She reached trembling fingers toward the wand.

"Do not do this for me," Yussuf said. "I can manage for a while longer. And here is Maridah, come to take up her heritage."

Maridah saw tears glimmering in Hadidjah's eyes as her cousin shook her head. Before Hadidjah could touch the wand, Maridah grasped it in her free hand.

Fire jolted up her arm. Every nerve flared into white agony. Her throat clenched around her breath. Her back arched in spasm. Waves of pain shook her. All she had to do was to let go . . .

The wand clattered to the tiled floor.

Maridah bent over, gasping. Her vision blurred, crimson, as if her eyes had been washed in blood. A gentle touch steadied her. She inhaled her cousin's perfume, the scent of rosewater and cloves.

Maridah was still unable to speak, but could stand on her own, when Hadidjah released her. Slowly, with resolve taut in every line of her body, Hadidjah bent to pick up the wand.

Slim fingers closed around the ivory rod. For a moment, the delicate engravings shimmered. Then the light passed from them. Hadidjah straightened up. Trembling shook her body. She looked up, an unnatural brightness in her eyes. She opened her mouth as if to speak, but no words came.

Maridah found herself unexpectedly moved by the sight of Hadidjah, ashen and resolute. She could not imagine what her cousin must be suffering. Moving stiffly, for her muscles had not yet fully recovered, she fumbled for her handkerchief.

Hadidjah waved it away and clasped the wand against her body. The chamber, empty except for a guard at the doors, had fallen very still. Maridah could hear nothing above the rasp of her cousin's breathing and the thrumming of her own heart.

Color seeped out of Hadidjah's skin, her hair, her beautiful hazel eyes. For an instant, it seemed that she had become part of the wand. Ivory, once living but now with only the memory of that life. Enduring, enslaved. Glistening with magic as if with tears.

Yussuf covered his face with his hands, his shoulders shaking, making no sound.

Although the gesture brought her a sadness she could not explain, Maridah bowed to her new sovereign. "You are now the Princess of Khazarand, and so I will say to the whole world!"

L ater, much later, the two cousins stood on a balcony overlooking the twin rivers. Dusk perfumed the shadows as Khazarand's thousand gardens released the heat of the day. The moon, just past full, cast a softly golden light.

Maridah, still in her favored robe of soft cotton, her hair simply dressed, breathed in the lingering sweetness.

"You have not yet made your plans to return to Samarkhand," Hadidjah said.

"Not yet." Maridah still dreamed of Samarkhand and, sometimes, a statue who had perhaps become a man, who spun tales of wonder more real than the stones beneath her feet. A wooden horse waited to carry her to her heart's desire, if only she knew what that was.

"There is something I would ask you," Maridah said, "although you may think it presumptuous."

Hadidjah's smile was a ghost in the gathering dark. "Dearest cousin, we know each other too well for formal courtesies."

"Well, then. When you took up the wand—you saw what it did to me, and I had come here determined to take the throne. I never realized how much greater was your own desire. You were never ambitious, not in that way. I thought you content with pretty clothes and ardent suitors."

"Of which I have many, all of them interested in power," Hadidjah interjected. "I must marry and provide our city with an heir, but I will choose carefully. I did not pick up the wand in order to give away everything I worked so hard to achieve."

"Why, then? Why did you do it?"

"Did I have a choice? How else could I put forth a lawful claim to the throne? I took it up because there was no one else, and to spare my father."

Maridah nodded silently. Uncle Yussuf would not have lain down the Regency until Khazarand had a rightful Princess.

Now that Maridah had abdicated in Hadidjah's favor, the throne was secure.

"I saw what the wand did to you," Hadidjah went on. "I had not the slightest doubt it would bring me even greater pain." She paused, blinking hard.

From the way her cousin spoke, and the coiling silence that followed, Maridah knew the pain had not abated, but it was of the heart and spirit, not of the body. She said, "I cannot envy you."

"You need not." Hadidjah paused. "Did Grandmother ever tell you—do you know what the wand does? How it grants power?"

Maridah supposed the wand bestowed some exceptional degree of prosperity, health, good luck, or invincibility in battle.

"It reveals the truth," Hadidjah said quietly.

"Surely that's a good thing. To know when your adversaries or even your own advisors are lying."

"You may say so, you who have lived for your philosophy, who breathed in Grandmother's tales of enchantment as a fish breathes water. Such stories are beautiful and bewitching. One forgets that not every true thought or every true word, spoken in haste or anger, is kind."

In Maridah's sight, moonlight turned Hadidjah into a woman of silver-washed ivory. Maridah remembered the wetness of the wand, how it had appeared to weep. She thought of the statue, animated by passion. Even as the stone had come to life, life now seeped from Hadidjah's human flesh as ivory, beautiful and hard, took its place.

Maridah's heart shivered. Were they not two sides of the same hand, the dark moon and the light? Truth bound one with barbed chains, scouring away trust and love; the other was seduced by a world of easy dreams, of riddles that tantalized and intoxicated.

By the grace of the Infinite, what were stories *for*?

All her life, she had wandered through a world of stories. And what use had they been, except to make her entirely mistaken about her uncle, the sorceress, the statue? Even Hadidjah.

Even herself.

Yet . . . if stories had the power to give life to stone, to comfort a dying old woman, to ease the loneliness of a royal child, might they not also give life . . . and hope . . . to this woman she loved, who was even now turning into ivory?

Smiling, Maridah laid her hand upon her cousin's arm. "I think we have, between us, more than enough truth and more than enough dreams, for any one lifetime."

Together they went into the old work room, where the brass casket whispered poisoned secrets in the wavering candle light. Together, they opened it. The ball and the top were in their proper places, no longer inert but charged, waiting.

Together, they put away the ivory wand and the little wooden horse, closed the casket, and sealed it with molten lead.

Together, they placed it back in the stronghold.

The next morning, Hadidjah would sit upon the throne, judging with her own mind. And Maridah would enter Grandmother's chambers and throw open the doors to the clear light of day. She would study, as was her talent; she would tell all the stories she knew, not to insulate and cripple, but to bring life to the ivory statues of men's hearts.

I will carry you
Wherever you truly wish to go.

Hadidjah would dispense justice, and Maridah would spin out dreams, and together they would create such an age that there would be no end to the tales of wonder.

MERLIN'S CLUTTER

by Helen E. Davis

There's really nothing quite like life with a great wizard—unless it's life with a disorganized bibliophile or a creative genius. The day I first saw Marion's house, most of the floor was not visible. The library was about a foot deep in papers and fabric scraps (it doubled as the sewing room), and the memory of her office makes me shudder to this day. So I can truly empathize with the protagonist of this story. It's like being given the responsibility for a job without being given the authority necessary to do it.

Helen E. Davis grew up in Northern Louisiana, graduated from Oberlin College in Ohio, and lives in Dayton, Ohio. She is a housewife, a mother of two teenagers, and an occasional substitute teacher. This is her second professional sale.

Adele lay in bed, listening to her husband's footsteps as he walked out the front door. After the slam a delightful silence filled the cottage. *Now,* she thought, willing aged muscles to unknot, *Now I can get up.*

The wizard she had married promised her riches and eternal youth—then went and lost the damn stone. He was searching for it, he claimed, as he hurried out the door each day. When he returned, usually after dark, it was to eat his chilled supper and go straight to bed, or else to shut himself into his study for hours. Meanwhile, the years carried off her youth and with it, her strength.

Pulling her shawl over her thin shoulders, she pushed her feet into slippers. The bedroom was cold no matter the season. The central room was a little better, with a fresh built fire and early dawn sluicing through the windows. A table stood before the hearth, and on it lay the remains of the wizard's breakfast.

Adele's eyes narrowed. Their fight last night had been about the clutter in the house, with Himself screaming that he couldn't live in such a disorganized place, for he had not been able to find a book he wanted. From there he had yelled about the pots piled beside the sink (there were no nails on the walls to hang them) and the jars of canned food stacked against the far wall (there was still no pantry to put them in) and her knitting yarn tangled in the basket beside her chair (his cat would not believe that yarn was neither living nor a threat) and then a dozen things more minor than that.

Meanwhile, he left his dishes for her to pick up, his robes for her to put away, and his papers on any flat surface. She gathered a set which he had dropped on the counter the night before and saw the book he had been bellowing about beneath them.

She dropped the papers back on it.

Shuffling to the hearth, she swung the kettle over the flame. If the wizard wanted a clean house, she would give it to him. But she was starting with *his* clutter first.

ଔଔଔ

His always being gone bothered her the most. Day in, day out, half the nights, and almost every weekend, he was off on that damned sacred quest of his. There was always a library he had to visit, an old hermit he had to talk to, a new scrap heap he had to comb. Meanwhile, to her fell the daily cooking, gardening, and cleaning.

Where to start? she thought as she wiped gnarled hands on a threadbare apron. The door to his study caught her eye, standing ajar with a pile of paper slumping over the threshold. Every day it was worse. She was forbidden to enter his study, lest she disturb the powerful spells within—but anything which crept out, she reasoned, was hers to deal with. So she fetched two baskets: one for things which should be kept, and one for things which could fuel the fire. A bright fire would truly warm the place. Knees creaking, she knelt and gathered the papers.

The first was a hand-written receipt for two jars of dried newt eyes, a packet of powdered frog toes, and a bottle of seaweed jelly. When had he bought those things? She looked at the date, shuddered, and tossed it in the refuse basket.

There were other things, equally ancient. Such as a letter from a long-dead king, and another from his grandson offering safe passage through a war fought for reasons forgotten. There were several invitations to baptisms, coronations, and funerals, often of the same individual, and more than one unpaid bill. All this went into the refuse basket without a second glance. Correspondence deserved a second look, but most of it was over such trivial things as the price of tadpole tails. The more solid objects she set aside, such as the scarf embroidered with the queen's mark and the jeweled ring in the shape of a lion's head. They could be sold to buy wood when the paper ran out.

Beneath a mass of unmailed letters of recommendation, she found a stone bowl that was too large for the save basket. It was carved of rough grey stone flecked with black glass, but the inside curve was polished. It weighed so little that it seemed to float on air, and her aged arms lifted it easily. A faint warmth tingled her fingers. This, she knew, was the perfect bowl for making bread. Setting it aside, she returned to the paper pile.

The sorting was good for her fingers. Her fingers moved more nimbly as she worked, and the stabbing pain in the joints faded.

Her next find made her glad that she had decided to clear the pile today. It was an egg, twice as large as a duck's egg, with a grey, mottled shell. Addled and rotten. She set it carefully in the bowl, praying that it would not break before she could bury it in the compost heap.

When the refuse basket was filled, she rose on creaking knees and shuffled stiffly to the fire. The old papers tumbled into flames that flared with delicious warmth. For several minutes she stood there, savoring the heat, then turned back to the pile. Despite her work it seemed no smaller. With a sigh she picked up the bowl and set it on the table, so that neither she nor the cat would accidentally knock against it and crack the egg.

Odd, the old eggshell seemed almost white when set against the dark grey of the stone.

Back at the pile she sorted out a treasure map with *El Dorado* scribbled across the top and a scroll of spells tied with string. Hints were scribbled in the margins. The wizard's attempt to write *Spellcasting for Imbeciles,* she remembered. Just beneath it lay a collection of letters that discussed the various uses of Dragon's Blood. From the notes he had scribbled on these, it looked as if he might have been planning a second book.

Hidden treasure and book royalties. With those, perhaps, they could afford coal in the winter and a servant to help with the house. She set these things carefully to the side, planning to bring them out the next time he complained.

Beyond the doorway, the pile crouched like a lurking beast. Dark hollows that could have been eyes stared at her above a mouth-like pit. The jagged corners of papers formed teeth, and it had a red scarf for a tongue.

Adele quickly shook her head to dispel the vision.

When she rose to empty her trash basket a second time, she heard the pile avalanche across the doorway. No wonder it wasn't any smaller. Now one long arm of clutter reached toward the table while bits of paper fluttered across her bare floor. With a sigh she bent and picked up a receipt for a room full of straw and a spinning wheel.

Thankfully the fire was unknotting her old muscles. She moved almost as freely as a young girl.

Another avalanche, and the pile of paper and trinkets crossed half the room. Just beyond the threshold, a baked clay cup lay in a nest of old envelopes. Its plainness was belied by the foreign words carved beneath the lip, and the shining fingerprints pressed into the sides.

Suddenly angry, she kicked the clutter pile. Of all the stupid stunts Himself had pulled, this was the worst. Years he had spent on that bloody sacred quest, and the cup had been in his study the whole time! Well, she would show him. She would take the cup, put it on her counter, and present it to him the next time he complained. It was his clutter, not hers, which was making their life miserable. But when she was two steps from the door the pile slumped backwards, pulling the cup from her reach. Too angry to stop her foot nearly touched the threshold—

—a sharp crack sounded behind her.

Several musical pings followed, the barest of tunes. Adele turned slowly, and watched as pearl shards fell from the bowl. Tiny yellow wings flapped wetly, and a scaled amethyst head peeked over the rim. Yellow eyes blinked at her.

The egg had hatched a dragon.

It swung its head around to examine the room, then stopped at the fire. For a moment it stared at the flickering flames, then uncurled from the bowl and whipped across the table.

"No!" Adele jumped for the dragon but it was faster, and with little splutting sounds it crossed the floor and dived into the flames. She felt her heart catch, but then the little creature settled itself on a burning log and gazed out at her, content.

Flames within, flames without. It was happy in the fire.

But how had it hatched from a rotten egg?

She picked up the egg shell, as white as clean sand, and suddenly noticed two things. Her fingers curled around it without any pain or stiffness, and they were as straight as a young girl's. And the wizard's dirty spoon, which she had accidentally set the stone bowl on, now gleamed gold.

This was The Stone. It had also been in the wizard's clutter pile for years.

She glared at the mound of paper, and realized it was moving with a purpose. It slid across the floor as the arm rippled toward the table, toward the stone. Trying to take back the thing which had given it life.

She snatched up the bowl, then grabbed her broom with her free hand and swept it across the arm. Papers scattered, flying up as if caught in a whirlwind, then returned to the arm. Other loose papers rose from every surface and joined it, until the monster grew three legs and a thick torso.

She tried to sweep it into the fireplace. Some of the papers lit, catching the interest of the dragon, but others returned to the monster and formed two long whips. One wrapped around her broom, the other reached for her bowl. She dropped the one and grabbed the other to her chest, kicking a paper leg as she did so. But other than a few scattered letters, the blow did no good.

Splut, splut. The baby dragon, now out of the fire, caught the letters and blew sparks on them. It watched in fascination as they smoldered.

The front door, could she make it? She took a step but the monster flowed in front of her. She was pushed back to the sink, back to the corner where it could trap her, back to where her cast iron skillet was within reach. She whacked it hard across the monster's torso, sending papers flying.

Splut, whuff. Splut, whuff. Now the baby dragon was firing the papers in mid-air, and jumping on the flames when they fell. How much longer before the house caught on fire?

Could she fend off the paper monster even that long? She swung again, knocked out more papers, and saw with satisfaction that it was shrinking.

The door blew open, sending eddies through the paper-strewn wind. Himself stood there, mouth and eyes open at the sight. "Woman!" he finally bellowed. "What are you doing?"

The dragon noticed him. Splut, splut, whuff.

The wizard yelled as he beat out the flames on his robe, and the dragon darted back.

"Trying to clean up *your* mess!" she shouted and swung again. By now the baby dragon was occupied with the wizard's robes and the papers blew back, unharmed.

"My mess!" he retorted. "Why do you say *my* mess?"

"It crawled out of your study! Do something!"

"Did you enter my private sanctum? Did you break the ward of containment?"

"No! Now *do* something!" She knocked the head from the monster, and watched it reform.

"Oh, very well," he sighed, lifting his staff. "I banish you to . . ."

The paper monster split itself in half, revealing the clay cup inside.

Arching his eyebrows in surprise, the wizard stopped his spell and reached forward.

Instantly an arm of paper whipped from the torso and snatched away the staff. Himself blinked in surprise, and looked at his empty hand. "Perhaps that's where things have been disappearing to."

"I imagine so!" Adele fought furiously, but realized she was getting wedged tighter and tighter into her corner. The baby dragon had at least returned his attention to the paper monster, but was only watching in a thoughtful, crafty way. "Help me!"

The wizard scratched his beard. "I could summon the guild, they might have some ideas."

"I need help now!" She glared at him.

In that brief pause, the paper monster grabbed the frying pan and swallowed it. Another arm curled around her, and all she could do was kick and thrash. Already a second arm was reaching for her bowl. If it was this strong without the stone, what could it do in possession of it *and* loose from the study? One kick in the center, probably futile, sprayed out papers.

Splut, splut, whuff!

One of the monster's legs burst into flame. The squat head shifted to look down at the flickering tongues that danced from one curling, blackened edge to the next yellowed sheet. The arms beat at the flames, and caught fire themselves. Popping embers sent sparks higher into the body, seeding more fires, while a sheet of flame roared up one side.

As it listed to its weak side, its mouth gaped wide and smoke poured out.

Trinkets and coins dropped from the crimson-flecked ash, then larger objects: stoppered bottles, ash-trays, and an assortment of long-lost lunch plates. The frying pan, red with heat, dropped at Adele's foot and scorched the floor.

As the flaming leg gave way and the monster collapsed into the fire, the wizard's staff rolled away, smoking slightly. He picked it up, saying, "I'll take care of this."

He promptly dropped the staff and sucked at his fingers.

Adele threw him a hotpad.

But the bonfire was already dying down, leaving a circle of burned floor, a mystical cup sitting on a hill of fine ash, and a very disappointed dragon.

"Quite a mess it made," the wizard said, dispelling the last of the embers. "I wonder how it managed to come alive?"

Adele held up the stone. "Perhaps you dropped this into your clutter pile?"

He looked hard at it, then shrugged. "It's possible. Everything else seems to have collected there. I'll take that now."

"I don't think so." It was hers, by right of discovery—and battle. "I'll hold onto it from now on."

ഓ⚮ജ

Adele smiled as she swept out the crumbs and the dust. Her house was now neat. The door to the study was finally closed, and all of the wizard's little piles of paper were gone. The pots hung smartly from each of a row of nails she'd hammered in herself. The windows were clean and bright, and everything was in place. It was so good to have youthful energy again!

And Sparks, bathing in his customary place on a log in the fireplace, was an enormous help.

Himself walked in, golden-haired and young, with papers in his hand. "I'll be in my study," he announced as he dropped them on the table.

Splut. Sparks jumped from the fireplace and climbed a chair to eye the papers.

"Is there anything important in that?" Adele asked innocently.

Himself wrinkled his brow. " Just one, I think."

Splut. Sparks jumped on the table.

With a sudden cry the wizard grabbed his papers and ran for his study.

Adele smiled at the dragon. "Good boy," she said, and crumpled an old receipt for him to flame.

SCEPTRE OF THE UNGODLY

by Elisabeth Waters & Michael Spence

Although this is the sixth story in the Treasures series, we're sort of circling back to where I began in SWORD & SORCERESS 14. Alyssa has been Guardian of the anti-Treasure the Blade of Unmaking for centuries now, which makes her the logical mentor for the next unfortunate soul destined to guard an anti-Treasure. Unlike a positive Treasure, such as the Grail, which chooses a Guardian and keeps him or her for as long as possible, an anti-Treasure is perfectly happy to change Guardians frequently—preferably with as much attendant chaos as possible. So the fact that Alyssa is still with us is no credit to the Blade, but to time spent under the world-centering influence of the Grail. But if she ever thought this would bring her life stability, she gave up that idea long, long ago.

Captivated by the Blade (fortunately not literally) back in SWORD & SORCERESS 14, Michael Spence suggested that we set our first collaboration, "Salt and Sorcery," in the same world, and the Treasures series was born. A writer-editor, teacher, and researcher, Michael writes on issues of faith, fantasy, and science fiction at "Brother Osric's Scriptorium" (http://michaelspence.us). He is currently adapting his story "One Drink Before You Go" as an audio drama. Michael lives in northern Indiana with his wife and their dog—who fancies himself the Guardian of them both, determined to provide all the chaos they will ever need.

One morning, within the space of eighteen minutes, Senior Thaumaturge Edward made two discoveries. First, his father wanted him to come home for the first time in six years. Second, he was about to become one of the most important people on the face of the earth.

He didn't know which one terrified him more.

Lady Wizard Alyssa, Guardian of the Blade of Unmaking, didn't know about the first item yet (indeed, neither would Edward for another seven minutes), but she was deeply apprehensive—all right, terrified—about the second.

"Both Logas and I have classes this term," Lady Wizard Sarras, Guardian of the Grail and Alyssa's mentor and best friend, pointed out. "And, as you of all people know, we do not send the new Guardian of a Treasure out to retrieve it by himself."

Alyssa nodded. "I know," she agreed. "It's hard enough to handle the Treasure itself—especially when it's an anti-Treasure—without having to deal with anything else. I could never have managed without the two of you helping me. Actually, I'd probably be dead if you hadn't been there. Now it's my turn to watch over and assist Edward." She looked around the Commons where the three of them were having an informal conference over breakfast. "They're going to stop serving soon," she remarked. "I hope he doesn't miss breakfast."

Lord High Wizard Logas looked at the doorway. "I believe that's Edward now." All three of them watched the young man who virtually sleepwalked through the serving line and then added a large mug of coffee to his tray. "I'll bring him over," Logas added, rising to collect his wandering protégé.

Edward sat down, still half-asleep, and took a long pull from the mug. "Metamorphose, O Morpheus! Secede, O somnolence!" he muttered.

"Is that a new spell to wake up," Sarras asked lightly, "or is there just too much blood in your caffeine stream?"

"Uh, the latter," Edward said. "I don't think I *want* to wake up." He sighed, extracted a letter from his book bag, and broke the seal. *He must really be asleep,* thought Alyssa. *Otherwise he'd be the first to consider that a breach of etiquette.*

The faux pas did not go unpunished. Two sentences into the second paragraph Edward choked on his coffee.

"Bad news?" Alyssa asked.

"My father," he groaned, and read aloud: "'. . .The Board of Directors will hold its annual meeting here during the Feast of the Nativity. Since you will one day take the helm of the Company, I believe it is high time they met you. I shall send a Company carriage for you on the twenty-third of December at noon.'

"Today. Just like that," Edward commented glumly. "Alexander Speaks, and it is Done."

Everyone at the table knew about Edward's father, who had a strong magical talent, an uncanny ability to influence public opinion, and ambitions for his son that matched neither Edward's talent nor his inclinations. Edward's one attempt to live up to his father and influence someone's thinking had occurred two and a half years ago, here at the University's College of Wizardry. The results had been disastrous, including serious magical injury to a fellow student that had nearly seen Edward expelled or worse. Only the compassion of Stephen, his victim, had saved him.

Edward had labored long and hard to undo what his magic had done to Stephen, and in the process the two of them had not only cemented a friendship but, as a team, were currently marking out new territory in academic magic.

Alyssa felt a strong sympathy for him. Even centuries after their deaths, she still remembered what her parents' disapproval felt like. Alexander was not likely to take Edward's new position well at all. She hoped there was someone else available to run the family import/export business, because after today Edward would no longer be a candidate.

"We have some news for you," Lady Sarras said, raising the subject of their meeting and their reason for waylaying their young colleague.

"Good or bad?" he replied with forced lightness.

"Good, bad, and bad," Alyssa said. "What do you know about Guardians?"

"Like Laurel?" Edward's ex-girlfriend was living in China now, having accidentally become the Guardian of one of its Greater Treasures.

"No," Sarras said. "Like us. Laurel's Guardianship comes from a different tradition. Remember how she wandered around using a Treasure to hold her hair in place for days before anyone realized what it was?"

Edward nodded. Laurel had found the Scholar's Pin in a crate of customs documents and used it to hold her hair up because the afternoon grew warm and the pin was sitting on her desk.

"It's different for us," Sarras said. "Unlike China's Emperor, we don't choose Guardians for our treasures; they are chosen for us. When a Guardian dies, all of the other Guardians know who has died and who the new Guardian is."

"Everyone except the new Guardian," Alyssa said. "I had no idea what was going on when these two arrived on my doorstep and told me I had to come with them."

Edward took another sip of coffee. "And you're telling me all this because you have *good* news." With somewhat forced cheer, he went on, "So may I assume, then, that all's right with the world, and no one has died?"

Logas smiled ruefully. "Would that it were so, young Edward. I *can* tell you that no one has shuffled off this mortal coil today, nor do we expect anyone to do so tomorrow."

Edward let out his breath. "Oh. Good, then. So—"

"It occurred last month."

Edward visibly sagged. "And you've come to me because . . . because the new Guardian is . . ." He swallowed hard. " . . . me."

The others nodded.

"I see," he said. He looked at his elders, one by one. "So what's the good news?"

"That *was* the good news," said Alyssa. "The bad news is that you, like me, have been chosen to guard an anti-Treasure." Before he could respond she went on, "The other bad news is that it has disappeared, and we have to find it."

"Let me get this straight," Edward said slowly. "You know who is *supposed* to be guarding it—"

The others nodded.

"—and where to find him—me—"

They nodded again.

"—but you don't know where the thing *itself* is."

Lord Logas nodded. "As one of our brightest young researchers," he said, "I doubt you will find this to be a significant problem."

"All right," said Edward. "So what is this anti-Treasure? And is it 'anti' anything specific?"

"It's called the Sceptre of the Ungodly," Lord Logas said. "Have you heard of it?"

Edward shook his head. "What does it do? For that matter, what does it look like? I have to be able to identify it before I can find it."

Lord Logas smiled in a *Got you!* way that made Alyssa wince. It wasn't fair to ambush Edward when he hadn't even finished his coffee, much less had a bite of breakfast. "I have in my workroom a number of sources concerning the Sceptre," Logas said, "and we can look at them after breakfast. In the meantime, may I offer you my congratulations, Edward. The fact that you've been chosen for this responsibility speaks well of you. It also shows that Stephen was right to put his confidence in you after his injury. I believe that even had we not already considered that matter closed, this would settle it."

"A Guardian," Edward said slowly. "I'm going to be an actual, honest-to-Tertullian Guardian. Who'd have thought it? Surely not—" he looked at the letter next to his tray. "My father!" he cried abruptly. "He expects me to take over the family business someday. And he's just ordered me to come home—*today*, at noon!—to a board meeting so he can make it formal. I can't do that and be a Guardian both! . . . Uh, can I?"

Lady Sarras and Lord Logas exchanged glances. "We haven't done anything like that before," Sarras said. "We try to stay out of commerce when we can. We prefer to keep a low profile, and portraits in an Annual Report available to anyone who asks for it are not something we want."

"Perhaps," said Logas, extending a finger to rub his lower lip, "this would be an opportunity to educate your father in the ways of mages. You've not spoken with him in a while, no? Something tells me this would be an auspicious time to do so." He looked at Alyssa. "You will go with him, of course. As I recall, you can do innocent and harmless-looking very well."

"That was more than five hundred years ago!" Alyssa protested. "And wherever I go, the Blade goes—and you have to admit it makes some people very uncomfortable."

Sarras said nothing for a moment, obviously considering the problem. "You'll need shield boxes," she said, "both for the Blade and for the Sceptre when you find it." She rose, picking up her tray. "Come to my office with me, Alyssa, and I'll find what you need so you can pack it." She cast a look of pity on Edward. "Eat your breakfast before Lord Logas drags you off to his workroom, and don't forget to allow time to pack."

⋆

"Could you thicken the weather shield, please?" Alyssa asked Edward, pulling a blanket tightly around her. "I haven't seen this kind of snow in a long while!"

Beside her, Edward spoke the appropriate phrase with the correct pitches. The unseen hemisphere around them grew denser, deflecting the snow from the passenger compartment yet not interfering with the sail that extended from the mast in front of the carriage. "You're kidding, right? I thought you came from the highlands!"

She laughed. "I did. I guess I've lived in the South a few hundred years too long. Thins the blood, or something."

The carriage had touched down, right on schedule, in the quadrangle behind the College's administration sector. The driver—his father's own chauffeur—had greeted Edward with a respectful grin, and had helped him and Alyssa place their bags under the carriage seats. Now the carriage soared through the December sky, the driver tacking as necessary to make headway through the less-than-friendly weather.

"Okay," said Edward, increasing the ambient heat within the bubble, "so I'm to take charge of this Sceptre thing and keep it from influencing the wrong people—"

"Try *any* people," corrected Alyssa. "Give me the psalm again."

"One-twenty-five, verse three," he recited. "For the sceptre of the ungodly shall not abide upon the lot of the righteous; lest the righteous put their hand unto wickedness."

Alyssa nodded. "Right. When someone other than its Guardian holds the Sceptre, not only that person but anyone under his or her authority tends to use whatever power they might have for evil rather than good. You see why we'd want to keep it out of the King's hands, certainly."

"I get it. Nebuchadnezzar, Belshazzar, Alexander the Great, Antiochus . . . ."

"And before them. If we're to believe the legend, Lamech made it and used it first, prior to the Flood. I doubt that even his great-great-great-grandfather, Cain, would have been pleased with him."

She watched Edward try to come to grips with the idea. "A king's rod, made of ash, thousands of years old—" he said slowly, "—and I'm its custodian." He let out a whoof of breath. "Why me? Do you know?"

"Not for certain," Alyssa replied, "but I do have a theory. How much do you know about the Blade?"

"The Blade of Unmaking . . ." Edward said slowly, obviously trying to remember information he hadn't paid much attention to in the first place. "Just pretend I don't know anything. What does *it* do in the wrong hands?"

"Usually it makes the person commit suicide," Alyssa said, "using the Blade. It's *very* messy." She shuddered at the memory. "It makes a person think that he or she is nothing, not worth anything, and shouldn't exist. So," she continued, "its Guardian has to be someone who can feel that and *not* kill herself."

"How does someone—anyone—develop that ability?" Edward asked.

"By feeling suicidal and not committing suicide," Alyssa said, remembering her childhood, now mercifully centuries past. "By learning that feelings are one thing, and action is quite another, and it is in no wise necessary—or desirable—to act upon every feeling that passes through you. And feelings *do* pass."

"So it doesn't make you want to kill yourself anymore?" Edward asked hopefully.

"Well," Alyssa shrugged. "I don't want to hold it in my bare hands. It's a distraction, to say the least. But, yes, the temptation weakens greatly over time." She looked at Edward. "As for the Sceptre . . ."

Edward suddenly looked horrified. "But if the Sceptre makes a person use his power for evil, surely someone who has *already* done that would be the worst possible Guardian . . ."

"Not," Alyssa said gently, "if the person learned from the experience. Remember what Lord Logas said at breakfast—that your being chosen for this responsibility spoke well of you? It's not the people who have never been tempted who become Guardians; it's the people who have learned to deal with the temptation." She smiled encouragingly at him. "I think that's exactly why you were chosen."

"I suppose that makes a certain kind of sense," Edward admitted. "So, once we're done at home, I can begin searching for it. Any idea where to start?"

Alyssa reflected. "Well, we know its previous Guardian knew he didn't have long to live, so he set out to bring the Sceptre to his successor." She grinned. "We didn't know it was you at the time, but he did."

"Okay, so he begins his trip; then what?"

She shrugged. "That's it. That's all we know. He told his friends he was leaving, but that they mustn't follow him. Apparently that was the way he did things. We don't even know which ship he boarded—only that no one ever heard from him again. Five days later, I'm preparing my lesson plans for next term's Historiography course, and right in the middle of working out lesson objectives I'm hit with the absolute certainty that *you* are the Sceptre's Guardian. I found Lord Malcolm, Lady Sarras, Lord Logas, and Lady Catharine, and the same thing had happened to all of them." She chuckled. "So yes, you're the one. If you disagree, it'll be your word against the five of us."

"And that was a month ago?"

"Yes. Perhaps we should have told you straightaway, but Lord Logas was hoping to find the Sceptre for you first."

Edward fairly cackled. "And he failed, did he? Hah! 'Brightest young researchers,' he says! 'I *doubt* you will find this to be a significant *problem*,' he says! The man was *conning* me!"

She managed a sheepish grin. "It's been known to happen."

He shook his head, looking up at the snowflakes blowing toward them and parting to pass by on either side. He stood and crossed to the seat opposite her, sitting down quickly so as not to lose his footing in the turbulence. Leaning toward the edge of the shield, he called out, "Andrea! Would you like me to take over?"

The voice came back, "You must be joshin', sir! 'F I did that, Master'd 'ave my 'ead, 'e would! You just stay back there 'n stay warm!"

He frowned. "All right. But if you change your mind . . ."

"Yes sir! Oh, and we'll be passin' Dermot's farm in a moment!"

"Dermot?" Alyssa inquired.

"An old friend of Father's; he grows wheat and barley near our home. About two hundred acres. Father has offered to buy the land several times—I know he'd like to add it to the estate—but Dermot won't sell. I have to hand it to the man. Father's hard to resist when he has his mind made up."

She believed it. An untrained yet strong magical talent . . .

Edward ventured a look outside and down. His eyebrows rose. "Andrea! Could you take us down, please? I'd like to show Lady Alyssa the farm."

"Yes sir!" The carriage began a shallow dive.

This didn't look like an active farm. The land had been plowed and seeded, but otherwise it seemed somehow neglected. Weeds grew indiscriminately, and the soil appeared a bit more windblown than one would expect.

A sign appeared in the distance. As they drew nearer, the words became legible:

UNDER DEVELOPMENT
TRIANGLE PROPERTIES

"Well, now," Edward said, settling back into his seat. "He wouldn't sell to Father, but apparently he sold to *someone*.

Unless he's quit farming and gone into management. I'll have to ask Father about it."

The driver's voice came back to them again. "The manor's in sight, sir! Only a couple a' minutes now."

Alyssa was impressed. The structure coming into view was no castle like the University buildings, but it was a large, well-designed and well-built house that exemplified the phrase *ancestral home*.

The carriage threaded the drive lane, passed under the arch, and came to a halt in the *porte-cochère* before the front door. Andrea was at the carriage door in a flash, helping Alyssa and Edward debark from the hovering vehicle, after which she returned to the driver's seat and floated it away toward the carriage house.

The front door opened and a tall, heavy-set man appeared, accompanied by another household retainer. They descended the few stone steps, and as the servant gathered the luggage, the man thrust out his hand for Edward to take. "Edward, my boy! It's good to see you." He turned to the unexpected Alyssa. "I don't believe I've had the pleasure."

Edward still clasped the proffered hand, clearly nonplussed. "Uh, Father, this is the Lady Wizard Alyssa, of the College of Wizardry. She's overseeing my . . . training." He turned to her. "Lady Alyssa, may I present my father Alexander?"

Alexander, ignoring the proper introduction, raised both eyebrows. "I must say, you seem rather young to be a professor. You must be quite gifted."

Alyssa smiled politely, but declined to explain. "It's nice to meet you, sir." That was a flat-out lie; something about the man made her feel extremely uneasy.

Alexander laughed, a boom of a laugh that echoed in the *porte-cochère*. "Gifted *and* graceful! She'd make quite a catch, Edward."

His son reddened and cleared his throat. "We saw Dermot's farm on the way in, sir. What's happened?"

Alexander smiled. "I'll fill you in on everything at the meeting tomorrow," he said. "Things are beginning to move around here. But I believe tea is waiting. Shall we go in?"

ෝ෬ඏ෭ෳ

Dinner that night was a sumptuous affair, but it was no comparison to the meal Alyssa knew would be served up on Christmas Eve at the College—they observed the "Feast of the Nativity" on more than one level there. She would miss the Lessons and Carols service that was scheduled for tonight, not to mention midnight Mass tomorrow night. Alexander had made it clear that they didn't "fool around with such trivialities here. Gets in the way of business. What's the point?"

"I've heard about your journal articles with—Stephen, was it?" Alexander said over dinner, as they sat at the high table. "Excellent stuff. Don't understand a word of it myself, of course—far and away too much maths in it—but they tell me it's brilliant. Your name will make a grand addition to the Company." Looking up at the life-size portrait that adorned the dining hall, he added, "Your grandfather would have been proud."

"Father," Edward said, ignoring his father's obvious expectations without actually voicing opposition to them—a trick Alyssa suspected he had practiced for most of his life—"I was hoping you might be able to help us. We're trying to trace one of our colleagues from the Continent who didn't reach us. He was traveling by sea, and I thought that since they send you the schedules and navigation plans from all the passenger and freight lines, we might use them to locate him."

Alexander shrugged. "Certainly. I have the current week's documents in my office, in fact. We can consult them after—"

A young woman appeared at his side. "Excuse me, sir; Mr. Hagen is on the scrying-pair for you; the weather still won't let him leave his city; he's afraid he might even not be able to attend the meeting at all—"

For the first time since they arrived, Alyssa saw the executive's face lose its cheer. Indeed, the man seemed to darken, with a sudden scowl that gave Alyssa a moment's concern for the safety of the wineglass in his hand. As quickly as the expression had appeared, however, it was gone. "Thank you, Joanna. I'll talk to him." As he rose from the table Alexander said to his guests, "This could take some time; I'll see you in the morning." He turned to the woman who sat with them at the high table. She had not been introduced to Alyssa, nor had she spoken a word during the meal. "Margaret, you'll show them to their rooms." He strode off without a backward glance.

Alyssa had wondered who the woman was, but she was stunned when Edward turned to her and asked, "How have you been, Mother?"

☙❧

That was one of the best beds she had ever slept in, Alyssa decided when she woke on the morning of Christmas Eve. Away from her husband, Margaret turned out to be friendly and even to have a delightful sense of humor. Alyssa wondered how she managed the latter while living with Alexander and decided it must be a survival trait.

Margaret had not only shown her to this elegant room, she had also found her a gown and suitable accessories for the Christmas Eve ball the following night. "I'm sure Edward forgot to mention that you'd need a ball gown—it's been so long since he's been home that I'm not sure he even remembers the scale of entertaining that his father insists on."

I suppose Alexander needs to hold on to some "trivialities" after all, Alyssa reflected, *although it also sounds*

*like a good opportunity for—what was that word?—
"networking"*—whatever that meant. She decided it was
probably a fishing term. The man owned ships, after all.
Apparently he also had the resources needed to provide her, at
the drop of a thimble, with a gown that fit both her tastes and her
figure.

Lunchtime came, and then the purpose of their visit: the
Meeting.

"I do think I ought to observe, don't you?" Alyssa asked
Edward. "After all, it affects us at the College too." *And we do
want to know what this man is up to.*

"I agree completely," said Edward. "But you know about
corporate board meetings—they're traditionally closed. Even
I'm here by invitation only."

She smiled. "Oh, that shouldn't be a problem. I have a
spell I can use—they won't even know I'm there."

The dining room, it turned out, doubled as a conference
room. Eleven men she'd never seen before were seated around
the extended table, along with Alexander and Edward, who had
been seated at his father's right hand.

One of the chairs near the other end of the table was
empty. *I suppose Hagen didn't make it after all*, she thought.
Rather that take that seat herself, however, she found another
chair along the wall.

The "ooh, shiny!" spell, as Stephen had dubbed it,
appeared operational. It wasn't that she was invisible,
precisely—they didn't know enough about light to bend it
properly without using a cloak or other bulky covering, and there
would also be the problem of seeing through a light-deflection
field. This spell deflected attention instead. Anyone about to
look her way would suddenly find something much more
interesting to look at in another direction.

She sat and watched the pre-meeting socializing. After a
time, Alexander stood and rapped on the table. "Gentlemen, let

us come to order. This joint meeting of Macedon Import/Export and Triangle Properties is hereby called to—"

He continued to speak, but Alyssa wasn't listening anymore. A glance at Edward's ashen face showed that the two items that had seized her attention had done the same to him. For one, there was the name "Triangle Properties." For the other—

Edward was staring at what Alexander had struck the table *with*.

It was a six-sided rod about eighteen inches long. Along its gray wooden sides she saw inscribed non-repeating patterns made up of oddly lengthened triangles in various arrangements.

It was an exact match to the drawings in Lord Logas's books.

The meeting could not be over soon enough for her.

ఴᎯᏏᏮ

Afterward, while the other board members took tea in the dining/conference room, she and Edward managed to take Alexander aside to the parlor. "I must say, I'm pleased that you're taking an interest in the business," the older man said to his son as he sipped his tea. "What's your question?"

"Two questions, really—and neither of them seemed appropriate in the meeting," said Edward. "How long have you been in property management? And where did you get your 'gavel'?"

"Ah," said his father. "Actually, I've been doing management off and on for some years now. The idea to make it a company in its own right, though, came at about the same time I acquired this." He reached beneath his short business cape and withdrew the rod from a sheath at his belt. "You like the triangle motif? It looked like the basis for a corporate symbol, so I used it."

Alyssa found herself captivated by the sight of the rod. In the back of her mind she didn't so much hear as *feel* a voice, speaking in low vibrations that seemed to rattle her bones ever so softly. *You can do it. Whatever you set your mind to do, you can do it. DO IT. DO IT.*

"It's cuneiform writing," Edward said absently, "used in Mesopotamia four thousand years ago." He reached out a hand. "May I see it?"

"Cu-nee-if—" the older man attempted the word, meanwhile pulling the Sceptre away from Edward's outstretched hand and cradling it protectively to his chest. Alyssa was sure he wasn't even conscious that he'd moved. "Eh, you and your maths. I just thought it had the sense of strength I was looking for. It reminds me that I have it within me to do anything I put my mind to. A good business *needs* that kind of attitude. The board certainly seems to have picked up on it. So I like to keep the rod with me. Call it a motivational talisman, if you like."

You have no idea, Alyssa thought. "Where did you find the rod?" she asked.

"A passenger on one of my ships," said Alexander, settling back in his chair and taking another sip of tea. Another young woman in livery appeared with a teapot to refill their cups, and also set a plate of biscuits on a nearby table.

"It seems he was quite elderly," the man went on, "and also not accustomed to sea travel. When *Atalanta* ran into a storm, he did his best to ride it out, but unfortunately he died. A combination of seasickness and dehydration, the captain told me. When the ship docked I inspected the situation, and I found the rod in a silk-lined box among his personal effects. He didn't list a next of kin, so I kept it. I had Margaret make the sheath."

It did look better on him than a sword would, Alyssa noted. Swords, on the other hand, didn't wield themselves.

"So you created Triangle Properties," Edward said. "But how did the company get Dermot's farm?"

"Oh, that. Our first acquisition. Dermot ran into some trouble over unpaid taxes, and the baron seized the land. The shock killed Dermot, sorry to say, but we were able to buy the property."

"Taxes?" Edward sounded incredulous. "But Dermot always ran an efficient operation. He never had a problem with unpaid taxes!"

"I know," said his father with a grin. "And he won't ever again. Our treasurer—you remember Janssen—has contacts on the baron's staff, and he's quite creative."

Edward fell silent, unable to speak. After a moment, he whispered, "He was kind to me when I was a child. He encouraged me when I asked how his tools worked. I played in his barn." He looked at his father. "He was your *friend*."

His father smiled. "Don't fret about it. There was absolutely nothing personal involved. It was just business."

⋘⋙

E dward and Alyssa retreated to the portrait gallery to make plans. It was out of the way of the preparations for the ball and large enough that they could see anyone approaching before the person could hear what they were saying.

Edward shuddered. "This is a nightmare," he muttered. "I expected to find the thing *after* I dealt with my father, not to have to take it away from him!"

"Well, there is one bit of good news. Two, actually: we know where the Sceptre is; and you don't have to take it away from him."

"I don't?" he said, nonplussed.

"No, you don't. It's not your responsibility until it's in your possession. It's *my* job to get it into your hands; that's why Logas and Sarras sent me with you."

"How are you going to do that?"

"I'm working on a plan," Alyssa said, wishing the plan she was coming up with was less risky. "What sort of dancing do we do at the ball tonight?"

"I forget what it's called," Edward said, "but we sort of walk forward and back very slowly. I think it's so people can admire—or sneer at—each other's clothes. Don't worry," he added quickly, "my mother has wonderful taste; I'm sure you'll look gorgeous."

"Somehow, Edward, that's not my biggest worry at the moment."

cs CR ℰ⟩ ℬⱺ

As Alyssa had expected, the dance Edward had been trying to describe was a pavane. Edward led her into the first set immediately behind his parents. The dance dated from Alyssa's youth, so she probably knew the steps better than anyone else in the room. This freed her mind to concentrate on other things: things like the Blade, which was in a sheath on her right forearm. She was very thankful for the long gloves the ladies wore and the loose, flowing "angel-wing" sleeves of her gown. As her partner, Edward was on her left side, and, despite the fact that she was careful to rest only the tips of her gloved fingers on his sleeve, she could feel tension positively radiate off him. She sympathized with the feeling, but she was glad of it. It meant that he wouldn't try to catch her when she "tripped."

It was still a big risk. Alyssa prayed with all her heart that Alexander had been a basically decent person before ambition—and the Sceptre—had overcome him. If he wasn't, things could turn deadly in seconds. But this was the only plan she had been able to come up with . . .

The dance was ending, and Margaret released her husband's arm as they turned to face each other for the final bow and curtsey. Alyssa lifted her hand from Edward's arm, but instead of turning to face him, she stumbled forward, sliding the Blade out of its sheath as she did so. Alexander's right side was toward her, and she caught herself on his forearm with both hands, brushing the flat of the Blade against the bare skin at his wrist. She was very careful not to draw blood; just a bare touch would be more than enough.

It was. Alexander screamed, reflexively flinging her away before falling to the floor and trying to pull his large body into a small ball. Edward caught her—it was that or go down like a nine-pin along with her. "Get the Sceptre!" she said urgently in his ear as she got her feet back under her. She pulled a silk-lined shield bag out of her left sleeve and pushed it into his hand.

Edward rushed to his father's left side—his mother was already kneeling at his right. As Edward plucked the Sceptre from his father's sheath and thrust it into the bag, Alyssa took a moment to put the Blade into the second shield bag she was carrying and secure it back under her sleeve before trying to help.

Margaret, however, had things well in hand. Already she was giving orders for Alexander, who was sobbing and raving, to be carried to his room. She asked the nearest board member to do her the favor of leading the next set of dances, nodded to the orchestra leader to continue, and told the butler to make certain that food and drink continued to be served. Then she walked calmly out of the ballroom, with Edward and Alyssa in her wake.

As soon as they were out of sight of the guests, she led the rush to Alexander's rooms. Edward and Alyssa could barely keep up with her. She dismissed the servants before Alyssa could protest.

"He *mustn't* be left alone," she said urgently to Margaret, as the sitting room door closed. "He's probably suicidal."

"We're lucky if that's all he is!" Margaret snapped furiously. "Whatever possessed you to commit such a gross breach of hospitality?"

"I'll sit with Father." Edward edged nervously toward the bedroom.

Through the door Alyssa could hear Alexander's faint sobs. "—so sorry—was just business, never meant for you to *die*—sorry, so sorry—oh, Dermot, Dermot, *Dermot!*"

"Do what you can," she told Edward, "but for the love of God, keep the Sceptre away from him!"

She faced Edward's furious mother, who glared at her. "I felt it when you brought the Blade of Unmaking into my house," Margaret said, "and I looked you up to see what it was you carried. You're a *Guardian;* you have been for a long, long time. Why did you misuse what you are supposed to keep safe? *Why did you harm my husband?*"

Alyssa looked her straight in the eyes. "If you're Sensitive enough to notice the Blade—especially when it's in a shield bag—you could hardly have missed what your husband has been carrying with him for the past month!"

Margaret dropped her eyes. "I lined the sheath with silk," she said, "and I was doing research to find out what it was."

"The Sceptre of the Ungodly," Alyssa said shortly.

Margaret went pale. "'For the sceptre of the ungodly shall not abide upon the lot of the righteous; lest the righteous put their hand unto wickedness.' Saturday, the midday Little Hour."

Alyssa nodded. "That's the one. It's nice to find someone here who knows the Daily Office. From the way your husband spoke of the Nativity, I wasn't sure anyone in the household was observant."

Margaret smiled grimly. "Alexander doesn't speak for me. He just thinks he does."

Alyssa eyed Margaret with new appreciation. This was a type of power she understood; in fact, it was the kind she had held during her parents' frequent absences when she was a girl. It didn't matter who had the fancy title; if you were the one people listened to, the person who made certain that things got done . . . *that* was the real power.

"I'm truly sorry, Lady Margaret," she said. "I would not have used the Blade if I could have found any other method of getting the Sceptre away from him and into the hands of its new Guardian."

Edward returned, carefully keeping the shield bag with the Sceptre on the side of his body away from them. "Father's asleep," he said. "And I have a feeling that he's going to be all right."

"God grant it," Alyssa said prayerfully.

"Who is the new Guardian?" Margaret asked.

"I am," Edward said. "That's why I'm holding this instead of passing it off to Alyssa like the proverbial hot potato." He looked sober. "It's my responsibility now, for the rest of my life." He closed his eyes briefly, looking suddenly very young and completely overwhelmed.

"I think it would be best for everyone if we got that into a proper shield box and took it back to the College as soon as possible," Alyssa said.

Margaret nodded. "I have no desire whatsoever to be lacking in hospitality, but I can think of nothing I'd like better at the moment than to have *both* of those artifacts out of my house. Immediately."

"We'll go pack right now," Alyssa assured her, "and we'll leave a soon as you can arrange transportation for us."

"Twenty minutes," Margaret said, reaching out to tug the bell pull.

"The company," Edward said. "You know I can't be the one to run it."

His mother smiled. "That should be no problem. Mr. Hartwicke would be the better choice, anyway. I think they'll see reason."

Edward leaned over and kissed her cheek, holding the Sceptre as far away from her as possible. "I won't be coming back here, Mother," he said, "but I hope that you will visit me at the College when you can."

"I'll do that," she said, standing on tiptoe to kiss her son's forehead. "And always remember, Edward, I love you. And I'm proud of you."

"I'll go pack." Edward practically fled from the room.

Margaret smiled fondly after him and shook her head. "I never expected this for him—"

"Nobody ever does," Alyssa said with feeling.

"—but I think he may be a good Guardian," Margaret said. "Running the family business was never something he wanted or had any talent for."

"True," Alyssa agreed. "He's a born academic. And there are several other Guardians at the College, so he'll have plenty of support as he adjusts to his new responsibilities."

"In other words, he'll have an easier time than you did."

"I certainly hope so," Alyssa said fervently. "I thank you for your hospitality," she continued, "and I am truly sorry for the breach of it I committed. I'll be going now." She turned to look back as she left the room. "I do hope that you'll visit the College."

⁂

Fifteen minutes later, having packed the Blade into a sturdy shield box, done a quick change from ball gown to travel dress, and thrown everything else hastily into her bag, Alyssa joined Edward in the carriage. As they took off into the bright star-filled sky, Edward said, "We should get home around eleven. Midnight Mass?"

"Fine by me," Alyssa replied. *We have a great deal to thank God for.*

MATERIAL WITNESS

by Brenta Blevins

The Great Tapestry that hung above the throne in Muirgana showed the history of the kingdom, but not as a normal tapestry woven by human hands did. With the proper spell, the tapestry could reveal the truth about past events, which was how Princess Valyra discovered that her father had been murdered. So when she found herself inside the tapestry, she tried to change what had happened. The results of her efforts, however, were not at all what she expected.

Brenta Blevins lives and writes in the Appalachian Mountains, where she enjoys hiking with her husband. She has written audio dramas that have been produced for public radio in the United States and aired there, in South Africa, and in Australia. Her short fiction has appeared in *ChiZine* and a number of anthologies. Her white longhair cat, Snow Crash, assists with her writing by helpfully placing his tail over her keyboard.

Eyes swollen with grief, Princess Valyra knelt alone before the Great Tapestry. Its amber background glowed with a rich golden light warming the limestone wall behind it, revealing the enormous textile was more than a normal wall-hanging.

Staring at the muted harvest scene, Valyra used her father's secret spell to will the blocky lettering across the top, "Testimony to Truth," to give her what she wanted, *needed* to see: how her father died. How could anyone believe he, the king of Muirgana, had been mauled to death when he'd killed his first bear at eight summers old? Had everyone fallen under a spell?

For most viewers, the magical tapestry hanging above the throne wove an incredible moving tableau of lessons from the kingdom's most historically significant events: King Deleon, Valyra's great-grandfather, protecting a village from invasion from an Eastern empire. Wrede, her grandfather, defending peasants from a band of outlaws. Ered, her father, sharing his crops with villagers in a drought.

At the least, Valyra would see her father again. Before she'd arrived home, her uncle Tolor—the new king—had already seen to the burial.

Valyra's heart leapt as the Great Tapestry transformed to show a new scene. At first, it seemed the firelight cast flickering hues on the embroidered golden shocks of gathered wheat with reapers raising silvery hooks to harvest more. The multicolored fabric appeared to sway from some breeze in the great hall, falling into shadow, then light again in fiber chiaroscuro. But, it became clear the vivid weft threads danced free of the warp, then dove again to re-weave together, forming new pictures. The threads knitted faster so the image of crop collection changed to one of glinting-armored knights riding across the castle's moat bridge. Again, the yarns unraveled and intertwined.

Valyra's eyes teared anew as the tapestry showed her father and her maid in the courtyard waving at her departure months ago. Her father had sent Valyra to study with her aunt after her mother's prolonged illness and death. As the sorrow of losing both parents in so few months swept over her, Valyra wrapped her arms around herself, the fire crackling in the knight-high fireplace doing nothing to warm her.

The wall-hanging changed, showing other events in the recent past: green-clothed entertainers dancing and juggling in the great hall, a courtier's wedding, delegations wearing the red and gold of Ramsa's northern kingdom meeting with her father to discuss . . . what? Valyra wished the magic tapestry emitted sound. The next scene showed her father riding his stallion over the moat bridge with a hunting party of dogs, courtiers, and nobles, including her mother's brother. They rode together into the rocky wooded White Hills, then pursued bears fleeing through the trees. The party split, divided, and separated again, chasing different bears until her father and his brother by marriage, Tolor, rode alone. Leading, Tolor reached into his saddle sack, then pulled on bizarre clawed gloves. He turned and suddenly clouted her father, knocking him from his horse. Before her father could rise, Tolor leaped down and beat Ered repeatedly, gashing him with long bloody streaks cast upon the tapestry in silken crimson threads, until the king lay immobile. Tolor then walked up the white rocky hillside to a tiny cave and cast the gloves inside.

Her uncle—the new king—had killed her father.

The scene unraveled and the tapestry again showed her great-grandfather. The yarns blurred as her Valyra's eyes filled. She would go to—go to—

Boot steps echoed in the great hall. Valyra's back stiffened.

"Valyra." Her uncle's voice filled the empty hall like the bitter wind before a thunderstorm.

She rose, whirling to face Tolor. "You!" Her body trembled—not with fear of a murderer, but with rage. "You killed my father!"

Tolor shook his head. "It's hard to be an orphan." He and her mother had lost their parents when they'd caught the fever that Ramsa traders had carried south. Tolor had always claimed the traders had intentionally brought illness with them. "You shouldn't be alone, not at your age. I will marry you into a good alliance."

"I will prove you killed him!"

Tolor's eyes narrowed. "Is this a desperate attempt to gain the crown? They'd never accept you—a child unprepared in governance, battle, or defending a kingdom." He twisted his hand dismissively.

Valyra's face flushed in embarrassment and anger. Her elder brothers, the trained and presumed heirs, had preceded their parents in death.

"Desperate? I didn't murder to become ruler!" Valyra's fists twitched with fury. Her combat experience was limited to playing swordfight against her brothers and cousins with the fireplace poker. She'd succeeded only in burning a hole through the Great Tapestry, creating a mar in the corner that her father had graciously forgiven. With Tolor now blocking the fireplace, Valyra had no weapons with which to defend the people from a treacherous murderer. If he'd killed to gain the throne, what might he inflict upon the residents of the kingdom?

"You should stop offering unsubstantiated accusations. As *we* might view such as treason." Using the royal plural pronoun, Tolor's lips twitched with arrogance.

Valyra's control slipped. She swung her fist at her uncle, desperate to make him hurt for his crimes of murder and deceit. All too easily, Tolor dodged the blow. In the blink of an eye, he punched her as he had her father. Her head spun and she stumbled backward. Her feet danced, struggling for purchase. Her heel caught on the uneven edge of a slate tile. Reeling, her hands flew out to catch herself against the tapestry.

Pain shot through her as pinpricks stabbed her entire body, as if she had been shot through by thousands of needles. They drove deep into her and she felt her mouth yawn toward a scream. The needles yanked hard, as if fighting to pull thread into her so she felt herself growing enormous and bound to explode. She felt the thousand perforations tugged apart, then together. A sound like fabric ripping filled her ears—and her scream fell silent.

She plummeted to ground softer than stone, her hands landing on damp grass. Valyra blinked, wondering how hard her uncle had hit her to make her hallucinate, but the green plants remained in focus. She gazed at trees, bushes. Patting herself, she was surprised not to feel blood spurting from thousands of wounds. She recognized the birches and limestone outcroppings of the White Hills, where the tapestry had revealed her father had bled to death.

Was this the afterlife? She gazed into the sky. Tolor loomed over her, enormous. She drew back, scuttling behind a rhododendron bush, wishing for more substantial protection, then peered around the glossy leaves, realizing he was impossibly taller than the trees and insubstantial as a ghost. She couldn't be dead; the forest felt too real. And there was no way her uncle could present so large in the sort of afterlife Valyra thought she deserved. Through puffy white cloud formations, she glimpsed faint outlines of the great hall behind him: the high fireplace, the pointed arches, the throne on its dais. Valyra realized she was looking through a window that was the tapestry. Somehow, she had fallen through the threads of the wall-hanging into textile memory.

Her eyes grew wide as she contemplated her situation in wonderment. She'd never known about this magic.

Her uncle raised an enormous diaphanous hand, poking the fabric as if searching for her hiding behind the cloth, but his ethereal fingertips didn't even stir the tree leaves overhead. His gaze never connected with hers, as if he watched some other scene.

She was safe from him. For now.

"Everything as planned." Tolor's voice from behind Valyra caused her to jump. Sliding through the dirt around the bush, she turned to face the scene the tapestry had shown her in the great hall. Her uncle stood over a man's immobile body. Her father! Valyra saw two horses, hunting equipment, blood. Too much blood. "The throne is mine now. You let Ramsa get away with the murder of my parents, *your* family by marriage. I will declare war finally to exact retribution."

She started to rise, to run to confront her uncle for whatever good it might do, but the man shouted and struck the horses' rumps.

The spooked animals galloped, their hooves beating a frantic tempo as they tore through the underbrush. Her uncle charged after them, screaming, "Bear attack!" Valyra beat her fists against a forest floor that felt all too real. She wanted to stop him, but knew she was only interacting with a recorded past. Nothing could change what had happened. Instead, she ran to her father and dropped to her knees beside him. His chest had already fallen still and he looked all too pale against the blood that darkened his neck and the soaked grass. She grasped his hand, which felt as real as everything here had, rubbed the calluses worn into a groove matching his sword hilt. Tears didn't streak her cheeks as she squeezed his fingers; they'd fallen for too many weeks before. Paying respect to him, she sat for a long time, contemplating what her father had meant to her (the time he'd surprised her with her first riding horse, the birthday he'd given her her own illuminated history book), how kind he'd been to her mother (bringing her flowers from the river, sitting with her at nights when she was at her sickest), and what he'd done for the kingdom (when no fighting was required in his ruling, he farmed as hard as he could for its residents). Finally, she knew she could honor her father best by carrying out his mission of protecting the kingdom—his people . . . her people—and ensuring Tolor would face justice for his treachery. She had to free herself from the tapestry. Finally, she released her father's hand and placed it over his heart, whispering "Good-bye."

The silhouette of her ghostly uncle still hovered behind the trees. She ran toward him, intent on jumping back onto the great hall's floor. Instead, she bounded through forest, dress ribbons streaming behind her, until she hurdled into a meadow. She shook her head, then turned and ran in the opposite direction until she reached the hill with the cave. Stopping herself from following the bearers of her father's litter, Valyra ran south, then west, but she ran only through the familiar White Hills until her quivering legs collapsed underneath her skirts. Her gasping breaths seared her lungs. A sob croaked through her ragged throat as she realized she couldn't separate herself from the tapestry's stored past.

She was trapped. As effectively as if her uncle had married her off to a tyrant in some distant land.

Everything went black, not like night falling or with the warning sparkles of a faint, but as if the sun and all the stars had been plucked from the sky.

When her vision returned, Valyra saw a village with gray thatched huts and fenced livestock nestled in a valley. The castle rose on a distant hill above—too distant to hear the sheep's baa-ing or the cattle lowing.

Or the pending attack.

Slithering through the tall grasses on the southern hilltop, men wearing animal pelts screeched and howled charging toward the village. She watched from the hillside as a man she recognized from the tapestry as her great-grandfather charged with a group of knights out of a barn and from around the northern ends of buildings to fend off the attackers. They all ignored her vantage point; she was merely a spectator to the conflict.

Blackness and she suddenly sat in a village and identified her grandfather stopping a band of thieves—dirty, desperate men—from stealing tools, foods, livestock, whatever they could fetch from one of the villages under the castle's protection.

Valyra realized the tapestry was replaying its chronicle of significant events. To return to the great hall, she only had to wait until the tapestry finished its current loop, then, when it reached near present, it would spit her out.

Time was cut again, and her father stood in the back of a loaded wagon parked amidst the brown, drought-stricken grasses and handed down sacks of grain and baskets of dried fruit to hungry villagers. As the magical tableau replayed the kingdom's history, she rose and prepared herself for her journey back to reality. Anticipating leaving the tapestry would be as painful as entering it, she steadied her breathing. She crouched, preparing to flee her watching uncle who assuredly planned to silence her.

Everything went black. Once she saw light again, she started running, sure she would feel stone flooring underfoot. But she didn't. Instead, she found herself running once again on the grassy hillside above the village her great-grandfather had protected. The tapestry had not released her.

Her legs folded. She was trapped in the magic embroidery, doomed to repeat history while her uncle carried on with his nefarious plans.

As the scene replayed, Valyra glanced over her shoulder through the tapestry. Time seemed to pass differently in the ghostly great hall than it did in the fabric. As the ages passed by her, Valyra saw her uncle seated on the throne, turned to study the tapestry, perhaps verifying she hadn't materialized or perhaps trying to learn some tactical advantage from past battles. In the hall, knights assembled to listen to her uncle. War would be coming. A war no more fair to one kingdom than the other. Valyra couldn't allow the attack on Ramsa. She had to escape before the knights marched to battle on Tolor's ridiculous campaign. She had to keep the tapestry from recording Tolor's coronation.

The abbreviated history repeated over and over. Valyra stewed in impotent anger that she couldn't inform the knights, the ministers, the other royals of Tolor's treason.

Tolor.

Perhaps if the same magic worked inside the tapestry as she had used outside it. . . . Valyra knelt and placed her palm to the ground, willing the magic to return her to the White Hills. Her vision went black and she cycled to that point. Before her uncle struck the blow that killed her father, she rushed from behind the bushes and shoved him, but he struck her hard, knocking her unconscious with a single blow.

She awoke in her great-grandfather's era. She focused all her anger on one target.

She replayed her father's murder, this time hurling a rock at her uncle, but it missed connecting with his fat head, and he dispatched her as easily as he had before. The next time, she ran into the scene, trying to distract her uncle from his murderous intent, but it still didn't save her father. She warned her father. She tried delaying him, but her uncle merely rode back to murder him. Nothing could change how fate had ultimately woven itself. The scenes inevitably started again at the beginning, just as the sun inexorably started a new day in the world in which she had once lived. She could do nothing to save her father and grew tired of watching him die time and time again.

For a while, she merely watched history take place as it repeated before her eyes. She ate when she felt the urge; the village crops seemed to satisfy her as food had in her previous life. She used her father's spell to slow the landscape's time so she could sleep an entire night in a village barn.

On the hundredth or so repetition of the tapestry's history, Valyra tired of waiting, tired of being a spectator. The time for grieving was over. She couldn't—wouldn't sit idly while her uncle planned a war. She yanked a sword from the hand of a prone knight. Weighing it, the weapon's heft was unfamiliar in her grip and she was as awkward wielding it as the fireplace poker. As with her father, she wouldn't, couldn't change the past, so there was no harm in learning and practicing in the re-created simulation. Was there?

She trotted down the hill toward an invader armed with a staff. As he turned from dispatching a villager, she hefted her sword, having to hold it in both hands. She lifted it to one side, hoping to swing it with force.

The invader took no note of her pretty dress as he swung his staff as if she were a soldier. She blocked its momentum, but the impact vibrated up her arms. Her fingers almost let the hilt slip from her grasp. Her efforts were as clumsy as the punch she'd aimed at her uncle. Rushing past, the invader took his staff and twisted her feet so she tumbled, cracking her head so hard on the ground that it bounced up before smacking the packed hillside a second time. Her vision went black and her mind had just enough time to wonder whether this was her end.

Though her head ached, she woke with relief to her grandfather's battle. As soon as the tapestry's memory returned her to a scene, history was as it had been—exactly as it had always played out on the Great Tapestry.

Again, she armed herself with a sword from a fallen warrior. She fell quickly. The next iteration, Valyra dispatched an invader, before falling to a second. She learned that anything on her transferred from each scene. She donned the cap and breast plate from a downed soldier to armor herself. The best sword stayed with her. With each recurrence, Valyra defeated more opponents. And wounds? She learned she could heal her own by using the magic in the tapestry to weave herself back together. She discovered from firsthand experience what the knights of a kingdom were expected to endure in the ruler's employ.

She knew the battles by name—not merely the conflict designations of Tea Creek, Rock Springs, or Night of Fire—but the names of the participants—Simac who'd warned Sweetwater of the attackers; Wad who'd organized the digging of trenches around Mana village to prevent the fire from destroying it; young Daba who'd brought water to the wounded at Cold Valley. She knew how each of the warriors fought and learned to recognize who would fare well or poorly. She learned tactics to try and strategies to avoid in all the battles since her great-grandfather's rule. She began to read the signs of drought and learned how to dry food, expand hunting, and store barrels of rainwater, actions that would mitigate suffering.

She practiced more than swordfighting. Helping her father feed the hungry, she respected him even more when she saw for herself the good he'd done for the poor people who offered him no additional tracts of land, no trade agreements, nothing.

She understood better than anyone how all the tapestry's stories came together to weave the history of the kingdom. Living here had taught her more about managing a kingdom than working with her mother or her aunt to host visitors, patronize entertainers, check medical needs, or monitor the supplies to run the castle. This experiential repetition was better than an illuminated history book.

She lost track of time, falling into the rhythms of the familiar conflicts and battles. She experienced more than just the primary tapestry scenes, visiting the era when her family was still alive. She decided to spend all the time she wanted with them.

They didn't recognize her. Why would they? She was older than in their memory. She saw herself, too, recorded in these times; she was young and immature, prone to slapping her brothers in anger then dashing off, her scarves waving behind her. She barely recognized herself. The magic was cruel in its own way; her family forgot her each time she returned to them. But to be with her father. Her mother. Her brothers when they were all alive and healthy.

She grew stronger parrying with her eldest brother.

"You're a tougher fighter than I am. Going to challenge me for the throne?" His voice was light and teasing.

Her reply come out low and her lips curled into a wistful grimace. "I would like nothing more than for you to sit on the throne."

She forgot there was once a world outside this one.

Following the long fight of Great Meadows that left her hot and exhausted, Valyra walked to the village's mill pond, laying her sword beside her. The weapon was now as common to her as hair ribbons had once been. Kneeling by the water, she scooped up handfuls and drank deeply. Once her thirst was quenched, she sat quietly, then noticed her reflection in the water. Grooves creased the corners of her mouth. She traced the lines with a fingertip. Turning her hands over, she stared at the rough flesh, her knuckles knotted and scabbed, her palms now as callused as her father's had ever been. How much time had she passed here?

She looked at the sword hilt by her knee. After hundreds of clashes, Valyra realized if she could again face off a cousin with a fireplace poker, she'd do more than burn a hole in the tapestry. She'd certainly do more than miss landing a punch on her uncle. What had Tolor been up to while she'd visited her family?

Wait. A hole in the tapestry.

A hole.

Everything went black and she was pulled into her grandfather's history. As he valiantly fought to protect a mother and child, Valyra realized she had to find a hole in the tapestry, the flaw in its magic, to break free. How could she do that? She'd explored all over the landscapes of the past and hadn't seen any holes. Or had she?

She knelt and willed the tapestry to display her father's murder. When the White Hills reappeared, Valyra ran through the woods without a glance at her father's murder, then jumped from boulder to boulder up the steep hillside until she reached the cave where her uncle had hidden his murder weapons. She dived through its opening, feeling as if she were being strained through a sieve, and then plummeted onto slate flooring.

Her ancient armor cushioning her tumble, she rolled upright as if under attack, but, blinking disorientation away, realized no battle took place; her uncle was holding court in the great hall. He looked no older than when she'd watched the tapestry reveal his murderous act in what seemed so long ago. As courtiers stared, she strode toward the throne.

"What is—?" her uncle's voice boomed. The hall rustled as knights and others in audience rose, shouting.

"Princess Valyra!?"

" . . . dove out of the tapestry!"

" . . . it showed a new scene . . ."

Valyra's armor covered a dirty, tattered dress, now too small for her hard, muscular physique. Her ribbons had long since torn loose.

"You murdered my father," Valyra said. This time, her voice wasn't shrill when she accused her uncle. "The people of Muirgana deserve better than you on the throne."

"Who are you?" Tolor shouted. "You are an impostor pretending to be our frail princess!"

She ordered the knights, "You must take that man into custody. He murdered the king."

The guards looked uncertainly between Valyra and Tolor.

She turned to them. "He faked the bear attack upon King Ered." When they still didn't move, her eyes met the faces of each of the knights. "You know your king wouldn't have fallen under those circumstances." She saw in their gazes a desire to believe her and a fear she might be correct about their new king.

"We didn't!" her uncle shouted.

"Let me show you." Valyra turned to the Great Tapestry, putting her hand against the thick fabric, commanding it to show the bear hunt.

"You've planted false evidence to accuse us!" her uncle protested, the crown on his head sliding askew. "Treason!"

He moved faster than she expected, leaping up, drawing his sword from its scabbard and charging her.

She acted without thinking. She drew her own sword and twisted it around Tolor's with such force that she wrenched it from his hand, sending it tumbling to the slate. The clattering of metal upon stone echoed throughout the great hall.

She raised her sword point to her uncle's throat, holding the blade perfectly steady. This was a far cry from throwing a clumsy punch.

"You dare raise your sword to us!" he protested.

"Wait." Valyra held her hand up toward the knights. "All I ask is for the truth to be known."

The yarns rewove and displayed the tragic scene in the White Hills, when crimson blood flowed over white stone. The audience gasped as they witnessed Tolor murdering her father.

The knights surrounded him.

"But I didn't—" he protested.

"The guard will find the murder weapons in the forest cave," Valyra said. On the knights' faces, she saw that she was no longer the spoiled youngest member of the royal family; instead of disdain or disinterest, she saw respect. "As we saw in the tapestry."

Slumping, her uncle fell silent.

Valyra smiled at the tapestry that had given her the power to offer testimony to truth.

The captain of the guard snatched the crooked crown from her uncle's head and then knelt, offering the royal emblem to Valyra.

ଓଔଔଫ୭

A month later, the tapestry wove its newest scene filled with knights and villagers, decorated in brilliant, festive colors: Valyra's coronation.

OWL COURT

by K.D. Wentworth

Jolice was away when everyone in her village was killed—except for the women and girls taken away by the raiders. She went to the Owl Court for justice, and the Lady Owl accepted her, but Jolice first had to change so that she could rescue her kinswomen, and then she had to decide what was truly a just solution for both the women and the raiders.

K.D. Wentworth has sold more than eighty pieces of short fiction to such markets as *F&SF, Marion Zimmer Bradley's Fantasy Magazine, Hitchcock's, Realms of Fantasy, Weird Tales,* and *Return to the Twilight Zone*. Four of her stories have been Finalists for the Nebula Award for Short Fiction. Currently, she has seven novels in print, the most recent being THE COURSE OF EMPIRE, written with Eric Flint and published by Baen. Her next book (also co-written with Eric Flint) will be CRUCIBLE OF EMPIRE, due out in March 2010. She lives in Tulsa with her husband and a combined total of one hundred sixty pounds of dog (Akita + Siberian "Hussy"). Her website is www.kdwentworth.com.

Jolice climbed the sacred mountain all day after the massacre, turning her face into the wan winter sun and doggedly tramping upward through the snow long after the light had given way to green-black shadows. Owls filled her mind, their wings gliding silently through the sky, their eyes immense and golden. If only she could reach the owls—

She could not think about the dead back in the village scattered across the bloodied snow, grandfathers and toddlers, the fathers and brothers with their bows and knives and short swords still in hand. Nor could she let herself remember all those not there, the mothers and sisters and baby girls obviously stolen by raiders. Mother and her sweet young sister, Larsi! They were all gone!

She made herself think only of the Lady Owl and her winged Court, the dreadful white stillness of her mountain kingdom, the promise of Owl aid, Owl justice.

Great-Aunt Mirna had spoken of the different sacred courts on long winter nights when the wind howled against the lodges, Bobcat Court and Wolf Court, Bear Court and Elk Court. Each had its own Lady and its own concerns, but the people of her village were Owl Clan. Owl Court was where they would always find justice.

The old aunt lay dead in the bloody snow now, her eyes empty, her hands fisted. She would tell tales no longer and no one remained in the village to listen. Jolice's boots crunched through the snow, step after step after step, and she was so cold, it seemed ice crystals filled her veins. Her feet were dangerously numb. She knew the signs of impending frostbite, but it did not matter. Nothing mattered save justice.

Long after darkness swathed the mountain, she skirted yet another jumble of boulders, then came upon a forest that matched Great-Aunt Mirna's tales, a stand of immense deep green pines growing so close together that the snow was markedly less beneath. Outside the trees, moonlight from the half-moon shimmered across untracked snow and it seemed someone, somewhere, watched her progress.

Jolice stamped the snow from her boots in a vain effort to get warm. "Lady Owl?" she whispered, her throat tight with misery.

Wind sighed through the pine needles, carrying their sharp aromatic scent. Nothing else moved, but still she had the impression of *eyes* watching. The air was thin up that high. Each breath cut through her lungs like a cold, cold knife.

"Lady Owl, please!" Ducking her head, she wove through the closely spaced trees. "I am Owl Clan, your kin!"

The White Owl is sacred, Great-Aunt Mirna said in her memory. *Go before her only with gifts.*

She had brought no gifts, she realized with a pang. Consumed with grief when she returned to the village and found the slaughter, she'd fled, seeking help, not thinking of tribute.

"I will make a gift," she said, gazing up at the stars dimly visible through the green-black needles. "I will! Just tell me what you want!"

Nothing answered. Perhaps all those winter night tales of Owl Court had been just an old woman's fancy. Fear coursed through her as strongly as when she had come back after a morning of gathering firewood only to find everyone missing or dead. She had been stupid, coming all the way up here when she should have hiked across the valley to Bobcat Clan or back down the river to Deer Clan and sought their help instead.

Hot salt tears brimmed in her eyes but would not flow. She was possessed of a sorrow so far beyond mere tears that her body did not know how to respond. Her legs gave way and she sank to the snow-covered needles beneath a huge pine. The corrugated bark was rough against her back. Weariness rolled over her like a great dark tide and then she slept in the ice-ridden shadows.

ೞೞೞ

*Y*ou *have brought me a gift,* Lady Owl said.

Jolice opened her eyes and found an immense white

owl, tall as a man, gazing down at her with golden eyes like suns. The wind gusted, loosening snow from the branches overhead to fall on her shoulder, but it only felt wet, not cold.

"No," she said, scrambling to her feet out of respect, "I was so upset, I forgot what my aunt said."

The golden eyes blinked. *Child, you brought yourself.*

The girl's head seemed so muzzy, she couldn't think properly. "I need help—" she said brokenly, unable to look away from that intense hot-gold gaze. "The women, the girls of the village, my mother and sister—!"

The owl spread its great wings, beating them so that she was inundated with cool pine scented air. Power tingled through Jolice's body as though every nerve in her body had been asleep all her life and had now suddenly woken.

I accept, the creature said, then faded into mist.

ψωψ

"**W**ake, sister." A hand touched Jolice's chilled face. Her eyes opened and she flinched back. Moonlight still gleamed on the snow just outside the pine forest. A woman stood before her, straight and strong, clad all in white leather and furs, shod in tall white boots bound with golden cord. Instead of hair, long white feathers covered her head, pale as moonbeams. Her brow was wide and smooth, her eyes fiercely gold. They gleamed in the dimness as though illuminated by some inner fire.

"Who—are you?" Jolice said, her throat still hoarse with grief. She was cold and stiff from sleeping in the snow and could not stop shivering.

"I am Sasalla," the woman said. She reached down to Jolice, grasped the girl's forearm and pulled her onto her feet with a strong sure motion as though she weighed nothing. "Until now, the youngest of Owl Court. I serve my Lady Owl." On her back, the woman carried a sinuous bow carved from ash and a quiver full of white arrows. "You seek aid from the Lady."

"Then—she is real." Jolice gazed around at the shifting moon shadows beneath the pines. Pairs of golden eyes blinked down at her from many of the branches overhead.

"If you did not know she was real, you would not have come into her court," Sasalla said. Stirred by wind, the long white feathers danced around her oval face.

Desperation had sent her up the mountain, not surety, hope that there might at least be some grain of truth in the old tales. Jolice did not know what to say. She bent down to brush snow off her leggings, then had to catch herself against the tree trunk when the snowy ground seemed to slant beneath her feet and her head whirled.

"You are hungry," Sasalla said. "My Lady Owl gives you leave to hunt her forest." She ducked her head and strode out from under the pines.

"But—!" Jolice darted after her, but the woman was gone. Jolice's chilled hands curled into fists. She carried only a small knife, totally inadequate for hunting. And even if she did catch something, how would she cook it? She had not thought to bring a flint when she fled.

She gazed around at the moonlit snow. The wind gusted and a spray of snow crystals pelted her face. Perhaps she should just go back to sleep under the trees until morning when it would be easier to find ground squirrel or pika tracks. But then she heard something, a faint thump, a rustling, and realized that she could see perfectly well even through it was still night.

A flicker caught her eye. She lowered her head and examined the snow. The whisper of paws lured her. Sharp curiosity drew her on as though, if she persevered, she would hear the end of an interesting tale. What *was* it making those intriguing sounds? She cocked her head, listening.

Then, careful to make little noise herself, she eased back into the aromatic pines, soon finding telltale tracks in the snow.

She recognized the pattern. Hare. A large one. If only she had a length of cord to fashion a snare!

Hand braced on the rough bark, she slipped around the tree's immense bole and saw her quarry, an snowshoe hare in its white winter coat, normally almost invisible against the snow. But now she could see that its whiteness was an altogether different shade from that of the alabaster snowfall.

Her mouth watered and it seemed season upon season since she'd eaten. The hare gazed back at her with terrified black eyes and froze after the fashion of its kind.

Eat, something whispered in her ear.

She turned her head, but no one was there.

You must grow strong, if you are to prosper in my court, the voice said. *Eat!*

Her hunger was suddenly a burning coal in the pit of her stomach, threatening to consume her from the inside out if she did not act. With a despairing cry, she threw herself upon the terrified hare, grappled in the snow, then wrenched its neck.

Well done, child, the voice said.

Numbly, she drew her knife to skin the beast. "What— about a fire, Lady Owl?" she said, her voice only a whisper.

There is no fire in my court.

She nodded and made the first cuts along the back legs, slipping the skin off the steaming carcass as Mother had taught her. Repelled, she watched her trembling, bloody hands work. After she finished, she sat on her heels looking at the meat, thinking about it roasted or cut up in stew as Mother would have served it. Her hunger surged, but she could not eat it raw. She could not!

My children are strong, the voice said. *They never look away from truth, however unpleasant. They always do what they must, as will you, if you wish to dispense my justice.*

Dead bodies scattered in the snow. The missing women and girls. Her family! As though her hands belonged to someone else, Jolice sliced off a bit of the warm raw flesh and raised it to her mouth.

It tasted unexpectedly delicious.

ϘϘϘϘ

A fter eating her fill, she buried the bones, skin, and offal in the snow, then curled up under the trees to sleep. She gathered a nest of pine needles, then closed her eyes and dreamed that her mother was looking for her, searching inside a musty unlit lodge filled with captive women and girls, going from each to the next, unable to believe that Jolice was not among them. She dreamed that her little sister, Larsi, sobbed with terror and exhaustion until her eyes were sore and red, calling out for her father and Jolice.

Father lay dead in the snow along with the rest of the village's men, boys, and old women, but in the dream Jolice tried to tell the child that she would find her with the aid of Lady Owl. Larsi could not seem to hear.

See where they are with your dream-eyes, Lady Owl said, and Jolice realized the immense owl stood beside her. *You cannot rescue my daughters until you know their location.*

Jolice tried, but the lodge was bare, the women and girls crowded together, theirs hands cruelly bound. She found nothing upon which she could orient herself. It could have been anywhere in the lands of the Nine Clans or beyond.

Walk outside the lodge, Lady Owl said.

"How?" Jolice whispered. The door flap was tied shut from without, the walls firmly pegged down against the chill.

It is your dream, the owl said. *Use your feet.*

Jolice looked down and it seemed her feet were no longer human. The boots that Father had made her were gone. She walked now on great talons like an owl. She willed her owl-feet to move and they carried her past the sobbing women, then through the lodge's hide wall which parted before her with no more substance than early morning fog.

Outside, two men stood guard. They had kindled a fire and now spoke to one another in low voices. The rest of the village slept. A brindle-colored dog rose as Jolice approached on her dream-feet, snarling, hackles raised.

One of the men spoke sharply to it and the beast slunk away, ears pinned, still growling.

"Brujel, some of them are so young," the taller of the two said. Jolice saw in the flickering firelight that his face was pocked as though he had survived a terrible fever. He looked to be in his thirties and wore a heavy coat trimmed in wolverine fur, the mark of a great hunter.

"They will grow," Brujel said. He was older, perhaps in his forties, and gray grizzled his long hair which was bound at his neck. "In a few seasons, our sons will need wives too."

Where, she asked herself, had she seen that style before?

"It will never be the same." The younger man glanced at the lodge and shivered. "If only they would stop crying!" He turned back to the dancing flames, his shoulders hunched. "We should have moved to another village and negotiated for new wives."

"Hirdlan applied to all eight of the other clans last fall after we buried the last Elk daughter," Brujel said. He jabbed at the fire with a stick and fat red sparks flew upwards with the smoke. "None of them would accept us because they feared we would bring the Choking Fever and then they too would lose all their women."

It seemed then that *sorrow* permeated the air, both Elk Clan's and Owl's, sharp and bitter. She edged nearer and the flames shifted, reaching for her hungrily.

The younger man flinched and craned his head, gazing past Jolice into the darkness. "Did you see that?"

"It was just a gust of wind," the older man said.

They had destroyed all the families in Owl Clan's village in order to replace their own. Now, two villages mourned! "Let them go!" Jolice cried. "You cannot amend death with more death!"

"The wind is rising," Brujel said. He huddled into his rabbit-fur coat. "We will have a storm tomorrow."

"Let them go!" She beat at them with her fists, but somehow she had wings now instead of arms and could only strike them with white feathers. They seemed not to feel the blows.

The younger man lurched to his feet, shivering. "It is so cold!" he said, rubbing his hands over his arms. "I'll get more wood for the fire."

Where are they, child?

She turned away from the guards. This was one of the Nine Clans. Their conversation had revealed that much. The Choking Fever, she had heard her parents talking of that this winter, how the terrible disease sickened everyone, but killed only women and girls, how no one would visit or trade with the infected village for fear of contracting it. But which one had it been? She had played with her sister, gossiped with her friends, fetched firewood and helped with other chores as required and paid little attention to the direr aspects of life.

Her owl-feet walked through the snow as the wind blasted down from the mountains, but, clad in white feathers, she did not feel the cold. She passed lodges, many empty with their untied doors flapping in the wind. Then she came upon a pole with an object fixed atop it. Though the night was dark, the moon occluded by clouds, she could see clearly. The stark bony hollows of an elk skull gazed down upon her.

She had come to Elk Clan.

Well done, child.

The scene faded into cloudy night sky and then she was asleep, white feathers caressing her cheek.

ଷୠଐଽ

She awoke at midday in her nest of pine needles. Sitting up, she ran fingers through her hair. "Lady Owl?"

A tall, elegant figure emerged from the shadows. Sasalla knelt in the snow beside Jolice. "My Lady Owl sleeps during the day as should you."

Jolice scrambled to her feet, which were still human, she saw, clad in the boots her father had made. "No, I have to rescue my mother and sister, now that I know where they are!"

Sasalla with her long white feathers and golden eyes gazed at her steadily. "Then go."

Jolice plunged out from under the cool pines into full sunlight. Brightness streamed down upon her, a great hot weight that threatened to burn out her eyes. Tears streamed down her cheeks and she could not see. Gasping, she stumbled back under the trees, heart pounding, seeing only searing spots as though she had looked into the sun itself.

"You are a child of the night, now," Sasalla said, "as are all who come to Owl Court. Sleep away the harsh day until the sweet cool dark comes again."

Her mother's tear-ravaged face rose in Jolice's memory. She heard her sister's sad voice again. "Then we can rescue them?" she said.

"We can try," Sasalla said. "But first you must learn to fly."

ଷୠଐଽ

Jolice woke again in darkness as the wind sighed through the pine boughs overhead. It seemed someone or something familiar and beloved had called her name.

"Mother?" She sat up and brushed pine needles off her shoulders.

The branches rustled, then Sasalla joined her. "She is still faraway, as are they all," the tall woman said, "in the village of Elk Clan."

"How could Elk Clan do that!" Jolice lurched to her feet, hands fisted. "They hurt everyone so that they could have what they wanted!"

"Humans often behave so," Sasalla said. "Young as you are, you know that." Her golden eyes gleamed through the shifting tree shadows and she took Jolice's hand in her cool fingers. Power tingled up her arm. "The Lady allows us to look into the past and see through other eyes when there is need. Look now."

Then Jolice glimpsed flashes of herself in that fiery gaze, times when she had been *thoughtless, even selfish, thoroughly heedless of the love that had surrounded her.* The viewpoint shifted and now she saw herself through her mother's perspective, *a willful, fey child who thought mostly of her own needs with little care for the future.* With a sob, Jolice looked away.

"You belong to my Lady Owl now," Sasalla said. "Those days are gone. You are one of Night's little sisters."

"I have to rescue them!" Jolice said, blinking away tears.

"Then come with me," Sasalla said.

Together they walked out of the pines and then hiked up the mountain. The moon had risen and now drifted across the blue-black sky, illuminating a few scattered clouds. Sasalla looked so lovely against the snow, her figure white and gold, each step quick and sure.

"How long have you been in Lady Owl's Court?" Jolice asked as they scaled the boulders.

Sasalla kept climbing. Her snowy head feathers trailed behind her like a cape. "I do not know."

"Months? Years?" She was falling behind.

"It does not matter," Sasalla said. "You will find that such accountings are no longer part of your life." She sprang from rock to rock, never faltering.

Jolice could not match the woman's grace, but it was strange, she thought, how the night's chill no longer touched her. The sharp mountain wind blasting out of the north felt merely fresh and invigorating.

"Now," Sasalla said, stopping on the highest, craggiest rock, "if you are to be of any use to your family, the Lady says you must fly."

Laboriously, Jolice climbed the last few rocks to join her. Pine-scented wind buffeted her face. She swayed, trying to keep her balance. "How?" she said, crossing her arms. "I have no wings."

"My Lady Owl has already given you wings," Sasalla said. "Now you must find them."

Jolice stared back down the snow-covered mountain, the groves of pines and aspen studded here and there, the naked gray rocks, the frozen streams. "Do you have wings?" she turned to ask Sasalla, but the woman was gone. Jolice stood alone on the rocks in the chill night beneath the crystalline stars.

The wind blew. Above, between racing clouds, the stars glimmered, so much wiser than she would ever be. How can I have wings and not know it? she thought. Her hands explored her shoulders but of course there was only human bone, flesh, and skin.

She closed her eyes and tried to see herself spreading arms that had turned mysteriously to wings, sailing back down the mountain to the little valley where what was left of Elk Clan lived. The winter wind would buffet her face. Everything below would be tiny and insignificant. She swayed . . .

But when she opened her eyes again, she was still only herself, a lost girl standing on rocks, all alone in the dark and foolish. She should have gone to Bobcat Clan and asked for help. If she started back down the mountain now, perhaps she could reach them by midday tomorrow.

But then she remembered the daylight's painfully burning light, how it had driven her back into the trees' sheltering shadows. She was changed. That way was closed to her.

You are so close, child, the voice said.

She knotted her fists and stared up into the endless night sky. "Tell me what to do, Lady Owl!"

Unfurl your wings.

As if it were that easy—just decide to have wings and then fly! Anger flooded through her, white-hot, searing, like a river that was about to carry her away.

And who is the object of your anger, child?

Not Lady Owl. Though Jolice didn't understand how the Lady intended her to rescue her family, the spirit at least had not turned her away. "I'm angry with Elk Clan!"

Are you?

She remembered what she had seen on that dream visit. The men of Elk Clan were mired in loss, much as she was now. Their wives had all died along with their sisters and daughters. Elk Clan's whole future had passed away while the other clans went on with their lives and refused even to trade with them, lest they put themselves at risk too. Elk Clan had done a terrible thing, but they had suffered as well.

But the anger was still there, molten and pent up. If she wasn't angry at Lady Owl and at least understood why Elk Clan had been so desperate, then all she had left as the focus of that anger was—

"I am angry," she said slowly, "because I was gone when it happened, because I couldn't stop them from killing my father and taking my mother and sister." She fisted her hands. "I should have been there!"

But then you would have been cowering in that Elk Clan lodge with the rest, your hands bound, your face wet with tears, the voice said.

The acknowledged anger stiffened her shoulders, made her hold her head tall.

Now, child, fly.

She raised her arms and it seemed the stars whispered encouragements in hard bright little voices. The wind gusted at her back, pushing, and then she *leaped* out into empty air—

Falling, falling. She had no wings. Air streamed through her outstretched fingers. Sasalla had lied. The rocks rushed up at her and then—

And then—

Something deep within her breast *tore* as though she were coming apart at unsuspected seams, a terrible wrenching, rending of heart, blood, and bone as Lady Owl's great cruel talons reached inside her body and pulled.

She blinked, suddenly freed, and then flew, wings angling up into the night sky, light as gossamer, light as breath itself. Down below, she heard something thud onto the rocks. The bitter scent of blood seeped through the air, oddly exciting. Jolice soared up the mountain, then circled back.

Take a last look, Daughter, then come away and look no more, the voice said.

The body of a girl sprawled across the rocks, arms akimbo, legs badly broken, brown eyes staring up sightlessly. The body wore her leggings and the decorated tunic her mother had made for her just last harvest. It wore her face.

"Am I dead?" she asked as she wheeled above the rocks.

Not the part of you that matters, Lady Owl said. *Fly higher. Inhabit all of the sky as do your sister owls.*

Jolice angled her wings upward so that the snowy mountain below dropped away. Abruptly, she was falling *up* into the starry night sky. With a shudder, she lost focus and could not remember how to fly. Her wings flailed until finally she leveled out.

You hold back, child, the voice said.

"I am—afraid," she said, gliding just above the pines.

That is because you cling to being merely human.

"I will stop if only you will tell me how," Jolice said.

You must find that path within yourself, Lady Owl said. *Now go and rescue my children.*

She soared back down to the valley, passing over her burned out village, then following the trampled snow to Elk Clan. The night was fine, the wind bold and pine-scented. She felt gloriously free as she stretched her new wings and yet troubled. Even if she rescued the women and girls of Owl Clan, her father and the rest of the men would still be dead. Nothing could ever be as it had been.

She found the village again, its watch fires banked, the guards nodding off. Dawn was near. She would have to hurry. She landed in the snow close to the pole and its overseeing elk skull. With a flutter, dozens of owls swooped out of the sky and joined her, each as snowy white as the Lady Owl herself.

The instant their talons touched the snow, they transformed into women. Long white feathers crowned their heads and their eyes were hot gold. "Youngest sister, what would you have us do?" Sasalla said.

Jolice looked down and saw that she had hands again instead of wings. "Over here!" she whispered and led them through the maze of lodges to the one where the survivors of Owl Clan were imprisoned. She used her belt knife to cut the hide wall, then slipped through the jagged tear. Inside, she could see perfectly well despite the lack of light.

One by one, she pulled the sleeping women and girls to their feet, slit their bonds, and guided them out through the torn wall to her sister owls.

Dazed with misery, the captives stumbled and fell, clung to her for support, asked who she was, snuffled and wept. Elk Clan had taken forty-three prisoners in all, including her mother and young tousled haired sister, Larsi. To the last, they seemed smaller and more fragile than she remembered. She could hear the blood pounding in their veins, the thud of their frightened hearts. Outside in the snow, the captives shivered in the moon shadows, then gazed at the owl rescuers with disbelieving eyes.

"Jolice, is that really you?" Larsi reached up and touched her sister's cheek with her fingertips. "What happened to your hair?"

Her mother held Jolice close, as though she were only three again. "Child, child, what have you done?"

"I went to Owl Court and gave myself to the Lady Owl," she said into her mother's familiar hair which was still redolent with the scent of blueberry soap. Her mother seemed so short! "We must go before the Elk Clan men wake."

"Go where?" her mother said, releasing her. She brushed at her tear-stained face. "They killed everyone, including your father, and burned our lodges. There's nothing left."

Two villages, each cut in half, Jolice thought. Her mother was right. Nothing could mend that.

Sleepy voices came from the front of the lodge. Footsteps stamped toward them through the snow. Larsi hugged Jolice's waist, sobbing.

"They have taken everything from us," her mother said, "including our future. They don't deserve to walk this earth with decent folks!"

Humans always want blood revenge, the Lady said, *but Owl Court is concerned with justice. These are my blameless daughters. Find a way to make them whole.*

Her former self, what she had been holding back from the Lady, that bit, like her mother, also craved revenge. She felt the truth of that down to her toes.

The older man who had been on guard the night before, the one called Brujel, darted around the lodge, torch in one hand, sword in the other. "Get back in the lodge!" he shouted. Several men joined him and she could hear more startled voices as the rest of the village awoke.

The Owl Clan women and girls huddled, helpless and terrified. Jolice smoothed Larsi's hair, then passed the child to their mother. "These Owl Clan daughters are not yours to command," she said, turning back to Brujel. She held her head tall and proud, for had she not flown the skies this night?

Her long head-feathers trailed in the wind and she saw his eyes widen as he realized they had come from Owl Court.

"They are Elk Clan now!" he said, his face reddening.

A line of pink glimmered along the eastern horizon. Jolice thought the humans would not even notice it yet, but the faint light was glaring to her new eyes. There was not much time left this night. "They are under the protection of the Lady Owl," she said, squinting.

He seized Larsi by the hair and dragged her close. The child sobbed hysterically. "Leave now or we will kill them all!"

He gave off fear-scent like the hare she had killed in the Lady Owl's forest. He was *prey*. She felt her interest sharpen, remembered the hot taste of blood. "Give back what you have taken," she said, circling him as though he were only a cornered rabbit.

Fear glinted in his eyes. He rotated, always keeping his sword between them though the tip wavered. "We did what we must—to survive! Their men would have done the same!"

She felt the fiery breath of dawn growing. She and her sister owls could kill these brutes, and part of her longed to just tear out their beating hearts or drive them over a cliff, but that would not provide for Owl Clan women and children who had no one now to fill their lodges with meat or protect them from further attacks.

Truth is a terrible thing, Lady Owl said. *Most prefer to look away.*

The truth of what they had done. Jolice saw in Brujel's eyes that he thought only of his own grief, his own need, his own future, as did they all.

The Owl maidens looked to Jolice with their gleaming golden gaze, hands clasped, waiting. With a flash, she understood. This was *her* justice, as they each must have had their own such moment when they gave themselves to Owl Court. She must shape this justice herself.

The night wind coursed through the valley, carrying a hundred intriguing scents. The Elk Clan men's eyes glittered with the last of the reflected starlight. Everyone, man, woman, child, and owl watched her. She gazed from face to face to face, trying to work out what to do.

Jolice's mother reached for Larsi, then dropped her hand. "You're just one girl," she said in a trembling voice. "Go back up the mountain. Live out your life with Lady Owl. We will take care of ourselves."

They would give in, she meant. They would lie with these criminals and bear them Elk children while Owl Clan's burnt lodges and dead husbands rotted in the snow.

She would not let that happen! Jolice cocked her head, then seized Brujel's wrist in cool implacable fingers. "Bring them and follow me!" she cried to her sister owls. She *reached* and then the men were all suddenly *elsewhere* standing in a burned-out village, the snow dark with frozen blood, the air acrid with ashes.

The startled Elk Clan men stared, each in the grasp of an owl maiden. Brujel gave a startled cry. "Wha—?"

She forced him across the blood-saturated snow to stand over her father's grisly corpse. Brujel struggled against her grip, but this new form had strength far beyond that of her old body, lying now broken upon the rocks. "See what you have done, Elk Clan," she said. "Look upon your deeds with other eyes."

Brujel fought harder to free himself, striking her over and over, though she did not feel the blows. She reached back in time, as Sasalla had shown her, and found her father's last minutes, seeing the carnage through his eyes *as he seized his sword and ran to fight off Elk Clan's attack, feeling his fear for his family, then moments later the stark agony of his wounds as he sprawled, bleeding away his life in the snow.*

Crying out, Brujel lurched back and then Jolice let him go. Many of the Elk men collapsed to their knees in the bloody snow. "You can never return what you have taken." Her voice rang through the darkness. "But justice demands that you make amends. You will build Owl Clan a new village at a location of their choosing, and then you will hunt for them, protect them against attack, carry out all the homely tasks their men would have done, never asking anything in return."

She stalked through the men still shivering from the pain they themselves had inflicted, each step precise. If they would not look at her, she pulled their fingers away from their faces. "You will take none of the women to wife unless they desire it," she said, "and I cannot imagine after what you have done that they ever will. None of their Owl daughters are to be promised to your Elk sons."

Brujel staggered toward her. "But how will Elk Clan survive?" His face had gone utterly white.

"You may not," she said. "Or perhaps the other clans will eventually take pity if you respect your new obligations. In the end, the Lady Elk and Elk Court will decide your fate."

She took the nearest man's arm, *reached*, and then they were back in Elk Clan's village. With a cry, the men dropped their swords, staring at their hands as though they were drenched in blood.

Jolice turned to her mother. "They will honor you now," she said, and her voice sharpened toward a screech. "It's little enough after what they have done, but it is all that I can give you."

Dawn was a hot red line along the eastern horizon now, the sky above brightening to gray. Her eyes had to turn away.

"Come with us!" her mother begged. Larsi was sobbing again.

"That life is over," Jolice said, feeling the enthralling lure of the open sky. "I have another now."

Larsi caught her hand and pressed it to her wet cheek. "Won't you ever come back?"

"Not unless you need justice," Jolice said.

The child's touch anchored her to the ground when she longed to fly. Freeing herself from Larsi's fingers, she felt the last of her humanity slip away. With a full throated cry, she leaped up into the sky and then soared on gossamer wings with her sister owls back to the cool green-black piney silences of Owl Court.

NELLANDRA'S KEEPER

by Teresa Howard

As anyone who has a sister knows, the answer to "am I my sister's keeper?" is a resounding yes, especially if your sister isn't doing what your family wants her to do. The mystery, however, is why adults think a girl can control her sister's behavior.

Teresa Howard is a teacher and school technology coordinator by day. Nights and weekends she morphs into a con-going Fantasy and SF fan and writer whose stories cover a wide range of speculative fiction and children's stories. The world of Aldebar and the magical Nelari people feature in many of these stories, and she is currently working on a novel set in this world. She shares her home with SuzieQ, a loveable Tibetan terrier. She says that she made the mistake of reading the bios of former "Sword and Sorceress" authors and is both honored and intimidated to be included in their numbers.

"Where is Nellandra? I told you to guard her until after the wedding." The high priestess's mind voice prickled uncomfortably in the back of my head.

"I'm sure she's just gone for a walk. I can find her." My answer was much calmer than I felt, a little trick of mindspeak that I employ from time to time.

"Nellandra should be preparing to meet her bridegroom, not wandering off. She must not be late for the betrothal feast, too many people will be watching." I winced as I felt her annoyance.

"Yes, Grandmother, I'll make sure she's there."

From the beginning, I had disagreed with Grandmother's decision to send Nellandra to the Degg Homeland for two years. She had resisted coming home. Now, Nelladra was back in Nelar and I was again her keeper and protector, a job I wouldn't wish on anyone. After assuring Grandmother that Nellandra wouldn't be late, I set out to bring the truant bride back from her wandering.

I pulled a transparent blue stone from its resting place in the bag at my waist. Rubbing it gently, I hummed the ancient seeker's song. The stone warmed in my hands until it gradually gave off a soothing heat of its own.

I have always had a special bond with Nell that even our Grandmother, the High Priestess, can't match or explain. If anyone could find the reluctant bride it's me, and finding Nell was my mission, at least part of it. I suspected that I would also have to convince her to go through with the marriage.

I focused on a mental image of Nellandra's face. Ah, there she was. I could see her in my mind, and seeing her, knew at once where she was hiding. I began moving purposefully in her direction.

Pushing through a tangle of creeping vines and leafy bushes, I spotted Nellandra stretched out lazily on a bed of blue-green egat moss beneath an ancient tree.

Alerted by my approach, she sat up and spoke wistfully, "I've missed this place." She stroked the velvety moss and continued as if I wanted an explanation. "Rishal is so dry."

"I thought you wanted to stay in the Degg Homeland?"

"I do, but I love Nelar too." She brushed back dark auburn curls from her fine-boned face and smiled.

I couldn't help noticing how the moss almost matched the color of her eyes. No one could dispute Nellandra's beauty.

And being taller than many Nelari men, she carried herself with an easy grace and assurance.

Recalling the purpose of my mission, I delivered my message. "Grandmother has been calling for you. You're late and if you don't hurry back, everyone's feast meal will be cold before we're dressed."

I watched embarrassment color her cheeks.

"Oh! I'd forgotten the time. I'd better hurry. Thanks, Galley!" She jumped to her feet and hurried away at a graceful sprint, heedless of the tangle of bushes that I had carefully maneuvered through.

Smiling to myself, I watched her retreating figure. That's Nellandra, brains, beauty, grace, but not a smack of magic in her bones. I ran after her, sure that she would need my assistance before long.

"You're not going to appear at the feast looking like that, are you?" I was out of breath when I caught up with her, but still mindful of my duties. "Your blue is faded."

Nell shrugged giving me a sideways glance. "In Rishal I hardly ever wear the blue. No one wears it there."

"Well, this isn't Rishal."

Nell nodded in understanding, and we walked in silence to the room we shared. She rubbed the silky cream into her skin until it shone blue and smooth. As she did so, I combed special oils into her auburn hair until it hung as black and sleek as my own. Glancing at her reflection in the mirror, I noticed there was a frown on her face. *Surely she realizes how beautiful she is. Her bridegroom can't help but love her, even after he finds out how we've tricked him.*

"I don't understand the hurry for this wedding." There was sadness in Nell's voice, as if marrying the most eligible bachelor in the Western Nelari Kingdom was some horrible sacrifice she was being asked to make.

"It's the first step in reuniting the two homelands," I reminded her. Nell isn't stupid, far from it, so I knew that there was something else bothering her.

"But, why me?"

Nodding at the ceremonial necklace she wore, I answered, "You're the First Daughter of the Stone. Grandmother has chosen you to be her heir."

Nell burst into tears. "But it doesn't want me, Galley. I've worn it for three days and nothing has happened. I haven't felt anything. Touch it, Galley, it's cold. It doesn't want me." She took off the necklace and held it out to me.

I stepped back in horror, staring at the glittering Stone hanging on the slender chain. It was the thing I desired more than anything in this world or the next. I shook my head. I knew I could never touch that Stone and let it go again. "It takes time to bond with the Stone, Nell. If Grandmother says that you are the chosen one, then it is so. Trust her. Give it time."

We finished getting dressed in silence, then set off for the feast.

As we entered the banquet hall, I stopped to speak to friends as Nell went on ahead. I saw her greet two young ladies, daughters of council members. I recognized both and knew that neither would wish Nell any good, so I left my friends and followed her in. Nell had gone into the dining area and they were watching her, heads together.

"The old woman is crazy if she thinks I'll follow that one. I touched her just now, and she is unbelievably weak." Basara smoothed her gown, arching her neck in a superior manner. "I could squash her with very little effort."

A rage boiled within me. I reached out with my mind. Basara jerked in fear as the strength of my magic pressed on her mind. I eased up only slightly as I approached them. My voice quivered with the anger I felt, "Such a weak mind, I could squash it with just a thought."

I released Basara and walked past, while they stared in disbelief. Nell's lack of magic was one of Grandmother's little secrets; I was the other. If we were going to keep Nell's secret, I was going to have to use every bit of the considerable magic I possessed. I reached forward and surrounded Nell with some of that magic now. Not a lot, but enough. Anyone else who decided to test her now would not find her aura lacking in magic.

The bridegroom, Lord Alcyon, was the tallest Nelari I'd ever seen, and was well muscled and handsome too. I stood behind Nell as she was presented to her future husband and felt the gentle touch of his magic as he reached out to her.

Nell's hand reached out, and before I could move or protest she had pulled me into the space between them. "This is my sister Gallandra."

I don't know which of us was more surprised. Lord Alcyon recovered first. I felt the touch of his mind again, this time its attention directed at me. He looked puzzled for a moment, glanced at Nell, then back at me. I changed the color of my magic slightly, and he smiled. "I'm pleased to meet you, little sister."

Normally being called little sister would have offended me. I am sensitive about my small stature, and being fifteen, I am a woman, not a child. However, Lord Alcyon's gentle tone and the warmth of his magic were irresistible. Nell didn't seem to agree. She remained nervous and formal throughout the dinner.

"Ladies, may I impose on you for a tour of the gardens? I'd like to get a peek at some of the rare flowers the High Priestess has acquired." He smiled teasingly at Nell. "There won't be much time tomorrow."

That was my cue to make a graceful exit and give Lord Alcyon some private time with Nell. I was just about to oblige him when Nell outmaneuvered me.

"I'm sorry, Lord Alcyon. I'm not feeling very well. I think I had better go back to my room and lie down. Gallandra can show you the gardens. She's the expert on plants in the family. Not even Grandmother knows more about herb magic than Galley."

I glared at my sister. "If you're ill, Nell, I can go back to the room and fix you something. I'm sure Lord Alcyon will excuse both of us."

"No, I'll go back to the room alone. I just feel a little queasy, and tomorrow is a big day. Please show Lord Alcyon the gardens." With that she turned and walked purposefully out of the hall.

Frustrated, I sent a wave of magic after Nell, and gifted her a little headache too, for being so rude to our guest. For his part, Lord Alcyon only looked mildly amused.

"Well, little sister, let's find these gardens. It's a lovely night for a walk."

So walk we did, and talk, and laugh. I pointed out several rare flowers. My nerves made me stumble a bit in the explanations, but Lord Alcyon was charming and never once made me feel like an unwanted companion. He shared wonderful tales of the Western Homeland and the ocean that separated it from the land of the Narr, our enemies.

I soon thought Nell was lucky in Grandmother's selection of first mate, and I meant to tell her so, even if I had to wake her up. Our room was empty so I quickly began the search for Nell again. The thin veil of my magic surrounding her made her easier to find.

"By my ancestors!" She was in the suite of one of the other guests assembled for the wedding. Basara's brother Nabar was charming, a charming snake. He was known in court circles for two things, his ability to cast a seduction spell, and the art of blackmail. I realized belatedly that the magic I'd left Nell wouldn't protect her against Nabar's tricks.

Minutes later I was banging on Nabar's door, my probing magic revealing that thankfully I was in time to prevent him from becoming Nell's first mate and spoiling any marriage plans.

"Go away," Nabar ordered as he opened the door the tiniest crack.

"I want Nell. Send her out now."

Nabar laughed. "Nell doesn't want you right now, she wants me."

I wasn't about to waste time arguing with Nabar and risk people finding out that Nell had spent even a short time in his rooms unchaperoned.

"Out of my way," I commanded and hit him with a fierce shaft of magic. The door flew open and Nabar tumbled back onto in the floor.

Breaking his spell over Nell wasn't easy or painless, and I didn't shield Nell from the pain either. That would teach her to be a little more careful. AS Nabar watched the scene in apparent good humor, he threw back his head and laughed.

"The old woman's picked the wrong sister." He got carefully to his feet. I felt the icy touch of his magic stroke my cheek. "Would you like for me to be your first mate, Galley? We would make such a powerful team." His seduction spell began to wrap itself around me.

I tried to shake it off in disgust, but it was a strong spell and I was inexperienced enough to be momentarily mesmerized by its tantalizing song. But before I gathered myself enough to react, Nellandra acted, coming to my rescue. Using a heavy vase, she hit Nabar a glancing blow on the back of his head. He crashed immediately to the floor, and the effects of his spell evaporated. Sometimes non-magic action is so satisfying. I helped Nell back to our rooms. She kept apologizing and thanking me for the timely intervention, but I disagreed.

"It's my fault, I should have gone back to the room with you. I shouldn't have left you alone. Grandmother warned me there could be trouble."

"And just when did you become my guardian?"

"I was five."

"Ancestors, Galley! No one gets magic that young. Why didn't Grandmother make you her heir? Surely she knows by now that I'll never come close to your magic." I flinched at the question. Nell fixed me with a look. "What is it? What's wrong?"

Tears streamed down my face as I revealed the truth. "Five sons. I'll bear five sons."

"That's good. You'll have lots of children."

"Not children, sons. No daughters."

Realization dawned on Nell's face. Without a daughter, the office of high priestess would fall for the first time on someone from another house.

"Poor Galley, she shouldn't have told you that. It is so unfair. But why me? Wouldn't it be better to select someone outside the family?"

"Your daughter will be a Silver Queen, Nell. Grandmother let me see. She will be the greatest priestess since Prenola. She will unite both the Eastern and Western homelands."

"I see."

"And Lord Alcyon really is kind. Grandmother is right, when he finds out that you don't have your own magic, he will protect you. You'll be safe with him."

Nell squeezed my hands. "And you? You will be free, right, Galley? Free to live your own life."

I wiped away the tears, nodding.

We talked a little while longer before I fell asleep. Surprisingly it was a deep sleep, and I woke up late. Nell was already gone. I found her in the temple seeking the wisdom of the Stones. That is always a private matter for a Nelari so I waited for her with the other ladies.

I was just beginning to fill our Grandmother in on the events of the previous evening when the door opened. There was an audible gasp from several of the ladies. I turned to see that they had stepped aside to allow Nell to enter the room. She walked in slowly, her head high, her skin a glow of pink and white, the auburn curls shining. She had forsaken the blue! Disaster!

I rushed to Nellandra's side and hissed a warning in her ear. "Don't do this! If you forsake the blue, you will be banished from the Homeland forever."

Grandmother started to come toward us, her mindspeak bombarding me with commands. "Get her out of here! Lock her in her room if you have to, just don't let anyone speak to her!"

Nell held up her hand. Her voice rang with its own magic. "I have freely accepted this Stone, and only I have the power to bestow it on another. That is the law of the Stones."

There was shocked silence in the room. Grandmother reached toward Nellandra, her eyes pleading. Nellandra shook her head, and the High Priestess of Nelar bowed in defeat.

Nellandra turned to me then. One hand gently touched my shoulder and pushed until I was kneeling. Leaning forward, she kissed my cheek and slipped the Stone around my neck. The power of the Stone surged through me as it came to life and blazed a brilliant blue. It was everything that I had ever dreamed or imagined. Nell laughed in triumph. "Hail Gallandra, First Daughter of the Stone."

My euphoria was tempered with sadness, of a vision of things ahead for both of us. Her daughter would be my heir. "I'll come for her, Nell. I'll have to."

"You can come." Nell's voice never wavered. "But she'll be free to choose. I promise you that, Galley, she will be free to choose."

So, Nell slipped away from her bridegroom and her people and I was left to pick up the pieces. Grandmother was no help. I had never seen the High Priestess so beside herself with grief. Not even the death of our mother had affected her so. It would be a long while before she came to herself again, and I doubted she would ever be the power she once was. She had been defeated without magic.

My thoughts turned to Lord Alcyon. He was waiting for his bride. He was waiting for the beautiful Nellandra. But technically that wasn't what the marriage contract specified. It only stated that his bride would be the heir of the High Priestess of the Eastern Homeland, the First Daughter of the Stone. With Nell's abdication, I became the chosen heir. I wore the Stone. I sent away the ladies and council members, even Grandmother. Then I sent a messenger to bring Lord Alcyon. He could reject the contract if he wished, and be blameless. He deserved to make that choice.

I felt his surprise when he entered and found me instead of Nell waiting.

"Where's Nellandra?"

"Gone." I touched my hand to the Stone. His gaze followed, then met mine, demanding answers. I related some of the events leading to her departure. "I'm not Nell, but our offer still stands."

"You're still a child! What can you offer?"

"We can be married. Not right away, but not long. I'm fifteen."

He shook his head gravely. "Fifteen. A woman, yes, but still too young. The Western homeland will be at war soon."

I hesitated, about to make a grand concession. My Stone urged me on. "I will increase the marriage contract to include five sons. Five sons with powerful DaWakanda blood."

His face struggled to convey the urgency of his homeland's need and control the insult he must feel at Nellandra's departure.

I raised my hand and added, "And the power of the Stones will be with your warriors."

I had been warned that the Stones had been all but forgotten in the Western Homeland and I could see that truth in his eyes.

"Power!" Lord Alcyon drew his sword and held it out, "This is the power I need."

My anger ignited and the Stone's magic soared through me. A bolt shot from my hand and the air sizzled with blue flame. Lord Alycon's sword, snatched cleanly from his hand, spun in the air as if consumed by the flames. Neither of us moved.

After a time my anger cooled and the sword fell at Lord Alcyon's feet. In its hilt, a small blue stone glimmered as if still reflecting the flames' power.

Lord Alcyon fell to his knees and grasped the sword, his thumb caressing the embedded stone. Magic hummed as he lifted the sword and touched its blade to his forehead in a pledge of fealty.

Looking up, he whispered, "My Lady."

SAGES AND DEMONS

by Catherine Soto

This is Catherine's fourth story about Lin Mei and the two cats she found in an abandoned temple. In the past few years they have grown from helpless kittens to partners she can communicate with. Lin Mei has learned to see with their eyes and hear with their ears, which is a good thing for her; during the same period she's gone from groom to caravan guard to semi-official secret agent for the Empire.

      Catherine Soto lives in San Francisco. She has developed an interest in Kyudo, the art of Japanese archery. She is still hanging out at the Asian Art Museum, but she misses the monks and the daily prayers (the exhibit this past spring was from Bhutan, and the two monks who came with it chanted scripture for an hour twice a day). By the time this book is published there will be an exhibit titled "Emerald Cities"—no, not Oz—art from Siam (now Thailand) and Burma (now Myanmar).

L in Mei and her brother Biao Mei walked into the great square before the Norbulingka palace. No sentries challenged them, for the Yar Lungs ruled there, and no Yar Lung would admit to danger or fear. An old man in a stall nearby was selling strips of roasted meat wrapped in barley bread. The smell tempted them, for they had just arisen and they had eaten a light dinner the night before after a long journey.

"Food, Grandfather," Biao Mei said gruffly, handing over two coppers. The old man snatched them out of his hand with an alacrity that belied his years and handed back two wrapped meat strips. Lin Mei bit into hers with relish. They moved to the side of the square and eyed the crowd around them. Already the square was beginning to fill with a crowd of merchants, shoppers, and beggars. Lin Mei shivered in the early morning chill despite her quilted jacket and the hot breakfast they were eating.

"That man is in a hurry," Biao Mei noted, nodding his head in the direction of a burly man in a long woolen robe making his way through the crowd. Lin Mei eyed him closely.

"Or running from someone, or something . . ." she said, noting the backward glance as he shoved someone aside. Automatically she eyed the rest of the crowd and saw another man, tall and lean, dressed in the leathers of a nomad and with a shaven head, striding through the crowd toward him. She tapped her brother's shoulder and motioned toward the newcomer.

It was over in moments. The two men seemed to brush against one another, and the short burly man fell, as if stumbling.

But the two had seen enough death in their short lifetimes to know it when they saw it. Shoving their half-eaten breakfasts into their jackets they raced forward into the commotion starting around the fallen man. Biao Mei raced after the killer as Lin Mei headed for the fallen man.

As soon as she saw the blood soaking into the ground she knew nothing would help. The wound was deep on his right side, just under the ribs. He coughed his last breath as she knelt by him.

"Does anyone know him?" she asked the crowd.

"Go Choden," someone replied. "A servant of the Kalden temple."

"The killer was tall, with a shaven head and dressed in the leathers of a nomad," she said. "Did anyone see him?" There were nods, but no one could give a name. Her brother returned, shouldering his way through the crowd.

"He got away," he said, "into the alleys in the lower town."

"Ah!" someone cried. "All the bad ones live there!"

"The chostimpas come!" someone else cried out, referring to the city guards. Standing, Lin Mei saw a group of tall ruffians making their way through the crowd. Eyeing the liberal use of their long staffs and whips on the people around them gave her little assurance of civil treatment.

"We'll go look for the killer," Lin Mei announced. "Let's leave," she muttered to her brother, who showed enough sense to follow her into the crowd. In moments they had slipped from the square into the alleys of the lower end of the town.

"He vanished into that area," Biao Mei said, motioning with his left hand. Lin Mei noted he kept his right hand near the hilt of the sword thrust though his sash.

"And we will not," Lin Mei replied. "We are here on another mission, not to solve random killings. We will leave it to the chostimpas. Let us go back to our room."

They had lodgings not far from the square, in the Norbu Ling quarter, almost in the shadow of the palace. Circling around the square through the outskirts of the city they arrived at the Inn of the Yu Thog, which had been recommended to them. The recommendation had been a good one. The place was clean and had private rooms at reasonable rates and good food.

As they entered the inn, the innkeeper's wife approached. "There was a message for you," she said, clutching a strip of paper. "It arrived just after you left." Lin Mei thanked her and took it, but waited until she and Biao Mei reached their room to open it.

Closing the door behind them they paused to take stock. Their few belongings were neatly arranged as they had left them. Lin Mei looked over at a corner to check on the cats, Shadow and Twilight. They were asleep in a puddle of fur on a worn horse blanket. Satisfied that there was no immediate danger, she unfolded the paper. After a moment she looked up from it to her brother.

"It's a message," she told him. "It gives the code phrase, and says to meet him at the Kalden temple. It's signed Go Choden." Biao Mei frowned.

"Let's go see that temple," he said. Lin Mei nodded.

⊰⚬⚬⚬⚬⚭⚭

The temple was grand, tall and imposing, with a bell tower in the square beside it. They stopped in the area before the steps. Lin Mei set her lips gazing up at it. Imposing as it was, it was in a barbaric style, meant to impress a less-sophisticated audience. It reminded her they were in the heart of a barbarian empire.

"I thought our contact was the Sage of Sakya," Biao Mei said, gazing around.

"We were to seek out the Sage," she said, "and that would bring us to the attention of the man we would meet. Not necessarily the Sage." Settling her sword and dagger in her sash she led the way up the stairs and through the wide doors. A young monk stood as they approached.

"We bring sad news," Lin Mei said. "Your servant, Go Choden, has been killed in the square by an unknown assailant." The young monk nodded.

"I have heard," he said. "Go Choden was a faithful servant. This is a sad moment."

"Last night we sought the Sage of Sakya," Lin Mei went on. "We were told he had retired and were instructed to return today. Is he available?" The young monk frowned.

"No, he is not," he replied. "Chostimpas from the palace came this morning and arrested him, on orders of Dorje Gyaltso, the Khan's advisor. He is being held captive in the palace."

CR80

The great temple bell had just rung the hour of the Dog when they met again in their room at the Yu Thog. They had spent the day in town, Biao Mei learning the lay of the land and Lin Mei gathering the gossip in the square and the surrounding areas. It was surprising how little concern was being paid to the killing that morning in the square. Apparently violent death was not uncommon. The arrest of the Sage was another matter.

"The Sage is charged with witchcraft against the Khan," she said. "All the square was filled with gossip of it."

"All of it conflicting?" Biao Mei asked. She nodded wryly.

"So many tales of dark wizardry that he is made out to be the most powerful and evil mage under heaven."

"And the advisor?"

"Very little said," she replied. "That says something." Biao Mei nodded.

"Fear," he said. "People are afraid to say anything bad, but can find nothing good to say." It was her turn to nod.

"And we were asking about him. That bit of gossip will find its way to the wrong ears soon enough. How went your scouting?"

"The palace is strongly built, but against the mountain," he said. "If attackers get above it in numbers, it would fall."

"The Yar Lung are building it mainly for ceremony," she said. "They still pride themselves on their nomad heritage, and spend most of their time in tented camps. At present the Khan is camped just outside the Temple complex of Sera, a few hour's ride from Lhasa. But his advisor, who is supposed to be a powerful sorcerer, is in the palace."

"Odd," Biao Mei mused. "Advisors like to stay close to those they advise."

"Truth," Lin Mei agreed. "Very odd." In the corner the two cats stirred, sparking an idea in her mind. "You said the palace is built against the mountain?" He nodded. "Night scouting," she said, bringing a grin to her brother's face. "But first, food, for all of us."

⋘⋙

The innkeeper's wife sold bowls of stew for a copper each, and Lin Mei and Biao Mei ate heartily. A bowl of stew in the corner fed the two cats, much to the bewilderment and amusement of the other guests. In truth the two cats were an oddity in their own right, being cream colored with dark faces, paws, and tails. Shadow had grown to the size of the wild cats of the mountains. Twilight was half his size, sleek and slender. Their odd looks had prompted many to call them devil-cats, and Lin and Biao had done little to dissuade such talk, although Lin Mei was cautious not to encourage it. Charges of witchcraft could cause them much trouble.

"What do you mean?" Lin Mei asked around a scrap of tsampa, the barley bread that was the staple of the high mountains. "I thought a Bonpa was a priest of the Old Gods." The old woman went by the name of Rabten, and was, like many others of her age, inclined to talk.

"That, and much more," the old woman said in a low voice. "But he has never been admitted to a temple or monastery for study. He is a Njalyorpa, a mountain wizard, who has learned his art from others like him. But some of them are very powerful because of their association with the spirits and demons of the country."

"Like lumas?" Biao Mei asked, referring to the stone serpent demons of lakes and rivers. The old woman nodded.

"And others. People say that Dorje Gyaltso has captured the demon of the mountain above Lhasa and keeps him in a room in the palace, bound with spells and magical charms."

"That is his name?" Lin Mei asked, wiping up the last of her stew with a scrap of bread. The old woman nodded, her eyes darting about the nearly empty room.

"Yes. He convinced the Khan to build the palace on the hillside. A bad idea, for the demons of the land were not appeased by the proper ceremonies. Instead he used his magic to capture the most powerful one and lock him up!"

"The Khan does not live in it," Biao noted, "preferring his tent city for a court."

"He is still a nomad at heart," the old woman replied. "And the palace is still being built. Dorje Gyaltso stayed behind to oversee the construction. And to ensure the demon does not escape."

"He sounds like a very powerful magician," Lin Mei said, encouraging the old woman to talk.

"He is," she agreed. "And he is distrusted by the Bonpas of the land, who dislike his power over the Khan. He is new to this region. He came suddenly less than two years ago and impressed the Khan with his magic arts and prophecies. Now he rules Lhasa, in the Khan's name."

"We have seen that before," Biao Mei muttered as they left the inn, the two cats scampering along beside them.

"Priests and magicians should be content to rule in the otherworld," Lin Mei agreed, her eyes gauging the darkening sky. A thought formed in her mind.

"Let's go see that young monk before we start," she said.

The temple bell had just rung the last hour of the day when Lin Mei and her brother ascended the stairs of the temple once more. The door opened as they approached, the young monk bowing them in, almost as if they had been anticipated. They entered, Shadow and Twilight slipping in behind them like ghosts as the door closed. The monk ushered them into a side room and motioned them to hard cushions on the floor. He took a small straw mat for himself.

"I am Jongbu Kunchen," he said. "Welcome."

"Biao Mei, and my sister, Lin Mei," Biao said, motioning with his left hand. His right nested comfortably in his lap, near the hilts of his sword and dagger. Shadow settled into a corner, his sister curling up quietly near him. Lin Mei noted that, and their alertness. So they sensed no immediate danger, but they were still not at ease. She took out the scrap of paper and handed it over to the young monk, who quickly glanced at it.

"Did you know of this?" she asked.

"Go Choden took orders from Penchen Rimpoche, the Sage of Sakya," Jongbu replied.

"The talk in town is that he was arrested for plotting witchcraft against the Khan," Biao Mei said.

"A lie," the young monk replied. "Sages do not practice witchcraft, or any other kind of sorcery. That is mostly done by the lower orders of Njalyorpas."

"Why would Dorje Gyaltso have him arrested?" Lin Mei asked. Jongbu frowned.

"He fills the Khan's mind with fears of plots and schemes against his rule," Jongbu said. "Many nobles and Bonpas have been arrested because of this. The Sage spoke out against the advisor's evil influence over the Khan."

"And now he has been arrested," Biao Mei said. The monk nodded gravely.

They thanked the monk and left, Lin Mei dropping a few coppers into the collection box just outside the door.

ଔେଔେ

It was now dark, and they took the less-traveled byways to the palace. An hour of careful work got them to the rocky hillside above it. Lin Mei noted the lack of sentries. Obviously the Yar Lungs' disdain for danger and attendant precautions was not mere talk. And then, the Khan was away, and the palace was still under construction. Biao Mei motioned to a door on a wall nearby. Lin Mei nodded and settled down into a comfortable position on the ground.

She was not sure how the bond between them and the cats had formed. Two years ago, they had found the young kittens in an abandoned temple near the body of their mother. Soon after adopting them, Lin Mei had started to be disturbed by dreams and visions. With testing and practice, she had learned to see with their eyes and hear with their ears. Biao Mei also had this ability to some extent, but he was content to let her exercise it. Now she reached out with her mind, melding her senses with theirs, and the two cats silently glided forward to listen at the door.

In moments they had ascertained that there was no one on the other side of the door, and Lin Mei motioned with her hand, all the while maintaining her link with the cats. Biao Mei worked a slender dagger from his boot top into the space between the door and the jamb and, after a moment opened the door. Lin Mei stood, following him into the dark entryway. A silent request sent the two feline scouts scampering ahead, their tails raised high like little flags. So they sensed no danger. Yet.

Lin Mei and her brother followed, silent in their felt boots. The corridor was spacious, with garish murals on the walls. It was what she expected in a barbarian palace. It was built to be imposing to a barbarian people, with little knowledge of, or concern for, esthetics.

She stopped for a moment, sending her mind forward with the cats. A vision of a vast canyon opened up, flat bottomed and sheer walled. She was used to a cat's-eye view of thing by now, and she identified a vast hallway, ornately decorated, and devoid of people. She frowned.

"No one ahead," she murmured. "The place is almost empty."

"No guards standing sentry," Biao Mei agreed quietly, "and no servants tending to the place, or enjoying it while the masters are away. Odd." He loosened his sword in the scabbard and led the way forward, Lin Mei following his lead. When it came to danger and battle, she was content to trust his instincts.

At an intersection of the corridor with a hallway they met the two cats waiting for them. Their mood had changed. Now they were tense, wary. Shadow eyed one end of the hallway where a dim light around the distant corner provided vague illumination. Twilight had her eyes on the other end, which ended in a flight of stairs leading down. Lin Mei sensed unease on the part of both cats. Looking into the darkness she felt the hair on the back of her neck prickle.

"The old woman said something about spells and magic," Biao Mei whispered uneasily. Silently he led the way to the stairs, while the cats prowled uneasily behind them.

The stairs led downward, the only light from small butter lamps set into the wall at intervals. The walls were bare down here where no one would have enjoyed murals or adornment.

At the bottom they found a massive wooden door, metal studded, barred with a thick beam. At first Lin Mei thought the marking on the planks were a crude attempt at decoration before she recognized it as the cursive writing of the mountains.

"Spells and magical charms," she whispered. Biao Mei nodded, his eyes taking in the thickness of the beam and planks. A sudden hissing from the cats caused them to turn around in a flash, their hands darting to their swords.

And just as quickly Lin Mei saw that their swords would be useless.

It was a woman, clad only in long, flowing black hair that fell past her waist. She stood on the stairs above them. Tall and slender, almost sinuous, she projected an air of menace and danger. Her eyes were cold and hard, and betrayed a high level of intelligence. And Lin Mei's blood ran cold. She knew exactly what they were facing.

"Lumas," she breathed.

"Yes," the creature replied, in a voice that was almost a hiss. "Why are you here?"

"We seek the Sage of Sakya," Lin Mei replied, in a voice that held only a slight tremor. Considering her true feelings she felt slightly proud of that.

"He is not here," the being hissed. "Inside is Akar Nawang."

"That is the Demon of the Mountain?" Biao Mei asked.

"The Master of the Mountain!" the lumas hissed. "And my Lord!"

"Where is the Sage of Sakya?" Lin Mei asked.

"Above," the lumas hissed, her eyes darting up the stairs. She grimaced and quickly vanished up the stairs in a movement that was simultaneously rapid and graceful. Lin Mei suddenly felt much better, the feeling of dread gone. A look at her brother showed he was relieved also, as were the cats, who had been crouched in a corner. But a memory rose unbidden in her mind. Such a being would not flee ordinary mortals . . .

"Dorje Gyaltso!" Lin Mei said. In a flash they ran up the stair, the two cats bounding up behind them, and raced down the hallway, silent as ghosts. At the corner they turned down the corridor just in time to avoid being seen by the approaching Njalyorpa and his guards.

In the dark corridor they both dropped to the floor, arms up to hide their faces. Only their eyes showed between their dark sleeves and their black hair. The two cats melted into the shadows.

The wizard passed by, intent on his thoughts, followed by two tall and lean chostimpas, armed with spears and daggers. No one thought to look down the corridor to where Lin Mei and her companions hid. As soon as they had passed she and her three companions slipped out the door and vanished into the night above the palace.

It was near dawn as they made their way back to the inn. They circled past the main square, avoiding parties of chostimpas patrolling the area. In the shadows a puzzled frown passed over Lin Mei's face. Setting her puzzlement aside for the moment she followed her brother back to the inn, the two cats scampering ahead as advance scouts.

Rabten was already up, starting the day's work. She nodded as they returned, apparently not concerned or curious about their night's activities.

"There's stew already," she said, setting out bowls and tsampa for them. Another bowl was set out for the cats. Lin Mei handed over a copper and thanked her.

"There are chostimpas prowling about," Lin Mei commented around a mouthful of tsampa. "I thought the Yar Lung disdained precautions."

"They do," the old woman agreed with a grin, "but Dorje Gyaltso does not! He is no fool. He knows he is disliked, and he fears attack. Also, I hear they are searching for someone." She gave them a sidelong glance before turning back to her pots.

"Who are the chostimpas?" Lin Mei asked. "They all look like a type."

"Most are from Kham, the land in the northeast," Rabten replied. "Like Dorje Gyaltso. He chooses men he can trust."

෴ශ෴

Alone in their room after their meal Lin Mei checked the door before turning to her brother. The two cats were already asleep on their blanket.

"All the nomads we have met have been short and bow-legged," she said. Understanding crossed Biao Mei's face.

"The killer was not," he breathed. "Tall, lean, and hard looking. Like the chostimpas."

"And Dorje Gyaltso is their master," she said.

"And he holds the Sage captive, along with the Demon, Akar Nawang. No wonder he prefers the palace to the tent city of the Khan. He has more to guard here." He yawned suddenly, and Lin Mei realized they were both very tired. Their young lives had been active and filled with danger. They were fit and trained, but the high altitude of the Tifun Empire took some getting used to.

"This will take thought, as well as action," Lin Mei said. "Let us follow the cats' example and get some sleep. Then we can plan our moves with a clear mind." Biao Mei agreed, and they went to sleep, taking care to set their swords and daggers within easy reach.

It was past noon when they awoke, Lin Mei stretching as she stood. Biao Mei was doing his morning exercises and Lin Mei joined him. Then they went out to the common room of the inn. Rabten was there, with more bowls of soup.

"The day is begun," she said, "and most people are out and about."

"It is a busy city," Lin Mei said. "Many people come here."

"Many people," Rabten agreed, smiling. "The Hind Empire is to the south, ancient and powerful. The Tang are to the northeast, and the Turks are to the north. This land has many names, one of them is the Navel of the World."

Lin Mei laughed at that. "Many gods and demons frequent it," she said. "The magicians and sorcerers must have much work here."

"They do," Rabten agreed. "It is a big part of their work. Many of them are very powerful because of the demons they capture and enslave."

"In the Tang empire we have come across demons and devils also," Lin Mei said. "Some are from the mountains. In Kendar we met a lumas who lived in a stone."

"They sometimes do," Rabten said. "If you want to know about them, ask a monk, or a Njalyorpa. But be careful! Not all speak truth!"

Lin Mei and her brother eyed each other at that. Thanking her for the meal they left the inn, the two cats strolling alongside.

"Let's talk to that young monk again," Lin Mei said, "and see if he speaks truth."

The circled the city, avoiding the more trafficked areas in the center and the chostimpas that stood watch there. Soon they were at the temple. Fortunately the area was clear of the prowling guards. The monks were at their afternoon devotions, so they waited in the shadows for the chants to finish. Lin Mei's mind went back to a nighttime meeting several months before in Kendar.

CRBDD

"There is talk of a new advisor to the Khan of Tifun," Ro Min was saying. Lin Mei and her brother were in a side room of the main building of the compound owned by Wang Liu, a wealthy merchant, and their sometime employer. With them were Ro Min and Kin Shin, expert archers, bodyguards to the merchant's young wife, and agents of the Tang Imperial Agency, the secretive spy service of the Empire. "He counsels the Khan and supposedly wants to foment a new war with the Empire."

"And we are to spy out the truth?" Biao Mei asked. Lin Mei and the two women suppressed smiles. Both Imperial agents were attractive women, and Biao Mei had a young man's infatuation with Ro Min.

"We already have eyes in Lhasa," Ro Min replied. "But we have received no messages in the last year. It may mean there is nothing noteworthy to report. And then, something may be wrong. We need to know."

"How will we contact your spy?" Lin Mei asked.

"Find lodgings at the Yu Thog Inn. Then seek the Sage of Sakya," Kin Shin replied. "You will be contacted when it is safe. The code phrase will be, 'The sunrise is brilliant here'."

"Wang Liu is sending a caravan to Lhasa later this month," Ro Min added. "You will go along as guards. When the caravan returns you will stay behind. Say that you seek the Sage's advice as to your destiny."

"Your mission is merely to learn if anything is wrong, and bring back word," Kin Shin said. Both Lin Mei and Biao had nodded soberly.

ങ‍ഊഃഓഃ

"Missions grow in size," Lin Mei muttered to herself now as they waited. "Like weeds."

The main door of the temple opened and a line of monks exited to their chambers for private meditations. Jongbu Kunchen was among them, but when he saw them rise from their place by the wall he motioned them over, a soft smile on his face.

"We seek wisdom," Lin Mei said, as they approached.

"One older than I can give you that," the monk replied smiling. "But I can offer tea."

The tea was hot, flavored with butter and salt. They settled on their cushions, while the cats curled up in the corner. Jongbu eyed them with amusement. Cats of any type were rare here in the mountains, Lin Mei had observed, although the forest held tigers and leopards. After some desultory small talk Lin Mei brought the talk about to more serious matters.

"We were advised by an oracle in Kendar that we should seek the Sage of Sakya to learn our destiny," Lin Mei began. "But if he is held captive, we cannot do that."

"Truth," Jongbu said, sipping his tea.

"Can someone else help us?" she asked. Jongbu set down his cup, his face thoughtful.

"Sakya is a monastery several day's march from here," he said. "It contains a large library of ancient manuscripts said to contain much lore and prophecy. The Sage studied there. Others have also, and perhaps one of them could be of assistance."

"Are there any here in Lhasa?" Lin Mei pressed on. The monk shook his head.

"Those who study such lore are reluctant to leave the monastery. It holds much to interest them."

"And yet the Sage did," Biao Mei said.

"A brave man," Jongbu said, nodding his head in respect. "He felt it was his duty to fight against evil. So he came here to speak out against Dorje Gyaltso, and his influence over the Khan."

"And now he is captive," Biao Mei said. Jongbu nodded.

"An evil event," he agreed.

"The palace is barely begun," Biao Mei said, "and already it has a dungeon for captives. A sign of what the Khan's advisor thinks is important!" The monk smiled at that.

"That is true," he said. "Always those in power seek to stay in power. But power can enslave as well as empower, and so the true sages avoid it, seeking wisdom instead."

"And Dorje Gyaltso keeps the Sage in a dungeon," Lin Mei said. "It must be uncomfortable." The young monk shook his head.

"The dungeon is guarded by spells and incantations," he said, "to hold the demon captive. The Sage is kept in a cell in the living quarters, near the advisor's own rooms on the top level. But even if he were in the dungeon, it would not matter. A true sage can contemplate wisdom in a cave in the mountains."

"We heard that the demon had a servant, a lumas," Lin Mei ventured. "What is the attachment between them?"

"Ah," the monk said. "The mountain reaches to the sky, and draws its power down as rain. The water flows down to the rivers and lakes, and the Lumas is empowered by that. So the lumas must be close to the mountain demon." Lin Mei and her brother shared glances at that.

With a final sip they finished their tea and left, taking care to leave a copper in the collection box.

It was already late afternoon and the sky was starting to fill with rain clouds. "There is no demon to harness the power of this storm," Biao Mei said, glancing up. Lin Mei nodded, deep in thought.

"We will visit the palace again tonight," she decided. "But food first. I think it will be a long and busy night."

Rabten was setting out food for the handful of guests, and she got three more bowls of stew as she saw them enter. By now the cats had become well known to the others there, and there were scraps of meat thrown to them to supplement the stew. Twilight earned a shout of glee as she snatched her scrap out of the air with a quick paw stroke.

"This is a good inn to stay at," Lin Mei said. "And the food is better than in most places." Rabten's wizened face split in a gap-toothed grin.

"My grandfather built this place," she said. "It has always been a good place to stay. We get many travelers from far places." Mei Lin and Biao smiled at that and finished their stew. Cups of tea rounded out the meal, and, suitably nourished, they left the inn, the two cats scampering alongside them as they made their way through the darkening alleys and side streets of the town.

It was just past the hour of the dog when they finally reached the hillside above the palace. The moon shone through gaps in the growing clouds as they made their way through the brush and boulders above the palace. They peered around a large boulder, letting their eyes grow accustomed to the darkness below. After a moment they made out two guards squatting by the door that had been unguarded the night before. Lin Mei pointed to the side wall of the palace, where a flat roof area indicated a terrace. Biao Mei nodded and led the way, Lin Mei following. The two cats ghosted through the darkness beside them, thoroughly enjoying the moment in a feline predatory way. They were going into battle.

Soon they were near a side wall of the palace, out of sight of the guards and hidden in the shadows. But the wall was almost twice their height here.

Silently Lin Mei called the cats. Biao Mei picked up Shadow and tossed him up on the terrace, followed by Twilight. Looking through their eyes Lin Mei ascertained the terrace was empty. She took her sword and dagger from her sash and set them down. Biao Mei cupped his hands for her foot, then vaulted her high enough for her hands and arms to hook on the wall. She pulled herself over the edge and then turned to catch the swords tossed up after her. She took her sash off and tied it around Biao Mei's sword, making a knot on the other end. She set the sword on the terrace top and dropped the other end over the side, standing on the sword as she did so. Her own sword and dagger were slimmer, lighter versions of the ones Biao Mei carried, and at the moment sturdiness was required.

In moments Biao Mei was over the edge. Sashes were once more wrapped about their waists and swords and dagger thrust through them. Lin Mei sent the two cats forward. A hatch nearby near the center of the terrace looked promising, and a few moments of listening through cat ears told her there was no one immediately below.

Biao Mei's boot dagger opened the hatch, and they looked down into the space below. Boxes and bundles showed in the shifting moonlight, but nothing else. Biao Mei caught the edges of the opening and swung down easily. Lin Mei followed, his strong arms catching her and easing the landing. The two cats jumped down unaided.

Another few moments of listening through cat ears told her there was no one outside the door. Biao Mei had it open in seconds, prompting Lin Mei to speculate privately that they might have a lucrative career as thieves if the caravan guard business ever hit a slump.

Cat senses told her there were humans beyond a turn of the hallway. Earlier the day before, while gathering gossip in the town, she had bought some tea at a stall frequented by day laborers. Seemingly casual questioning of men who worked on the palace had given her a good picture of the floor plan. That end of the hallway led to the living quarters. But she intended another direction first.

"The dungeons first," she whispered. Biao Mei looked puzzled for a moment, then led them down the hallway and down another set of stairs.

They met no one. Flickering butter lamps cast an eerie illumination that made odd shadows of them on the walls and floor. Despite herself Lin Mei shivered, the hair on her skin prickling. It needed no town gossip to tell her that powerful magic was being worked here.

Another set of stairs led to the dungeons. Soon they were at the door covered with the odd, cursive script used in that land. Once more there was a feeling of fear and foreboding, the cats hissing in a low tone and looking about. But in an odd way that made her feel better.

"Last night, as soon as the lumas left, so did the feeling of fear," she whispered. "The bad feelings were gone. So it was the lumas that caused those feelings, and not the spells that hold her master captive."

"And?" her brother asked.

"The spells are meant to hold the demon captive, and keep the lumas away. But we are mortal, and they do not affect us. And a demon on the loose will give us a good distraction when we rescue the Sage." He grinned in understanding.

"She is nearby," Lin Mei said. He nodded, then went to the door.

The beam barring it was massive, as thick as a man's torso, bound with iron. He stripped off his weapons and jacket, laying them on the floor near him, then stepped to the door. Squatting he shoved a shoulder under the beam and lifted, grunting as he did so. Lin Mei watched, impressed despite herself. She knew her brother was strong, but even so, it was something to watch. It was the work of a strong young man, conscious of his strength, and knowing how to use it.

Slowly the beam lifted, then shifted outward as he slid a foot out from the door. Carefully he dropped to one knee, lowering the beam down so one end rested on the floor. He stood to catch his breath, then stepped to the other end and took that end off the bracket, laying it carefully down on the floor.

And, slowly, the door started to open, creaking on the hinges. The cats spat and hissed in fury, and Lin Mei felt her hair stand on end.

"Let's leave!" she said, leading the way up and out. Biao Mei already had his jacket on. Grabbing his weapons and sash he followed her up the stairs, the cats running ahead and vanishing into the shadows.

At the top of the landing they ran into the lumas, startling them into stiffness. But she had no time for them, running past them with a sinuous grace, her long black hair streaming behind.

"The living quarters!" Lin Mei said. "The Sage is next!" They ran up another flight of stairs and down the long hallway leading to the rooms occupied by Dorje Gyaltso, and hopefully, the captive Sage of Sakya.

They ran into a group of men running their way; the ones in the lead were armed guards. Without stopping Lin Mei dropped to the floor, using her momentum to roll forward into the path of the foremost guard. Tripping over her, he fell sprawling to the floor right in front of Biao Mei, who drew his sword in one swift move and swung down, splitting the chostimpa's skull with a meaty thwacking sound Lin Mei had heard all too often.

She was now busy with the next guard. Coming up on one knee she drew her dagger and thrust upward at the guard, who had continued his rush forward without seeing that the point of his spear was now past her, and therefore useless.

There is a point on a man's inner thigh where a strong kick, or blow, will stun. Her dagger found that point through long experience, and he fell in a heap on her. The next guard as no match for her brother, who dispatched him with a swift stroke of his short, heavy sword. Lin Mei stood to face the fourth man.

"Jongbu!" Biao Mei said in surprise. The monk, now clad in armor and helmet, grinned and stepped forward, drawing his sword as he did so. Faced with a familiar threat Biao Mei's surprise gave way to grim necessity, and he stepped forward. Jongbu's sword thrust out in a skilled move, one that bespoke countless hours of training.

But there is a big difference between training and actual combat. Biao Mei had been fighting for his life, and his sister's, almost all his life. For all his youth, he was no neophyte. He thrust aside the monk's sword with a practiced sword stroke of his own, stepping forward, using all his strength to press forward against the monk, and drawing his dagger as he did so. A swift thrust pushed the dagger point through a gap in the armor. The monk went pale, gasping for breath. Biao Mei twisted the dagger free and thrust again, driving it deep under Jongbu's jaw. The monk in armor fell in a bloody heap to the floor.

That left the last man, who was dressed in a black robe hung with amulets carved from what appeared to be bone, human from the look of some of them.

"Dorje Gyaltso?" Lin Mei asked. Automatically the man nodded, stunned by the sudden loss of his companions. His surprise did not last long, as Biao Mei's sword slashed once more.

"Let's go!" Lin Mei gasped. Biao Mei nodded, following her down the hallway.

Just beyond were the living quarters. Behind the second door they found the Sage of Sakya. He rose from a cross-legged sitting position as they burst open the door.

He was a tall, slender man, shaven headed, clad in the red robe of the Bonpas. A string of prayer beads hung from one hand. "We've come to rescue you!" Biao Mei said. "Please follow us!" The Sage nodded, almost as if amused. He picked up an amulet-studded bag. Slipping it over one shoulder he followed them down the hallway, carefully stepping around the bodies of the dead men. The Sage paused for a moment to gaze sorrowfully at the dead Jongbu, making a sign in the air as he did so. Then he followed Lin Mei and her brother down the hallway.

At the landing he stopped. "You have done well," he said. "But here we must part. You have duties of your own to perform. I must stay and deal with the demon below." As if to make his point there was a dull roar far down below, almost as if a storm was howling through the mountain passes. He smiled at their looks of concern.

"I was taken captive because Dorje Gyaltso used the power of the captive demon to aid him," he told them. "But I can deal with the demon alone, now that the Njalyorpa is dead. And I must. Do not worry, I will be safe. This is work I have done all my life." Lin Mei nodded, and she and her brother raced away down the hall. Behind them the roaring intensified as the Bonpa descended the stairs, his fingers working the prayer beads as he started a singsong chant.

The rear door was unguarded. Apparently the two guards had decided to find another place to be as the roaring of the demon in the dungeons below had reached them.

Here the cats rejoined them. With a firm grasp on essentials they had conducted a raid of their own, apparently on the kitchen. Shadow was carrying a meaty rib almost as long as he was, while Twilight carried what looked like a cooked fowl almost half her size. They bounded alongside, tails high in triumph. *Lunatic beasts*, Lin Mei thought.

The temple bell had just sounded the hour of the dragon. Biao Mei was outside saddling their horses and adjusting the loads on the packhorses, with Shadow to supervise. Lin Mei was settling their bill.

For the past two days the town had been abuzz with the tale of how the demon Akar Nawang had broken free of his enchantments and killed Dorje Gyaltso, the Khan's advisor, and how Penchen Rimpoche, the Sage of Sakya, had fought the demon, finally defeating him and gaining his submission through the use of strange and powerful sorcery. The demon now dwelled quietly in his mountain. The storm which had raged over the town had passed, and the bright morning sun shined outside.

"I will miss your stew," Lin Mei said to Rabten, who squatted by the fire and the pots over it. The old woman grinned.

"You have been good guests," she replied, looking up. They were alone in the room. She looked up at the window where sunlight streamed in.

"The sunrise is brilliant here," she said. She looked up at Lin Mei, whose face was now carefully expressionless. "You do not seem surprised," the old woman went on.

"A temple and an inn," Lin Mei said carefully. "Both places where strangers can come and go, with no one thinking it odd. And good places for people to meet and talk. And both you and Jongbu Kunchen were free with information. Perhaps to assist, perhaps to lead us into an ambush. When I saw Jongbu in the palace with Dorje Gyaltso, I knew." Rabten looked up at her with sunken, rheumy eyes, dark and shrewd.

"You are wise beyond your years," she said. "Good, as you walk a dangerous path." She stopped to look over at Twilight, who sat near the door, eyeing the scene with casual alertness. "And with interesting companions."

"Who was Go Choden?"

"A messenger. Penchen Rimpoche was helping me in this matter. He too does not wish to see war break out between our two empires. Dorje Gyaltso sent one of his men to intercept the message, but it had already been delivered."

"Any messages?" Lin Mei asked.

"Just report what you saw, heard, and did," the old woman said, turning back to her pots. Lin Mei turned to go, shouldering her pack as she did so.

"Give my regards to the ladies of the long bows," Rabten said without looking up. Lin Mei grinned, and walked out the door.

THE CASE OF THE HAUNTED CITY

by *Josepha Sherman*

Tallain and her partner were secret agents working for the Organization of Magical Sovereignties, a group dedicated to keeping the world safe from the Dark. Sometimes these jobs are less interesting than they sound. Unfortunately, there are also times when the job is much *more* interesting than it sounds.

Josepha Sherman is a fantasy and SF writer/editor, storyteller and folklorist, who has written everything from Star Trek novels to a bio of Bill Gates to titles such as TRICKSTER TALES and DEEP SPACE SATELLITES, as well as short fiction and articles on science. She has told stories all over North America. Her most current titles include the STAR TREK: VULCAN'S SOUL trilogy with Susan Shwartz, the reprint of the UNICORN QUEEN books, and FOLKLORE FOR STORYTELLERS. She also edited THE ENCYCLOPEDIA OF STORYTELLING. You can visit her at sff.net/people/Josepha.Sherman.com or at her business site, www.shermaneditorial.biz.

Tallain, wiry, dark-haired and youngish, reined in her horse in the still-cool desert morning. The large yellow hound that had been loping alongside stopped with her, going back on his haunches. They both sat for a moment looking up at the city walls, stark against the bright blue sky-less impressive when seen straight on. Many of the stones were cracked or crumbling.

"Kansillaydra," Tallain said with just the smallest touch of irony. "What's that quote? 'Her towers are tall and stately, full of grace'—well, once upon a time, maybe."

Now, the city was just another trading stop, slightly crumbling, populated by sturdy olive-skinned people who were related to the desert nomads with whom they traded.

The hound grunted, not impressed.

"I agree," Tallain said dryly. "But the report said that this is the place, so . . ." She prodded the horse forward.

Even in these less glamorous days, the city was still supposed to be pretty prosperous. "Prosperous" was hardly the word that came to Tallain's mind as she approached what had probably once been quite an elegant stone gate but was now just another time- and weather-worn relic. Funny. There were no other travelers, no caravans, and there should be at least someone taking advantage of the relative coolness of morning . . .

"Halt! State your name and reason for being here."

It was a guard. Guards, Tallain corrected silently, watching them move forward in a line to bar her entrance. Their uniforms were . . . adequate, the sort of well-worn mail that looked as though it had been passed down through several generations. The outfits of folks used to peace.

Formerly used to peace, she corrected silently. Noting their uneasy glances and the too-tight way they were gripping the hilts of their swords, Tallain thought, *All right, show time.*

"Oh my, I am *so* glad to see civilization again!" she all but twittered. "I am the Lady Tallain, and it's been, oh, one long *nightmare* out there."

"You are alone?" one guard asked.

No, you idiot, there's an invisible army with me. "Well, yes, of *course* I am. That's been part of the nightmare. When those ruffians attacked—why, I thought I was going to just *faint* from the horror. I do believe they slew everyone but me. And my wonderful Serein, that is, my hound here." Serein shot her a wry look. "Why, if it wasn't for him," Tallain continued, ignoring him, "who *knows* what might have happened to me! Do you know, I shiver when I *think* of it? But I'm here now, and safe. So if you gentlemen will please just step aside . . .?"

"Our apologies, lady." The guard didn't sound particularly apologetic. "Before you may enter our city, you must pass a test."

"A test? What sort of test?" If they meant to try searching her to see if she bore some enemy tribe's tattoos, the hell with the lady disguise. "Gentlemen, I've been out in the desert a long, *long* time. I really would like to rest."

"The test is neither painful nor time-consuming," the guard assured her, and held out something that glinted—

Tallain bit back a laugh just in time. What he was holding as though it were all-Powerful was nothing more than one of those worthless Iratni amulets, marketplace stuff, silver so thin she could bite through it. The guards couldn't really believe it could ever hurt anything with any real Power—yes, come to think of it, they could. What did they know about magic, after all?

And what, I wonder, are you trying to hurt?

You didn't interrogate a group of uneasy men holding swords. Tallain took the amulet from the guard with a flourish, touching it to head and heart—might as well make a production out of it—then wryly touched Serein and even the horse with the useless thing. "Satisfied?"

Evidently they were. The guard took back the amulet without a word, and the men stood aside just far enough for her to ride through. "You test all your visitors this way?" she tested.

"It's—needed."

Tallain tried her most innocent, I am so puzzled frown. "But why? Is there something I should be worrying about while I'm here?"

One guard said gruffly, "Just don't go out alone. Especially not after dark. Not safe—"

"Not safe for a lady like you," another guard amended hastily.

Uh-huh. As if you mean there's nothing to fear than honor in peril.

But it really had been a long journey here. "I *don't* suppose you could recommend an inn?" she asked.

"The *Travelers' Ease* might be open," a guard suggested. "Down that street, right-hand side of the road.

"'Might?'"

He shrugged.

Tallain rode on down a dusty, empty street, eying locked doors and barred windows. Serein growled, deep in his throat. "I agree," she said. "Looks like the report was accurate as far as it went."

There were people in the streets, but not as many as might be in a trading city. And they all had the hangdog looks of those in a city under enemy occupation.

"*What* enemy?" Tallain murmured. "Where? I don't feel anything unusual. Serein?"

He whined: No.

Tallain tried her most charming smile on the locals, but received only glares or nervous glances in return, and even a few warding-off-evil gestures.

"They're scared all right," Tallain said. "I don't know about you, but I'm just too worn out to go interview the local equivalent of a mayor."

A grunt of agreement from Serein. While they'd gotten most of the way by other than ordinary methods, the last stretch of the journey had been by most mundane means so as to attract no unwanted arcane attention.

"Exactly. Hah, but there's the inn."

She assumed that it was the inn, although the sign had been taken down. It had the general shape of one: a wall with a gate that would, Tallain saw, open onto a central courtyard and the inn itself. But the place wasn't exactly alive with commerce, either: Not a guest, or even a worker, in sight in there. She glanced down at Serein, who gave her a canine equivalent of a shrug.

"At least the windows aren't barred," Tallain said, and rapped on the side of the gate, delicately, as a lady would do.

Nothing.

She rapped again, more forcefully, then gave up being lady-like as a lost cause and banged on the gate with one booted foot. The sound rang out like a flattened bell, and after a moment, a worried-looking fellow came scurrying. He made the mistake of opening the gate a crack, and Tallain kicked her horse through, Serein closely following, before he could stop them.

"My lady—no—you mustn't—"

Dismounting, Tallain tossed him the reins. "See to it that your boy gives him a good rubdown and the best grain."

"But—my lady—"

"What? Have I made some mistake? Is this not an inn?"

"Uh, yes." At his frantic gesture, a boy came running to take the horse from him. "Yes, but, uh—please, lady, wait!" He caught up with Tallain at the door to the inn. "We're closed."

"Really? I seem to see tables set up in the common room."

"W-we have no available guest rooms."

"Odd. I don't see any other guests."

"That's because we're . . . we're under renovation."

Lord, he was clutching another of those silly amulets. Someone in the market must be cleaning up with them. Yes, and granted, innkeepers were often superstitious, but they rarely let that fact stand in the way of a profit.

"That," Tallain said flatly, "is the most ridiculous excuse yet. I passed that stupid test at the town gate, my dog and I have been on the road a long time—"

"We don't allow war dogs!"

"Oh, Serein here is just an overgrown puppy. Aren't you, boy?"

Serein gave her a long-suffering look, but he grudgingly let her scratch him behind the ears, even (when she pinched one ear in warning) giving his tail a perfunctory wag.

"Now," Tallain continued, "as I was saying, we have been on the road a *long* time. You are either going to explain what's frightening you—"

"Nothing!"

"Then you are going to give us a room. *Now!*"

ଔଓଃ

The room actually wasn't that bad, plain but clean, with a bed that looked (and smelled) like it actually held fresh straw and a chest for clothes. The nervous stable boy brought the saddlebags then left, not even waiting for Tallain's thanks.

"Great," she said.

Dumping the saddlebags on the chest, she began rummaging. Behind her, she heard a sigh of relief, and tossed a cloak over her shoulder, then turned in time to see Serein finish shifting out of dog-shape back into his tall, rangy, yellow-haired self, wrapping the cloak about himself.

"Next time," he said, "you do the shifting."

Tallain grinned. "But you make such a cute puppy."

"Hah."

It was said without heat. They'd already agreed that in this land of dark-haired people of average height, a tall blond man would have been a little too memorable.

As her fellow agent slipped into his trousers and tunic, Tallain murmured the proper spell-code over the gem in her ring, and then said into the gem, "Code 545. Special Agents Tallain and Serein reporting—HQ? Come in, HQ. Repeat: code 545. Anyone home?"

"Well?"

Tallain shook her head. "You try it."

He did, but then frowned. "Interference. Much too much for what we've seen so far."

"Or not seen. Or, for that matter, sensed." She didn't need to add that just because they hadn't sensed anything arcane didn't mean that it wasn't here.

Serein stretched wearily, and then let himself fall back onto the bed. "Might have known it wasn't going to be anything so simple as a would-be warlord or marauding bandits."

"Something that only comes out after dark," Tallain commented. "Bet me. Something that, as a result, can only be detected after dark."

"No bet. It's going to be an interesting night."

"There's an understatement." Tallain hunted in the saddlebags for a fresh outfit, one that didn't smell so strongly of horse. It really, truly was too bad the inn didn't come with bathing facilities.

As she pulled out a tunic, her hand closed about a familiar insignia. OMS agent: Special Field Operative. She and Serein had to carry ID, of course, even if they were undercover—and even if Tallain and Serein, equally of course, weren't their real names. Acting across boundaries and authorized to use all necessary force, the Organization of Magical Sovereignties hunted down illegal spell-casters, eliminated demons, and in short, worked to keep the everyday world safe from the Dark—at the same time, without letting the everyday world know what they did.

Sounded dramatic, Tallain thought wryly, the stuff of ballads. More often than not the cases boiled down to this, long treks over dusty roads or stakeouts in boring villages. And the job wasn't made any easier by the need to keep their missions secret from the ordinary citizens.

She and Serein had been agents together too long to worry about niceties. It would be full night all too soon, and a wise agent snatched rest whenever she could. Tallain flopped down beside him and closed her eyes.

ඝ෪ℛℰ෪ಜ

They both woke with a start to find the night nearly fully there. In one smooth leap, Serein was at the window—then backed off, remembering in time that he wasn't in dog-form. Tallain joined him—ah. The innkeeper's boy, balanced precariously on a ladder.

"What, pray tell, are you doing?" she asked.

"Nothing, nothing, lady. Just, well, you know. Putting up the barricade. For, uh, your protection."

Uh-huh. Silver bars. Silver-plated, her senses corrected.

"Wouldn't hold off even a thirtieth ranked imp," Serein muttered.

"Or in," Tallain corrected wryly. "Come on, Serein, walkies."

He raised a wry yellow brow. "And maybe the innkeeper will actually let us back in afterwards."

"Just change, all right? You can change back once we're away from the inn."

"Next time, you are definitely doing the shifting," he said, and shrank back into dog-form. Tallain gathered up his discarded clothing, and they headed out into the night. They stopped at the stable: only one horse, theirs. It whinnied at them, as if glad of the company. Tallain couldn't resist scratching it under the jaw for a moment. "Sucker," Serein's dog mouth managed.

"Yeah. Soft touch. That's me. Nothing arcane in here."

They headed on out into the quiet streets. Serein took only a few moments to shed the dog-form and dress, stretching in relief. The city seemed utterly asleep, its citizens safe—or at least thinking themselves safe—behind their barricaded windows and doors. Not a sound.

A hot, savage wind swept down the streets from out of nowhere tearing at Tallain and Serein's hair and clothes and stinging their eyes with dust. Suddenly the dark night was ablaze with reddish light.

"What the hell—"

Then they heard the voices. Faint, insidious, they were part of the wind itself. They murmured words too soft to be clearly heard and they laughed, and there was no doubt to either agent that they were evil.

"Class Four Phenomenon," Serein noted tersely. "Sounds and voices. Nothing tangible visible."

"Doesn't feel right," Tallain said. "True Class Four shouldn't have that weird lighting. Come on."

They headed straight into the weirdness. A turn up ahead brought them out onto the wide main marketplace.

"Ah. Definitely not Class Four."

They had come upon a scene from some disordered dream. Dust swirling up in endless clouds, swept by the fierce, hot wind, filled the air with a reddish haze. Through the haze, the marketplace was filled with a milling, terrified crowd, shrieking and running. And through the crowd moved dimly seen figures, like so many thin, inhuman shadows.

"Overlap," Tallain said after a moment. "Some of it past illusion, some of it real stuff."

"And which is which?"

For a few moments neither she nor Serein, trained investigators though they were, could have answered that. Then Tallain snapped, "Look."

Some of the shadowy beings were vanishing into houses, finding openings that had not been completely barricaded, shrinking and slipping through cracks that would have blocked a rat.

"If they get out again . . . yes."

One of the figures had broken open a locked door, another a flimsy barricade.

"Spirits don't need to do that," Serein drawled. "Illusions don't, either."

"Not unless they're carrying off stolen goods that can't shift shape with them," Tallain added. "Great. We've got supernatural thieves."

One of the creatures, still shadowy and undefined of form, came swooping towards them, carrying a pack, and Tallain cried out a quick Spell of Binding. With an angry, wailing cry, the thing dropped the pack, raced right through the two agents, making them shiver with its chill, and vanished.

"Well," Serein said. "That was . . . interesting."

"One way of putting it. But you don't get so much fear in a city from mere thieves, no matter how weird. There has to be more—"

"Hell. There is."

Tallain rushed a being that was bearing a shrieking child, tried the Spell of Binding again-ha, yes, that made the thing drop its burden. Instantly, the other things swarmed them. Tallain grabbed the child and Serein shouted out a Word of Power that opened up a clear circle around them.

"Dammit," Tallain snapped, "where are the parents?"

"Too scared to leave their homes?"

"Or . . . oh hell, it's a sacrifice: take our gold, take our child, but let us live."

She knew, with a Special Agent's keen psychic senses that this was the truth, and knew that Serein felt it, too. How long had this been going on? How many kids sent off to who knew what-

It ends here. Now.

"Serein. Look. Up there on that rooftop."

It—he—was a weirdly romantic figure, tall and wild, apparently human, with robes and long dark reddish hair swirling in the wind. Human-like, at any rate: His eyes glinted with flashes of red like those of a wild thing.

"There's the source."

"He's not aware of us."

"Not yet."

Tallain shoved the child into a shadow and whispered a quick Concealment about it to keep it safe. Serein shouted out his Word again to get the shadow-things out of their way, and Tallain and he forced their way through the dust and wind to the building on which the figure stood. He still didn't seem to be aware of them: probably casting too much Power himself to sense them. Just the same, the two agents climbed up the side of the building without using magic. Mud brick wall, fortunately, with plenty of handholds worn by time. They stepped out onto the roof—

And stopped, hit by the unbelievably strong wave of Power surging from the figure. He whirled to stare at them, revealing a sharp-planed, triangular face and those savage red-glinting eyes. Human? Not human? Hell, a hybrid. No way knowing what powers he wielded. He shouted, and the red haze of dust swept down over them, choking them, hiding him. A sudden roar of wind made Tallain stagger, and a sudden *emptiness* warned her—

Whoa, where was Serein?

"Watch out!" she yelled. "Open Portal!"

No textbook spell, nothing balanced, no clean edges or shape to it, no way to judge where the distortion between realms began or ended—

She heard Serein's surprised shout, instantly cut off. "Oh hell," Tallain said, and sprang after him.

It wasn't the textbook jump between realms, either. Instead of a clean transition to another place, a red haze suddenly surrounded her, and she couldn't get through the cursed stuff no matter how hard she tried.

Dammit! She couldn't back out to reality, either. And no way in hell was she going to abandon her partner. Risky to work magic in a Portal, but Tallain couldn't figure out what else to do, so she called out a Transfer Spell—

Whoa! She'd done *something*. The red haze swirled back into black and gold shards, then vanished into a blaze of golden light and—

—she was through, colliding with something that felt like flesh, bouncing off and landing with a grunt on something hard with a force that bruised her rump. Enough light for her to realized that she was in a room with stone walls and floor. She'd just collided with Serein—but his head had collided with greater force against the floor. He was out cold. Concussion? Tallain put a hand on him, willing *Shift!* Shapeshifting, for some reason the OMS techs had never established, restored the body's pattern, which meant that wounds got instantly healed. *Shift, dammit!*

No time. Tallain turned sharply to find herself facing a tall, hooded figure . . . ah, the fellow from the rooftop, and she wasn't going to worry about how he'd gotten into a closed room. Seen up this close, he no longer had that wild splendor, but he was decidedly still worth seeing, with the sharp lines of that intriguing face.

Uh-huh, and those red-black too-wide eyes that definitely said, *hybrid*. Yes, and madness, too, Tallain realized suddenly, feeling a coldness shiver down her spine. If his breeding was what she guessed, no wonder he was mad. Madness and magic together . . .

"I do not have guests," he said.

Nice voice, rich and deep. Too bad he was as crazy as the wind. That explained those shadow-things, tangible and intangible at the same time: crazy, indeed. "Leave Portals open like that," she said, "and you're bound to have more."

He gestured, and Tallain was slammed back into a wall. "You will learn respect!"

O . . . kay, fellow, anything you say. Basic rule of agenting: Play along with the enemy till you had him figured out. She gave him her most innocent stare. "But I do not even know who you are."

"I do not waste time in banter!"

"But I am Tallain." She could be free with it since it wasn't her true name. "Surely you . . .?"

"If you wish a name, let it be Arag. But I am no mere human. In me runs the blood of demons!"

I was right. Wish I wasn't. Demon-human crosses don't make sane offspring. Or give those offspring predictable powers, for that matter. "I see," Tallain said somberly.

"Ah, you show no fear! You are wiser than the other fools."

By now, Tallain's senses had recovered enough to tell her this wasn't a demon realm, just one of the many pockets of non-reality between the realms. That wasn't as comforting a thought as it might have been, because it was *his* pocket, and that mean it gave him extra strength.

Ah, including the strength to change the whole scene without effort, because they were now in a cavern like a great open mouth, reddish and shadowy. No, not shadows, Tallain's senses told her, just vagueness around the edges. So, now! His will couldn't extend far enough to keep the whole scene solid. Not infallible, then.

As long as Serein doesn't slide away into that vagueness. Come on, dammit, guy, shift!

Not a sound from where he lay. Where she hoped he still lay, not that she could risk a glance over her shoulder to find out.

In the center of the cavern stood a chair that was only one grade less grand than a throne, elegantly worked out of dull red stone. It was surrounded by random heaps of the riches that had been stolen from Kansillaydra's people. Arag took his throne, his robe falling in smooth folds around him, and studied her with cold interest. Fighting the impulse to pirouette, Tallain said, "Now what?"

"You still show no fear. The others do, and that makes them victims. But you . . . who are you to show no fear?"

Then he *didn't* know she was an agent, or that Serein was her partner. "I am too impressed to be afraid."

"Impressed! By what? By *this*?"

"Revealing this new scene," Tallain said carefully. "That was truly amazing."

"That is nothing! There should be much more—and there will be much more!"

"Is that why you . . . farm the city?"

"'Farm,' ha. Yes. I like that. They are sheep, and I am the scythe that takes their lives."

Why oh why didn't I take that course on abnormal minds? One of those things she had planned to get around to doing—assuming there was an around to get to after this. "You take their riches," Tallain prodded delicately.

Arag shrugged. "They have no right to such things. They infest the city, no more than that. My mother's people built it! I take what belongs to me, but mere riches are not enough. Their young, their vermin, their life forces are strong and sweet, but *they* are not enough!"

Oh hell. Those poor kids. At least, she reminded herself, she'd saved one of them. It strained her self-control to the limit to do nothing more than ask mildly, "But why?"

He suddenly stood, looming over her with eyes like smoldering red coals. "I am of the true blood, the dark blood." His voice was barely a whisper. "My father no mere demon. No, he was nothing less than a demon prince, and he must be honored in me. And then I will be a prince as well!"

Not if I have any say in the matter. Not that I have a clue as to what I'm going to do to stop you.

Second rule of agenting: Keep them talking. Sooner or later they trip themselves up or give you a clue about weaknesses.

"That's amazing," Tallain said. "I mean—a demon prince."

"Do you not believe me?"

"Of course! I . . . simply have to wonder . . ."

She let that trail off, gambling that there was enough human blood in him for curiosity.

There was. "What? What are you wondering?"

"Well . . . it's not my place to criticize, but . . . your father . . . a demon prince, I mean he has to be someone really important."

"He is!"

"Yet he left you here."

"Of course! He is testing me, waiting for me to show my worthiness."

Sure he is. Demons didn't think like that. Daddy would either have taken the newly spawned hybrid baby with him, or come for him at puberty, when a kid's potential for magic and/or evil were strongest. *Sorry, guy, you're just another byblow.*

A crazy, murderous one.

Keep him talking. "You grew up in that city, didn't you? Poor Arag, how terrible for you."

"They never knew what they scorned. They never understood what they thought merely mad. But they will weep. And then they will die."

The words would have been trite if they hadn't been said in such an utterly reasonable voice. "I am not one of them. What do you want with me?"

"Surely you should know. The people who infest the city now are weak, inferior. You are not of them, and you are not weak. You shall give me your life force."

Oops. Should have seen that coming.

No help from her partner. He wasn't going to—

The idea struck her with the force of a blow. *You idiot! He can't, but you can!*

"I am honored," Tallain said somberly. "Do you wish me now?"

Arag blinked. "You are . . . willing?"

"Willing to put an end to waiting," she said truthfully. "Shall it be now?"

Aha, she really had him stunned. Perfect. Either he'd forgotten he had sensed magic from Serein and her, or just wasn't registering it any longer with his mad mind.

"Let me do this properly," Tallain purred, and began taking off her clothes.

"What—"

"Oh, you wouldn't want this to be a less than perfect sacrifice."

Damn, she wasn't having such an easy time of it. How did those dancing girl types manage this? She was struggling with laces, hopping on one foot to get out of—

Good enough!

"Perfect," she repeated.

And lunged at him, shifting as she went: something with fangs, something with talons. Biting at him, clawing, forcing him off-balance.

Mustn't let him recover, mustn't let him get off a spell—

No! He had a demon's ridge of bone protecting his neck!

With a roar, Arag backhanded her against a wall. Tallain screamed as fire blazed over her. Shift, hurry, shift before the pain overwhelmed her—

Yes, something else, not sure what, but it gave her new strength and claws that raked Arag's side and—ow, broke against a demon's scales.

Has to be a vulnerable spot—

He had claws of his own, the retractable kind, and they dug deep into her side, pulling her to him.

There was the weak spot, there, right under his chin, no bone or scales there, but she couldn't reach—

Shift!

Just in time, because she heard teeth snap together where she'd just been. His fangs were rudimentary, but sharp enough to—

More fire! Tallain hastily continued the shift into something armored.

Can't keep this up! He's too fast, too damned strong. If Serein—

Serein! Inspired, Tallain threw herself at him. She willed strength into Serein, drawn from her life force. Really dangerous to weaken herself right now but hell, what was a little more peril?

Serein stirred, opened his eyes—and instantly understood, shifting into yellow hound once more. He sprang at Arag, darting in, darting out, and harrying him like a true hound after a bear. Tallain struggled into one last shift, ignoring her pounding heart and labored breathing.

Arag was shouting something harsh and ugly, and things demonic were shimmering in the corners—great, he was calling on his kin.

One crisis at a time. Serein leaped, fangs catching Arag by an ear and some hair. The hybrid shrieked, but his head was forced back for a crucial instant—

Tallain lunged, claws extended, and struck home.

As blood fountained over her, Tallain was thrown sideways by Arag's frenzy. She hit hard, said the hell with it, and stayed put. They'd either lost, and the demons would be forming, or they'd won, and either way there wasn't anything more she could do about it.

Shift, someone was insisting, mind to mind, *shift! You're not dying on me, dammit!*

That had to be Serein, and he wouldn't leave her alone until she did something about it. With one great effort that forced a gasp from her, Tallain shifted one more time.

And found herself in her right form, stark naked on a rooftop in Kansillaydra, with Serein, stark naked, with a supporting arm around her.

"Case closed," he said.

"Not quite. Going to be interesting to see how we beat the indecent exposure rap."

Serein burst into weary laughter, and after a moment, Tallain joined him. The two agents stood shivering but triumphant as the sun rose over Kansillaydra.

PAX DRACONICA

by Cate McBride

"Another day, another dragon, another damsel in distress . . ." Oops, that's not a damsel; that's a dragonslayer. On the other hand, "another day, another dragon, another kill" can get tiresome, too. But dragons are evil and destructive, so you have to kill them all, right? Well, maybe not . . .

Cate McBride has worked for the Canadian federal government in a variety of policy and program delivery positions for the past 22 years. She spent eighteen of those years working with Aboriginal communities, mainly in the Arctic, and her work has taken her all over the country: all twelve provinces and three territories. She currently lives in Ottawa, Canada's capital, with her young son Sean who has begun to make up his own bedtime stories. They share space with Big Blue the fish and a big black dog named Dingo who is terrified of kittens.

Dara Dragonslayer sighed as she slowed her roan gelding at the crossroads. Behind her lay Kingstown, where Ional waited patiently. Ahead lay yet another village ravaged by one of the Great Reds. Another dragon to slay.

Her worn leather armor crinkled and cracked as she dismounted to read the signs in the early morning light. The armor had been new only last year, but now it was charred, drier than field rations and smelled of sulphur thanks to the last five dragons she had killed for the King. Dara took off her helm and ran her fingers through her short brown hair, wincing as she touched the dried strands that had been bleached white by dragon fire.

After confirming that Innsbeck lay to the east, Dara turned to remount. The roan was skitterish and danced away from her. Dara caught a whiff of dragon stench and led the horse off to a small copse of trees near the east road. There was no use trying to ride to the village if the stench was that strong. She sighed again and wished that once, just once, a dragon would nest far enough away from its kill that she could ride to the rescue instead of arriving on foot, heavy dragon lances deadweight across her shoulders and feet sweating in her heavy riding boots.

The horse jumped and pulled back on the reins as they approached the trees. A small squeal rose from the grass below.

"Watch where you're stepping, you great ox!"

Dara dropped the reins and pulled her swords from the scabbards across her back. She looked down to see a small Gold dragon poking its head out of the long grass. She flicked her right sword forward and the beast dove back into the grass.

"Pax, Dragonslayer. I have been sent to parlay with you."

Dara snorted but cautiously lowered her blades. A request for Pax had to be respected, no matter who—or what—asked for it. "Give me one good reason why I shouldn't kill you now, before you grow big enough to kill entire villages."

The dragon moved slowly out of the grass, stopping just out of sword's reach. It sat up on its hind legs and sketched a low bow towards Dara, its undersized wings fluttering between its shoulder blades like flower petals. It should have looked ridiculous, since it only came to her knees, but the Gold's sinuous grace made the bow as elegant as that of a courtier.

"My kind does not grow big enough to ravage one of your human villages. We too have been attacked by the Great

Reds and offer our services in helping you rid this land of those who break your laws."

Dara snorted again. "You're a dragon. I'm the Dragonslayer. Why would you want to help me?"

"Should all humans be punished because some are thieves and murderers? Or should those who would live in peace work together to protect each other? I have been sent to negotiate with you: our aid in ridding this Kingdom of the Great Reds who break the peace, in return for safe haven for those of dragonkind who pledge to your King."

Dara wanted to believe the little dragon. If it was telling the truth, this could be the change that allowed her to settle down with Ional. But if it was lying . . . She quickly made a decision.

"Prove it now, dragon. Help me destroy the Great Red that lies ahead and I will personally escort you to the King to negotiate your Pax."

"Grevel. My name is Grevel."

"Fine. Grevel, then. Do we have a deal?"

The little dragon nodded and dropped back to the grass. Dara heard her horse whinny and she whipped around to find Grevel curled around the saddle's pommel, oblivious to the fact that the roan was shaking in fear.

"If you mount quickly, it will calm the animal and we can be on our way."

Dara shrugged, sheathed her swords and pushed her helm back onto her head. After pulling the reins free of the bracken at the horse's feet, she mounted in one fluid motion. As as soon as she felt the horse relax between her legs, she pulled slightly on the reins to turn it east towards Innsbeck, praying that the animal would stay calm long enough to get her a little closer to her goal.

"Go north," Grevel demanded.

"But the Great Red is east, near the remains of the village."

"Before we confront it, there is one with whom we must speak. Go north."

"You better not be leading me into a trap, dragon," Dara snapped back, but she followed the dragon's directions.

The roan calmed as they road up the northern road and the stench from the Great Red faded from the wind. They rode on in silence, Dara concentrating on keeping her horse relaxed and moving, until the land around them began to shift from fields to rocky outcrops.

"Turn left here," Grevel broke the silence as they approached a dirt path leading into the rocks.

She kneed the roan down the path which ended at a cliff-face riddled with small caves. A sandy clearing stretched from the end of the path to the cliff with a circle of low rocks in the centre. A Gold dragon perched atop each rock, expectantly facing the path. They were all at least three times the size of the little Gold, their wings full sized and folded elegantly across their backs.

Grevel flowed down the horse's side and moved toward the largest of the waiting dragons. It rose on its hind legs and bowed, deeper than it had to her, Dara noticed.

"The Dragonslayer as requested, Eldest" Grevel said, turning to beckon her without breaking its bow.

"Well done, little one, and well come, Dragonslayer. You do us great honor with your trust and we hope that you will find that trust well placed before this day is done." If its faded color was an indication, the Eldest was truly old. And big for a Gold, about the size of a small pony.

Dara shifted in the saddle, fighting the urge to draw her swords and attack. "And how will I find this out?"

"Fighting a Great Red alone, you risk injury or death, is this not so?"

Dara nodded in agreement. "A full company of trained soldiers was used before the war, when the Great Reds were fewer. But now the King must divert all troops to the west and the number of Great Reds grows every year. Those of us trained in dragonslaying must work alone to deal with them all before too many villages and farms are lost."

"We too are prey to the Great Reds," the Eldest continued, "and while we can send more warriors than you to each battle, we are too small to succeed without many facing certain death. We are not so numerous that I would send my subjects on suicide missions."

Dara's eyes widened. The Golds must be serious if their King was willing to risk meeting with a dragonslayer in person.

"What do you propose?"

"Given the ravages of the Great Reds, we understand that you and your King will need proof of our sincerity before accepting our proposed arrangements. We will, therefore, help you defeat the Great Red who has destroyed the village south of here. You will then escort our emissary to your Kingstown to arrange a formal meeting between our two peoples to finalize the Pax."

"And how do you propose to defeat your murdering kinsman?" Dara was hard pressed to see how dragons small enough to be taken by hunting dogs could have any effect on a Great Red.

The Gold King turned to Grevel and nodded. "Explain your proposal, child."

Grevel moved to the fore and bowed once more towards Dara. "If you were to dismount, Dragonslayer, it might be easier for us discuss battleplans."

Dara smiled. "Dara. My name is Dara."

Grevel flipped back its wings in acknowledgement. "Very well, Dara. Your horse would be happier downwind, I think," and its tail pointed to some scrub on the left of the clearing near a stream and a pile of fodder. "Please see to the beast and join us."

It took several hours of discussion, with some arguing, to agree. Dara thought that Grevel's plan was too simplistic to work but in the end, the little Gold convinced her to take the chance. If it didn't work, she thought grimly, she could always handle the Great Red her usual way.

The other dragons had left the clearing after providing Dara with simple rations and water, but the dragon King relaxed on its rock, watching but saying nothing. When Dara finally nodded her agreement to the amended plan, the King sat up and bugled. In an instant, six dragons appeared in a semi-circle around Dara.

"Go with my blessing," said the King, "and lead them well, child," it added as it turned to Grevel.

"Good hunting, Dragonslayer," it added as Grevel bowed one last time and turned to slide up the roan. By the time Dara reached her horse, the dragon wing had lifted into the air and was heading south.

The roan once again refused to near the village, so Dara and Grevel trudged on foot from the crossroads, reaching the burnt-out shell of Innsbeck as the sun sank behind them. Dying fires that mirrored the red sky above glowed on either side of the road, testaments to the heat of dragonfire that they still smoldered this long after the Great Red's initial attack. Dara scanned the sky but their aerial escort was nowhere to be seen.

"Don't worry, Dragonslayer," Grevel said, dismounting from its perch on the lances balanced across Dara's shoulders. "When the time is right, they will appear as planned."

Dara grunted in response and moved into the village, not bothering to look behind to see if the little dragon was following.

They found the Great Red sleeping on a makeshift nest next to the open well in the village square. Beside it the well looked like an empty beer cup next to a drunk snoring at a tavern table. As Dara paused to shift the lances to her hands, ready for throwing, Grevel snaked past her and skittered towards the larger dragon's nose.

"Dragon." Grevel stood on its hind legs, its voice suddenly loud enough to echo off the remains of the larger buildings around the square. "I come to hold you accountable for your actions and misdeeds."

Lazily, the Great Red opened one eye to peer down on its smaller cousin and chuckled low. "And who are you, pest, to disturb me, bringing a dragonslayer to my nest?"

"I am sent by my King to tell you that the Gold dragons will no longer sit idle while you and your kind ravage our lands. We wish to live in peace with our human neighbors and will do whatever we must to keep that peace. My King commands me to tell you to leave this place or face his wrath."

The Great Red surged onto its feet, mantling its wings. It towered above the village ruins, making Grevel look like a mouse by comparison. "Dragons siding with humans? You dare to say this to me?"

It turned its head towards Dara. "And you, Dragonslayer. Have you become so weak that you must rely on this vermin?"

Grevel answered before she could. "The Gold King has called Pax with the ruler of this land and has declared you and your kind outlaw. What say you? Do you go or do we fight?"

The Great Red roared its response and slammed one front leg onto the smaller dragon. Dara shifted the lances slightly in her hands and prepared to attack.

Grevel danced away from the Great Red's descending foot and bugled. The wing of fighters rose from behind the building shells on then west side of the square, each with a large rock between its forelegs. One by one, they began to drop their loads onto the head and back of the Great Red, circling out of range as the beast reared to its full height, breathing fire into the air.

As soon as it exposed its underbelly, Dara darted forward with her lances, weaving to avoid the falling rocks and the dragon's thrashing tail. The Great Red was distracted by the circling Golds who were returning with second and third payloads and didn't notice her until she was between its feet.

Too late, it turned its attention back to the ground, snapping at Dara as she planted her feet to throw the lances. Before it could connect, one of the falling rocks hit it between the eyes and its teeth snapped the air above her head. Ignoring the rocks falling around her and the Great Red's thrashing tail, Dara calmed her breathing, took aim, and let her lances fly towards the dragon's heart.

The left lance bounced off the dragon's scales, but the right one hit the small soft spot under the dragon's right foreleg. With a bellow, the Great Red tried to lift from the ground, its wings beating faster with the effort of taking off from a standstill.

Unable to see due in the dust clouds raised by the dragon's wings, Dara heard it twist in its death throws and fall on its back towards the ground. She turned and ran back the way she had entered the square, racing to get out of the way of the falling giant. A force thudded against her back, pushing her forward and onto her knees. Behind her the ground shook as the Great Red landed, wings splayed out and tail thrashing one last time.

Dara was winded, but otherwise unhurt. She stood and turned to look at the Great Red stretched out behind her, its head only a few feet away from where she landed. There was no sign of Grevel, but a small lump under one of the dead dragon's wings was feebly moving, a tip of dusty gold sticking out.

Dara ran forward and heaved the wing upwards. Panting heavily, Grevel slowly pulled itself out from under the Great Red's body. When it was free, Dara let the wing thump to the ground and quickly bent down to the Gold.

As she checked the little dragon over for injuries, the fighting wing backwinged to a landing around the corpse and every member reared up and bowed. Dara dusted off her armor and watched with amusement as Grevel pushed her away—gently this time—to accept the accolades of its betters. She was certain she saw a faint blush rise on its face.

The fighters stepped back, freeing space for the Gold King to land in front of Grevel. Dara stepped away from the pair as the King himself bowed to the little Gold. Grevel hung its head, unable to look the King in the eye.

"Well done, little one, well done indeed." The King gently nosed the smaller dragon until Grevel shyly looked up. "You have proven that a female can be as brave a warrior as any male."

The King turned to Dara. "Will you accept our Pax and present it to your King, Dragonslayer?"

"I will indeed, your Magesty," she responded, "on one condition. I promised Grevel when we met that if we killed the Great Red, I would personally escort her to Kingstown to negotiate your Pax. My horse has accepted her, which will make the journey easier. And I think she has earned it."

The Gold King bared its teeth in what Dara hoped was a smile. "What do you think, daughter of mine? You have earned your right to join our warriors, as you requested. Would you set that aside to act as my emissary to the human King?"

Grevel bowed once. "Gladly, father, if you so wish."

"I so wish, my dear." With a nod to Dara, the King and its fighters launched themselves into the air.

Dara turned to pull her lance from the Great Red's breast and debated searching for its mate but decided that it had become too dark to bother. She settled the lance across her shoulders and beckoned to Grevel.

The little gold scurried up her back to take its perch on the lance. Once it was settled, Dara carefully picked her way down the road towards the copse where the roan waited for them.

Grevel had obviously recovered from saving Dara's life. "So what to warriors do after they make a kill? Does it involve drinking and wenching? Is there a village near here where we can find some wenches? Just what is a wench anyways?"

Dara smiled in the dark. Ional could wait another day or two. She doubted that any of the locals would live up to Grevel's expectations as "wenches", but she was sure that with some effort, she would think of an appropriate reward for her kingdom's newest warrior.

SEA-CHILD

by Cynthia Ward

A pirate attack upon your village is generally not considered a good thing. But this attack, and her reaction to it, ended up giving Vekki both the family she had ceased to hope for and a position in life that she had never expected.

> Cynthia Ward (www.cynthiaward.com) was born in Oklahoma and lived in Maine, Spain, Germany, the San Francisco Bay Area, Seattle, and Tucson before moving to the Los Angeles area. She has sold stories to FRONT LINES, *Asimov's SF Magazine*, and other magazines and anthologies, including some previous volumes of SWORD & SORCERESS. She publishes the monthly Market Maven eNewsletter, which covers market news in the science fiction, fantasy, and horror fields. She is working on her first novel, a futuristic mystery tentatively titled THE STONE RAIN. With Nisi Shawl, Cynthia coauthored the writing manual WRITING THE OTHER: A PRACTICAL APPROACH, based on their fiction diversity writing workshop *Writing the Other: Bridging Cultural Differences for Successful Fiction* (www.writingtheother.com).

When the pirates attacked, they came by land, where the villagers of Grunnett kept no watch.

Vekki and her mother were the last to know, when the raiders' axes struck door and wall, cracking open their lonely shack on the isolated spit. The pirates broke in, laughing and bloody from their assault upon the village, and they fell upon Vekki and her mother almost before they could rise from their pallets in the lone room of their salt-bleached shelter.

"Do not fight a man who would force you," the fishwives liked to say, but the old herbwoman told the village girls, "Fight, because it may stop the rapist, and not fighting never did."

So Vekki fought, shouting, writhing, clawing. She struggled to win free, to go to her mother's side and defend her. But five pirates bore Vekki down painfully upon the hard sand floor, more men than even a girl as sturdy and strong as the seventeen-year-old could oppose.

"The blubbery sea-cow has sharp claws," cried the pirate straddling Vekki, whose beard-patched face dripped blood from the furrows she'd dug.

"I'll not have a female so unnatural," said another pirate, looking on. "There's skin between her fingers."

Vekki remembered overhearing the old herbwoman scolding gossips, when they'd speculated upon whom Vekki's unknown father might be, long years ago.

"Not one of our men," one of the gossips had been saying. "With the webbed fingers, she's one of the fish-people—"

"Vekki's no scaled mer," the herbwoman had said. "Nor seal-girl, either, with that long, blue-touched hair. Her father's a nereus. And you don't want to anger the nerei. So be silent. Don't even think of them."

The patch-bearded reaver pulled the cutlass from his belt and pointed the notched and bloodied blade at one of Vekki's pinned wrists. "I'll clip the sea-cow's talons for her—"

But a pirate hung with gold, higher-ranking than the crudely dressed men who had invaded the shack, stuck his head through the shattered boards and driftwood of the wall. "Belay that," he cried, "there's an Imperial warship on the horizon. They'll see the smoke of this stinking village. Fall back to the ship, or be left behind!"

Most of the pirates cursed and rose up, binding Vekki's mother's wrists to carry her away with them, for she did not look as old as her thirty-two years, and was pretty and hale; she could be sold to some distant merchant or nobleman of the Imperium. But the marauders marked by Vekki's nails lingered, four of them holding her fast as the patch-bearded reaver laughed and raised his cutlass for the swing that would sever Vekki's hand from her wrist.

But as the cutlass rose and the retreating pirates bore Vekki's mother through the door, she screamed at the threat to her only child.

The scream and disappearance of her mother raised new heights of anger and fear for her mother in Vekki, as if raising a storm in her very soul. And the sensations she felt became strange. For it seemed that the storm poured out of her, invisibly, yet with the shattering fury of a winter northeaster, which brings the gray ocean surging out of its bed, to drown villages and smash cabins and snap great pines many miles inland.

And the five pirates' faces twisted suddenly, and their hands rose to their throats, releasing Vekki. The cutlass, dropping abruptly from loosened fingers, thumped upon the pale sand. And in the red dawn light pouring through the open doorway and split walls, the pirates' expressions turned to confusion and terror; and each man's hands clutched at his throat, as if he were strangling upon a too-large draft of ale.

The five men opened their mouths, as if to scream, and water spilled over their lips. It drenched their beards and shirts and the entirety of their bodies, and spread in puddles that joined in a pool on the sand. Dark streaks and swirls, as of blood, showed in the dawn-lit pool. And there were seaweeds in the pool, and in the water bursting from the men's gaping mouths; and the smell of brine filled the broken shelter.

The men toppled over, one by one, as if felled by powerful cutlass blows. In wonderment and apprehension, Vekki touched each man upon the wrist, seeking a pulse as the

herbwoman had taught her, after pirates had struck the village
five years ago. And as Vekki confirmed that each man was dead,
a fierce elation rose in her breast; and she ran out of her mother's
shack, seeking the pirates who had captured her mother.

They were not in sight.

"*All* the pirates are gone," Vekki whispered in horrified
realization.

Upon the horizon she saw a war-galley of the Imperium,
a vessel seldom seen in northern waters, but always recognizable
with its grand size and purple sails and great banks of oars. On
the land above the rocky shore, villagers wandered through the
burning ruins of Grunnett, or saw to the wounded, or wept over
the dead. But Vekki was alone on the barren spit where her
mother's shack stood, as isolated as she and her mother had been
since Vekki's birth. Yet large footprints showed where the
pirates had fled, and Vekki, running, followed them to the edge
of the forest, which hemmed in the village and its fields and
orchards on three sides.

"They have gone into the woods," Vekki whispered; shy
and shunned, she had the developed the habit of talking to
herself. "And I know little of woodcraft."

She sometimes wandered the woods alone, since the
other children had rarely played with her, and her isolation had
increased as a woman's budding curves made her more shy. The
villagers were not supposed to hunt or forage in the forest, which
belonged to the count. But Grunnett was far from the county
castle, so many of the villagers hunted or gathered, and knew the
forbidden wood-skills. Save occasionally for the herbwoman, no
one had seen fit to teach these skills to Vekki.

But, looking more closely, Vekki realized she had
learned enough to follow the pirates' flight through the forest.
For in their hurried retreat, they broke branches and pulped
rotten deadfalls. They left footsteps in the dust of decayed pine
needles and disturbed fallen leaves so their undersides showed
wet against the dry leaf-mold. They rubbed moss and lichen

from the dark trunks of trees and the gray outcroppings of granite.

"But I move so slowly," Vekki whispered as she searched for the signs of the pirates' passage.

Grunnett and its sheltered cove were enclosed to the north by a long, low, thickly forested point of land. Vekki came to the far side of the point, drawn by the damage of the raiders' flight to the place where their little caravel had stealthily moored. But when she emerged from the forest, she saw no pirates or boats or captives upon the shore; only the caravel, under sail, absconding before the Imperial war-ship might spot them.

"They are fled with my mother," Vekki cried. "And surely they have taken others. But perhaps I can still—"

She tried to rouse the strange surging storm in her soul; and she felt a stirring within. But it was weak, and the sensation never flowed out of her. She realized she could not use her newfound power over such a distance.

"I might have drowned the pirates," she concluded in despair, "were I not too slow—"

She fell silent, for the cold gray waves were calling to her, as they always did when she looked upon them. She might not run fleetly, with her muscular, clumsy-looking body; but she had always swum swiftly and well, so that the other children of Grunnett, and even the adults, had quickly learned not to race her in either river or cove. And so, with a wild, impossible hope kindling in her breast, Vekki flung herself into the ocean.

She swam with strong, rapid strokes. Her arms cleaved the ocean as if they were slim oars. Her long, webbed fingers and toes seemed to grip the water as if it were so many deep handholds in the cliff that rose south of the village. Her skin, which seemed curiously sleek and slightly blue in bright sunlight, shed the water more readily even than that rare foreign substance called glass. Her lungs took in great breaths and held them longer than anyone else in the village might. Her wool shift, however soaked, did not impede her progress. Nor did she mark the cold that would have sapped the vigor from the muscles of the other villagers, trapping them in a strong current or sinking them to watery graves while Vekki continued steadily onward, warm and unwearied.

Gods, grant me aid, Vekki prayed as she swam. *God of sea, keep me buoyant. Goddess of earth, keep me strong. God of sky, fill my lungs.*

And the old memory of the herbwoman scolding the gossips came back to Vekki, and brought her a new thought.

Father, if ever you cared for your shore-born child, aid me now!

She mocked herself. "Maybe the gods will help you. But your father, who has never cared to meet you? Who may not be within a thousand leagues of the Northern Ocean? Who may not even be nereus, despite what the herbwoman thinks? No," she told herself, "he's never had an interest in you. And you've no chance of catching up with a caravel under sail."

But she prayed for her father's assistance, as she prayed for the gods' assistance.

Do the gods answer my prayer? she wondered, realizing that the winds had died, becalming the single-masted ship, which had neither oarsmen nor oar-ports. *I pray you, gods of sea and earth and sky, keep the caravel dead in the water.*

And the winds did not return, and Vekki drew close to the caravel. Then, worried that someone might glance over the side and spot the speck of her upon the ocean, she took a great breath and dove beneath the glassy surface.

Rising close beside the barnacled hull, Vekki rejoiced that she had not recently trimmed her nails. She hated her fingernails and toenails for being so thick, and for tapering to sharp, obvious points. Once, she had cut them often, trying futilely to hide her inhuman claws from the other villagers.

It is good I grew tired of forever trimming them, Vekki thought, sinking the points of her fingers and thumbs into the slippery planks of the hull. Then she drew her feet forward and sank their talons into the wood, and began to climb.

But she had labored long and hard in her lengthy swim into the open ocean with its powerful currents. And the cold had penetrated her slick hide and the thick layer of fat over her muscle. So she was shaking as she ascended the side of the caravel; and her muscles jumped under her skin, as she had seen muscles jumping under the coat of a messenger's exhausted horse.

She rested, clinging to the wood. She ignored the ache in her fingers and toes as she bade the sun god to warm her. She prayed all the gods would fire her strength. She pleaded with her father to rise from the depths with all his nereus strength and magic, and use them to save the woman he had loved, at least for one night.

Then, as Vekki resumed her ascent, a corsair glanced over the side and saw her there. "Invader!" he shouted, drawing his cutlass. "A sea-woman boards us!"

"You'll not harm another woman," Vekki retorted, feeling the strange sensation rouse to furious life in her soul.

A sudden waterfall poured from the pirate's lips, and with a gurgling cry he swayed and toppled over the side, nearly striking Vekki as he plunged to the sea.

Then Vekki swarmed over the side of the caravel, and her heartbeat rose to a painful pace as she saw the deck. It was aswarm with pirates, near fifty men who were running to meet her with cutlass and hatchet and harpoon. And the pirates had no care for whether they trod upon the women and girls and boys who lay bound upon the deck, with Vekki's mother among them.

"Stand down, you scurvy rogues!" Vekki said, feeling new strength at the sight of her mother alive. "And turn this ship for land, if you would spare yourselves the wrath of a nereus!"

Some of the pirates hesitated, and a few glanced back, as if they feared to find more sea-folk behind them. But they all came forward, roaring for the girl's blood.

Then fear and anger grew in Vekki, enwrapped with the ferocious desire to rescue the mother who had loved her and protected her, despite all the hatred and suspicion of the villagers. The strange sensation swelled strongly within her breast. And water began to spill from the pirates' mouths.

Screams rose from some of the villagers. The pirates could say nothing, only fall upon the deck. But most twitched or writhed upon the boards; for Vekki's magic had not the strength or training to fill them all with brine sufficient to slay them.

Then the captain, who had been hidden by the ranks of his raiders, strode forward, a tall burly man with a four-foot greatsword. He was hung with gold and silver and gems, showing he had begun his reaving in the days when the pirates plagued the Central Sea, before the Imperium augmented its navy and drove the marauders to the hardscrabble north. In the morning light, his skin showed a tinge of blue, even to the top of his shaven pate, and he raised a hand from the grip, spreading his fingers to show the skin that stretched between them, and the claws that armed them. And no spot of water showed upon his skin or lip.

"Stupid halfbreed," said the captain, advancing toward her with both hands once more upon the hilt of his greatsword. "Your paltry magic has no effect upon a skilled nereus!"

Vekki quailed; but if she fled, her mother died or fell into the horrors of rape and slavery. So, as the captain drew close enough to strike, she flung herself upon him. And though the seventeen-year-old was slow with her muscular, fat-sleek body that was ill adapted to land, she was not so slow as the nereus, who looked two decades older.

Though he was larger and more muscular, the captain staggered at the impact of Vekki's body against his. Then he shouted with surprise and pain as her toenails dug into his belly and her fingernails sank into his throat. Her action had put her far too close to cut or stab with his greatsword; so he raised it up in his hands and smashed her with the pommel.

Vekki grunted as agony flared across her back like the fire of the sun-god's chariot; but the blow served only to drive her claws more deeply, and to make her limbs jerk spasmodically. The captain howled at the worsening pain; and Vekki felt the movements of his torso muscles and knew that he was readying another pommel-blow. She tightened her fingers on his throat and, like a cat, dragged her feet down his belly; and she put all her strength into piercing his layered fat and muscle.

Blood washed hot over her feet and hands, and the captain toppled heavily backwards. The impact jarred through Vekki's body, knocking her breath from her lungs and her nails from his flesh. But she scrambled to her feet and leaped back, red fingers raised against a renewal of the captain's attack.

He lay thrashing upon the deck, with no interest in her any more. All his attention was for his throat, which she had ripped open, and his belly, which she had disemboweled.

"Good work, daughter," came a stranger's voice, a man's, low and dark as ocean depths. "The half-nereus is finished."

"Perreo!" cried Vekki's mother, her voice half-strangled.

Vekki wheeled, her back arching as her battle-fury turned upon the newcomer who crouched on the rail of the caravel.

"He's finished no thanks to you, who abandoned his lover and babe almost before the babe was conceived," she spat like a cat.

"Your words are fair," said her father, who was looking upon her with an intent and curious regard. "Yet they are not truth. May I come aboard?"

Surprised that he would ask, Vekki nodded; and the nereus, Perreo, stepped down onto the deck. He was taller and broader than any land-man, and very handsome yet very strange, with the long bright blueness of his hair, the sea-blue hue of his skin, and the gills to either side of his neck. He was naked save for a breechclout of some scaled hide and a sharkskin belt and knife-sheath; and his ornaments were of gold and nacre and pearls. In one hand he held a trident of some hard-looking white substance that was not metal, and upon his brow he wore a simple gold circlet.

"Not truth?" Vekki said to her father. "What excuse have you, then, for abandoning lover and babe?"

"That I could not return, for my younger brother usurped my throne and bound me in fell enchantment," Perreo replied. "I have but recently won free, and ere I could claim my woman and child, I had to reclaim the throne of the Northern Ocean. Once I had slain my brother, I made haste for the shore with my men, to seek for you and your mother. Then I felt your thoughts, and knew you were my daughter."

He looked over the rail, and gestured; and nerei appeared at the rail, man after man of them, tall and muscular, clawed and webbed, bearing tridents.

Alarmed at the sight of them, Vekki cried, "They do not have permission to come aboard!"

Vekki's father never addressed nor looked at his nerei— he was looking instead upon Vekki's mother, as intensely as she looked upon him—yet the warriors did not come over the rail. Had Perreo made some gesture of command that Vekki had missed?

Perreo looked upon his daughter. "Will you let my warriors take this caravel to your village, and return the captives home?"

"And have the Imperial war-ship patrolling our waters see the caravel in our cove and kill us all for pirates? No, nereus, you will leave the caravel and pirates at sea for the war-ship to find," Vekki said. "Your warriors may come aboard this ship, but only to free my mother and the other villagers, so we may take to the boats and take ourselves to shore."

"Of course," said Perreo, graciously. Then wonder came into his face. "I did not dare to hope you survived, daughter. I did not dare to hope you would be so fine and beautiful and brave."

At his words, a warm feeling sprang up in Vekki, a sensation she had known before only when her mother spoke kindly to her; it was a feeling she had never known what to do with. So she spoke roughly to her father: "Get your men aboard, so they may free the villagers."

Vekki's father said nothing; but his web-footed warriors spread quietly across the deck, moving to the bound villagers and drawing single-edged white knives from sharkskin sheaths. Carefully, the nerei severed the ropes on wrists and ankles, freeing the captives more easily, Vekki thought, than if the curious white substance that formed their knives were steel.

Our knives and tridents are made of porcelain, a sort of ceramic, and forged by magic to be sharper than steel, and stronger. Sometimes they snap, but they are stout weapons, and have made the nerei lords of the deep.

Vekki stared at Perreo, horror warring with shock. "I heard your voice only in my head!" she exclaimed. *Can you read my mind?* she silently asked.

A nereus can sometimes sense strong thoughts in another who is near, he answered. *But the mind-speech is something else, that all sea peoples have, for speaking aloud does not work underwater. Daughter, will you share with me your name?*

Vekki, she told him at last, warily.

Thank you, he replied. *Vekki, I would ask a favor of you.*

Vekki regarded her father narrowly, and said, "What is it?"

"I would go to your mother's side," he said aloud, his vivid blue eyes turning to Vekki's mother.

And seeing the longing on her mother's face, Vekki lowered her gaze and gestured with an open hand; and her father surged to her mother's side. He cut her bonds with his knife. Then it fell to the deck, sticking upright in the wood, as he swept his long-lost lover up in his arms; and they embraced with such joy that Vekki, looking to them, looked away again, knowing that this was a moment for them alone.

Her father's warriors moved across the deck, freeing all the captives, and using the severed ropes to bind the pirates' wrists and ankles. The villagers rubbed the circulation back into their hands, and stamped their feet, all the while looking warily upon the nerei. In turn, the nerei moved back from the villagers, gathering in the center of the deck so that none might interpose himself between the villagers and the ship's boats that hung at the rails. The villagers took the weapons from the bound pirates, and such ornaments and gems and coin-pouches as the pirates had. Then, murmuring among themselves, the villagers went to the boats, and began lowering them to the sea.

They did not look upon Vekki or her mother, or the sea-king. They did not call to Vekki or her mother to join them.

The sea-king spoke into Vekki's head. *Your mother has agreed to come away with me, to my kingdom, and see if she would care to stay. For, though the King of the Northern Ocean may not wed a land-woman nor name their child as heir, his land-woman may live in honor and splendor—*

"If she does not drown!" Vekki exclaimed furiously.

There are spells and amulets that will let her breathe in the water, Perreo answered, regarding Vekki gravely. *And my kingdom has islands. If she chooses, your mother may dwell in a castle above the sea. And, if you choose, Vekki, you may live with her in air or under sea.*

"What if I choose not to let you take her away, sea-man?" Vekki demanded.

"You have no say in this," said her mother softly. "Only I can decide if I will stay with your father, or no. But you can come with us, and see whether you would prefer to live in your father's kingdom, or your mother's village." Her eyes grew damp, looking upon Vekki. "Come with us, daughter, please."

You have these in your blood, Vekki, said Perreo, stroking his fingertips along one side of his throat, tracking the curve of the gills there. Vekki's mother glanced at him, and Vekki wondered if she heard his mind-speech, as well. *Because you are half nereus, they are in your blood, and so I may grow them in your neck by magic, if you choose.*

Would you make of me an even greater freak? Vekki demanded, so pained by the idea that she could not speak it aloud.

No, daughter, said the sea-king, a strange look suffusing his face. *I sought only to make you more comfortable in the sea. And if you decided you did not like the gills, I would seal them away again.*

And can you make me wholly a land-girl? Vekki demanded.

No, he said, with an unexpected sadness to his mind-tone. *I wish to make you happy. I would do anything I could for you. But I cannot take away all that is nereus in you. I cannot eradicate half your body and soul.*

Vekki looked upon him and upon her mother, who seemed so happy by his side. Here, suddenly, Vekki had everything she had wanted: her father with them, her mother happy, her father wanting them both. And she had more than she had dared imagine: he was a king, offering them a far better place in the world than they had in the village, the shunned peasant harlot and her ugly, inhuman bastard.

Perreo's brow darkened, and Vekki realized he had sensed her thought. *I should kill anyone who scorned my woman or my daughter, or made either of you think you are less than whole and beautiful and perfect.*

"But you will not kill them," Vekki heard herself saying with surprise. "You will not kill them, if you would have any chance of your daughter visiting your kingdom."

The anger did not leave Perreo's face; but he inclined his head. "As you will, Vekki. I will not harm the villagers, so long as they do no further harm to you or your mother."

Vekki stared at her father. She had not thought of the villagers' treatment of her and her mother as harm. She was bastard; her mother was unwed, the abandoned leman of a sea-man, who slept with village men in trade for food and clothes, that her daughter might survive. Of course the villagers had behaved as they had.

Yet they should not have, Vekki had always thought. Though she had not thought the villagers harmed her or her mother, she had ached for them to behave toward her mother and herself as they behaved toward each other.

And her father *expected* that she and her mother should be treated well, and would *enforce* that treatment with death?

Vekki could hardly speak for the feeling in her, that had grown so warm. *Joy*, she realized. *It is joy*.

"Father," Vekki said, "I will go with you and Mother to see your kingdom."

GHOST MASKS

by Jonathan Moeller

It's not easy being one of the Emperor's Ghosts. It's not just the spying, or the occasional assassination; it's making certain that the person you kill is the one you really should be killing. It's avoiding the ever-increasing number of people who want to kill you. And you *must* be so inconspicuous as to be virtually invisible, because if enough people can identify you, your usefulness as a Ghost is at an end.

Jonathan Moeller wrote the novel DEMONSOULED (Gale/Five Star, 2005), and his short fiction has appeared in *Apex Digest, Aoife's Kiss, MindFlights, AlienSkin, Deep Magic,* and LILITH UNBOUND. Some of these publications are even still in print! He wrote "Black Ghost, Red Ghost" and "Stolen Ghosts" for *Sword & Sorceress 22* and *23,* and is pleased to return for *Sword & Sorceress 24.*

Caina knew that she might die before dawn came again.

A man sat before the hearth, staring into the flames, chin resting on the pommel of a broadsword. Caina had not seen him for over a year, but he looked as she remembered, his face and his eyes grim and hard. White scars stood out as his thick hands flexed against the sword's hilt. Caina had seen him use that weapon, seen him strike down foes with brutal strength.

He might do the same to her.

"Ark," said Caina.

Ark's head snapped around.

"They're going to kill the Emperor," she said.

Ark sprang to his feet in a single smooth motion, broadsword flying from its scabbard. Before Caina could react the sword rested against her neck. She could almost feel her pulse throbbing against the razor edge.

"Hello, Ark," whispered Caina.

"Caina?" said Ark. The sword did not waver. "The Ghost circlemasters told me that you were dead."

"Not yet," said Caina.

"They said that you betrayed the Ghosts," said Ark. "That you turned traitor and murdered old Halfdan."

"No!" said Caina. "The magi murdered Halfdan. As they will murder the Emperor, this very night, along with the Kyracian princes who came to make peace. The Kyracians will declare a war of vengeance, and in the chaos the magi will try to seize control of the Empire."

"How do you know this?" said Ark.

"This letter," said Caina. Slowly, carefully, she reached into her cloak, withdrew a tattered paper, and handed it to Ark. "I found it on the body of a magus who came to kill me. We have to act. The Ghosts don't know about this. They can't protect the Emperor from the assassin."

"Why should I believe you?" said Ark. "The magi could have reached into your mind, used their sorcery to twist your thoughts into whatever shape they wished."

"But they didn't," said Caina. "Listen to me. Halfdan was as a father to me. How could I have killed him? You know me. We've been through too much together. You've saved my life a dozen times. Halfdan may have been as my father, but you are as my brother, Ark. I swear to you I am telling the truth."

Ark said nothing, but his sword did not move, and his eyes did not soften.

"Do as you think best," said Caina. "Take me to the circlemasters. Or kill me. But I beg you. We are both sworn

Ghosts of the Emperor, his spies and servants, and the magi are going to kill him. You must stop them."

Still Ark said nothing. Despite herself, Caina began to tremble. The blade felt cold against her neck, so cold.

"Do you remember," said Ark, "the day you saved my wife from the slave traders?"

Caina surprised herself by laughing. "How could I forget? It is the only time I have ever seen you weep."

"I thought she was dead," said Ark. He blinked, once. "And I thought you were dead, too."

He lowered the sword, caught her by the shoulders, and pulled her to him in a rough hug. Caina's breath burst out in a startled cough. She had forgotten how strong he was.

"It is good . . ." Ark sighed and let her go. "I never thought I would see you again."

"Nor I you," said Caina.

"And I believe you," said Ark, returning his sword to its scabbard. "The Magisterium has been up to something for months. They've been killing Ghost spies left and right. But to kill the Emperor . . . we must go to the circlemasters at once."

"No," said Caina. "I have the death mark on my head. They'll kill me, and they won't believe me. If you go by yourself, they won't believe you, either. By the time you convince them the Emperor will be dead. We have to act, now."

Ark nodded. "What sort of sorcery will the magi use against the Emperor?"

"They won't. Too obvious." She pointed at the letter in his hand. "Read it."

He did. Then his brows knotted in an alarmed scowl. "Sicarion?"

Caina nodded.

She knew the name. Every Ghost did. Sicarion murdered for money, and he did it well, specializing in the murder of rulers. He had assassinated a dozen Lord Governors, a score of Imperial magistrates, Arthag kings, Kyracian princes, Carthian emirs. And numerous Ghosts who had gotten in his way. No one had ever caught him. No one had ever come close.

"Gods," muttered Ark. "We are overmatched."

"Yes," said Caina. "But it is still up to us."

"Very well," said Ark. A hard grin flashed across his face. "I'd follow you into hell, if need be. You figure out who needs killing, and I'll do it. Just like the old days."

"Yes," said Caina, smiling back. It was absurd. They might both die within the next few hours. Yet Ark's support cheered her more than she could say. "Let's go. The Emperor will greet the Kyracian Princes at the Praetorian Basilica. We need to get there before sundown."

"How are we going to get in?" said Ark.

Caina shrugged. "We'll lie. How else?"

"Ah. Just like the old days, then."

CR

Ark had supplies on hand, and Caina made use of them. A dagger in either boot, and knives strapped to her forearms, hidden beneath her sleeves. She changed to the flowing gown of an Imperial noblewoman, dark green cloth with black-slashed sleeves. While she prepared, Ark dressed as her man-at-arms. He had a coach and horses, and together they rode through the broad streets of the Imperial capital, past temples and mansions and the monuments of Emperors long dead.

"How will Sicarion do it?" said Ark.

"I don't know," said Caina. "Whatever method he thinks is appropriate, I suppose. He used a crossbow on the Lord Governor of the Pale. He poured ground glass into the dinner of an Arthag king. He . . . may even have access to some level of sorcery."

Ark scowled. "How do we find him?"

Caina didn't know.

At last the coach stopped before the towering edifice of the Praetorian Basilica, a massive stone pile of arches and buttresses and crenellated towers. Imperial Guards stood before the doors, imposing in their black armor, purple cloaks, and gleaming silver shields. Caina strode towards the doors, Ark trailing after her.

One of the Guards blocked her path. "A moment, my lady."

"What?" said Caina, speaking in the accents of a highborn noblewoman. "What insolence is this? Do you not know who I am?" She extended her ring for the Guard to kiss. "I am Countess Marianna Nereide, and my lord father will be most displeased with this."

"Pardons, my lady," said the Guard, "but when did you leave the Basilica?"

"Leave?" said Caina. "What are you babbling about, man? I just arrived, as you can plainly see."

The Guard looked at her, at Ark, and back at her. "Ah . . . forgive me, my lady. I must have been mistaken. Please, enter at once."

The Guards pulled the doors open, and Caina swept inside without sparing them another glance. Inside the cavernous hall other lords and ladies stood under the vast arches, speaking to one another in low voices. An empty throne sat on the dais as the far end of the Basilica, alongside three slightly smaller thrones for the princes. Caina hooked her arm through Ark's and guided him to a darkened alcove where they could talk.

"What was that about?" said Caina. "Why did he think I had already entered the Basilica?"

"There are numerous young noblewomen in the city," said Ark. "Perhaps he mistook you for someone else."

"By name?" said Caina. "There's no such woman as Countess Marianna Nereide." It meant something, and Caina did not like that the Guard had asked after her. She looked over the Basilica, trying not to scowl. Each of the nobles had brought their own guards, but Imperial Guards stood at the base of every pillar and in every arch, watching the lords and ladies through their black helms.

"There is a Ghost among the Imperial Guard," said Ark, following her eyes. "A centurion named Tylas. I will speak to him, have him urge the Guard to greater vigilance."

"Good," said Caina. "Look. What do you see?"

Ark frowned. "Lords of the Empire, high magistrates, Imperial Guards . . ."

"And no magi," said Caina. "They always attend when the Emperor holds court."

She did not like that, either.

Ark's mouth twisted. "So they do not come, lest they are implicated."

"Or," said Caina, "they don't want to get caught in the chaos."

"That," said Ark, "or Sicarion is going to do something that will kill everyone here."

Caina liked that even less.

"Go warn Tylas," said Caina. "I'm going to have a look around."

"Will the Guard let you wander?" said Ark.

Caina shrugged. "What threat is one unarmed woman? They will not care. Go."

Ark nodded and walked towards the Guards. Caina stepped after him, her skirts whispering against the marble floors. She wandered among the pillars, making a show of looking at the ancient carvings while scanning every nook and cranny.

Where would Sicarion hide?

She could not guess how the assassin planned to kill the Emperor and the three Kyracian princes. According to the letter from the magi, he would kill them all at once. Caina did not see how that was possible. No one with a drawn weapon could get anywhere near the Emperor. An archer would get only one shot before the Imperial Guard covered the Emperor with their shields. Sorcery? It would take potent sorcery to kill four men at once, and Caina doubted Sicarion had access to that kind of power.

Poison, perhaps?

Or did Sicarion plan to kill the Emperor and the princes before they even reached their thrones? The Basilica's roof rose four hundred and fifty feet over the plaza, with a narrow balcony running above the clerestory windows. A man perched there would have a clear view of the plaza and streets below.

Along with a clear shot. A barrel of stones pushed from the balcony at the right moment could wipe out half the Imperial court.

She looked for Ark, but he was deep in conversation with a centurion of the Imperial Guards. Tylas, no doubt, and Caina didn't dare show herself to another Ghost. She slipped around a pillar and walked to the base of the Basilica's northern tower. An Imperial Guard stood before the steps, watching the nobles with a blank expression. His eyes shifted to her, and widened a bit in surprise.

"You there," said Caina. "Has anyone come this way?"

"Yes, my lady," said the Guard. "Your sister said she had a headache, and went up to take some fresh air."

Caina hid her surprise. Sister?

"Yes, thank you," said Caina. "I had best bring her back. My lord father will be wroth if we miss the Emperor's arrival."

The Guard stepped aside. "Hurry, my lady. His Imperial Majesty will arrive at any moment."

"Hurry," murmured Caina, "yes."

She took her skirts in both hands and started climbing, cursing the long gown with every step. Damnable skirts! Four hundred feet later the stairs ended in a narrow wooden door, light leaking through the gaps between the boards. Caina pushed it open, the hinges groaning.

The wind hit her at once. The long balcony stretched along the Basilica's side, offering a splendid view of the city and the Imperial Palace on its high crag. Statues of long-dead Emperors stood atop the railing at regular intervals, gazing over the city.

A lone woman rested pale hands on the marble rail, her black hair billowing like a banner, the skirts of her rich green gown rippling. She seemed sad, haunted by some heavy grief. The woman looked up as Caina approached, blue eyes narrowing.

Caina stopped, shocked.

The woman was her exact double in every way, down to the smallest feature.

"Well, well, well," said the woman in Caina's voice. "We've worn the same face to court, haven't we? How dreadfully embarrassing! But don't worry, I'll take care of that . . ."

The double's hand blurred, steel flashing. Caina dodged as the throwing knife whirred past her head, spinning so close that she felt it brush her hair. She went to one knee, yanked the dagger from her right boot, and leapt up just in time to deflect a second throwing knife. Caina lunged at her foe, dagger leading. The double caught her wrist in both hands and twisted. Caina growled with pain, but slammed the heel of her free hand into the double's face.

Her palm struck wood, not flesh. The double staggered with a grunt, a mask of polished black wood clattering against the wall. And then the double vanished. In her place stood a lean man in dark leathers, weapons at his belt. Hideous scars crisscrossed his shaven head, making his face look as if it had been stitched together from leathery scraps. Either he had been mauled or someone had taken a knife to him with vigor.

Sicarion.

A heavy locket of red gold hung from a chain around his neck, bouncing against his chest.

His knee came up and slammed into her stomach. Caina stumbled back, wrenching her wrist free from his grasp. Sicarion drew daggers in either hand and backed away six or seven steps, watching her. Caina slipped a throwing knife into her free hand and held it ready.

"Strong, for a woman," said Sicarion. His voice rasped and hissed; perhaps one of the scars had damaged his throat. "Though perhaps overly proud."

"Overly proud?" said Caina. "This from a man who calls himself 'of the dagger' in the ancient tongue?"

"Recognized that, did you? I've earned that name," said Sicarion, daggers tracing slow designs in front of him. "Did you like my disguise?" He gestured at the mask lying between them. "The magi enspelled it for me. Part of my advance payment. A useful little toy, no?"

"Oh, very useful," said Caina, mind racing. If she shouted, would anyone hear her? She didn't think she could take Sicarion in a straight fight. Damn it all, but she shouldn't have come up here alone. "Right up until I saw you. What do you think would have happened if someone had seen us together?"

Sicarion laughed. "The magi told me that they killed you. So disguising myself as you seemed safe enough. That's what I get for trusting a band of sorcerers. They can't do anything right. Which, of course, is why they had to hire me."

"They shouldn't have hired a money-grubbing incompetent," said Caina.

"Money? Money is meaningless. Do you want to know why I like to kill kings?" said Sicarion. "Or princes, or emirs, or Emperors, whatever they like to call themselves. I've killed more people than I can remember. Every last one of them deserved to die screaming and sobbing in terror. But there are so many more of them. I'm only one man with a dagger. I can't kill them all by myself. But kill a king, kill a king at the right place and at the right time . . . thousands of people die. Maybe tens of thousands. Sometimes for generations. And all of them will have died by my hand." His eyes kindled as he spoke, filling with glee. "All from one thrust of a dagger."

"Are you insane, or merely wicked?" said Caina, keeping her eyes on him. Madman he might be, but he was talking for a reason, she knew, to throw her off balance or to distract her.

"Neither. This world deserves to die screaming. And I'm just the man to do it."

"You'll meet death firsthand if you don't lay down your weapons," said Caina.

Sicarion smiled and slid his daggers back into his belt.

Caina blinked in surprise. He had no defense now. One quick flick of her wrist and she could bury her knife in his throat.

But he had to know that, didn't he?

"You want to know how I'm going to kill your Emperor and those princes?" said Sicarion.

"You won't kill anyone," said Caina. "You'll have to go through me first."

"If you wish," said Sicarion. He lifted the strange locket hanging from his neck. "Another payment from the magi. The mask's just a toy. But this . . . this is different. It's a mirror for mind. The sorcery laid upon it is such that whosoever looks upon me will see their mind's blackest fears and worst regrets reflected back upon them. They often die, or go mad. Sometimes their hearts burst within their chests from the terror."

"Sorcery can be fought," said Caina, making up her mind. She tightened her grip on the knife, ready to throw.

"No. Not this kind," said Sicarion, opening the locket. Within, Caina glimpsed something like a ruby ablaze with its own inner flames.

And then Halfdan stood between her and Sicarion.

Caina flinched, her throw freezing halfway through. Blood oozed from a wound in Halfdan's neck, another from a gash across his chest. His eyes were glassy and empty, his mouth pulled back in the rictus of death. He looked just as he did on the horrible day when the magi had seized control of his mind, forcing him to attack her.

"You killed me!" he screamed at her, the words thundering inside her skull. "You killed me, I loved you as the daughter I lost and you killed me!"

"No!" said Caina. "No, no, I didn't, I tried to save you, I would have saved you if I knew how, I . . ."

"Your fault!" shrieked Halfdan, blood bubbling from his lips. The words plunged into her mind like knives. "You could have saved me. If only you had been smarter. If only you had been braver! You could have saved me, but instead I am screaming down in hell because you killed me!"

"No!" repeated Caina. Some small part of her mind insisted that something was wrong, horribly wrong, but the sorrow and guilt strangled her. "No . . . I'm sorry, I'm sorry, I . . ."

And then Sicarion rushed forward and seized her by the neck and shoulder. Too late Caina remembered, and she yanked back her dagger for a stab. But Sicarion shoved her, and Caina tumbled backwards over the railing, the plaza rushing up to meet her.

The dagger fell from her grasp. Caina just had time to scream before her head struck something hard, and darkness swallowed her.

ଓଈୄୄ୧ଓ

Caina awoke to the taste of blood in her mouth, the world spinning around her. The plaza rotated above her, painted red with the sunset. Was she still falling? Her hands flailed above her head . . . or were they below her head?

After a moment she realized that she was hanging upside down.

Caina spat out a mouthful of blood and looked up. She had only fallen thirty feet or so. A statue stood upon a ledge, brandishing an upraised spear, and Caina's skirt had caught upon it. She felt the seams straining, but the gown had been well-made, and the fabric held.

Well. Heavy skirts had some use after all.

She peered up at the balcony and saw no trace of Sicarion. Why hadn't he finished her off? He needn't even have bothered with a weapon; a dropped brick would have done the job.

Caina grinned.

Sicarion had erred. He should have just stabbed her and hidden the corpse, rather than playing with his sorcerous trinkets. It might have taken weeks to discover her body. But if the Imperial Guard saw a mangled corpse lying before the Praetorian Basilica, they would take the Emperor to safety, and Sicarion would miss his opportunity to strike.

Her grin faded.

If Sicarion realized that his cover had been blown, he would move to strike at once. And Ark, the Emperor, and the Imperial Guard would have no defense against that damnable locket. Little wonder the magi had not attended. The locket's power would drive everyone in the Basilica mad with terror, and Sicarion could butcher the Emperor at his leisure.

But only if Caina didn't stop him first.

She swung up, trying to catch a grip on the statue. Twice her hands slipped. On the third try she felt her skirt start to tear. She threw herself forward, her arms clinging to the statue's ankles, her legs wrapping around the spear. Bit by bit she climbed the statue, until she could lever herself onto the ledge.

Her head hurt, and her limbs ached. But that didn't matter. She knew how to be hurt. She had been hurt worse than this.

What mattered was stopping Sicarion.

She looked around. The clerestory windows were twenty feet below the ledge, and she had no way to reach them. That meant she had to go up. The stonework here was weathered and cracked, the mortar crumbling away. Caina slid off her boots, shoved her remaining dagger into her belt, and started to climb.

The wind lashed at her, tugging her hair and tattered skirt. Caina gritted her teeth and kept climbing, fear driving her faster. For all she knew Sicarion had slain the Emperor and the princes already. Inch by inch she climbed, trying not to look down. At last she heaved herself over the marble railing and collapsed onto the balcony, breathing hard.

The wooden mask was gone. No doubt Sicarion had taken it to resume his disguise. Caina wished that she had thought to kick it over the railing. She hurried down the stairs, bare feet slapping against the worn steps. Music drifted up from the Basilica, the sounds of drums and the blaring of trumpets.

The Emperor had arrived.

She had just reached the Basilica proper when a centurion of the Imperial Guard stepped before her, leveling a dagger against her throat. Caina twisted in his grip, intending to drive her knee into his groin. But he anticipated her move and sidestepped, ramming her into the wall. Caina gasped, stunned, and the Guard pinned her in place, dagger returning to her throat.

It was Tylas, the Ghost that she had seen with Ark.

"What is this?" demanded Caina. "I am the Countess Marianna Nereide, and you will release me at once or my father . . ."

"So old Ark was right," breathed Tylas. "Someone was coming to kill the Emperor after all."

"You're a Ghost," said Caina. "Listen to me. I . . ."

Tylas pressed the blade against her throat. "You murdered Halfdan, and the magi sent you to murder our Emperor. What did they promise you? Gold? A title? Lands? Or did they just break your mind?"

Caina blinked. Ark had done just as she had instructed. He had warned Tylas of the assassin without mentioning her. And Tylas knew of her death mark, and so assumed that she was the assassin.

Perhaps Sicarion was not the only one who had erred.

Caina scanned the hall, trying to think. All eyes were on the Emperor and the Kyracian princes. They stood on the dais, the Emperor in black armor and purple cloak, the princes outlandish in their blue robes and silver diadems. One by one the lords and ladies processed to the dais and bowed, paying their respects. She spotted Ark a third of the way down the line. Sicarion stood besides him, again wrapped in the mask's illusion, the locket resting against his chest.

Caina hoped she did not really look like that when she smirked.

"Look," said Caina. "Look. Just look at Ark."

Tylas frowned, but glanced over his shoulder. "So?"

"Who is with him?" said Caina. "Just look."

Tylas scowled at Caina, but looked at Sicarion, and his eyes grew wide. "What sort of trickery is this? This is sorcery!" He pushed Caina out before him. "Come with me . . ."

But this time Caina had anticipated his move. She seized his armored forearm, spun, and yanked the dagger from her belt. The hilt slammed into his jaw, and his head snapped back. Caina surged forward, driving her shoulder into his armored chest, and Tylas lost his balance and fell against the stairs, his helmet clanging against the wall. He moaned once, but did not get up.

Caina raced into the Basilica, the marble smooth and cold against her bare feet. Ark and Sicarion had reached the dais. Ark bowed, while Sicarion gripped his illusionary skirts and did an elaborate curtsy.

"Countess Marianna," boomed the herald, "of House Nereide."

"My Emperor!" said Sicarion in Caina's voice, his words ringing over the crowd. "It is an honor to stand before you and your august guests on this most auspicious day. I have brought a gift that I wish to lay before the princes of the Kyracian people, that friendship may bloom anew between our two nations."

Caina ran faster. She heard someone shout for her to stop, heard armored boots clanking against the floor in pursuit.

"You are generous, Countess," said the Emperor, his voice still strong despite the lines of age and weariness that marked his face. "Present your gift."

Sicarion smiled and lifted his hand to the locket.

And there was no more time. Caina threw herself forward and tackled Sicarion. The breath exploded from his lungs, and they toppled to the floor. Ark drew his broadsword with a shout of alarm, and a score of Imperial Guards converged on them. Caina clawed at Sicarion's face as they fought, trying to wrench the mask away. His fist connected with her cheek, throwing her back, but not before the mask went flying.

Armored hands seized Caina's arms as Sicarion scrambled to his feet, his true appearance revealed, his scarred face twisted with fury. She saw the Guards look at her, at Sicarion, back at her in confusion.

"Kill him!" shouted Caina. "The Magisterium sent this man to kill the Emperor. Ark! Kill him now!"

Sicarion wheeled back, cat-quick, as Ark came at him. Some of the Guards approached, swords drawn. The rest formed a wall before the Emperor and the princes, shields raised and swords ready. Sicarion backed against a pillar, a dagger in one hand, his other reaching to take hold of the locket.

His eyes met Caina's, and he winked at her.

"Ark!" said Caina. "Listen to me, kill him now, kill him . . ."

Sicarion opened the locket, its hellish light spilling out.

A shuddering gasp went through the crowd. Ark stopped, the blood draining from his face. A woman began to scream, high and shrill and terrified.

And then Halfdan stood before Caina, chest wet with blood, dead eyes filled with accusing fury.

It was only an illusion, only a trick, but still the sorcery sent sorrow and terror pouring into Caina. The Guards holding her arms sagged, moans coming from their throats. Screams erupted through the hall, mingled with cries of grief and desperate appeals for mercy. Ark fell to his knees, sobbing. The Emperor collapsed onto his throne, face white with horror.

Every man and woman in the Praetorian Basilica had just seen their deepest terrors come to life.

Caina wrenched free from the Guards, who made no effort to stop her. Her hand dipped into her sleeve and drew out a throwing knife. Her arm arched back, her eyes fixing upon Sicarion . . . and again she saw Halfdan's dead eyes staring into her.

"Your fault!" his voice screamed at her, "your fault, your fault my death was your fault, I made you what you are and you let me die . . ."

Caina stumbled to one knee, sobbing. She flung the knife at Sicarion, but her trembling hand sent it spinning into empty air.

"Still trying to kill me?" shrieked Halfdan, the words throbbing inside her skull. "Traitor and faithless, I curse myself that I ever thought of you as my daughter . . ."

And she heard Sicarion's voice too, hard and mocking.

"You know, I don't even know what you're seeing," said Sicarion. He stepped before her, dagger dangling from his hand, the locket on his chest ablaze with fiery light. "A dead lover, perhaps? You should see your face!"

Caina growled, and tried to stand, but the sorrow crushed her, and she felt herself sobbing. She glimpsed a noble on his knees, weeping and begging mercy from someone unseen, while an Imperial Guard threw himself upon his sword with a scream.

"You're stronger than the others, aren't you?" Sicarion said. "Strong enough to fight, if not strong enough to overcome. I respect strength. So I'll give you a little reward. You'll get to watch as I kill the Emperor and his Kyracian friends. Assuming the old fool's heart doesn't burst before I get to him." The scarred leather of his face split in a grin. "A hundred thousand men will die screaming because of what I do today . . . and you'll get to watch it begin."

He turned and walked towards the dais. An Imperial Guard stepped in his path, trying to hold a steady sword. Sicarion reached out, yanked back the Guard's head, and sliced his throat. The body fell with a clatter of armor and a spray of blood.

Caina staggered back to her feet with a scream, pulling another knife from her sleeve. But as she looked at Sicarion, Halfdan's face filled her vision, accusing her, condemning her, and her concentration shattered. She fell besides the slain Guard, weeping, the wails of the terrified nobles and Guards filling her ears. It was no use. Whenever she looked at Sicarion, the mental mirror of his sorcerous amulet ripped her darkest fear from her mind and flung it into her face, and she had not the strength to fight. She saw herself in the dead Guard's polished shield, saw herself weeping like a stricken child . . .

The shield . . .

Caina blinked.

Wait.

Sicarion climbed the dais, the dagger waving. Caina seized the shield in both hands and lurched to her feet. She hurried towards the dais, weaving like a drunken woman.

"Sicarion! Look at me. Look at me, damn you! Turn around and look at me!"

Sicarion turned, laughing, and Caina held the gleaming shield up before her face.

"So the fear has broken your mind after all?" said Sicarion, still laughing. "Hiding behind a shield like a child, hoping that I won't see you? So pathetic that . . ."

His words trailed off. Caina waited, not daring to look over the shield's rim.

Sicarion's voice became a shocked whisper.

"No . . ."

His voice rose.

The grief and horror vanished from Caina's mind, like a shadow disappearing beneath the noonday son.

"I killed you!" shrieked Sicarion. "I killed you! Don't touch me. Don't touch me!"

And Sicarion began to scream.

Caina risked a look over the rim. Sicarion bent backwards, still screaming, his hands shielding his scarred face from something unseen. Caina wondered what he had seen in the polished shield.

She could wonder later.

Caina sprinted forward, shield held out. Sicarion shook his head, and his expression cleared in alarmed realization a heartbeat too late. Caina slammed the shield into his face with all her strength. Sicarion's head snapped back, blood flying from his mouth. Caina struck again, swinging the shield like a board, and caught Sicarion across the side of the head. The assassin snarled and slashed with his dagger, and Caina jumped back just in time to avoid getting gutted. But he overbalanced, and Caina's foot caught his knee. His leg folded, and Sicarion tumbled down the dais. His shoulder struck Caina as he fell, and her bare feet slipped on the slick marble.

She landed atop Sicarion, and his scrabbling hands closed about her throat. Caina wrenched back, but his iron fingers held her fast. She pawed at her sleeves, trying to pull a knife free, but Sicarion began to shake her. She raked at his face, and her hand closed about something hard and cold, terribly cold.

The locket.

Caina ripped it free from its chain.

A puzzled expression crossed Sicarion's scarred face. Then his eyes widened. With a shriek he shoved her away, scrambling to his feet.

"Don't touch me!" he said, his voice thick with horror. "Don't touch me or I'll . . ."

Caina never found out what.

Ark's broadsword swept down and plunged into Sicarion's back. The assassin toppled with a yell, falling before the dais. Ark looked at Caina and blanched in sudden horror. She dropped the amulet, picked up the shield, and brought it hammering down.

The locket shattered. Its hellish light flickered, sputtered, and went out.

"Wait," whispered Sicarion, his voice faint. "Don't kill me. Don't . . . don't kill me. I'll . . . I'll . . ."

"You told me," said Caina, "you told me that the world deserved to die, that all men deserve to die." The fury welled up in her. "I tried to save Halfdan, and the magi murdered him. You were only half right. Only some men deserve to die."

Sicarion's eyes widened. "Wait! Wait . . ."

And then the Imperial Guards shoved past Caina, roaring their rage, swords raised.

Sicarion died at the foot of the dais, his hundred thousand murders stillborn.

ൟൟൟ

"I think it is safe to say, my child," said the Emperor, "that your cover has been blown."

"Of course, your Majesty," said Caina. "Beating a man senseless with a shield in front of a thousand witnesses will do that."

She sat slumped in a couch in the Emperor's private apartments, Ark standing by her shoulder. The Emperor's personal physicians hovered over her, cleaning and bandaging her cuts. She knew how to fight through the pain. But, gods, it still hurt, and the exhaustion had caught up to her.

"Halfdan often spoke to me, of you," said the Emperor, voice quiet. "He always spoke very highly of you." He smiled. "As I would be dead and the Empire plunged into war had you not acted, I can see why."

"Thank you, your Majesty," said Caina. "Halfdan was . . . Halfdan . . . was as a father to me. My only wish is to do honor to his memory."

"And you returned in the face of a death mark, no less," said the Emperor. "Well, that must be dealt with. In light of today's events, you shall no longer serve as a spy within my Ghosts."

Caina flinched.

"And as a reward, you shall be elevated to the rank of a Countess of the Imperial Court," said the Emperor. "Unofficially, you shall serve as my adviser." His thin mouth twisted. "The magi aren't done. They will not rest until I am dead and they hold the Empire in slavery and tyranny. The horror we endured today . . . how many more shall they inflict upon the Empire, if no one stops them? I shall need your cunning mind, my child. Will you accept?"

Caina laughed. "I've spent enough time masquerading as a Countess, so why not become a real one?"

"And you," said the Emperor, looking at Ark. "You seem marvelously efficient with that sword, and people keep trying to kill our clever young Countess. Will you serve as her bodyguard?"

"I shall, your Majesty," said Ark. "It will be like old times."

Later Caina walked to her new lodgings in the Imperial Palace, Ark following her.

"No longer a spy," said Ark. "What will you do with yourself?"

"Oh, I don't know," said Caina. "But I'm sure something will come up."

She suspected that advising the Emperor might well involve a great deal of subterfuge. The Magisterium still lurked with their plots and sorcery. Someone would have to ferret out their secrets.

Caina smiled and touched the hard shape hidden beneath her skirt.

Sicarion had planned to use his mask to murder the world, but she would put it to better use.

THE VAPORS OF CROCODILE FEN

by Dave Smeds

Alexander Pope said "A little learning is a dangerous thing;" but he didn't specify to whom—and a student may well learn lessons that the instructor never intended to teach.

Sword and sorcery works by Dave Smeds include his novels THE SORCERY WITHIN and THE SCHEMES OF DRAGONS, and shorter pieces in such anthologies as LACE & BLADE and RETURN TO AVALON, as well as eight previous volumes of SWORD & SORCERESS. He writes in many genres, from science fiction to contemporary fantasy to horror to superhero and others, and has been a Nebula Award finalist. He lives in the Napa/Sonoma wine country of California with his wife and children. In addition to being an author, he has been a farmer, graphic artist, and karate instructor.

I was raised here in the bog. Not many can say that. Few families have chosen to tie their lives to this peat, to these sulphur mists. Would *you* raise your daughter where crocodiles roam? You have seen for yourself how well the creatures thrive here, where the hotsprings and honeycombed channels cure the river of its snowmelt chill. Their pervasiveness is one of the two things for which this place is famous. The other is the Tale of the Dwarf Rebels.

You have not heard that story? The Duke of the Narrows had defeated all his rivals but one, his younger half-brother,

Strawhair. Having barely escaped the battle at Founders Knoll, Strawhair fled to a stilt house deep in the bog. Feverish from wounds, bereft of all but two of his fighting men, Strawhair was undone, but the duke was not satisfied. He tortured Strawhair's vassals, learned of the hiding place, and set out with a contingent of knights to eradicate this last challenger of his claim to the fief.

The duke saw no threat in the marshdwellers. We are not dwarfs, as the legend would have you believe, but most of my folk are short and slight, the better to propel our rafts over masses of lotus and water hyacinth. The welcoming party cowered before the knights' drawn blades. When the duke ordered a group to ferry him and his contingent to Strawhair's refuge, they complied in all apparent meekness. But once they were deep in the swamp, they leaped into the water and rocked the vessels from below until the duke and every one of his warriors fell overboard. Burdened by their armor, the invaders sank into the muck and drowned. It was a trap of Strawhair's design. His first victory among many. Eventually he reigned over the neighboring duchy as well, whereupon he came to be called Thrame Half-King.

Ah. You have heard that name, I see.

My grandfather told me that his grandfather was one of the men who sent the duke tumbling. But nearly every bogdweller will make a similar claim and swear it is the truth, no matter that the ambushers were rewarded by Strawhair with good farmland and fine houses. Which is another way of saying, they did not linger here among their kin, siring their babies by the glimmer of witchfire upon muskrat dames like my mother. There has only ever been one noble estate here, and it did not originate from Strawhair's grant. It was founded by Lithra, Countess of Orchid Mire.

Lithra had not been born into the nobility, but she was a sorceress of such caliber that many rewards came her way, including this property and its appurtenances. You might say that I was part of the latter. I was ten years old when I was indentured to her as a potion wench.

For eight years I assisted the countess in making her concoctions. She taught me much during that span. Many rich and influential folk craved her services. She needed to accommodate at least some of them lest she give up the trade of wealth and favors she had come to enjoy, but she had wearied of collecting ingredients, extracting their essences, then mixing and measuring everything just so. She would leave the dull parts to me, stepping in when the limits of my skill were reached, or when lesser results might harm her reputation.

Whether her clients wished for a philter of seduction, a salve to cure hairiness, incense to poison a spouse, a tonic to ward off plague, she could usually accommodate them. Yet many left disappointed. They wanted what she had—enduring youth. She had been born when Strawhair still reigned, and yet she appeared no older than twenty.

"That drink requires ingredients that no longer exist," she would tell them. No matter how high the bribe she was offered, her answer was the same.

What she said was the truth, as far as it went. The ingredients did not exist. What she did not say, not even to me until she had to, was that on a given day and in a given place, they *would*.

❧☙☙

My first hint that something was looming occurred as I was reading aloud from Lithra's grimoire deck in her study. The countess was standing by the window. When I reached the bottom of the tablet and looked up, the sunlight caught her face in profile.

Her jowls had slackened. I would not have noticed in dimmer light. The change was slight. As soon as she raised her chin, the looseness vanished. I wondered, had I truly seen it? But then I noticed new moles on her upper shoulder, revealed by the cut of her dress—Lithra loved to display her long, sculpted neck. The moles were small. No more than freckles, really. But they marred what had been, as recently as the previous morning, a swath of unblemished skin.

She turned to me. I quickly restored my gaze to the tablet.

"Why is licorice root included in that potion?" she demanded.

I hesitated. "To mask the taste of the hoar moss?"

She clucked her tongue. "That's not even a good guess. Nothing masks the taste of hoar moss."

I winced.

"There *is* no licorice root in that potion," she scolded. "Not if you want it to work."

I looked again at the line of text. It said licorice root. But I should have known better.

Lithra strode to the sand table and raked it smooth, erasing the previous lesson. "When you know the true ingredient, write it fifty times."

"Yes, m'lady."

She marched out, leaving me to my punishment. I sat at the sand table and began to contemplate what rune I would etch.

It was a familiar place to be. Even after years of study, I made errors. I needed to be able to recognize thousands of ingredients—some of which had several names. I needed to know whether to apply them as powders or shavings, hot or cold, for inhaling or for swallowing. Hardest of all, I had to recognize which parts of the instructions in her grimoire were rendered in code. No elixirist writes down his or her lore in such a way that parties uninvited may make free use of it. Fail to recognize the cipher, and a remedy becomes a poison.

I wrote nothing in the sand. I could not concentrate.

Lithra was aging.

ಚಿC33ಲಿನ಼

Over the following week, Lithra grew agitated to a degree I had never before seen. She had always been quick-tempered, but she had the cook whipped for over-salting the soup. When a footman stepped on her hem as she dismounted from a carriage, she threatened to have him castrated. Knowing how his predecessor had ended up, he pissed himself on the spot.

She was quick to snap at me when I arrived in the courtyard the next morning for our daily stroll.

"About time you arrived."

I was startled to see her there. I was in fact early. The countess usually lingered at breakfast—a meal sometimes not taken until noon.

I curtsied. "Your pardon, m'lady."

She held her body stiffly. Her eyes were bloodshot. Had she not slept? Nor eaten?

She launched herself down the main garden path. With my shorter legs, I had to scurry to keep up. I found myself staring at the nape of her neck. The hair was grey at the roots, and the skin cobwebbed by fine wrinkles. By now, she looked to be at least sixty.

Or perhaps only fifty. She seemed older because she had grown plain. I had not realized before that the magic that maintained her youth was also responsible for her beauty.

I glanced back, anticipating the company of servants or one of the guests the countess sometimes invited to keep her amused, but no one emerged from the manor. Soon we could not even see the building through the foliage.

"You have seen the changes in my appearance," she said.

The statement came without warning. I trembled as I answered. "Yes, m'lady. I have."

"All will be well. I need another dose of the Wine of Consorts."

"The—" I tripped on the raised edge of a flagstone, and nearly fell. "Did I hear you say—?"

"The Wine of Consorts. One of the Elixirs of the Numinous Mages."

"Everyone says the art of making those was lost."

"That is what they say."

Yet Lithra had mastered at least one of them. She was telling me she was at the level of the sorcerers of legend.

"I can hear your mind working," Lithra said. "You are remembering the nature of the great potions."

She had read me. Just as existence is expressed in solid, liquid, and gas, the highest magic bestows its abundance in three aspects—the internal, the external, and the threshold between. Plainly, in Lithra's case, the bounty of the internal aspect was her enduring youth. Her body had been altered so that it no longer suffered the effects of passing time. Her beauty was surely the bounty of the threshold. It wasn't that her form itself had grown lovely, but a glamour affected the way observers perceived it.

That left the bounty of the external. "You have some kind of power over the world around you, or over the people around you," I said.

"Yes. But if you haven't guessed what it is, I shan't tell you. I am already sharing more than I care to." She extended her hands. "Do you see how they shake?"

"Yes." I had already noticed the tremors.

"I need you to be my hands. I can't trust my grip. Were it not for that, I would not have brought you along. Be thankful you learn anything at all today."

"Yes, m'lady."

It was an odd place to be in. My fingers were short, like the rest of me, and the countess had on occasion been displeased with my dexterity.

"Is it always like this?" I asked. "Do you have to endure this decline?"

"It was safe to take a new dose weeks ago. It is because of my partner that the timing is so inconvenient." She spat into the hedge. "May he dine on goose dung at every meal."

"Your partner?"

We stopped. Lithra fixed her stare upon me. "You will repeat none of what I am about to tell you, do you understand?"

"As you command, m'lady."

At the quickness of my answer, she grew more calm.

"The Wine of Consorts is called that because it must be made from a pair of catalysts—one supplied by a female, the other by a male. In a few minutes we will rendezvous with my ally. I would be happy never to have to look at him again, but I do not have that option."

We continued on in silence. I was too stunned to dare more questions. Lithra was the last person I would have expected to have a partner of any sort, let alone one whose contribution was so key to her success and station in life.

She ignored the usual meandering garden paths and mazes and led us onward in as straight a route as we could take toward the edge of the estate, where it melted into the bog. The groomed landscape fell away. We shifted to a gamekeeper's track, a narrow thread of native clay that forced us to lift our skirts to make it through the nettles and berry brambles. The stench of simmering peat grew stronger.

"Do you smell the frogs?" my pa used to say as we returned from our regular treks to the market henge. Lithra's manor house was surrounded by garden flowers and every room scented with bouquets or spiced candles. It was only when I ventured out into this amphibian miasma that I felt at home.

The morning sun was banishing the mists as we reached the end of the path. Ahead lay an expanse of lagoons, shallows, drowned trees, islets, and brush. Slightly to our left a short pier thrust into the deeper channel that bounded this fringe of the marsh. A dinghy was tied to it. Standing on the dock, arms folded and head high, as if he were commanding the gloom to lift, was a large man.

Our movement made no real sound that I heard, but he turned toward us immediately, his right hand darting to the hilt of his sheathed sword. He moved like a fighting man.

He relaxed as he saw who had come. He removed his nondescript travelling cloak and tossed it, along with a campaign duffel, into the boat.

The attire he had revealed was far from nondescript. His shirt was finest silk. His tunic was linen, embroidered with such intricate detail it must have taken a seamstress months to complete the needlework. Many of the colors were more vivid than can be teased from plant dyes, requiring sorcery to achieve.

A warrior he might be, but he was no common soldier. Even at this distance, I recognized his likeness from the proclamations his scribes and messengers had distributed through the land. He was Obur. The King.

"*He* is your partner?" I gasped.

"Yes," the countess replied.

I suppose I might have guessed, if I'd had more than a few minutes to speculate. There were only a few dozen known immortals in the land, and surely her partner had to be one of them. But the *king*?

His gaze settled upon me as we approached. I was unaccustomed to such scrutiny from a male. I felt as though my gown and shift had evaporated, leaving me naked in front of him. The feeling was not unpleasant.

"Who is this young fawn?" he asked.

"My potion wench."

I curtsied. He smiled. I blushed.

"Let's be done with this," the countess declared, clambering down the ladder and into the dinghy.

"After you," the king said.

My hand trembled as I took his. He held me securely as I lowered myself down. I felt . . . royal.

"Control yourself," the countess snapped. "He's just a man."

Obur began untying the knots that secured the vessel to the dock. "She knows that's not true." He winked at me. Despite what my mistress had demanded, I blushed again.

"Stop smiling," Lithra told me.

And instantly, my lips flattened. Suddenly. As if of their own accord.

All at once, I understood why.

"That was foolish of you," the king told Lithra as he stepped into the dinghy and gave us a push away from shore. "Now she knows."

For eight years, I had obeyed Lithra unfailingly. When she was harsh—which was nearly all the time—I saw her venom as justified. When she treated servants and visitors poorly, I saw it as their fault, and—though my opinion was of course never solicited—I took her side.

Loyalty. That was the final gift the Wine of Consorts had given her. She commanded the loyalty of those around her. Only now, with the magic growing weak, could I even summon the perspective needed to be aware of the compulsion I had been under.

"You be silent," the countess told the king. But he just laughed. That was when I understood the rest—he was immune. He was the one person who could freely choose to be disloyal to her.

Obur took the center bench and picked up the oars. My mistress and I faced him, side by side on the aft bench.

"Well?" he asked.

Lithra pointed. "That channel. Keep to the north as we skirt the mangroves."

So even Obur did not know where we were going. This did not surprise me. It would not have been like Lithra to keep her catalyst within her own manor, where a thief—or an untrustworthy partner—might succeed in locating it. It was hidden more elaborately than that.

The king propelled us on with steady, powerful strokes. We rounded the first bend and the dock vanished behind the mangrove tangle. Ravens called out to warn of humans penetrating the marsh. Turtles abandoned their logs as we approached, to hide in the clouds of algae.

"You've looked better," Obur commented.

Lithra bristled. "I have you to thank."

He chuckled. He stroked his close-cropped beard. It was shot with grey, but only a little. The elixir's grace had not yet abandoned him as much as it had Lithra.

"Perhaps you should have inhaled more deeply last time we were together," he said.

"If I failed to do so, it was because I was holding my nose at the need to be next to you."

"Have care, my orchid in the mire. Or I will think you do not love your king."

"Spare me your blathering," she replied.

A muscle in his jaw twitched, and for an instant, I thought he would pick up an oar and pound her across the skull. Nevertheless his voice was mild as he said, "Your wench wonders how you keep me coming back each time, when you nurse me on such sour milk."

Hair rose on the nape of my neck. He had precisely described how I viewed their bickering. Could he see within me?

Yes. That must be it. People said the king could sense what vassals and courtiers were sincere in their support of him, and that he had an uncanny ability to ferret out traitors. Some believed this insight sprang from a magical source, like his youthfulness. It appeared they were right. It seems the Wine of Consorts had given him the ability to see the true desires and opinions of those around him—his bounty of the external.

Lithra, though, was opaque to him. That irked him.

Surely at one time they had been on good terms. Had time alone changed their attitudes? Or was it that Lithra couldn't bear the thought of someone she couldn't sway, and he couldn't bear the uncertainty of not knowing if a person near him was arranging to betray him?

All I could do was stare at the power of the king's hands as he gripped and pulled on the oars, and know I would be afraid of attempting to betray such a man. If I ever did and the plan went awry, he would be the most dangerous of enemies.

He studied me. I saw him ferret out my mood, sense my conclusion. He smiled again.

And then he frowned at Lithra. Did she have some trap in mind for him? If so, I didn't know. And therefore, Obur couldn't know, either. It was her secret to have.

"We are going very far in this time," Obur observed after an hour of threading through the lacework of navigable channels. I heard suspicion in his tone.

"I am just following the scent," she replied, "and it has led us this way. It's not much farther. I can tell we're close."

In fact, another quarter hour dragged by. But then, as we rounded a cluster of cattail reeds, Lithra let out a pent-up breath.

"There."

Ahead lay a fallen cypress, one broken, half-rotted limb jutting well above the waterline. From a beetle niche grew a large, strikingly handsome bog lily, its stalk strung like foxglove with blooms, their hue saffron near the crest, deepening to copper at the base. The flowers were like cups, and each hung low, bowed down by unnaturally heavy loads of nectar.

As well as I knew the swamp, I had never seen such a flower.

"It blooms only when I need it to," Lithra explained to me, with not a little pride in her tone. "And never in the same part of the bog."

It was ingenious. Most of the time, she had no need to hide or to guard the catalyst, because it simply didn't exist.

Obur ceased paddling, letting the boat ease to a gentle drift. This was enough to bring us right under the jutting branch. The king took hold of a knobby projection of the tree trunk and held us in place.

Lithra reached into the campaign duffel Obur had brought and withdrew three items—a flask, a funnel, and a chalice. She put the funnel into the mouth of the flask.

"Tip out the contents of the blooms," she said, handing me the items. They fit together so snugly that it was as if they were one piece. "And need I say? *Be very careful.*"

I made my way to the prow. I had grown up riding in boats such as these and my balance was good, but nonetheless I concentrated on my steadiness. The lower blooms of the stalk were right at the height of my bosom. I decided to begin with those.

A butterfly sailed in. It hovered as if to sample the lily's provender, but it had no sooner come close enough to smell the full aroma than it shot away as if bitten.

I realized gnats and midges were no longer dancing around my face as they had throughout the journey. They were keeping at least four or five feet away from the flower. I saw none of their drowned carcasses in the pools of nectar. Nor any pollen or other impurities.

I tipped a bloom. Four or five drops of syrupy amber liquid fell into the funnel. I realized it would be a lengthy process. The bloom, the largest, was no larger than a pinkie thimble.

A searing pain, like pepper juice in a knife cut, soaked into my index finger and thumb, where the stickiness of the nectar clung. I blew air, but it only served to spread the stickiness a bit further, and added to the agony.

"Yes," Lithra said coolly. "I always hated that part. It's difficult not to get a little on one's skin. Don't be a baby. It will cause no permanent damage."

"You might have warned her," Obur remarked.

"Nothing teaches like experience," the countess replied.

I tried to be even more careful as I harvested the second and third blooms, but a trace more liquid touched my skin. I stifled a whimper. I was sure blisters were rising.

I wondered how something so caustic could be swallowed. Did it become palatable upon being combined with Obur's catalyst?

Abruptly, the answer came to me. One did not drink it. One breathed the fumes.

I said nothing. I was certain I did not want Lithra to know I'd guessed this aspect of the process.

"Well, child," she said. "Do not sit there chewing your curls."

I went back to work, trying to lose myself in the task so as not to notice the discomfort as much. Finally, when more than half the flower's yield had been depleted, Lithra said I had gathered enough.

She accepted the flask from me with care, conscious of her unsteady grip. There wasn't much opportunity to spill any, however. She immediately raised the flask to her mouth, exhaled into it, and tightened the cap.

The flask began to glow—not to the eye, not so that any non-mage would notice a difference, but I had no trouble sensing the aura. From the nods of satisfaction from Lithra and Obur, they perceived it even better than I. Within a few more minutes, Lithra's catalyst would be ready to be combined with Obur's.

How like her, to hide her treasure not only in place and time, but to require one last manipulation on her part to bring it to full strength.

"Your turn," the countess told the king.

He chuckled. "We will see. You might have to be patient."

"Perhaps this time you will choose a different benefit," Lithra grumbled. "One that will make this process easier."

"You would love to see me weakened. No. I will keep the same set of gifts. They have served me well. And being patient will do you good. Spirits know you don't get much practice."

Lithra shot him one of the glares I had borne the brunt of over the years, though the puffiness of the bags beneath her eyes reduced the intensity of it. She tapped her finger against the flask. "Get on with it."

Obur drew his dagger. I hiccupped at the sight, but he did not point it at either of us. He splayed his thumb on the bench, nail side down, and placed the tip of the weapon in the center of the fleshiest part.

He pressed down hard.

His skin held. The knife did not penetrate.

"Hair in my soup would be more use than you," Lithra complained.

Obur shrugged. To me, he explained, "When the magic fades, it goes quickly. But until then, it is as strong as if I had just taken a dose."

"What were you trying to do?"

"His blood is the catalyst," Lithra said.

Obur grinned. "Can you think of a better way to keep it safe?" He jabbed his palm with the dagger. Again, the tip would not penetrate. The bounty of the threshold protected him. The tales of his invulnerability in battle were well-known.

"The sea folk raiders once coated their swords with oils their shamans swore would let them cut me. They tried and they tried. I killed two-thirds of them, and told the others to go back and kill their shamans. I'm told they took my advice."

To pass the time, he told other tales. Lithra sighed and rolled her eyes. After he had described his plans to seize the mines of the southerners on his next campaign, he handed me the dagger and laid his thumb down again.

"Put all your weight into it," he told me.

I was not sure I, small as I was, could press any harder with all my weight than he could with his one arm, but I took the knife, set it on his thumb, and bore down.

At first, the skin held. Then the very sharpest part of the tip sank down a fraction more. A bead of blood formed.

"That will do," he said. He took back his knife. "Hold out the chalice."

I did so. He held his thumb out and squeezed three drops into its gleaming gold receptacle.

The power in the drops radiated over me. It made me sway. Obur liked that.

But I kept the chalice extended.

"No more is needed." Obur said. "Unlike some, my potions are *concentrated*."

Lithra sniffed. "You just don't like to bleed."

They would have kept sniping at each other, but I interrupted them. "That was not enough," I told the king.

"Eh?" he asked.

"You will need more," I repeated, my voice failing as I reached the last word and realized to whom I was speaking.

"How could *you* possibly know that?" Lithra asked. "Let me see, child. Be prepared for a strapping when we return to the manor." But as I held the chalice to her nose and she inhaled, her brows rose.

She scowled at Obur. "More, fool. Unless it's your intent to ruin the spell."

Brows furrowed, Obur checked for himself. He grunted. "So it seems."

He squeezed out one more large drop. "There. That will do." He pressed the chalice closer to me. "Do you agree?"

"Yes. This is enough," I said.

Obur chuckled. "It's not like you to have such a talented assistant, Lithra my sweet."

"She is more gifted than I guessed," the countess admitted. I knew that sour tone. I had not won a reprieve from the strapping.

"There is more, though," Obur said. He was radiant with cheer as he spoke. "Did you know she craves to take your place?"

My heart began to pound. I turned to Lithra, and saw her eyes widen. It was the last expression she would ever wear. In a single efficient move, Obur stood, drawing his sword as he came up. He whipped the blade sideways. Lithra's head tumbled off her neck into the water. It disappeared into the duckweed and flotsam.

I screamed while Lithra's body teetered and spasmed, blood spurting from the severed neck. As calm as a cat on a pillow, Obur snatched the flask of nectar from her fingers before her thrashing could send it flying.

My screaming lasted until after the body had gone limp and flopped to the bottom of the dinghy. Then I began to sob.

"I didn't mean . . . I didn't want . . . what have I done?" The words burned as they came out.

I was a murderess. Obur had seen within my heart. It was true, I had longed to be in Lithra's place. To be mistress of a fine house, my life fixed with riches, beauty, admirers? I had always wanted it.

"You will get over it," Obur assured me. "You will thank me, soon enough. Here. Hold this while I deal with the dregs."

He handed me the flask. Somehow I summoned enough composure to grip it securely.

Obur hefted the body onto the gunwale. Another shove, and it would fall overboard. But in that moment, all the weight of it was at one end of the boat, along with the weight of Obur and his accouterments. Before I gave it thought—before Obur could sense my intent and move to thwart me—I flipped backward into the water.

When I surfaced, I saw an upside-down dinghy. The water beyond it was churning. Obur's head and arms shot into view. He thrashed about, eyes wild.

"I will feed you your own toes!" he roared. I remembered the stories of how he dealt with captured enemies, and I nearly vomited. He had not been pulled to the bottom by heavy armor like the Duke of the Narrows and his men. Of course not. Obur did not wear armor. His skin was all the protection he needed from blade or arrow.

Somehow, terror did not paralyze me. While he tried to work his way around the dinghy to get at me, I let go of the chalice, ripped open my bodice and wriggled out of my servant's gown. Buttoning the flask into the lady's friend pocket of my shift, I launched into the fastest swimming stroke I knew.

When I had fled a full skipped-stone length of distance, I dared to glance back. Obur was still next to the boat. He had dispensed with his cloak and was trying to remove his boots, but the weight of his remaining garments sent him under whenever he turned his attention away from treading water.

Any swamp girl learns to swim well. The king, like most folk of our realm, where local waters usually run cold, had obviously never learned to swim at all.

I aimed for the one speck of dry land I had spotted while we were approaching the magical flower. I knew I had to reach it without delay. Dark reptilian forms were converging from the right and the left. I hoped they would ignore me, tasty morsel though I was, and head for Obur, who was still in water crimsoned by Lithra's blood.

A tangle of lotus vines suddenly blocked my way. I knew them as a type that grows only along banks, not in open water, so I thrust my feet down. Finding I could wade, I fought my way through the tangle onto land.

A stirring in the vines in my wake alerted me. I sprang high. Jaws snapped right behind my heels. I sprinted forward and began clambering up the twisted ropes of a strangler fig tree.

The tree shook with the impact of a large body. Only when I had reached a branch in its heights did I look down.

A crocodile was leaning on the tree at its base, gazing up at me with what I felt sure must be hope that I might tumble from my perch. Splatters of mud, flung by my scampering feet, dotted its snout. It opened its mouth, and I saw a piece of torn cloth in its teeth. At just that moment, I became aware that the breeze was wafting freely over my bottom. I reached back. My hand came away covered only by mud and swamp scum—and maybe a bit of crocodile saliva—but no blood.

Gradually, my heart ceased pounding, and my breathing steadied. The whole time, the crocodile regarded me. Only when it determined I was not going to plummet into its maw did it stalk back to the water, emitting an almost doglike snort.

Once through the lotus vines it swam with lethal purpose to join of its companions near the overturned dinghy.

The spot was a chaos of churning water, thrashing crocodile tails, and bloody foam.

"When the magic fades, it goes quickly," he had said. With luck, he was already dead. If not, at least he was too preoccupied to deal with me. I was determined to make good on my reprieve, and find places to hide where even a man with a king's resources would not find me.

ೞ൫ഔ౩

It took me a quarter of an hour of sloshing across brackish channels and crossing isthmuses of matted vegetation to reach one of the larger islets I knew I would find in the interior of the bog. The whole way I kept alert for crocodiles. Now, finally, that danger was receding. Reaching a spot well clear of the bank, where there was no brush to hide a large predator, I exhaled the terror I'd been hoarding.

Behind me, water sloshed. Something parted the reeds.

I spun around. The fear plunged right back into me.

Obur stood at the edge of the islet. His grin was all teeth.

His clothing was in rags, and what still held together was red and sticky. His skin was no better. He was oozing blood from dozens of punctures and bleeding freely from several gashes. But clearly, his magical invulnerability had not entirely forsaken him. His attackers had not been able to tear him to pieces, nor had they been able to hold him under and drown him.

"Do you know what it takes to fight off crocodiles?" he growled. "You simply kill enough of them that the living decide they would rather feed on their dead brethren than bother with you anymore."

He had lost his sword and his dagger in the struggle, and his right hand was one of the many parts of him that had been badly gnawed. He reached out with the left—an appendage easily capable of throttling the life from me if I let him get within range.

"Now," he said, pointing to the place where my shift bulged from the presence of the flask, "we will finish our business. Don't worry. I'll let you live. One good whiff of the elixir and I will heal completely. How could I stay angry with you after that?"

I turned and raced away.

He snarled. I heard his heavy footfalls as he pursued me. He was gaining. His long legs gave him the advantage in a footrace.

But ahead was the reason I had come here. A large cypress tree rose at the far edge of the islet. A circular platform awaited thirty feet up its trunk. At the same level, a stout rope was anchored, with a pair of thinner, parallel ropes attached higher up. The lines crossed over to a tree rising from the shallows to the west.

I would like to think a squirrel could not have scaled that cypress as quickly as I did. There were no branches down low. I had to shimmy up. But my brothers had taught me well. I was too high for Obur to grab by the time he reached the spot.

Now I had the advantage. I was far lighter than he, and I was not wounded. Reaching the platform, I began scurrying across the main rope, lightly grasping the thinner lines for balance. I was nearly halfway across the gap by the time Obur finished climbing.

He tried shaking the ropes, but the main one was too thick, and the others too taut to let him succeed. Livelihoods depended on maintaining this arboreal highway, for many valuable parts of the bog are inaccessible even by rafts and canoes. If he had been able to use his sword, he might have been able to sever the lines. As it was, he was forced to continue the chase.

Below us, a pair of crocodiles raised their heads off their sandbar and regarded us with interest. One of them opened its jaws. At the sight of the teeth, sweat burst from my palms, but soon I was past them and, breathless and trembling, reached the next platform.

Obur was leaving a bloody handprint behind each time his right hand gripped the guide rope. He was making better progress than I had hoped, his natural agility compensating for his inexperience.

I hurried on. From tree to tree we went—platform to platform through the mid-canopy. I was faster. Bit by bit my lead increased. The great danger was that I get careless and slip. I made sure not to go so fast I let that happen.

Obur, on the other hand, threw caution to the wind and pushed harder. Gradually I understood. At least one of his wounds was deep. He was bleeding to death. If he did not catch me soon, he never would.

Finally I was an entire rope-length ahead. I paused at a platform, ready to launch myself onward, but I saw that Obur had stopped at the preceding one.

His breath was coming hard and ragged. He held the tree's bole for support.

"Wench!" he cried. "You don't want to flee. Stop and think. What's done is done. You can't bring Lithra back to life. You must think of yourself now. Don't you want to live forever? I know you want it. Cooperate with me, and you will have it."

He had realized the only way left to catch me was with persuasion. It wasn't a bad strategy. He was right in believing that I wanted the bounties of the Wine of Consorts.

But I could not get the image from my mind of Lithra's head sailing off her shoulders into the mire. And I had heard the stories of Obur. They called him the Bloody.

"What will you do, if I save you?" I asked.

"I will give you what you desire. What more do you need to know?"

"No. What will you *do*? For yourself? What will you fill the years with? What will you accomplish?"

He brushed away flies from his face. Drawn by the blood, they were nagging him incessantly. By his delay, I knew just how much his power had faded. He was trying to look within me, to see what answer I wanted to hear, and then he would say it aloud. He could no longer do so. Instead, he had to guess.

"I will do what I have done all along. I will make my realm greater. It is my destiny. Share it with me. I would like that."

He had such a seductive tone. It was said that for all his love of battle and conquest, he had never forced himself on a woman. I saw how that could be true.

But he had given me the wrong answer.

"It is often said, the people of this land were happier before you came to rule," I said.

He tried to rise, to come after me again. He did not have the strength.

"You doom yourself," he snarled. "Can you not see that?"

"I will have as much as I had before," I said. And more, because it would be a better world, with him gone from it.

He pleaded for another hour, whenever he rallied enough to regain consciousness. I cannot say it was easy to keep to my choice. I cannot say I did not continue to be tempted. But my resolve remained intact long enough. I was, after all, of Dwarf Rebel ilk. We choose our dukes and kings with care.

Finally the blood loss had its effect. Obur died there on the platform, hugging the tree.

೫ಎⴲೞೞ

Only when the flies were crawling over his distended tongue and moving in and out of his open mouth without any reaction from him, did I realize I might not have to forego the riches he had dangled in front of me. After all, blood was still oozing from him—blood that might yet be able to be a catalyst for the Wine of Consorts.

I retrieved the flask from the pocket of my shift. It still glowed with its eldritch energy.

Tentatively, fearing that Obur might jump up after all and seize me, I crossed the rope bridge to his platform.

Up close, I was able to perceive that his blood had not yet lost its magical potency. True, the power was fading, but only as fast as his body was cooling. I looked about, and as expected, found that the platform was equipped with a cooking pot, a brazier, and charcoal—swamp folk often spend days at a time on their foraging expeditions. I squeezed blood from his wounds into the pot until I was sure I had enough. It took far more than four drops, but that was no problem. I added the contents of the flask.

The elixir quickened.

In the end, I had to heat the mixture like tea in order to inhale enough of the fumes. I suspect Lithra and Obur would have found that step unnecessary. But it worked. I felt the energy radiating from my lungs into the rest of me.

I shoved Obur's corpse from the platform. Descending, I dragged it to the edge of an embankment and let it tumble into the water. It was only right that Obur and Lithra end up together, even if it had to be in the bellies of crocodiles.

Back on the platform, I studied the dregs of the elixir, learning what I could of its nature. I saved what did not steam away, but the dregs, once cool, became inert. I understood the one dose might be all I would ever enjoy. The effects would eventually fade. In ten years? Twenty? I did not know.

In the meantime, the enchantment manifested. By the time I made it out of the marsh and back to the manor house, I was transformed.

I was eighteen. I have not grown older. I doubt you are surprised that I chose endless youth as my bounty of the internal. Who would not want that? And in truth, I am not sure I could have influenced the magic to produce a different result, because the internal aspect is not entirely determined by reason and calculation. My body chose for me, seeking survival above all else.

Second, I chose beauty. I could not help it. I was like Lithra in that regard. I had no love of being plain.

The third bounty, regarding the aspect of the external, now there was where I applied what wisdom I could muster. I had carefully contemplated my options while harvesting Obur's blood.

I did not need to have influence over people. I make friends easily. I had no desire to see their secret desires or to coerce them to loyalty. Instead, I gave myself power over magical lore. As I pored over Lithra's grimoire deck of tablets and unfurled her collection of arcane scrolls, passages that I needed would catch my eye, and I would study them until I grasped the implications hidden between the words. I was drawn to particular shelves in the libraries in particular cities where I would find the right page of the right volume to bring forth critical information I otherwise lacked. I would succeed in locating the right mages with whom I could bargain for advice or written materials that had other elements of what I needed.

It took me less than three years to achieve the first of my two great goals. By then I had the knowledge necessary to create a viable catalyst for the Wine of Consorts. That is, I could make the female half. With a little practice, I found I could do it as well as Lithra, if not better.

The rest was far harder. If it had been easy, others would have done it earlier in history. But after many years, I have achieved the second goal. I know I can teach a male adept of even moderate magical talent to craft the other catalyst.

And so now we are here, my sweet man. Now you understand what it is I have to offer you. Tell me, what gifts would you have? What suite of three powers? Think carefully, for much depends upon your answer.

LORD SHASHENSA

by Therese Arkenberg

The Dhoth had attacked Treseda's estate and burned her fields, and their armies were still nearby, so the slave boy her steward found on her lands seemed to be the least of her worries. In fact, the boy proved to be amazingly helpful—and not just with the household chores.

Therese Arkenberg is a student from Wisconsin. Somewhere between school, work as a page at the local library (oddly enough, that was my first job), and reading—she spends more time with a good book than sleeping, she manages to scratch out a paragraph or two of science fiction or fantasy. She has no pets, but keeps an extensive collection of stuffed animals. Her work has appeared in *Kaleidotrope* magazine, on the *Raven Electrick* website, and in the online anthology *Thoughtcrime Experiments*.

Treseda Nudoath never looked outside her window anymore. The fields were out there, the fields the damned Dhoth had burned, the fields her people had relied on to see them through the year. A thousand questions ate at her every time she looked at them—how would she pay taxes, what would they eat, why had the Dhoth ever considered *her* crop a threat? And she remembered the raid, the sick fear that turned to cold dread as her summer green fields blossomed in orange flame, then faded to dead gray ash . . . So she avoided looking at the fields, if she could.

Unfortunately, that was hard to do when they lay outside her bedroom window.

She could just change rooms, she reflected as she stumbled down the halls of Poncenet estate, rubbing sleep from her eyes. But that would be like an admission of defeat, and far too close to cowardice, in her own mind at least.

"Your Grace." She looked up at the speaker, a tall man with slick black hair and eyes like chips of green glass. Treseda smiled at her steward.

"Good morning, Jahennes."

He returned the smile brilliantly, but his bow was apologetic. "Ah . . . I hate to disturb you so early, but . . . Faraden caught someone sneaking around the grounds last night."

Her heart skipped. "Dhoth?"

"No," he said quickly. "Rather, an escaped slave, Your Grace. We kept him in the loft over the stables, not wanting to disturb your sleep."

"Thank you. I'll see him over breakfast."

Breakfast, served in the dayroom by a sad-faced Heria, was modest: a bowl of porridge made of grains from last year's harvest, served from a communal pot, and a small yellow fruit from Treseda's garden in the courtyard. The Dhoth had burned the orchards.

Jahennes and Faraden, the stable master, arrived as she was finishing her meal. The slave boy was with them: slight, black-haired, dark skinned, with large pale eyes, obviously foreign. But his features weren't Dhoth, and he stared at Treseda's feet without defiance.

"Let me see his tag," she said.

Jahennes gently tipped the boy's chin up and took the bronze slave tag hanging from a cord around his neck. "*I am the property of Lord Shashensa,*" he read aloud. "Nothing else."

No directions for return, and Shashensa was a foreign name if Treseda had ever heard one. Not Dhoth, though.

"What's your name?" she asked the boy.

"Caiyo, Your Grace."

She exchanged a glance with Jahennes. Whoever this Shashensa was, possibly he might offer a reward for the return of a slave. And with the fields and orchards burned, and war-taxes coming, such would not be unwelcome. But something about the boy, a dull *distance* in his words that she had never heard before in even the most listless slaves, troubled her. It was as if he wasn't truly speaking, any more than a speaking-trumpet did when it echoed words called into it. What could have made him that way?

"And why did you run from your master?" she asked.

Caiyo shrugged.

Heria's hands shook as she poured Treseda's tea. Her daughter had been captured by the Dhoth, Treseda remembered, in their raid that summer. Who knew where the girl was now?

But if she had somehow escaped, and made her way to a stranger's estate, Heria could only hope that the thought of a Dhoth lord's reward was not worth the girl's freedom. And if Shashensa had wanted his slave back so badly, he should have made tags with directions for his return.

"Let him stay here," she said. When Jahennes looked at her oddly, she added, "Well, we have no idea how to return him, do we? And we don't have any idea what nation Shashensa could be from. The tag tells us nothing—every one of the Three Hundred Kingdoms uses the same alphabet, and I'm not ready to shift through two hundred languages looking for *Shashensas*."

"We could let a magistrate sort through it," Jahennes pointed out.

"We have Dhoth to deal with before then."

Heria set down the teapot with a gentle sigh.

"If he wants to go, let him leave," Treseda said. Caiyo shook his head. "Very well. Go and find something useful for him to do. Treat him gently. I'll have him considered a free man now." She rose, and on her way out, thought to add, "and take off that tag."

⋘ C⟨R⟩ℌ ⋙

"There's a messenger here to see you, Your Grace."

"Is he from Lord Shashensa?" She had said the words playfully, but Jahennes didn't smile.

"No. He's from Anderum. He's waiting in the salon."

The messenger from the capital, a short, dark-haired man caked with sweat-cemented dust, didn't waste any time on pleasantries after she entered. "Your Grace, several days ago, the King's Protectors intercepted and translated a Dhoth message. Their army is on the move. Your estate is directly in their path."

She cursed, but her anger was only bravado. She felt her heart plummet as she said the foul word. What more did they want? What more damage could they cause?

The messenger tactfully chose not to hear her. "The fortress of General Galadsten is five days' journey to the north. On behalf of the Protectors, I advise you to go there, and to start your journey soon."

Galadsten. Wasn't he supposed to have sent bread, after their fields had been burned? She hadn't received news from him since the beginning of the war. What good was he?

Begging the gods, why did the Dhoth have to come across her lands again? Hadn't she suffered enough?

"Thank you," she said. "I will gather my people tomorrow. We shall do as you say. I . . ." With nothing more to add, she sighed and said, "Thank you."

He bowed and left the room.

When she was alone, Treseda knew she could safely cry, but did not.

⋘ C⟨R⟩ℌ ⋙

Treseda tried very hard not to look out her window that night. Some time after she gave up tossing and turning, the dream began. It started with the pounding of surf on the shore, a sound she had heard often as a child, visiting paternal relatives in the seaside kingdom of Adbara. And then she knew she was standing in Adbara, on a wide stretch of white sand cupping a sapphire bay, fading inland into a lush green forest.

Adbara had fallen to the Dhoth, Treseda remembered through her dream. As she remembered it, she saw a black line far in the distance, moving down the beach towards her. A Dhoth army, she knew, but was untroubled. She took a bronze sword from the scabbard at her waist, a sword that rested in her hand as if familiar to her, and went out with the surf lapping at her ankles to meet them.

Others might have marched with her, she thought, though she never learned for certain. But the Dhoth warriors fell before her, and she fought as if she were an entire army, all the defender Adbara would ever need. And as she sliced and struck, she knew Poncenet was safe, because no nation could ever recover from the blow she was giving the Dhoth, not ever . . .

θʆζʑ

The sword hung in an ornate case above her study door, Treseda discovered. It was her grandfather's sword, and had been mirrored in the dream down to the last detail, though she didn't take it down to test its heft.

Her study was strangely clean this morning—the furniture glossy with wax, the scrolls rolled and placed in their cupboards or spread smoothly on her desk, the inkwell filled and the quills new-trimmed. The mystery went unanswered until Jahannes came around midmorning, bearing the breakfast that she had forgotten. "The new boy's been cleaning up the house."

"Caiyo?" she asked, shoving aside a scroll that listed the provisions needed for a five-day journey taken by a group the size of Poncenent's population.

"Yes." He set a bowl of eggs before her and added, "You told me to have him doing something useful."

"So I did," she said between sips of black tea. "He's kept with his decision to stay, then?"

"He must have." Jahannes peered at the scroll on her desk and frowned. She hated to see him so troubled, but could think of nothing to say to comfort him.

"When do we leave?" he asked.

"As soon as we can." She spooned egg in her mouth. A single laying hen had survived, hiding in her garden during the Dhoth attack. It was a shame her worry turned the luxury bitter.

Someone knocked on the doorframe. Looking up, Treseda saw it was Caiyo, leading a man in messenger's robes. It took her another moment to realize that he was the same messenger who had spoken to her the night before. Whatever had happened since then didn't seem to have gone well for him.

"Sir." Treseda rose and pulled out a chair for him. The messenger sank down, half-helped by Caiyo. She shot a grateful look over his head at Jahannes, who was pouring another cup of tea.

"Thank you. I had planned to travel on to General Galadsten," the man said, almost inaudibly. "I couldn't get through . . . there is another Dhoth army, pushing south towards Galadsten's fort."

"Where did they come from?" Treseda sputtered.

"Does it matter?" Jahennes asked. To Treseda's surprise, she felt his hand on hers, and gave it a heartening squeeze.

"We will do what we can," she whispered.

"That's little enough," the messenger said. "I hear the king himself is reduced to praying to the Valadherat."

"The what?" Treseda and Jahannes said together.

"The gods of the Valadhen people. His wife's gods. I thought you'd know, your boy here's Valadhen. The dark skin shows it. They're religious people. May I . . ." Caiyo caught the messenger by the arm as he sagged, nearly falling to the floor.

Treseda and Jahennes rounded the desk to him, but he waved away their concern. "I'm just a bit shaken. I had a close call, nearly riding into a Dhoth camp."

"And now you're trapped here with the rest of us." Treseda turned away restlessly, and almost regretted it when Jahennes dropped her hand. "With Dhoth on both sides . . ."

"Poncenet will have to prepare for a siege," the messenger murmured.

"I'm not sure we can withstand one," she said.

He met her gaze squarely. "I'm not sure we have a choice."

⋐⋒⋑⋒⋑⋑

Treseda sent out riders, bearing the message to all of her scattered fiefs to gather in the walls of Poncenet. Her servants and tenants set to work fortifying those same walls—built for privacy, not defense. Heria, helped by Caiyo—the boy followed her like a shadow—prepared rooms and spare corners to receive the new arrivals.

The plans for siege were left to her.

Assuming the walls could hold—which she did, lacking the heart to do otherwise—the next thing Poncenet needed was food and supplies to last. With the fields and orchards burned, their only source of such was Treseda's garden, mostly ornamental, and whatever the inhabitants of the fiefdoms could bring with them. The king had offered generous recompense to any whose property or estates were harmed by the Dhoth, but that would have to wait until the war was over, or at least passed this place. And assuming they won it. In the meantime, it was up to Treseda to see that what they had would stretch and make do.

At least her dreams were pleasant.

She wouldn't have thought of them as such only a few days ago—too violent, with her dream-self engulfed in a bloody rage that the waking Treseda could barely recognize—but it felt good, very good, to harry the Dhoth from Adbara. From Calada. From Selita. From Anderum, from Poncenet. Even if she must awake every morning to know that they weren't really gone, but approaching from every side.

She gazed out the window and immediately wished she hadn't—it looked onto her burnt fields. Most of the charred grain stalks had crumbled now, and gray ash mixed with the sandy soil. She had heard that burned fields were rich when replanted. If they could be replanted.

"Your Grace." It was Jahannes, standing at the door. With a brilliant smile—brought by memories of another dream that, even if it did not involve driving Dhoth into hell, was strangely pleasant—she waved him in.

He did not smile back. "Your Grace . . . there's a problem."

Sergeant Banfelh, the messenger from Anderum, stood behind him, accompanied by Caiyo. The dark former slave boy had seemed to be everywhere lately, but he was a helpful presence and Treseda didn't mind.

"Which problem are you referring to?" she asked, unsure if she sounded weary or bitterly amused.

"The area cut off by the Dhoth armies is larger than we first realized," Banfelh said, "with many more inhabitants."

"And not a soldier among them," Jahennes added. Number of possible troops was normally something the sergeant should remark on; coming from her steward the observation was all the more unsettling.

"So we have that many more mouths to feed, and not a single hand more that can protect us." Treseda sighed and sank back in her chair. It was only one more complication, and not the largest one by far. "Is there anything more?"

"We're talking about *a great deal* more inhabitants," Banfelh said. "And there is the matter of feeding them." His gaze flickered to the window; all others followed it.

"Can the serfs bring their own food?"

"Do you think your fields were the only ones burned?"

"Everywhere," Jahennes murmured. "Everywhere we could reach. Every field, every orchard, every garden. Some have been reduced to gathering from the forest. We have our winter stores, but this late in autumn . . . we had depended on the harvest to see us through."

"Do you think I didn't know that?" Treseda snapped. She was immediately sorry. Her head felt overbalanced; she rubbed her throbbing skull. "More to feed, less food, no defense." Well, what else did she expect? Unable to stop herself, she spoke her thoughts aloud. "We didn't really think we could win this, did we?"

"Your Grace?" Jahennes green eyes widened.

"We can't." She bounced her fist on the table, looking out the window with a glare that seemed fit to burn the fields again. "There's no way. We're surrounded by two legions of Dhoth. We're holed up in a farming estate, not a fortress. And— begging the gods—look at what happened the last time we faced the Dhoth!" She was shaking, almost angry, beyond fear.

Jahennes and the messenger exchanged glances but said nothing. With a sinking heart, she realized they agreed with her.

"Go," she said. They went. Caiyo gave her a strange look before following them out. He was always underfoot, she thought, knowing she wasn't being fair. He was trying to help.

"You'd have been better off with Lord Shashensa," she said to him. He turned back for a moment, but said nothing.

Treseda looked at her desk. When she thought he was gone, she spoke again, just to hear the words aloud and prove they were real. "If only they hadn't burned the fields . . ."

CRICRSICAN

She went to bed on an empty stomach, her abdomen growling and sore from hunger pangs, the knowledge that if she ate others would soon be starving gnawing at her far more viciously, and her appetite lost. Sleeping hungry wasn't sleeping well, but she didn't care. She was tired, and as she fell asleep she knew she never wanted to wake up.

She opened her eyes at the sound of wind. Deep wind murmuring through the leaves of the forest, low wind moaning around the stone walls and pillars, and there—high, soft wind whispering to something that bowed at its passage. Treseda rose and looked out her window.

Golden in daylight, it bent silver-white in the shine of the moon. Seedheads heavy, stalks long, sprouting from earth so rich and black that it seemed she could see it even in the darkness: grain in her fields. She went to the window and peered farther out, there—down and across the road—she could see the tall trees of the orchard, red and heavy with fruit. A cloud passed the moon and her heart skipped; only when the shadow vanished and the fields remained could she breathe again. Her fields and orchards, her livelihood, the lifeblood of Poncenet, were returned.

For a moment, Treseda Nudoath could feel perfectly happy.

ଔଔଔଔ

Why?
Who had caused this? Why must one of her final nights be wasted on comforting delusion? Was it her own mind betraying her? Her own weakness? Or *who*?

Treseda's eyes burned as she walked the halls with blind steps. The dreams of killing Dhoth, of loving Jahennes, and now this . . . all her desires played out delightfully. Uselessly. She awoke to find nothing changed, but with her heart aching from knowing what the change might have been.

Who? There must be someone to blame. For dreams this magnificent, there must be someone responsible.

Treseda realized suddenly that her feet were leading her somewhere. And, reflecting, she found that it all made perfect sense.

He was always there, could see what she wanted, knew the things she saw in her dreams. Her grandfather's sword in her study. The way Jahennes clasped her hand. He had followed her gaze out the window . . . did he even hear her whisper, when she thought they had all left her?

She climbed the stairs to the loft above the stables, and raised her hand to the door to Caiyo's room.

It swung open at her touch. The inside was dimly lit; an oil lamp with chains for hanging rested beside a pallet on the floor. Caiyo sat there, legs crossed, staring into nothing. He looked up as she entered.

"You," she whispered. "You're causing the dreams."

"I am." His voice was clear, calm, a counter to her own fury. Treseda sucked in breath.

"Why?"

"I thought to thank you . . . for letting me in. For letting me stay."

"This is your thanks?" she spat. "Can't you see that it only hurts more—to have hope, and have it snatched away in the morning?"

"It hurts less than nightmares," he said.

"How can you know?" Her voice broke. She must relax. This fury wasn't good, it wouldn't help her, wouldn't help anyone . . . it was as useless as the dreams. Caiyo sat impassively. Something glinted at his neck—the slave tag. The one that marked him as the property of Lord Shashensa. It had not been taken off as she ordered.

"Get out," she said at last, thickly. "Go. Now. I don't want you to spend another night under this roof."

He rose and left, silent—didn't plead, didn't weep, didn't stop to gather anything. He had nothing to take.

The gates were closed. She knew she should go and order their opening herself, spare him the shame of directing his own exile. But she was tired, suddenly, and felt about to weep. And she was stung with shame, black and sharp as a Dhoth's whip.

Will he die out there? she wondered. And realized that she cared, cared far too much for his fate, the way she cared for all of Poncenet: she cared so deeply that she was worn out from it, as if she didn't care at all. So she could prophesy its doom, and send him out to his own, with no feeling inside her at all. Except for something akin to rage.

She succumbed to her anger and began weeping.

಄ౠ಄ಞ

Treseda sent out scouts the next day. She didn't know why she bothered, knowing how a siege from the Dhoth would end, but perhaps others would want to watch their death approaching, and perhaps spying on the Dhoth let them feel useful. They reported the north advancing steadily—they were past Galadsten's fort, no knowing what had happened there—and the south rested, waiting.

She spent the night with Jahennes.

If he was surprised to find her at his door in her nightshift, he didn't show it. He stepped aside to let her in with a faint smile. They didn't speak much, but there was a sense of familiarity between them, as if they had come together before. She remembered the dreams—but pushed the memory aside.

Afterward, she paced across his room. He sat in the bed, watching her, saying nothing. She studied the furnishings, the lamps, the small clay sculptures and ink bowls and long quill pens, learning him by his possessions. Thinking of him, instead of everything else.

She stopped at his desk, covered by the sprawl of an unrolled map. There, sketched in green in the southwest corner, a cluster of domed tents: the Dhoth. A red army was marked in the north, with arrows showing the lines of advance. Closer, around the black square of Poncenent estate, fields were outlined in charcoal gray—the burned ones.

Treseda pulled another scroll over the map. It was covered in cramped cursive script, composing a hymn cycle to—

"The Valadherat?" she asked.

Jahennes chuckled, but he sounded embarrassed when he said, "I've been praying . . . to whoever might hear. Sergeant Banfelh mentioned the queen's gods, and I was curious."

She wondered if he remembered what the messenger had said of Caiyo's origins, but didn't ask. Instead she turned back to the scroll. It was a translation, but a very literal one, stilted and hard to understand in places. She whispered the words aloud, reading titles of hymns. "For the Bringing of Rain . . . Defense Against Plague . . . For Fruitful Sleep." Treseda laughed humorlessly; she could use some of that.

"Read it," Jahennes said. "I haven't looked at that one before."

She did, quickly and with an air of self-consciousness. Struggling with the awkward translation, she stumbled over several words and came to a halt when she found the name of the god petitioned.

"What is it?" he asked.

"Shashensa."

"That *is* a tongue-twister, but—"

"Doesn't it sound familiar?"

"No. What is it?"

"'Property of Lord Shashensa,'" she quoted from memory. "I declined to return it. Remember?"

"Oh." He chuckled. "I suppose the Valadhen are one of those peoples that name their children after gods."

"Yes. I suppose so." They were very religious, Banfelh had said. She looked over the scrolls. "You found these in the library?"

"I did. Remember your father's old steward, Sihenna? He had an interest in foreign religions. I think these were his."

She scanned the scroll, not admitting what she was looking for, but knowing when she didn't find it. "Are there more of these?"

"Probably. I'll look." He frowned and rubbed the back of his neck. In a low voice, he said, "Treseda. Why did you send him away?"

"I . . ."

Because he caused the dreams.

Property of Lord Shashensa.

"I don't want to talk about it," she said. "I'm sorry."

"No . . . it's all right." He shrugged. "Would you like to stay here tonight?"

"No. No, thank you."

He got to his feet. "Then let me see you out."

Too late she remembered the windows of her room, the fields. She turned her back on them, but could not close her eyes, unable to bear the images there. Ignoring the moonlight outside, she stared into the shadows of her room until her eyes fell shut.

She stood in her char-blackened fields, her grandfather's sword in hand. And there, at the edge of the road, in bronze armor and with a steel spear, was the Dhoth minor general, the raider, the murderer, the one who had ordered her fields burned.

She charged, flew to him with sword thrust before her, cut into his face and limbs until he fell at her feet, shapeless and dead. But when he was gone, there were others, more Dhoth coming, if too late to defend him, to avenge him. She cut them down. They would not win—this was *her* land, and she would defend it, and she would be victorious!

Her fields would never grow again, not even in dreams. But she would water them with blood, turn their earth with churning feet and the thrashing of dying bodies, and she would have her own revenge.

Treseda smiled in her dream, and awoke with her teeth bared in a feral grin.

ↃↃↃↃↃↃↃↃↃↃ

O ver the next days, she found herself frequently napping. She could get no rest at night and her days were exhausting. It was from one of those naps, which she had dropped into over garrison reports in her study, that Sergeant Banfelh awoke her.

"The Dhoth are retreating," he said.

She raised her head, blinking. "What?"

"The scouts you sent out yesterday have returned. Here, speak to them yourself." He stood aside, revealing two young men holding their caps respectfully in their hands, and looking at her with eyes buried deep in shadows.

"Good afternoon, Your Grace." One bobbed his head. "When we came to them, the Dhoth were breaking camp, Your Grace. We watched them go—this was the north army, you understand, and should be heading south. But they went north, Your Grace."

She picked up a pen and twisted its feathery top. "When was this?"

"When we came on them yesterday afternoon they were packing, Your Grace. They pulled down the tents this morning and turned north."

"You watched them all night?"

"Yes."

"How did they sleep?"

He swallowed, paling. "Not well, Your Grace."

"They had nightmares," his companion whispered. "Screaming ones, some of them."

"Some stayed up all night. There was a light in the general's tent—we could see him pacing."

Treseda sat back, smiling thinly. "So their sleep is troubled. Good. Mine is, too."

ଓଓଃ୫ଓ

She sent more scouts to the army in the south. They found the Dhoth sleeping in fitful snatches during the day. They had nightmares, too.

In her dreams that night, she saw Jahennes in the fields. And others—Sergeant Banfelh, Heria the cook, the two young scouts who followed the north army. All carried weapons: swords, pikes, fanciful blades with curving edges and hilts studded with gems, ornate but deadly. All of them were deadly.

They fought in a twisting landscape, sometimes the fields of Poncenet, sometimes the shores of Adbara, sometimes forests or foothills or the streets of a city she somehow knew was Anderum. In the eaves of the trees, on the crest of a hill, or in the shadows of alleys she sometimes saw the dark face of a young man watching them. She was unable to reach him in the fighting, and never knew for certain who he was.

Like her, Jahennes had little rest at night, and often slept fitfully during his spare daylight hours. She came to speak with him once, but he was too tired for a mere social visit. She asked, but he had not had the chance to read more of the Valadhen scrolls.

She remembered the prayer for *fruitful sleep*, and wondered if there was a hymn to be said for the restful kind.

ଓଓଃ୫ଓ

The Dhoth retreat continued. She sent out more scouts, and they were gone longer each time, having to follow the armies farther and farther away.

Once she sent them out and they were gone for ten days. They returned at dusk, dusty and exhausted, not bothering to wash, rest, or take refreshment before reporting to her.

"They're gone, Your Grace. We were following the southern army, and went along their route for days, but saw nothing. We passed around other estates and asked there. They saw the Dhoth moving south through the forest, avoiding roads, as if they were hiding from something. They said they moved quickly."

She called Sergeant Banfelh to her room, and had him relay her message to the serfs sheltering in Poncenet's walls. They could go home.

She would have told them herself, but her eyelids were already dropping.

That night Treseda slept peacefully, and the only dream she remembered on awakening was one about the horses she used to ride with her grandmother in Adbara.

She went to her study and took down her grandfather's sword. The size of the hilt was almost right, but the wire grip stung her smooth palm and slipped awkwardly in her hand as she swung it. So it was only a dream, after all.

Someone knocked as she returned the sword to its place above the door. She opened it and found Jahennes standing there, a scroll unrolled in his hands. Treseda recognized the cursive of the Valadhen hymns.

"Is there one named Caiyo?" she asked.

"Prince of Sleep. Lord Shashensa's servant. At first I thought it might have been a poor joke, naming the lord after the god, and he naming his slave boy after . . . but no. Not with the dreams."

"No." She bowed her head. "I sent him away because . . . I dreamed of the fields. Growing."

"Oh." She felt his hand gently close over hers. "They will one day, you know."

"Yes. Winter will be hard."

"It will. But we'll make it."

They would, she told herself and believed it. In the spring, she would plant the fields again.

"Jahennes," she said, "Is there a hymn to Caiyo?"

"There are many of them on this scroll. All 'for the good dreams'. Would you like to read them?"

"Only asking for good dreams? Are there any in thanksgiving?"

He smiled slowly. "We can make one."

"Yes." She returned his smile.

Thank you, Caiyo. And thanks to the one who sent you— Lord Shashensa.

THREE ON A MATCH

by *Michael H. Payne*

Joining a new study group at school is always a challenge: meeting your fellow students, adjusting to the group dynamic, avoiding the death spells . . .

Michael Payne says that nothing much has changed from last year—he's still living in southern California, still clerking at the library, still broadcasting at the UCI radio station, still singing at church, still writing reviews for sfwa.org and other websites, and still doing his online comics. This year, however, he can direct folks to hyniof.livejournal.com, the official "Hey, Your Nose is on Fire" Industries site where all this stuff comes together.

In front of the fireplace, the big wolf growled, and Cluny couldn't keep her tail from frizzing, her claws digging into the arm of Crocker's chair. Shtasith, stretching black and gold and sinuous across Crocker's shoulders above her, drew back his neck and hissed, every one of his tiny pointed teeth showing, but as far as Cluny could tell, Crocker just swallowed, his gaze fixed on a point about a foot to the left of Master Gollantz's desk.

"None of that, now, Raine," the magister said, and Cluny felt very glad he was standing between her and the wolf. "This is to be a private meeting, so on your way."

Raine got to her paws slowly, her voice gruffer than usual. "Keeping secrets from your familiar, master?" She made a show of sniffing the air. "A frightened human, a disgruntled firedrake, and a self-possessed squirrel hardly seem matters to jeopardize a partnership now entering its fourteenth decade."

Master Gollantz pointed to the office door. "Out, beast."

"Of course, master." Ears folded, the wolf turned and leaped through the wall with a pop of sparkling dust.

Cluny stretched her whiskers into the magical residue. A nice little teleportation spell. And if Raine could do it, maybe Crocker could learn.

"Familiars!" Master Gollantz stumped back to his red velvet and mahogany chair. "But then . . ." He gestured with several fingers, and the room, warm and bright, a beautiful late winter midday showing through the windows above the cases holding the magister's extraordinary collection of magical tomes, grimoires and artifacts, went suddenly dim and shadowy, a fog bank springing up all around them. "I certainly don't need to tell you about difficulties of *that* sort, do I, novice?"

Cluny blinked at him, her ears perking. Had he just called her 'novice'? But that would mean—

"Ah." A faint smile creased the magister's cheeks. "I see you know that word." Every trace of the smile vanished. "Might I suggest you next investigate the meaning of 'inconspicuous'?"

Her ears wilted. "Sir, I—"

"You are an *animal*, Cluny, admitted to Huxley as a potential familiar! That you instead display a wizard's grasp of thaumaturgy is absolutely unprecedented, and I've been researching the subject these nine weeks since you manifested your power in that unfortunate incident with the Queen of the Ifriti!" Sparks shot from the edges of Master Gollantz's eyes, Cluny's fur crackling with static. "Add to that the way you and Crocker mesh so perfectly that one might be tempted to call him your familiar, and you . . . he . . . it . . . you're twisting the union that lies at the very core of practical magic!"

Crocker stirred. "Sorry to be a disappointment, sir."

Gollantz waved a hand. "What you *are* can be hidden! What you've *done* cannot! Upsetting all of Powell House and taking this firedrake as familiar? How could you think—??"

"With respect, sir?" And Cluny meant it, too: she thanked the Squirrel Mother every day that it hadn't been someone like Master Watts who had found out about her and Crocker. "We've both apologized to Novice Steiverson for causing her binding to fail, but if I hadn't acted the way I did, Shtasith would've gotten loose! And I didn't know it would make him my familiar: how many wizards even *have* more than one?"

Master Gollantz settled back and pressed his fingertips together. "The last we had here at Huxley was 136 years ago, a young woman with a raven who bound a glass cat her senior year."

Cluny's whiskers bristled. "You mean—Esmeralda Stone? She was a Huxley student?"

"It's not something we advertise." Master Gollantz's gaze hardened. "In fact, after the Sorcerous Council finally defeated Ms. Stone and her army of the undead, they suspended Huxley's entire staff for allowing her to graduate. Master Watts and I both came in as junior faculty at that time."

He pointed to his "in" box, and a scroll popped into the foggy air. "Which is why, I'm certain, Master Watts this morning presented me with a petition co-signed by 15 other senior faculty members demanding that Crocker here be removed from regular classes and placed under the strictest possible independent training regimen." The scroll unrolled and wafted like an autumn leaf onto his blotter pad. "Any thoughts?"

Cluny looked up at Crocker, saw him looking down at her, his face as plain and pale as uncooked bread dough, his power around her more comfortable than the afghan her mother had knitted her when she'd first been accepted to Huxley. Of course, Shtasith looked back as well, his reptilian eyes slitted, his power hot inside her and wanting to get hotter, a pressure she'd kept a tight clamp on the whole week the firedrake had been hers.

She swallowed and faced the magister. "That sort of program might actually be best for us, sir. I—"

"What??" Crocker's voice cracked, the sour stink of his fear sharp in Cluny's nostrils. "But . . . I'm barely making it *now*! I mean, writing out what Cluny tells me so our homework won't trip the cheating wards is easy, or flowing with Cluny's doppelganger spell so it looks like I'm doing the magic in class instead of her, but if anyone starts paying closer attention—!"

"Silence, you simpering simian!" Shtasith hissed, his tail lashing, its black barbs tangling in Crocker's dark curls. "My master's wasted more than enough time coddling you and catering to your fears! You're nothing but dead weight, the basest sort of leech upon her power!"

Cluny cleared her throat. "Guys? Could we maybe not take up the magister's—?"

"Stupid lizard!" Crocker's face flushed, and he flicked a finger into Shtasith's snout. "Why don't you go back to—??"

"Insolence!" The firedrake roared and sprang into the air, his talons spread.

"Enough!" Cluny sent a jolt of power along the tether that bound her to Shtasith, but she also zapped Crocker a little— just to be fair. They both gasped, and she shook a claw at them. "D'you want me to disown you both? Is *that* it??"

Crocker's eyes went wide, Shtasith's wings missing a beat, but Cluny knew it was an idle threat. Like Master Gollantz had said, she and Crocker just meshed, and the flow of power had gotten even better since Shtasith's arrival. This past week, any time she'd thought about trying to separate herself from one or the other, panic stabbed her as hard as the time she'd been playing with some friends in an old dead oak tree, lost her grip on a moldy branch, and fallen thirty feet into the creek.

She whirled on the magister, embarrassment making her fur feel too tight. "I don't know what kind of help we need, sir, but I know we need something! And *quick*!"

Master Gollantz gave a crisp nod. "Correct answer, novice." The fog vanished, Cluny wincing at the sudden flood of daylight, and another scroll popped from the box to drop into Crocker's lap. "Your new class schedule. I'll continue as your advisor, of course, so should Master Watts or Mistress Shurtri become a nuisance, kindly direct them to me." He made a dismissive motion. "Now, I believe you have ten minutes to get across campus to meet your study group."

Cluny allowed herself one blink, then jumped from the arm of the chair and cast a quick shrink spell on the scroll before tucking it under her forearm and scurrying up the lapel of Crocker's robe to his right breast pocket: she'd reinforced the stitching and enlarged it for easy access since Shtasith needed both Crocker's shoulders to ride on. "Yes, sir, and thank you!"

Crocker stood—he'd *definitely* gotten better at recognizing cues this quarter—and bowed to Master Gollantz, Cluny doing the same over the edge of the pocket. Shtasith settled grouchy as a miniature thunderhead into his usual place, and Cluny began examining the scroll while Crocker turned, carried them through the outer office, down the steps of the admin building, and out into Eldritch Park, the patch of wild woods at the center of campus. She heard Crocker take a breath then, but before he could speak, Shtasith snorted. "If you're about to whine, simian, may I remind you how flammable human hair is?"

"Listen, you—" Crocker started.

But Cluny held the scroll up, let it burst to its proper size in front of him. "Look, Crocker. I think this'll work."

He took the scroll, and she went on: "We meet every day at noon and dusk with our study group and an advisor for what they call 'assignments and assistance,' but the rest of the time, we're pretty much on our own. We can request lab space, use all the libraries, make appointments with any faculty members whether they're teaching this term or not . . ." A wonderful little shiver scuttled up Cluny's tail. "It'll be just like our experiments back in the dorm room trying to find spells you can do, only now, since I'm sure we'll be under observation, we won't have to worry so much about accidents!"

She heard a whistling sort of gasp above her and looked up to see Shtasith staring down. "The magister mentioned summoning the Ifriti Ranee. I'd heard the story, but . . . was it truly *you*?"

Cluny blinked. "You . . . heard about that?"

Steam puffed from his nostrils. "It was the talk of the Firelands! Our Lady would howl with laughter when she spoke of the hapless mortal children she'd frightened nearly to death after they flooded a section of her lava pits with some sort of enchanted water!" He stretched his long neck toward her and whispered loudly, "The simian's doing, I assume, master?"

Crocker's mouth went sideways. "I do have a name, y'know, Teakettle."

Shtasith's acorn of a head snapped back, his needle-sharp teeth bared less than an inch from Crocker's right eye. "When you have demonstrated that you are more than a slightly mobile and alarmingly malodorous perch, you will have a name! And in the meantime, you will refer to me as the Immolator!"

"Uhh, Shtasith?" Cluny waited till the firedrake swung around to meet her gaze. "As long as we're talking about names, I've told you to call me 'Cluny.'"

His pointed little ears went limp. "I . . . I cannot!"

She let a whiff of power touch her words. "But you will."

"I . . ." When he swallowed, Cluny could see the lump travel all the way down that neck. "I will try . . ."

"Good." She gave them both her sunniest smile. "See? Now we *all* have things we can work on!"

"Oh, really?" Crocker grinned back. "What's *your* assignment, O mighty wizard?"

She crooked a thumb-claw over her shoulder. "I've got to look up the word 'inconspicuous,' remember?"

He laughed, and Cluny let herself relax, breathed in the pre-springtime air, tangy with the first stirrings of sap and flowers. And who knew? Maybe this actually *would* work . . .

They came out into sunlight not long after, five or six avian familiars ranging in size from a pigeon to a pelican squawking and laughing and tossing a ball back and forth in the blue sky over south campus, the oldest part of Huxley, the buildings squatting like ivy-covered rock formations among the trees covering the hillside ahead.

Crocker stopped to consult the scroll. "'Podkamennaya Hall, 2nd floor' is all it says."

Cluny shaded her eyes with a paw. "Podkamennaya is Huxley's original library, so we're looking for something that's more than a thousand years old." She spread her whiskers into the breeze, let the quiet power of the place wash over her, and crooked a claw at a grassy lump the path wound past before disappearing around a row of lichen-covered two-story brick piles that she guessed were classrooms. "I think that's it."

"What? Where?"

A hiss from Shtasith. "Must you question *everything*?"

"I just wanted to know—!"

"Trust!" Shtasith had a hard note in his voice that Cluny had never heard before. "If you do not have utter faith in our . . . our Cluny, you do not deserve to be her creature!"

Crocker's blush this time was so warm, Cluny could feel it. "You think I don't—??"

"Guys?" She dug her claws into his robe and hauled herself up so she could look easily from one to the other. "We're not doing this right now. I'd prefer we not do it *ever*, but since I know that's asking way too much, let's just put every bit of discussion on hold till we're alone again." Far across the park, Huxley's carillon began chiming sext. "Right now, it's noon. We need to be inside that library; you, Crocker, need to be the eager young wizardry student; and you and me, Shtasith, we need to be the ever-so-helpful familiars. Got it?"

Shtasith gave a snort without meeting her gaze, and Crocker straightened up, blinked, focused past her. "You think they'd have a door or something if they wanted people to get in."

Cluny slid back into Crocker's pocket and felt the flow of power a bit more, the way it swirled around a little outcrop of rock beside the grassy lump ahead of them the way river water swirled around a submerged log. "There. I'll bet you can use that airball spell we worked out to pop the illusion over it."

Crocker nodded and walked along the path to the outcrop. She could already smell his sweat, so she muttered, "Like a soap bubble, remember?"

He nodded again, made a circle with his left thumb and forefinger, raised it, and blew through it. Cluny felt her fur rustle as he drew upon their shared power, and she breathed a little prayer to the gods of aeroturgy: practicing this spell had left the west wall of their dorm room looking like the surface of the moon, though it had given her the chance to develop this neat little scouring and spackling spell . . .

The bubble was invisible, of course, but she could tell it had hit the outcrop when the stone surface peeled away like a banana skin to reveal a round door in the side of the hill. Crocker pushed through to a short corridor beyond, dust dancing in sunlight from windows that hadn't shown outside. The door clicked closed behind them, but other than that, all Cluny could hear was Crocker's shoes shuffling over the carpet, the air dry and musty and just exactly right for a library.

At the end of the corridor lay a room criss-crossed with bookshelves, a mass of granite jutting up in the center with the word "Information" carved into it. A dark-haired girl with a flannel shirt over her robes sat cross-legged on top of the stone reading a magazine printed with runes; she glanced up when Crocker stepped in, and Cluny had to poke him before he blurted out, "My group! I mean, I'm, uhh, starting with an independent study thing today, and, uhh . . ." It took him three tries to unroll the scroll. "Second floor?" he got out at last.

The girl looked at him some more, her search spells very sharp and defined; Cluny admired their designs while carefully blocking each one. She nodded, then, hopped down from the stone, and stuck out a hand. "Tzu Yin," she said. "I've been waiting for you. Stairs are over here."

Crocker blinked, shook the hand, and managed to say his name before she turned for the stacks. "Eubie bet a silver you wouldn't even get here," Tzu Yin was going on, Crocker hurrying to catch up. "But everything I've heard about you says you break things, not that you get lost." She shrugged. "He'll try to weasel out of paying since you're late, but Tangle, his familiar, is a stoat, so I guess it's natural." She glanced back at him. "Having both a squirrel and a firedrake isn't natural at all, so I don't know what to make of you yet." Cluny deflected a couple more search spells, and Tzu Yin grinned. "Not knowing's a new thing for me. I kinda like it."

Cluny could feel Crocker's heartbeat pick up. "Well," he said, "when you *do* figure me out, make sure to let me know."

They came to a flight of stairs, and Tzu Yin led the way up to a high-ceilinged room, tables and bookshelves scattered at what seemed to be random intervals over such an expanse that Cluny could just make out the far walls, lost in shadows cast by light trickling in from the narrow, dirty windows. Under the nearest of these windows, three tables sat in a loose triangle, five more students in their robes shuffling books and papers, the power washing around them making Cluny's whiskers hum.

A boy who looked even younger than Crocker scowled at them. "He's late, so the bet's off!"

Tzu Yin glanced back at Crocker and waggled her eyebrows. "That's OK, Eubie," she called, moving toward the tables. "As long as he's here, we can get started."

"Oh?" The blond girl waved her hand, and Cluny saw she was Jeanette Ahern, the star of Huxley's scrying team, and that the boy next to her was Ric Ibarrez, captain of both the academic decathlon team and the track team. Jeanette went on: "You planning on giving Mistress Ippolitov's lecture, Tzusy?"

The other girl at the table snickered, her long black fingernails tapping musical notes onto a piece of lined paper. "If we're voting, I'd rather hear Tzu Yin talk about *anything* instead of Polly going on about the proper way to comb one's hair before astrally projecting." She turned a grin at Crocker. "Or maybe Newby here can tell us about squirrel maintenance."

Cluny felt her ears go back and heard a little puff of breath from Tzu Yin. "Be nice, Meeshele."

A snap of fingers made Cluny look at Ric. "I remember now! Terrence Crocker! You're the frosh who's so strong, you've gathered two familiars, but so weak, you can't function unless they're with you even when you're in class!" He stroked a thumbnail through the little patch of beard between his chin and lower lip. "I'd be interested in hearing what *that's* like."

They were all looking at him now, and Cluny felt Crocker's heartbeat kick up another notch. "It's a learning experience every day," he said.

His voice didn't waver, but Cluny could smell his sweat, so she tugged his lapel and said quietly, "Maybe we could sit down, Crocker? Get settled and like that?"

Jeanette's eyebrow arched. "Your familiar uses your name?"

"She doesn't want to." Crocker grabbed at the nearest chair. "But I insist." He sat, and Cluny suddenly noticed something odd. The four students who'd already spoken—and Tzu Yin, too, now that she'd taken a seat—were bunched up together at one table. The second, right under the slit of a window, had a single empty chair at it while the only occupant of the third table—other than Crocker now—was a silent, nondescript boy, his hair very nearly the same sallow shade as his face and eyes.

A ghost! Cluny thought for an instant, but then those eyes moved and focused on her, and she felt his power flow past a little jagged but otherwise normal for a regular human wizard. She nodded to him, but he didn't seem to notice, his gaze already sliding upward to fix on Crocker.

The tiniest pin prick of pain between her ears shocked her into looking up as well. Crocker was smiling at Tzu Yin rather than the pale boy, but Shtasith was glaring straight at him. The firedrake drew back his head and hissed, and Eubie at the other table gave a snickering laugh. "Same thing ev'ryone says, buddy, first time they see Ghouly."

Out of the corner of her eye, Cluny saw the pale boy raise a finger, and Eubie's laughter choked off. "It's Goulet," the boy said, and his voice, flat and drab as a piece of cardboard, made Cluny's tail frizz up behind her. She hadn't learned to read auras yet, but something about this kid—

Crocker shifted, seemed to notice the boy for the first time, and stuck a hand out. "Hi, Goulet. I'm Crocker."

"So I heard," the boy said, lowering his finger. "And I have to say I'm not at all pleased to meet you."

A snort from Jeanette. "Gods and goddesses, Ghoul! Are you ever happy about *anything*??"

The boy sighed. "I was going to be *very* happy about today. But, well . . ." Goulet reached into a backpack beside his chair, and set a lop-sided glass globe onto the table in front of him. "Killing the five of you won't be nearly as satisfying with the death of an innocent attached."

For half a heartbeat, Cluny could only stare. Then Goulet poked the glass thing, and fire pulsed across her every nerve ending, the squeak that tore from her throat covered by the strangled gasps of the students at the other table.

The pain vanished immediately, though, burned to ashes in the fire she felt from Shtasith and smothered under Crocker's warm softness. She managed to take a breath just as Crocker

254   *Michael H. Payne*

cried out, "What was that??" and Shtasith hissed, "Foul magics, master! Shall I incinerate this beast??"

Goulet raised his finger again. "If your creature moves, Crocker, I'll set this thing to maximum and kill every living being on this entire campus." A smug smile pulled his lips. "I'd tell the rest of you jerkwads not to do anything, either, but I've never seen you show any intestinal fortitude before. So I'm not going to worry about it now."

Cluny chanced a glance at the others and thought for an instant they'd been frozen. But they were twitching slightly— Eubie's eyelids, a tendon in Meeshele's neck—and while Cluny could feel energy all around as spiky as a paw full of nettles, she couldn't begin to guess what Goulet had done.

She looked back at the boy, Crocker above her saying: "OK, let's just . . . take it easy, OK? No one wants to kill *anyone*!"

Goulet gave a strangled laugh and rubbed the silky hair along his chin. "I'm going to disagree with that. I'm also going to be momentarily intrigued as to why my mana flayer seems to have no effect on you."

The very thing Cluny had been wondering. Was it the strange way she and Crocker and Shtasith were linked? Or maybe this mana flayer thing was one of those spells mitigated by the presence of familiars: since regular students weren't allowed to have theirs in class, she was the only one here with that support right now. So how could she take advantage of—?

"Oh, well." Goulet sighed again and brought both his hands up. "I've been planning my revenge for far too long to let your resistance threaten it. So I'm afraid I'll have to—"

Crocker's burst of laughter caught Cluny by surprise. "Me? A threat? No, it's just that I'm not really a wizard: *that's* why whatever you're doing doesn't bother me."

The boy's pale forehead wrinkled. "Not really a—?"

"I'll show you!" Crocker spread his arms. "If I send my familiars away, you can see I've got less magic than a baby!"

"Send them away?" Goulet's frown deepened. "So they can call for help? How stupid do you think—?"

"OK, not *away*!" Crocker's voice kept getting more and more frantic, but Cluny could feel his heart beat slow and steady through his robes, not a whiff of panic in his scent. "Just across the room or something! Then you'll see I'm not a threat to anyone, and maybe . . . I mean, I just . . . I don't wanna die without knowing why! Please? Can't you . . . can't you tell me what they did to you?" He gestured to the others.

Goulet slowly moved a hand to start stroking the fuzz on his chin again, and Cluny felt a spark of hope. If Crocker could hold Goulet's attention, she and Shtasith could—

Do what? Well, *something*, certainly!

"Fair enough," Goulet said then. "Send your familiars to sit on those rafters." He pointed, and Cluny stretched, peered past Crocker, saw a place above the stairwell where several beams jutted from the wall. "If they move from there, I'll trigger the flayer and kill us all—no matter *how* little magic you have. But yes, you do deserve to know the reasons."

Crocker nodded, and Cluny felt his hand behind her, lifting her to his shoulder beside Shtasith, the firedrake's front claws digging into the rumpled cloth of his robes. "You heard the man, Cluny," Crocker said. "You and Shtasith. Up there. OK?"

"OK," she managed to squeak, wondering for the first time if Shtasith *could* carry her. The firedrake was looking a little doubtful, too, but he sprang into the air, the wind from his wings washing her fur. She reached up, thinking to climb his hind legs onto his back, but he was suddenly swooping over her, his front claws sliding around and scooping her off of Crocker. She couldn't stop another squeak, the tables falling away, the walls spinning closer, then he was dropping her; she grabbed the rough wood of the beam and blinked at Crocker and Goulet below and a good twenty yards across the room, Shtasith curling into the space behind her.

She almost panicked at the emptiness inside where Crocker's warmth usually glowed, but she swallowed it down, saw Crocker spread his hands. "Check me out however you want to."

Goulet focused on Crocker, and Cluny clenched her paws. Even if she and Shtasith *could* sneak out somehow to bring help, the students already here would still be trapped. No, she had to get the others out first while Crocker kept Goulet—

Misdirected! Her doppelganger spell! The one she used in class to transfer her spell-casting movements to Crocker!

She'd need to modify the parameters, and—Furiously, she started scratching the formulae into the top of the rafter. Include an invisibility component, some sound dampening and power shielding, a bit of blood magic to attract and hold the flayer's effects and any search spells Goulet might send out—

Gritting her teeth, she jabbed a claw into the base of her tail. What little she knew about blood magic said she wouldn't need much; she squeezed two drops onto the beam, then spun on Shtasith. "I need you to cut yourself!" she whispered.

"What?" His eyes whirled with specks of red and black. "How? And why? I—"

"Shtasith!"

Too loud! She cringed, glanced over her shoulder, saw that Goulet still had his attention fixed on Crocker: "A nothing like you," the pale boy was saying, "praised over a genius like me!"

Looking back at the firedrake, she did her best to keep her voice quiet. "I know you can bleed 'cause I stabbed you with that lance when I first captured you! Now do it!"

Eyes still spinning, he crooked his right foreclaw and scratched the top of his left forepaw. Cluny dabbed at the welling blood, tapped two drops onto the wood beside her own, and recited the cobbled-together spell.

Dizziness splashed over her like sudden rain, and Shtasith gave a little gasp. She grabbed his neck to steady herself and whispered, "OK! Pick me up and fly us down there!" She gestured toward the tables where Goulet was now waving his arms, Crocker nodding, then shaking his head, then nodding again.

"But—"

"No time!" She thrust her muzzle into the firedrake's ear. "You get us under that table right now!"

He tried to pull away, and she was just about to send a blast along their connection when he hissed, "You must release me, Cluny, or I'll have no chance to get either of us aloft!"

She wrenched her paws away, and he was suddenly slithering sideways, his wings billowing, his head sliding around and between her legs, swooping her up again; Cluny found herself clinging to his back as he shot swift as an arrow through the air to the library floor, hard and black with layers of filth so old, she couldn't tell where the dirt stopped and the wood began. Leaping off the firedrake, she cast a quick glance back at the rafter and felt like cheering when she saw herself still sitting there, a double of Shtasith peering over her shoulder.

The doppelganger part was working! Now to see if . . .

Cluny motioned Shtasith to follow her and scampered over to Tzu Yin's sandals. A murmured apology, and she slashed the top of the girl's toe, drew just enough blood to splash two drops onto the floor, and with a breath to center herself, whispered the words to activate the spell again.

She was ready for the dizziness this time, but the spell apparently had a larger effect on humans: Tzu Yin jerked sideways, fell right out of the chair—and left her image behind, frozen in place by the flayer. The real Tzu Yin stared up from the floor at the doppelganger, her eyes going wide, and Cluny ran forward, a foreclaw pressed to her snout: the sound-dampening component of this piecemeal spell was *way* too fragile to muffle anything as loud as a gasp.

Tzu Yin's stare shifted to Cluny, and the girl didn't cry out; Cluny scrambled up the arm of her flannel shirt, whispered,

"He can't see you! Get help! Hurry!" and sprang away for Eubie's blue canvas and rubber lace-up shoes, the dizziness not quite abating as it had before.

Eubie's socks were filthy but so loose, Cluny didn't have to reach very far up his leg to find bare skin; she slashed him and was setting the blood drops onto the floor when movement made her look up, Tzu Yin getting to her feet and starting unsteadily for the stairwell. Cluny sent out another quick prayer to the gods of invocation and muttered the spell for the third time.

The world spun crazily in front of her, and something smacked her hard in the side of the head. Blinking, she realized it was the floor, though her inner ear wanted her to think she was still upright . . . as if the floor was a gigantic wall she was somehow stuck to. Eubie lay upside down in front of her, his chair, occupied now by his doppelganger, jutting out into the empty space on Cluny's left, but the Eubie on the floor was already stirring, sitting up—except it still wasn't *up*! Frozen with vertigo, Cluny couldn't speak, couldn't even find her paw to put it to her lips to tell Eubie—

But Shtasith suddenly hung from the front of his robe, the firedrake's mouth moving, one front claw gesturing to the stairwell. Eubie stared, his chest pumping, but he nodded; Shtasith let go, and Eubie started crawling for the stairs.

Along the *floor*, Cluny realized, her jangled brain finally telling her that she was indeed lying down. She managed to get her paws onto the ancient wood, Shtasith quickly fluttering to her side, helping her stand, his power an electrical tingle over every inch of her skin. "Three more, my Cluny!" he whispered.

Casting the spell on Jeanette spun Cluny around like a kick to the head; doing Ric slammed her as hard as a baseball bat; and after Meeshele, she lay sprawled on the floor under the table for what felt like minutes, sure that she'd broken all her ribs. The pain just kept pounding, power tearing out of her, pouring forth in torrents to keep the spells in place. Huddled there feeling like glass about to shatter, she could scarcely hear

Shtasith's whispered instructions under Goulet's continuing oration, but the shuffle of robes moving away all three times told her it had worked. Everyone was out and safe.

Except for her and Shtasith and Crocker, of course . . .

Swallowing a groan, she forced her paws to brace her up, blinked and blinked and blinked until she could see her claws digging into the blackened hardwood. No way she could cast that spell again, so how—?

Gentle claws around her, balancing her. "Oh, my Cluny," Shtasith whispered, the raging fire she usually felt from him barely a flicker now. "We must get you away from here!"

"Not without—!" Her stomach fluttered, and she clenched her lips shut. If only she knew what a mana flayer did! Mana was the fundamental force underlying all magic, of course, but how could you possibly *flay* it??

Frustrated, she let her claws gouge curls of accumulated filth from the floor, her mind racing through every bit of theory she'd learned this year—

And it was like a series of dominoes in her head suddenly went flipping over, a pattern of definitions and connections and forces that made her gasp and grab Shtasith's neck. "Fly me up there! Right into Crocker's lap! Now!"

She heard his intake of breath, saw fear swirling in his eyes, but—"Yes, Cluny," was all he said, his grip tightening, her balance going haywire again as the floor dropped away.

"They'll rue the day!" Goulet's shrieks rang in her ears, and as they came out from under the table, she saw the boy had one foot up on the back of his tipped-over chair, his fists waving in the air. "My name will be whispered with fear and—!"

Shtasith dropped with her into Crocker's lap, Crocker hitching back in his chair and saying, "Whoa!"—she'd forgotten he couldn't see her. Now that she was touching him, though, she severed the power to her spells, all five doppelgangers disappearing, and pushed herself to stand on Crocker's left knee.

"I have had," she panted, Goulet staring at her with his mouth hanging open, "*more* than enough . . . of you!"

"Cluny!" Crocker cried behind her. "What're you—!"

"Damn you, Crocker!" Goulet screamed, and he lunged for the table, for the crooked glass globe he'd left sitting there, his finger jabbing the same indentation as before. Cluny braced herself, prayed to each and every thaumaturgical deity that she'd guessed right, and with the last vestiges of power pulled from herself and her two familiars, she cast her scouring and spackling spell across the floor of the entire library.

The effort buckled her knees, collapsed her across Crocker's legs, and the lump of glass went black, a darkness more absolute than any cloud-choked midnight. Cluny's ears popped, and the darkness began to swirl, a sudden breeze plucking at Cluny's fur.

No, not a *breeze*, she realized, the air as still and musty as ever. It was the deepest of deep magics plucking at her, a power stronger than anything she'd ever even imagined lurching into existence. "Hang on," she managed to say, and with a roar she felt rather than heard, the black spot sucked itself inward, became a void, walnut-sized and hungry, she knew, for all things magical. Just looking at it made her whiskers prickle.

Of course, she, Crocker and Shtasith were pretty much empty at this point, but she doubted the flayer would be much bothered by the fine line between mana and life energy that Mistress Otembe had talked about in BioSci. No, Cluny felt sure Goulet had spoken the truth: this thing would kill anyone, no matter *how* little magic they had. Fortunately, though—

A groaning, snapping, crackling sound, and the black wood of the floor directly beneath them began to ripple, Cluny's scouring spell starting to loosen the grime accumulated over the past thousand years or so. But not just grime, she'd known the first time she'd set a paw onto it. Century after century of students testing, casting and shaping magic of every sort had trod this floor, power sloshing onto it like water overflowing hundreds of thousands—maybe millions—of tanks.

Pried free, this power drifted upward, tickled Cluny's whiskers like pepper and spice before getting sucked into the maw of the flayer. Cluny couldn't help digging her claws into Crocker's robes, could almost hear the black spot sniff, following the trail of magic shaken loose by her scouring spell. It shifted, aimed itself downward, and with a whoosh like all the winds of the world rushing past, every blackened foot of the library floor was stripped down to bright shining wood. Vertigo pulled at Cluny again, clattering thunks echoing from all around as tables and chairs dropped an inch, and the flayer, as Cluny had hoped and prayed, gave a little burp and flickered out, apparently full to the level Goulet had set it for.

Silence for a moment, then Shtasith's quavering voice behind her: "We . . . we're alive?"

"Yes!" Crocker shouted, and Cluny flailed as he grabbed her up into a hug. "I *knew* you'd think of something!"

His warmth wrapped around her externally and internally, and she closed her eyes, held him as tightly as she could for a moment before she could find her voice. "Is Goulet—?"

"He breathes," Shtasith said, and Cluny forced herself to look back, the pale boy lying in a heap beside the now empty table, not a flicker of magic reaching her whiskers from him. A little rumbly sound, and Shtasith turned his gaze up past her. "Crocker, I . . . I must offer you apologies. You truly—"

A flood of light, a rush of air, voices a sudden tangle around her, and she saw they were outside, Crocker craning his head, Shtasith wings unfurling. A pink and green pixie in a white coat spun into view, a quarantine wand in one hand. "You're all right?" the pixie asked, tapping them each with the wand. "How can you be all right?"

More emergency personnel bustled about what Cluny now recognized as the main quad outside the admin building, a phalanx of blue-coated ogres converging on Goulet, groaning on the ground a few yards from where Crocker stood. "Crocker!" a voice called, and when he turned, Cluny saw Tzu Yin rushing over, a small silver-gray sparrowhawk hugging the side of her head. "That was amazing!"

Crocker spread his hands. "I just kept him talking. Cluny and Shtasith did the rest."

Cluny watched Tzu Yin look from her to Shtasith and back again, then the girl held a hand up to the sparrowhawk. "Jian?"

The hawk hopped onto her hand. "Yes, master?" he asked.

"I'd like you to call me Tzu Yin from now on."

Jian's eyes widened. "Master?"

"Yes." Tzu Yin nodded once. "It seems to have an interesting effect on a familiar."

It took some effort for Cluny not to burst out laughing, but then she saw Master Gollantz glowering from the other side of the security cordon. "Uh-oh," she heard Crocker say.

Shtasith gave a gust of steam, and Cluny put a paw on his head, dug the other into the folds of Crocker's robe. "Y'know, guys, I'm starting to think we might not be cut out for this whole inconspicuous thing."

A CURIOUS CASE

by *Annclaire Livoti*

These days law enforcement personnel and guns have replaced swordswomen. But, in real life, private investigators don't generally practice magic, and they don't have succubae as clients—at least I certainly hope not.

This is Annclaire Livoti's first professional sale. A recent graduate of Radford University, she currently resides in Loudoun County, Virginia.

You might say I have a passing acquaintance with the supernatural. Every so often, a succubus will drift into my office, throw a case on my desk, and drift back out again.

She called herself Diana, and I didn't mind when she visited. Well, I didn't mind *much*. It meant that I earned some respect in the eyes of the police, and that was always a good thing. They despise cases involving the supernatural community—means extra effort, extra danger, and extra paperwork, all of which they could do without.

There was usually a year or two between Diana's visits, so when she strolled into my office one Monday morning only six months after our latest case, I was a little surprised. She looked stunning as usual, being the type of woman that made men drone on about "legs that go on for *miles*" and "a stomach you could bounce a penny off of"—the sort of thing that came with being a succubus, I suppose. Today, she wore a black leather jacket, nearly see-through white blouse, and skin-tight blue jeans, and her blue-black hair was piled in an artful bun on top of her head like she'd just come from a runway in Paris.

"Diana."

"Virginia." Diana glanced around my office, taking in the little changes I'd made. "Business is booming, I trust?"

I just nodded. I liked to pride myself on being witty, but somehow it seemed pointless to try for a quip whenever Diana was around. She'd just smile that megawatt smile at you and ignore the wisecrack. I leaned back in my chair, trying to feign nonchalance and probably not succeeding. Couldn't blame me— Diana's cases were always interesting, and she paid extremely well. Plus, my car needed repairs to the tune of almost a grand. "What kind of problem is it this time?"

To my shock, Diana hesitated. Now, this might not sound like a big deal, but during our twenty-year acquaintance, I'd never once seen Diana at a loss for words. Ever. Each gesture, each word she uttered came out effortlessly, like she'd somehow gotten a copy of her life's script and constantly read five lines ahead.

"Diana?"

Diana looked away, her slate gray eyes shadowed. Tension suddenly radiated off her in waves, making my stomach do a nervous somersault. Well, crap. I was beginning to think I wasn't going to like this job.

"My sister is dead."

For a moment, shock gripped me by the throat and kept me silent. When I finally could speak, all that came out was a horrified, "How?" I already knew the answer even as the question tumbled from my lips. Succubae died only one way.

Violently.

"Lily is the fourth succubus murdered this month. You and I are going to find the killer." She smiled, but it was one with too many teeth and no particular warmth in her eyes. "I trust you don't mind if we avoid involving the police in this particular case."

I took in a deep breath. Released it. "You know I can't promise that, Diana." The police might be glad to fob off an unpleasant case or two on me, but that wouldn't stop them from arresting me for interfering in open murder cases, especially not ones that looked like a serial.

Diana was silent for a moment. Then something in her shoulders eased, and a wry smile curved her lips. "I shouldn't have asked."

I accepted that for what it was—the closest Diana could come to an apology—and motioned for her to sit down. "Tell me everything you know about the four victims."

She pulled a manila envelope from beneath her jacket and handed it to me. "The first was Ala, on the third. After that, Oza on the eighth. Then Verrine on the twelfth. Lily—" There was a barely discernable pause as Diana swallowed. "Lily was killed last night. The twenty-first."

I opened up the envelope. Four photographs spilled onto my desk. I studied them for a moment. Even if Diana hadn't told me they were succubae, I would've known. Unlike vampires, whom the cameras never seemed to detect, succubae and incubi came out crystal clear in photographs. It was simply everything else that blurred, like all the color and light longed to wrap themselves around that form—one reason succubae and incubi didn't make for good models.

All four succubae looked young, but that didn't mean anything. Diana hadn't changed at all in two decades; not a single wrinkle or gray hair had corrupted her beauty in all the time I'd known her. My gaze lingered on Lily's photograph. They looked a little like sisters, if you knew what to look for. It was in the tilt of their heads and the shape of their jaws.

Along with the photographs were police reports of the murders. I barely managed to keep from raising an eyebrow.

These certainly weren't legal. Then I thought about the dark look in Diana's eyes, a coldness that made my hindbrain want to hide under the nearest bed, and decided not to question how she'd gotten her hands on them.

Diana tapped a manicured finger on my desk, and I looked up. "I have three witnesses to Lily's murder."

Of course she did. If there were witnesses to be found, Diana would find them. Though I didn't spend too much time dabbling with the supernatural community, I knew enough to realize that Diana had connections.

"When can I interview them?" I asked, skimming the report on Ala. Single stab wound to the heart that punctured the aorta. She'd bled out in minutes. No witnesses.

"They're waiting outside."

I stared at her. "They're waiting—right. Just let me read over the police reports and then show the first one in." And let me work a spell or two to detect a lie, but that was understood.

Ψ͓⁊

The first witness was a soft-eyed tourist named Céleste Travere, who spoke English with just the barest trace of an accent.

"I was lost," she explained. Her long, delicate fingers plucked at the top button of her shirt, unbuttoning and then buttoning again as she spoke. A nervous gesture, not a guilty one—Ms. Travere had just arrived in the country two nights ago and couldn't have committed the other murders. "The driver of the taxi took me to the wrong restaurant. I was walking, trying to find another taxi, and heard someone shout, and—" She stopped and closed her eyes for a moment, pale freckles made obvious by the sudden blanching of her skin. When she continued, her voice was unsteady. "I did not see who killed that poor woman. I saw two men running over to the woman, but I did not see anyone running away."

"Were there any buildings around that the murderer might have ducked into?" I asked, and watched a frown twist Ms. Travere's mouth.

"There was a bar across the street," she said. "Everything else was dark and looked closed."

Diana interrupted. "The next witness had been visiting the bar *Vixen* when he heard the shouting."

Vixen? I raised an eyebrow, and Diana nodded. Yes, a bar that catered to incubi, succubae, and their groupies. Wonderful. I had a feeling I wasn't going to like this next witness.

Sure enough, Isaac Ferguson was a sallow-faced guy with the restless eyes and trembling hands of an addict. Only what he was addicted to wasn't drugs or alcohol, it was sex, carnal pleasure from either succubae or incubi or maybe both.

"Sit down, Mr. Ferguson." I kept my dislike out of my voice, but he flinched at the order anyway, gaze flickering towards the door like he was reassuring himself that he had an escape route. "Please, tell me what you saw."

"Not much," he said quickly. He didn't meet my eyes. Either he was lying or he needed a fix. "I was just about to leave *Vixen*, was getting my coat and heard someone shout. Went out to see what was going on and saw this—body on the ground." His Adam's apple bobbed jerkily. "There was a lot of blood. This guy was by the door too, and we both ran over to see if maybe we could save her." He paused, and then gave a brief, twitchy look in Diana's direction, licking his lips. "She was already dead, though."

"Did you see anyone else on the street?"

He jerked his head back, bony shoulders rising. It took me a second to realize he was shrugging. "We started running and I saw the French lady you just talked to coming over to see what was going on. Nobody else, though."

"And you didn't see anyone entering or exiting the bar when you got your coat?"

Ferguson shot me a look like I was an idiot. "I was getting my coat. Had my back to the door the entire time. You'd have to ask the other guy in the hall."

"All right. Thank you for your time, Mr. Ferguson." I handed him one of my cards. "If you think of anything that might be useful, just give me a call."

He gazed blankly at the card and tucked it into his pocket, but I could tell the words on the card weren't sinking in. He was too ready to get out of here, probably already thinking about going back to *Vixen* or another bar. "Sure," he muttered. Then his gaze flickered back over to Diana and lingered. He licked his lips again, and this time the truth spell glowed blue for honesty when he added, "I'll let you know if I remember anything."

The last witness was Sam, an incubus. He made his entrance by a wave of lust that hit me in the gut like a sucker punch. I doubled over, gasping a little and grateful that I was sitting, not standing, because falling over would have been fairly humiliating. I closed my eyes, gritted my teeth against the ache in my belly, and remembered exactly why I only consorted with Diana when it came to the supernatural community. Incubi tended to be male chauvinists wrapped in pretty packaging.

"Virginia?" Diana sounded startled at first, and then furious. *"Sam—"*

"Sorry," I heard Sam say in an offhand, careless way. My discomfort eased and then vanished completely, leaving only tension behind to tighten my shoulders and turn my knuckles white. "Old habits and all that."

I opened my eyes, resisting the urge to wipe away the sweat that had broken out on my forehead. "Just tell me what you saw," I snapped. At least Diana would forgive me for skipping pleasantries after *that* disgusting display.

Sam sat down, stretching his long, muscular legs out in front of him and apparently making himself comfortable. "I had grabbed my coat and started outside. I saw the body and shouted for someone to call 911. Then I ran over to see if there was anything I could do. There wasn't."

He paused, and then startled me by frowning and turning an earnest look upon Diana. "Meri, I am so sorry. Lilith was—"

Meri. Diana. Meridiana. Why did that name ring a bell? Well, it wasn't actually important to the investigation; I tucked that knowledge away for another time, when we *weren't* trying to catch a serial killer.

"Thank you," said Diana, and bowed her head. Her hands clenched at her sides, and then relaxed. "The funeral will be tomorrow if you can attend."

"Did you see anyone running from the scene?" I asked, drawing Sam's attention back. "Anything suspicious?"

"No. Just the other two witnesses and Lily."

After another soft apology to Diana, Sam showed himself out. As soon as the door shut behind him, I let myself slump in my chair and wipe at the sweat on my forehead. "I'm going to double-check Travere's alibi, look into Sam and Ferguson's history."

"I'll—" Diana began, and stopped at my raised hand.

"You are going to go home and arrange everything for tomorrow," I said firmly. "I've got things under control here."

"But," Diana said, and then stopped, shoulders slumping in an inelegant way. She looked tired now, and impossibly old. I wondered how old she actually was. A hundred? Five hundred? A millennium? It had never exactly come up in conversation. "That's probably best."

Diana turned to go, and I reached out and caught her hand. It was cool and smooth in my grip as I squeezed it. "I'll let you know as soon as I learn anything."

"Thank you," she said. Her smile didn't reach her eyes.

ଔ୯ଅଚ୦ଈ

First things first. Travere's alibi for the other murders held up—she'd flown in from Paris two nights ago. She also wasn't known to frequent supernatural bars.

By all accounts Ferguson was addicted only to the wiles of succubae, not incubi, so that possible connection between him and Sam was out. It did make him a possible suspect—maybe he was getting his revenge on the succubus who had addicted him? I called Ferguson's apartment to schedule another meeting and check his alibi for the other murders. No one answered. I'd have to call back later.

Sam was well-behaved for an incubus. There had been no complaints made against him since he'd come to the city, no rumors he fed too long and too much on a single human, no suspicious deaths—until now, of course. He worked at *Vixen*; the manager told me he'd just gotten off-shift when the murder occurred.

He'd also been working the night Ala was killed, which disappointed me a little. I kept thinking about his offhanded comments as he twisted me up inside with his powers, and wanted him to be the murderer, if just to see the look on his face as he was shoved into a police car.

What? I can be vindictive when I want to be.

ᘓᗞᘓᗞᘓᗞ

The next day came too quickly, and arrived gloomy and overcast. I thought about skipping the funeral—it wasn't like I'd known Lily, and Diana and I weren't exactly *friends*— but then I remembered Diana's empty eyes, and decided that she needed even business associates around her today.

The funeral turned out to be a quiet, sober affair. The majority of the mourners were Lily's fellow succubae and incubi, but I saw a couple of sunken-eyed humans who were obviously addicts as well.

Afterward, Sam sidled up to me. "Ms. Levine." He somehow managed to turn my name into an insult, a slight emphasis on *Ms.* as though I was one of those women who demanded equality until the right man came along.

I offered him my best screw-you smile and ignored the hand he offered me. "You were working the night Ala died."

He shrugged, apparently taking my statement for a question. "Probably. You'd have to ask my manager. I'm afraid I'm hopeless with dates."

"Sam. Virginia." Diana's face was pale, her eyes glistening with suppressed grief but her face and voice were composed as she walked over. "You both made it."

I nodded as Sam touched Diana's arm and quietly murmured his regrets.

Diana accepted them with a half-distracted air, her too-bright eyes focused on me. "Anything new?"

I shook my head, all too aware that Sam was standing right there, listening with grave interest. "Just checking alibis and looking for connections between the victims. Did you know Lily and the other victims were all part of the Celibate Succubae Organization?" It was an odd connection, I admitted—who would want to hurt succubae that *didn't* kill? — but it was the only one I'd found so far. The victims hadn't frequented the same bars or even lived in the same parts of town.

"The CSO?" said Sam, sounding scandalized and a little pained. "Oh Meri, tell me that Lily wasn't caught up by those idiots."

Diana's gaze darkened. "They're not idiots, Sam. They're trying to improve human perception toward us."

"By calling for the *executions* of those who make a mistake or two," Sam snapped.

"A mistake or two? Is that what you call killing someone, Sam?"

"They're just—" Sam stopped, and exhaled sharply. After a moment, he relaxed and offered us a rueful look. "No, you're right. They're doing what's best in the long run."

"So, a good angle," I said. It wasn't a question. "Know anyone in particular who hates the CSO?"

Sam snorted, a surprisingly harsh sound. "Try pretty much every succubus or incubus in the city. Everyone knows someone the CSO wanted to kill."

When I looked at Diana, she was nodding in agreement. "The CSO are not well-liked by the majority of our community. They're seen as too extreme." Some animation had returned to her eyes. "I'll ask around, see if anyone seemed particularly sincere in wanting the CSO destroyed."

"Good," I said. Meanwhile, I could go knock on Ferguson's door, see why he hadn't answered my three calls yesterday. If he'd run away, it was a good guess he was somehow involved, and I could give the tip to the police and be done with that particular thread of the mystery.

I left with a smile to Diana and a curt nod to Sam.

෧෬෩෧

No one answered when I knocked on Ferguson's door. Great. The landlord turned out to be a scruffy, sleepy-looking guy in his mid-fifties, who endeared himself to me forever by grunting at Ferguson's name and saying, "I'll let you into his place. Guy's about to be evicted anyway. A month behind on his rent."

We walked back to Ferguson's apartment, and I answered carefully when the landlord asked me what trouble Ferguson was in. "Witness to a murder. Just need to ask him a couple follow-up questions."

The landlord looked vaguely impressed, like being a witness to a murder was something to boast about, and then unlocked the door. "There you go. I'll have to go inside with you, of course."

"Of course," I agreed, and pushed the door open.

Ferguson wasn't home. Céleste Travere was, though, and the landlord's horrified yell filled my ears as we both stared into her lifeless eyes.

Well, crap.

∽⃝⃝∾

"It's Ferguson," I said as soon as Diana picked up. "Céleste Travere's body is in his apartment."

There was a long stretch of silence, and for a moment I thought the call had been disconnected. Then she said, "Have you called the police?"

"They should be here any minute." There was another long hush, and I sighed, frustrated. "I *had* to. The landlord saw the body and started screaming for the police." Plus, coming across a crime and not reporting it was a quick and easy way to get your license revoked. "Travere must have seen something." I winced, thinking about it. Poor woman. Wrong place, worst possible time, and she wound up dead thousands of miles from home because she'd seen something she shouldn't have.

Diana inhaled sharply. "Virginia. Sam is probably—"

"I'll check *Vixen*, see if he's working," I said, and then Luis Martinez and Natalie Carson walked in. Well, at least they were on friendly terms with me. "Sorry, police are here." I hung up and turned to Luis and Natalie. "How much do you know about the string of succubus murders?"

"Not a lot, it's Henderson and Mitchell's case," Luis said, and then stared at me, eyebrows trying to climb to his hairline. "How'd you get caught up in that mess?"

"The last victim—well, the last succubus victim—was Diana's sister."

Natalie whistled, wide-eyed. She touched the back of her neck, where a pale scar peeked out from under her collar. I didn't think she realized she was doing it. "How's she doing?" Her voice was soft. Of course it would be. Diana had helped me round up the rogue werewolves killing cops five years back, saving Natalie's life in the process.

"She wants the murderer."

"Then let's get him for her." Natalie grinned. For a moment my breath caught at the wolfish quality to it. Then I summoned up the lunar calendar I kept in my head. Quarter-full moon tonight. No danger.

"This is Céleste Travere, age 29. She just arrived in the US three days ago, witnessed Lily's murder Sunday night." I waved a hand at the apartment. "This is Isaac Ferguson's apartment. He 'witnessed' Lily's murder too. He also enjoys the company of succubae."

"Right. Got a description for me?" Luis asked, and I rattled it off, which Luis promptly repeated to his dispatcher.

I gave Luis and Natalie my statement as quickly as possible, and then excused myself. Time to call *Vixen* and see if Sam was working today.

His manager, sounding more annoyed than he had last night, told me that while Sam had been scheduled, he hadn't deigned to show up today. A quick explanation that I was calling about the succubus murders and believed that Sam might be the next target got me Sam's home address and phone number.

I tried calling. As soon as his voicemail picked up, I hung up and bolted for my car. I paused just long enough to take my Taurus from my shoulder holster, check how many bullets I had, and murmur a spell that would strengthen the blessing Rabbi Wirth had bestowed last month.

Sure, regular bullets would go through Ferguson like he was made of paper instead of flesh and blood, but I liked to be on the safe side.

CRCSO

S am's door was open when I got there, and I pulled out my gun, flicked off the safety. Hopefully I wasn't too late.

I peered around the door, but this time no dead body greeted me. The living room was empty, with no sign of a struggle. Maybe that was a good thing, maybe not.

"Sam?" I called, easing around the door and taking a few cautious steps into the room. "I've just come from Ferguson's, and—"

Again, Sam's presence struck me like a fist to the gut, and I doubled over, just barely managing to keep my grip on my Taurus. "You stupid—" I snarled through clenched teeth, locking my knees and refusing to fall to the ground. "Ferguson killed Travere and now he's after you, so just quit it."

Sam came into the living room then. I could just make him out in the corner of my eye. "Virginia, Virginia, Virginia," he sighed, and made a motion that could've been shaking his head. "I'd heard so much about you from Meri and others. I thought you were clever. Did you really think a *human* could kill succubae?"

I glared at him, lust and fury muddling my thoughts. One thing I knew: always trust my instincts. Sam had thrown me off with his trick in my office, made me think I disliked him because he was loathsome, not because my senses were telling me he was the killer.

I tried to raise my gun, but my hands were shaking too badly to aim.

Sam laughed and walked closer, tugging the gun from my unresisting fingers. He admired it. "Lovely. A Taurus PT-945, if I'm not mistaken."

"You—" I tried to think of a spell, any spell, but I was only a part-time practitioner, and we both knew it. I could do truth spells and strengthening spells, but using an offensive spell against an incubus was far beyond my talent.

My hands ached for my gun.

He looked around, frowning. "I suppose I could make it seem like you died here, surprising Ferguson as he waited for me," he murmured, half to himself.

Damn it. I closed my eyes, pushed back the ache in my stomach and the emotions swamping my mind. I had to do *something*. I wasn't going to die like the others, too surprised or overwhelmed to fight back.

Cold metal stung my face as he tapped my chin with the Taurus. "Get up," he commanded, and in his voice I heard all the power and assurance that the serpent must have used on Eve.

My legs moved, and I stood, wondering vaguely when I'd fallen to my knees. I stared into his pale blue gaze, willing my hatred to reach my eyes.

He laughed again and gestured toward the door. "Come on. I think the alley behind a succubae club will work better. I don't want to get my carpet dirt—"

And then the terrible pressure and lust were gone, and I stood there, blinking like someone blinded by sunlight. Someone snarled, a woman, and I thought dazedly, *Of course. Diana always has perfect timing.*

I blinked, the last of the mist leaving my mind, and watched Sam and Diana grapple for the weapon, expressions twisted into ones of loathing.

As the two struggled, I looked around. There was a nice paperweight on the coffee table, made of quartz. It looked expensive. I picked it up, moved my arm experimentally. Yes, that would do nicely.

Then I turned and slammed the paperweight into the back of Sam's head.

The incubus stilled, eyes going wide with surprise and just the beginning of pain. The pain was just starting to contort his face, his legs beginning to crumple underneath him, when Diana pulled the gun from his grip and coolly shot him twice in the chest.

I didn't have to look to see where she'd shot him. Sam had killed his victims all the same way: a single knife thrust to the heart.

Sam fell, and if he had any final words, Diana and I weren't going to bother listening to them.

I turned to her, shaky as a newborn lamb and probably white as a ghost. "How did you—"

"Sam was one of the loudest opponents of the CSO," Diana said simply. She looked down at the gun and grimaced. "This is going to be an awful lot of paperwork for you, I'm afraid."

"It's fine," I said, taking my Taurus and placing it on the coffee table next to the bloodstained paperweight. "I don't mind." I paused, looked mock-thoughtful. "Though if you want to pay for my car's tune-up, I wouldn't object."

Diana smiled then, and for the first time in days it reached her eyes.

I smiled back, and then went to look for Sam's phone, already anticipating the yelling Luis and Natalie were going to do.

SOUL WALLS

by Julia H. West

One of the things I look for is original magic. In this story art and magic mix inextricably together, which makes sense; both artists and magicians see things differently than other people. Learning *what* to see can be a real challenge. How you deal with adversity is another— can you be patient when it appears that you are making no progress? And then there are things that truly determine who you are: How do you behave when nobody is watching you? Do you strive to do the right thing? Are you kind, and do you deal fairly with people outside your own group?

Julia H. West, like many authors, has held a wide variety of jobs: quality control technician for ultrasound heart machines; genealogical researcher; office manager; secretary; desktop publisher; digger at an archaeological dig; quality assurance tech; webmaster; and aircraft electrician for the Air Force Reserves. She graduated Magna Cum Laude from the University of Utah in 1993 with a BA in Anthropology, and when people asked what she was going to do with her degree, she said "Write Science Fiction." She sold her first story in 1989, so she was already heading in that direction. Julia is also active in the LDS (Mormon) church. She is married to fellow science fiction and fantasy writer Brook West and has two daughters, both of whom also write.

Tiva and the other apprentices sat cross-legged on mats in front of Yongosona's house, eating rolled corn cakes and enjoying the dawn breeze teasing the mesa top. Behind them the sun rose hot, its rays painting Red Cliff, far to the west. The girls had been up since before dawn, plastering the wall at Chumana's house, so the breeze was welcome.

Yongosona, their teacher, pushed the woven door hanging aside and stepped out. She was the oldest woman Tiva had ever seen—wrinkled and stooped, hair wispy as summer clouds—but still bright of eye and steady of hand. Her fingers, tunic and skirt were all daubed with the paints of her profession.

Paints, Tiva thought in dissatisfaction. I run to collect materials for them, I grind them, I mix them—but I never get to use them.

"Today," Yongosona said, "we paint Chumana's Soul Wall."

Tiva glanced up at her teacher. Yongosona usually did not say 'we' when she spoke of painting. Would she allow her apprentices to do more than plaster walls or mix paint? Tiva pushed the rest of her corn cake into her mouth, dusted her hands off on her skirt, and rose to her feet.

The other apprentices also stood, from Honovi—already a woman and looking forward to having her Soul Wall painted—to little Pamuya, in her eighth summer, who had come to Yongosona at winter's end.

Yongosona stared at the girls for a long time, never blinking. Her gaze was distant; she obviously thought of the Soul Wall to be painted. Finally she said, "Honovi, bring the gold earth and white. Tiva, brilliant red and black. Kawaina, all the greens. Lomahansi, light blue and jewel blue. Pamuya, the basket of brushes and scrapers."

The girls scrambled into Yongosona's house. The inside back wall was covered with shelves holding pots and stone boxes, and pegs from which baskets and tight-woven bags depended. All the girls, even Pamuya, knew where every piece of equipment belonged.

Tiva took down the pot of brightest red paint, lifted the lid, and peered inside. There was little left—Yongosona had used much in the last Soul Wall. Maybe that would be enough; it seemed this wall would have much green and blue in it.

She put that pot and the larger one of black paint in a small basket, padding the pots with straw so they wouldn't strike against each other and break. Usually she had more to carry. Yongosona always took an apprentice with her when she painted a Soul Wall, but most of the girls were sent off on errands, or stayed at Yongosona's house making paint. Excitement rose in Tiva's chest. They were all going today!

The girls followed their teacher along the plateau, through sandy lanes between attached houses plastered in brown, cream, and red. Chumana's brothers and other kinsmen had just finished adding her new home to her mother's, and were plastering it in the same warm orange-red shade.

The men stopped their work and stood aside, nodding and murmuring "Grandmother" as Yongosona and her apprentices passed into the house. It had no door hanging yet; that was still on Chumana's intended husband's loom, at least a day from completion.

Chumana and her husband-to-be, Mikwliya, entered after the apprentices, their faces shining with excitement. Chumana carried an armload of cushions; Honovi accepted one from her and helped Yongosona to seat herself cross-legged on it, then the apprentices all lined up behind their teacher, still holding their burdens.

"Esteemed elder," Chumana said, touching her forehead at Yongosona. Mikwliya echoed her.

"Sit." Yongosona pointed. They dropped cushions and sat before her, side by side, shoulders touching. Yongosona reached out, her multi-colored tunic's loose sleeves falling back as she spread fingers and rested them on the foreheads of the young couple before her. All three closed their eyes.

Tiva quietly pulled straw from the basket she carried. Beside her, she felt Honovi doing the same. They never knew how long this part would take, but when Yongosona asked for paint it must be ready to set into her hand.

Yongosona took a long time. Pamuya fidgeted, shifting her weight from one foot to the other. Yongosona's arms were shaking now, and sweat ran down the faces of the young couple.

Yongosona began to hum, a monotonous up-and-down sound. Tiva wished she knew what Yongosona was doing. Somehow, she was discovering what to paint on the Soul Wall, but she never told her apprentices *how* she knew. Did a god tell her? Tiva could never paint Soul Walls if she didn't know *what* to paint.

Abruptly Yongosona dropped her arms and opened her eyes. "Go," she told Chumana and Mikwliya.

Chumana—only two summers older than Tiva— staggered to her feet and pulled Mikwliya up with her. Silently, they left the house.

Tiva and Honovi helped Yongosona to her feet. The old woman took a paintbrush from Pamuya's basket and stood surveying the wall they had prepared that morning, blank white. She gestured with the brush, then said, "Red."

Tiva took the lid off the red pot and placed it under Yongosona's brush. What did the old woman see as she surveyed the unblemished wall before her? Did the painting live behind her eyes, merely needing to be copied onto the surface? How had she known, before she came, what colors she would need?

One long curving line, then another, red on the white surface. Then, "Black." Tiva held out the other pot, and Yongosona took another brush from Pamuya.

Tiva watched carefully. At this stage in Yongosona's Soul Walls there was no discernable design. Tiva couldn't look at a section and say, "This will be a spine tree, this will be a gazelope." Later, when it was nearly finished, the parts came together, and she would be able to see that this black line was the gazelope's hip, and that brown one traced an eagle's wing.

Today Yongosona *told* them what her lines meant. She murmured as she painted, and Tiva had to listen hard to understand. "Swiftness for their children, like the sandrat over the desert," she said as a line in gold earth, then a few more, became a sandrat's supple length. Tiva's heart began to pound. Yongosona was explaining what she painted! She had done this seldom since Tiva became her apprentice.

The other girls didn't seem to notice. They held paints for their teacher and Pamuya clutched used brushes. They fidgeted and yawned as the painting grew before their eyes and Yongosona's voice, quiet as a breeze, described sandrose and corn stalk.

Then Yongosona said "red" once more, but instead of dipping her brush into the pot, she squinted at it. "Not enough brilliant red," she said. "Need more tomorrow." She looked up at Tiva. "Go to Red Cliff now. Get the brightest red earth."

She turned away from Tiva, asked for green, took another brush, and traced a line—part of a cornstalk—close to one of earth gold.

Though Tiva wanted to stay and listen to Yongosona's explanations, she set her pots down next to Honovi and ran out the door. She held her hand up, gauging how high the sun stood above the village. It was already a few handwidths above the horizon. Red Cliff was half a day's run away, and after she gathered the earth she would need to grind and mix the pigment. She must make the most of the daylight.

She hardly paused when she reached Yongosona's house. Food bags hung on pegs, already filled. Water bag here, basket for the earth she would collect here. Already on the run, she dropped the bags into the basket and left dark coolness for sunlight as she settled the basket on her back.

The path from mesa to desert below was steep and zigzagged down the cliff side. But the men and boys who ran it daily to reach their fields below had pounded it hard and smooth with their feet, so Tiva sped up. Getting her stride now, she slowed little at each turn for the next long downward slant, ignoring the dizzying drop an arm's length to one side.

Red Cliff, as far west as Tiva had ever been in her sixteen summers, was the western border of the land claimed by Tiva's village, Ayantavi. They shared it with their neighbor to the north, Shokitevela. Boundaries had been negotiated between their Talker Chiefs generations before, since both villages obtained earth for pigment at Red Cliff.

Reaching the desert floor, Tiva settled into a steady pace, running with a long stride. She had learned that if she *tried* to run fast, she just tired herself. So she ran, face toward Red Cliff, thoughts wandering far from the desert she traversed.

Yongosona would not let her paint, but that did not mean Tiva did not paint. Red Cliff had many caves and there was one—far up the cliff, a hard scramble—where she had smoothed and plastered the wall and sometimes tried painting for herself. But her lines were wobbly, and no matter what curves and lines she added, she rarely saw plant or animal. She had plastered over many attempts, but was beginning to think she would end up like many of Yongosona's other apprentices. She would find a nice boy in another village, bring him home, and Yongosona would paint them a Soul Wall. She would turn to decorating pottery or making patterns for weaving.

Red Cliff was closer now, and Tiva sipped from her water bag, never breaking stride. She adjusted her headscarf so the sun, directly overhead, wouldn't burn the back of her neck. The basket on her back was beginning to chafe through her sweat-damp tunic. When she stopped, she'd adjust it.

The desert, under the mid-day sun, was quiet. Animals, smarter than humans, hid in their cool dens when the sun was fiercest. Always running, breathing deeply but without panting, Tiva surveyed the area. Yellow sand everywhere, dotted with gray-green brush, with now and then a darker rock poking through. Nothing moved, no breeze stirred sparse branches; even the dust of her running sank almost immediately. She was alone with her discontent.

Yongosona had told them things as she worked today. Usually she merely grunted words—requesting paints, brushes, or other materials. What were the others learning while Tiva was off gathering earth? In eight summers of helping Yongosona, Tiva could count the times when the old woman had explained her paintings on the fingers of one hand. Yongosona taught them to make materials, then bade them watch and think on what they saw.

Tiva watched. Tiva thought. But she had not learned how to paint. She had not learned what made a Soul Wall the heart of a home, not just a decoration like a painting on a pot.

"You run well, girl," said a voice close to her ear.

ೞೞೞೞ

Almost, she broke her stride. Almost, she stumbled. But she caught herself and stared, open-mouthed and startled, at the young man running beside her. He must have been resting in the scant shadow of one of the rocks, or she would have seen him earlier. Now he paced her easily, running alongside, grinning at her shock.

"Thank you," she said finally. "I have far to go."

"You do," he said, words smooth, breathing easy, though he ran as swiftly as she. "May I run with you?"

His face had a familiar look to it. Like the runners in Shokitevela, he had waist-length hair tied with a cloth striped in red and yellow, but his trousers and tunic were white, not the bright colors most men favored. Perhaps she had seen him before, at the races with Shokitevela last fall. There should be no harm in his running alongside her. "If you wish," she answered.

They ran together, the only sounds their sandals swishing through the sand and the slight *huff, huff* of their breathing. Soon the young man's silence began to disturb Tiva. Why did he want to run with her, if he had nothing to say? Did he spy out where Ayantavi got their colored earths, to take for his own village? Men did not paint, but they did weave, and the brilliant red earth would color his yarn far better than the faded red in his head-cloth. She began to regret allowing him to run alongside her.

"Sensing souls is difficult," he said, startling her from uneasy thoughts.

"Yes," she said, to cover renewed shock. "I . . . I don't know if I have the right soul to sense others." Why had she told him that? It was her most private fear, one she had told no one else, and now she had blurted it to a stranger.

"You try too hard and not hard enough." He said the words casually, as if he knew her, as if he were not a stranger from another village, with no business to know what she did or why.

It stung her, his response, and she answered again without thinking, "I watch, and I think, as I have been taught."

"What do you watch?" he asked.

What *did* she watch? Yongosona. How she mixed colors. How she drew curves and lines. How she shaded paint into paint, how she used colors, what colors she used. What brushes she chose, which feathers and sticks she used to smooth and delineate. Tiva had watched this for eight summers, and thought she knew well enough what Yongosona did. But she still did not know *why*.

"I watch my teacher," Tiva told him, to break the silence.

"Do you watch what she does *not* do as well as what she does?" he asked.

Why did his questions fret her so? She remembered this morning, standing bored and restless as Yongosona touched Chumana's and Mikwliya's foreheads. She had *not* watched when Yongosona was not painting. Something stirred deep in her mind. *Watch and think.*

"You have far to go," the stranger said, and his stride grew longer, his steps quicker. She lengthened her own stride to keep even with him, and he sped up even more.

"Are you a painter?" she asked, and noted with shame that her voice was breathless with their current pace.

"I am a painter, yes," he said, "and more. As are you." His voice was as even and easy as it had ever been, though he ran as if he were in the fall races, sprinting to prove his village's superiority.

Her lungs began to feel the pace, as did the joints in her hips, knees, and ankles. Her arms pumped at her sides, as if to pull her forward through the air.

"Look to your walls," he said, and with satisfaction she heard him panting slightly. But then she frowned. *My walls?*

"What do you... mean? I'm not... married yet. I don't... have a Soul Wall." She didn't think she could run faster. She was sprinting, not pacing herself for the rest of her journey to Red Cliff. He was drawing ahead, and for some reason she could not let that happen.

"Change how you watch. Change how you think." He turned his head, grinned at her, and put on a greater burst of speed.

She could not keep up. He must be his village's champion runner, sent out to gather earth from Red Cliff. He had seen her, and chosen to tease her on his way. Regaining her normal pace, she fought gasping breaths back to steadiness. He ran on toward the cliff until sight of his dark hair and white clothing was lost in desert heat shimmer.

Now Tiva slowed for a moment, to adjust her headscarf, smooth the wrinkle out of her tunic where the basket rode on her shoulders, and take another sip of water. She had allowed herself to become overheated; that was bad. Her tunic was soaked with sweat, and her skirt flapped clammily about her calves.

What had he said to her? Change her way of watching and thinking? Again something—an idea—flickered in the back of her mind, but she could not catch it. She set out again in her accustomed stride, and slowly the ache eased from calves and hips, and her throat ceased burning.

୫୦୫୫୦

Red Cliff was much closer than she had expected. How far had she run while sprinting against the man? The ground underfoot changed, from yellow-white sand to gray earth streaked with red. There were more stones here. She had to watch her footing, not lose herself in thinking.

At the cliff's base she paused, shading eyes with a hand to peer at the sun. She had arrived more rapidly than anticipated. If she dug quickly she might have time to practice painting.

Practice painting. What could she change to make her paintings better? Always before she had painted as Yongosona did—starting with bold lines and working from them. But what if painting worked differently for her? She had never tried painting what felt right for *her*; she had always tried to copy her teacher. Was that what the young man meant, when he said, 'Change how you watch, change how you think'?

Excitement swept through Tiva. She wanted to try *now*, try to paint with her own eyes and mind, not Yongosona's. She ran down the long cliff, away from where most apprentices collected red earth. Then she scrambled up the wind-carved stone face, fingers and sandaled feet easily finding places. She had often wished she didn't have to paint the way Yongosona did. She had pushed that desire away, thinking she *had* to paint like her teacher. If she *changed.* . . .

The cave was cooler, out of direct sunlight. She didn't have time to plaster the wall, didn't have many pre-mixed paints available. That wasn't important. Today she wanted to try something different, to *experiment*. Her heart pounded against her ribs, and she laughed breathlessly. To get so excited about something she did every day of her life. It was only painting, after all.

But today it wasn't *only* painting. In fact, she didn't even open the tightly covered paint pots hidden in a niche. Instead, she took a charred stick and stood before the fresh white wall, the wall she had covered over so ferociously after her last failed attempt.

Think. *Change* the way you think. Instead of drawing a line and expecting the painting to emerge from it, think first of what should be there. Cornstalks in Father's fields, heavy heads waving in a slight evening breeze? Mother's cat, curled in the exact center of a woven rug with an expression of extreme satisfaction? Youngest brother, half-asleep against Father, finger in mouth as he listened to evening tales? All these things were part of her family's soul.

Is this how Yongosona knew what to paint on a Soul Wall? But Tiva's thoughts were of how her family was *now*. How could she draw what was to come? How could she draw a family's destiny before the family even began?

Change the way you think. Yongosona had lived in Ayantavi, and painted Soul Walls, since Tiva's grandmother was a girl. She knew everyone, watched children born and grow. She had seen boys leave for other villages, seen girls bring home their excited young husbands-to-be. Yongosona's husband was dead. Her sons lived in other villages. Was the whole village now her family, so she could see into their souls as Tiva could see her own parents and brothers? But what about the boys marrying in? Yongosona couldn't know their souls. She had not watched them grow up, did not know if they were smart or lazy or rambunctious.

Tiva shook her head. Too much to think on. She'd never paint anything if she thought too much. For now, something she knew, and knew well. The little peach tree outside the front door of her house. It was near the end of its life, but its gnarled branches yielded the sweetest peaches in the village.

She closed her eyes and smiled. She pictured the curve of the tree's trunk, one side uneven where her brother had hung on a branch and broken it off. Now it was in full leaf, and peaches hung heavy, nearly ripe. Her father had propped the branches up with forked sticks. That curve—the branch, the twigs, the leaves. . . .

The curve she drew on the white wall wasn't wobbly or aimless. The next curve, although making the branch thicker than it was in real life, was pleasing. She sketched on, adding hints of leaves here and there, shading fat peaches with her thumb. When she finally stood back and looked at her work, excitement gripped her again. Here was the first thing she had ever made that looked as she thought it should. And she had done it merely by changing her thought. What power in the grinning young man's suggestion.

She shivered a little—not from cold, but from the force of what had just taken her over. Then she looked up in alarm. It was cooler in the little cave than it had been. The sun was behind Red Cliff now, and the day was passing quickly. She had still to find red earth and get back to Ayantavi.

Assuring herself her basket was in place, she backed carefully down hand- and footholds in the stone. The best, the brightest red earth was at the northern end of the cliff, near Shokitevela's territory.

Tiva jogged along the cliff's base, searching out veins of bright red in ochre and gray. There—near the ground. It was very trampled here—other girls must come here often. She dug the darker earth with her wooden paddle, and found very little bright red. She packed it into her basket and covered it with straw, then ran on along the cliff side.

She found one other place, also very trampled, with a small vein of brilliant red. Had Yongosona used so much of it lately that her apprentices had dug all the easy-to-find earth? A glance behind at the cliff's long shadow told her she had little time to find enough and begin her long run home.

The ground began to rise, and Tiva saw only gray stone for stride after stride. She had come too far north; she would have to turn around and see if she had missed other places to dig brilliant red. Ah! There, just above head height on the side of the cliff, where scattered stone showed a recent fall, was the brilliant red she sought.

Tiva headed for it eagerly, but then paused, uneasy. She *had* come too far north. She was in Shokitevela's territory. This was their earth; she couldn't take what didn't belong to her village. She stopped, irresolute. The cliff's shadow spread far across the desert now, the sun long past zenith. She had little time to find more earth, get back to the village, and prepare pigment for tomorrow's painting. Would Shokitevela begrudge her a basketful of earth? There were no footprints—it seemed Shokitevela's painters had not come here. And the vein was large—she could see that.

She stooped to gather stones that had fallen from the cliff face, to pile them up to stand on so she could reach the red earth above. A lizard scampered from beneath one and raised its head, gazing at her. She stared back. Usually lizards were so shy of people that the whisk of a tail and tiny footprints in the sand were all she ever saw. This one sat still, just out of reach, black eyes staring. It was beautiful, sand-gold hide beaded with black and tan, banded with red. Its sides expanded and contracted as it breathed, and it gazed at her steadfastly as she stared back.

"Kukutsi," she breathed. This lizard was sacred to Shokitevela. She knew, seeing it here, that she was *not* to take their earth, no matter how great she thought her need. She let her head drop. "Yes, Kukutsi. I will leave."

Kukutsi turned its head, surveying her with each bright eye in turn, then whisked out across the sand.

Tiva took a deep breath, released it, then ran back the way she had come.

അ൏ൠ൏ౠ

Back in her own territory, there was a little more brilliant red earth far overhead; she found hand and footholds, but had to hook her basket over one arm—very awkward. Added to what she had, the basket was less than half full. But it would have to do; the cliff's shadow reached so far across the desert now that the sun must be little more than a few hands above the western horizon. Tiva packed the earth carefully, drank more water, and ate a corn cake. In her earlier excitement to paint, she had forgotten to eat.

She started back through rougher ground east of the cliff, stumbling occasionally. She was tired. The journey back to Ayantavi seemed almost more than she could accomplish. She took another sip and stretched her legs, knowing she must not delay.

She ran out of the cliff's long shadow into late afternoon heat. She was surprised to see another runner heading out from the cliff, angling more to the north and already farther east than she was.

The runner saw her and slowed. Tiva put on a burst of speed and soon was running alongside the other girl. It was Nakwanpa, one of the apprentices to Koloh-Pohu, Shokitevela's Soul Wall painter.

"You're out late," Nakwanpa said, rather breathless.

"As are you," Tiva returned. "Your village is farther than mine—you've a long run ahead."

Nakwanpa ran quietly for a moment, then answered, "I sought the brightest red earth and found little. I stayed overlong in the search."

"Ah, then we are alike!" said Tiva. "I, too, was looking for brilliant red, but the veins are almost gone." She stopped there. Should she tell Nakwanpa of the large new vein she had found in Shokitevela's territory? To do so would admit she had gone beyond Ayantavi's boundary. But it had been an honest error, and she'd taken nothing.

"I searched so far up Red Cliff that I strayed into your territory," Tiva admitted. "At the north end of the cliffs, where the ground rises, there is new-fallen stone. A large vein of brilliant red was uncovered."

Nakwanpa turned her head to Tiva, a smile wreathing her dusty features. "Thank you, Tiva, for telling me this. May your painting go well." The other girl sped up, angling north again. Just before she was out of earshot, she turned her head and called, "In your territory, halfway back along the cliff, there is a crevice with three sandrose bushes at its mouth. Follow it back and see if the brilliant red is as plentiful as it looked from its mouth."

Tiva waved her thanks and ran on, her spirit lighter. Each had found red earth in the other's territory. She thought Nakwanpa hadn't entered the cleft, hadn't taken any earth from Ayantavi's territory. She was doubly glad she had not dug any of Shokitevela's earth.

೫ఊఴ

It was nearly dark when Tiva ran the last long path up the cliff and reached her village. The smell of savory sauces cooking made her stomach growl. Cheerful voices rang over the plateau as families gathered at day's end. But she could not go to her family yet; she must bring her basket to Yongosona.

Yongosona sat on a mat outside her house grinding pigment in a stone mortar, lamps flickering in niches to either side of her. She looked up as Tiva, panting from the effort of the last long climb to the village, halted. "Late."

"Yes, Grandmother," Tiva said, bowing her head. "The sources of brilliant red are almost used up."

The old woman held out her hands for Tiva's basket. Without looking inside, she weighed it in her palms. Her face seemed to sag into more wrinkles than usual.

"There was more," Tiva blurted. "But I found it after I wandered into Shokitevela's territory. I . . . did not think it would be good to take their earth."

Yongosona looked up at Tiva, reflections of lamp flames dancing in her eyes. She studied the girl for a long time, as Tiva tried very hard not to fidget. Tiva's mouth grew dry, and sweat broke out on her brow despite the cool evening breeze.

The old woman said finally, "Shokitevela's earth would not suit an Ayantavi Soul Wall." She handed the basket back to Tiva. "All will be needed."

Tiva took the basket, pushed the doorflap aside, and hurried into Yongosona's house for another mortar, to grind the red earth for tomorrow's paint. As she settled down beside Yongosona, she tried not to feel the hollowness of her stomach and the aches in shoulders and legs.

ॐ ∞☙

Tiva was up before dawn with the other apprentices, preparing new plaster for Chumana's Soul Wall. She had not slept well, and her calves still ached, but the brilliant red had all been ground and mixed. It rested now in covered pots, ready for Yongosona's use.

Plastering complete, they ate, and Yongosona assigned tasks. Tiva was sent to Dry Gorge to gather insects for bright blue paint. Tiva wasn't sure if Yongosona had assigned her this task because she was displeased with her performance of the day before or not. Dry Gorge was much closer to Ayantavi than Red Cliff, but gathering gembugs was an unpleasant chore.

Tiva took a tight-woven bag as well as the carry basket, for gembugs were small and sifted through basket mesh or the weave of normal cloth. She set off quickly. Today she would make Yongosona proud of her. She knew where the best spine trees were, and should be able to gather many gembugs and be home long before dusk.

The air was still and hot as Tiva raced down the path to the desert below. The little hairs on her arms crawled, and Tiva scanned the sky for clouds. It felt like thunderstorm weather.

As she ran, the uneasy feeling that someone was watching plagued her. She scanned the terrain ahead, looking for telltale puffs of dust from running feet. No one. It must be the tickly, itchy feeling of the air.

Dry Gorge was a long, deep crack, waterless most of the time. In spring, snow melted in far-off mountains and filled the gorge with roiling water. The only other time water flowed in the gorge was when it rained heavily in those same mountains, sending water down the gorge even when the desert got no rain at all. The thunderstorm feel in the air made Tiva cautious.

She traversed the path worn into Dry Gorge's steep side carefully; it was not hard-packed and reliable as the one down the cliff at home, for most of it was destroyed every spring. Once on the gorge's pebbled floor, she trotted down relatively clear ways between spine trees, candleplants, and sandrose.

Many plants grew here, for there was water deep underground. The oldest spine tree roots must reach halfway through the world, searching for water. They were so well rooted that even flash floods did not dislodge them. These elder trees were the best places to seek gembugs.

Tiva found the huge, many-branched spine tree she sought. It was so tall its highest branches could be seen above the lip of the gorge, almost the same yellow-brown as the sand. Yongosona had sought gembugs here when *she* was an apprentice. Spines longer than Tiva's middle finger grew from trunk, branches, and twigs. They were sharp, and their sap made any scratch or puncture itch and swell.

It was easy to tell where gembugs made their homes in the tree. When a spine tree was damaged, spines grew like bristling whiskers from the wound.

The first bristly area Tiva found was in the trunk, just above head height. She wrapped her arm in a piece of leather and carefully angled her hand, holding a stone knife, in toward the swollen area where the gembugs lived. It was awkward, as she couldn't see above her head. Spines brushed the leather around her wrist, but she kept them from puncturing it.

She got her knife to the base of the swollen area, and was startled by a sharp chittering. A sandrat poked its slender nose out of the hole in the spine tree's trunk and cursed at her. Tiva froze in place, not wanting to get scratched by spines, but also wary of the sandrat's teeth. So this wasn't a gembug nest, but a sandrat den! She didn't remember seeing sandrats nesting in the spine trees before. Again, she had not been watching, or had watched the wrong things. She needed to remember what the young man had told her yesterday: *Change how you watch.*

"Carefully now, little sister, Tuwakala," Tiva told the sandrat. "I will leave your house alone." The sandrat pulled all but the tip of its nose back into its den, and Tiva snaked her hand out from among the spines. "I will go elsewhere to hunt insects."

She circled the tree, looking for more bristly spots. There was one as high as she could reach, but it would be too hard to get past the spines and cut out the insect nest at the end of her reach. Finally, she chose a small nest on a branch about chest height. As she cut the nest away and dropped it into her bag, she heard a cracking sound above her.

A sandrat—perhaps the one she had seen before—stood perched on one of the largest spines. Its long slender arms and hand-like paws were perfect for reaching past the short bristles of spines and into a gembug nest high above Tiva's head. The rat cracked a gembug between its teeth, then dropped the jewel-like carapace into the sand at the base of the spine tree.

Tiva dropped to her knees in the coarse dirt. It was littered with gembug carapaces. Why had she never noticed this before? The bright blue gembug armor glittered in the sunlight like tiny jewels. She scooped them up, dirt and all, into her sack. She could winnow them like grass seed to remove the dirt.

The sandrat chittered above her. "Thank you, Tuwakala," Tiva said. She followed the rat as it moved around the spine tree trunk, found another gembug nest, and started cracking more insects open.

A low rumble rolled over the desert, and girl and sandrat paused to peer at the sky. Clouds had rolled in while Tiva had been occupied gathering gembugs. The thunderstorm Tiva had felt earlier had arrived, unnoticed.

Quickly, Tiva scooped up as much of the gembug-bright dirt as she could, then tied the bag securely and lashed it into her basket. If the thunderstorm was here now, had it rained earlier in the mountains? She had not thought to watch, to notice if there were clouds over the mountains.

She started up the narrow, dusty trail, then paused when the sandrat chittered. The low rumble of thunder came again, louder. The sandrat had run to its den and hung outside, clutching a long spine and scolding.

If a flash flood came down Dry Gorge, the tree would survive the crushing force of the water, but the sandrat's home would be flooded. Did the rat have babies in its den? Would it come with her? Heartbeats later she stood beneath the tree once more, reaching up into the den. "Tuwakala, help me save your babies," she told the anxiously chittering sandrat. "I can't see into your den."

Did the sandrat hear? Did it understand? Tiva felt something warm and wriggly beneath her hand, picked it up, and transferred a sandrat no longer than her little finger into her basket. Another, then another, until seven squeaking youngsters crawled over one another in her basket. An adult—the father?—leaped from the mouth of the den to her basket, followed by the original sandrat, who had kept watch clinging to a long spine halfway up the tree.

As Tiva raced for the path there was different rumbling, not thunder accompanying the clouds. Tiva risked a look up the gorge, then turned back to watch her footing in the treacherous gravel. She saw nothing yet, but the noise grew ever louder. Higher she climbed, glancing nervously backward every few steps. Then a wall of water, dirty brown and full of sticks and stones, thundered down the gorge toward her.

She stopped looking back, spent all her energy scrambling up the chancy path. In her basket, the sandrats were quiet now, and she couldn't even feel them moving. Heart pounding, she used hands and feet to drag herself up.

She was almost to the top when a hand reached down and pulled her over the gorge's rim and into gusting wind. She stood, breathing hard, staring down at the murky depths of the water racing through the gorge.

"Thank you," she said when she had caught her breath and no longer trembled. She turned to see who had helped her.

It was a woman, middle-aged, plump and rosy cheeked. Her headscarf was woven in green and brown zigzags, her tunic green, and her skirt, whipped against her legs by storm winds, was brown. No village Tiva knew used those colors.

"You're a long way from home," the woman said, helping Tiva brush dirt from her skirt.

"I came for the gembugs," Tiva said simply. All the villages shared Dry Gorge, for it was the best source anywhere for gembugs and other plants and animals that thrived between its walls.

"So I see." The woman smiled. "And do you also gather sandrats?"

"Ah. No, I was saving them from the flood. Mama rat was cracking gembugs for me. . . ." she trailed off. That sounded absurd, even though it had seemed, at the time, as if that was exactly what was happening.

"I am sure they are grateful not to be down in that." The woman indicated the roiling water below them with a nod.

"Ye-yes." Tiva watched the water with a little shiver of horror. What if she hadn't made it up the path quickly enough? Whole trees floated down the once-dry gorge, smashing into the walls with the water's force. The flood hadn't reached the top of the great spine tree, but Tiva was sure the sandrats could not have carried their babies up the trunk in time.

"You were watching well today," the woman told her.

Tiva stared at her. The young man yesterday had spoken of watching. It was because of his words that she had noticed the gembug carapaces glittering in the dirt. But she had almost let the flash flood take her because she hadn't been paying attention to the sky. "Not as well as I could have," she muttered.

Thunder rumbled, and Tiva looked up at shining gray clouds hurrying across the sky, sped on by the wind that threatened to pull her headscarf off. "I need to get home," she said.

"As do they." The woman waved a hand at Tiva's basket.

"Oh, the sandrats." Tiva looked around. There were spine trees here, gnarled by wind and lack of water. Strong trees, survivors in a way different from those in the gorge bottom. When she walked over to inspect one, one of the adult sandrats leaped from basket to branch. It ran along the branch, avoiding spines the length of its body with ease. At the trunk it paused, then scampered upward. Around the trunk, along another branch, it explored the tree from top to bottom.

It stopped at a whiskery growth tucked between the trunk and the base of a branch. Twisting its long, supple body around the spines, it reached a paw into the nest and brought forth gembugs to crunch. It chittered, and the other adult sandrat followed it to the nest. Tiva watched in fascination as the two opened up the gembug nest and made themselves a hole to hide in. In the doing they spilled what must be generations of gembug carapaces into the sand at the tree's base.

"Little brother, little sister—Tuwakala—do you want your babies there?"

The response of the longer, yellower of the pair—the mother, Tiva thought—was to reach out a slender paw and chitter some more. Tiva took the basket off her back and, one by one, transferred squirming, squeaking youngsters from the folds of the sack into the hole.

When she'd moved them all she thought for a moment, then pulled her headscarf off. Storm wind whipped hair into her face, but she ignored that and handed the fabric to the sandrat. "To soften your new nest," she said. It was appropriate, she thought, for the blue stripes in the scarf came from gembug dye. The sandrat pulled the scarf into the hole, blocking the entrance so Tiva could no longer see the sandrat family.

Thunder crashed, overhead it seemed, and Tiva couldn't help cringing as she looked up. Strands of hair stung her face, and she shivered.

"A fine storm."

Tiva started. In her concern for the sandrats she'd forgotten the woman. Now she glanced over to see her standing tall, head thrown back, arms raised above her head. She'd taken off her headscarf, released her knee-length hair from its braids, and it writhed around her like something living. Tiva wanted to hide behind the tree, spines or no. Surely this was no normal woman, but a god. What would a god see in Tiva, the painter who never painted?

A gust tore the headscarf from the woman's hand, and Tiva seized it before it could be blown away.

"Keep that," the woman said, turning her face to the wind.

Tiva also faced into the wind, that her hair would be blown back from her face and she could tame it with the green-and-brown headscarf. What should she think, that this powerful being had given her a token?

"We must go now." The woman set off running through the desert, angling against the wind. Her destination seemed the line on the horizon where the cliffs of Ayantavi lay.

Tiva looked at the gembug carapaces spilled beneath the spine tree, wanting to pick them up. But the woman had said they must go *now*. She could return for the gembugs another day.

She shouldered her basket and, feet sure in the harder dirt past the gorge's lip, ran after the woman. The woman was already far ahead and she pushed herself, lengthening her stride. The wind shifted, pushing at her back rather than her side, as if to help her catch up.

Breath came easily now, the itchy thunder feeling of the air gone. The wind, damp with rain that never touched the desert floor, caressed her arms and back, helped her along, as her strides steadily shortened the distance between herself and the other.

Then she was nearly even with the woman, who ran well for one so plump. "Who are you?" she called.

"A friend," the woman said, and the distance between them began to grow once more. "Who are you?"

Normally she would have answered 'Tiva of Ayantavi,' but she was certain that was not what the woman really asked. *Who am I?* She was Tiva, daughter of her parents, sister to her brothers, apprentice to Yongosona. She would be those things no matter what—they were external, not something inside. Who was she inside? Who was the real Tiva?

Like a gust of damp wind, the answer came. "I . . . am a painter." She ran on, then said with more conviction, "I *am* a painter." Even though she was still an apprentice, even though she had painted only one thing that satisfied her, she knew she was a painter. The conviction raced through her body and left it tingling with a feeling like the earlier thunder itch, but much stronger.

"And. . . ?" The woman was farther ahead of her again, the wind shredding her words.

"And much more," Tiva said, unable to put feelings into words. She had pushed a doorflap in her mind aside and found a whole room of being behind it, and the things there dizzied her. There was the seeing that Honovi would never be a painter, and that the shells on the west bank of the Sikanvahu River yielded a better pigment than those on the east. There was the touch of her mother's hand on her cheek and her father's strong grip as he lifted her higher on a cliff to reach an abandoned bird nest. There was the comfort of a purring cat and the discontent of never painting a Soul Wall. This and much more swirled into a cord that tugged her forward.

As she struggled with that innerness, the woman had become a distant brown-and-green figure, moving across the desert with the grace and speed of a gazelope. Tiva pushed some of the tingling energy into her legs to strengthen her stride, and satisfaction washed through her as she gained on the woman once more. A question burned in her mind, one she thought the woman could answer.

The woman seemed to sense that Tiva approached her, and she sped up. Tiva drew breath deep into her lungs, and the muscles of her legs adjusted to a new, faster rhythm. Her arms moved easily, open-handed, at her sides, and she sucked damp storm wind into her nostrils to fuel her body.

The woman ran, and Tiva followed, gaining over time. Their speed grew, and burning began in Tiva's calves, the bones of her hips, her shoulders and back. Still she pushed to go faster, faster than she'd ever run, even in a sprint. It was harder to drag the damp air into her lungs now. In the dizziness beginning in her head, she almost lost the question she must ask. But the woman was just ahead, and in a moment would be close enough that Tiva could call out to her.

Tiva did not think the woman was running; she skimmed the ground like a low-flying eagle. Even the swiftest runners of all the villages had never raced an eagle, but now Tiva ran, ran until she could almost touch the woman's green tunic. She gasped out her question. "How . . . do . . . I . . . see . . . souls?"

The woman turned her head, on her face a grin like the young man's the day before.

"You have already begun," she said.

Darkness surrounded them. Tiva had not been watching where the woman led her, had just run, run with all her strength and will. The ground beneath her feet turned from the sometimes tricky desert sands to something firmer. The woman was a moving shadow among shadows, and Tiva poured everything she had left into staying with her. If she lost sight of the woman in this darkness, she would never see the harsh desert sunlight again.

Tiva ran, straining body and lungs. The walls around her—for she was in a cave now, a cave that stretched on and on—glowed with pale green and yellow designs. There was no opportunity for Tiva to look at them; she noted their existence and ran on. *Have I begun to see souls?* she asked herself as burning pain and exhaustion coursed through her body. *I do not understand Tiva; how can I understand others?*

A flicker of movement ahead in the pallid glow. The woman had disappeared into one of many openings in the cave walls. Tiva fixed her eyes on that one opening, indistinguishable from all the others, and pushed herself harder than she had yet. Pain shot up her legs, her lungs seared, but she reached the opening just as her strength failed.

The effort was as difficult as if she had pushed through a solid wall. Then something blazed through her, from aching feet to the top of her head. She stopped, swaying and gasping, then took a deep breath that wasn't desperate, that didn't struggle for acceptance in overtaxed lungs.

She was in a small cave, rounded like the inside of a pot, as she imagined the interior of the sandrat's den must be. The walls and ceiling shone in patterns and colors so bright that she had to squint to look at them. She followed the flow of a woman's hair as it became a mountain in a range, designs on a lizard's back. But the lizard was a cornfield, and the ears of corn, blossoms on a peach tree.

One section drew her with a sharp internal sense of recognition. The painting flowed and built with the other patterns, but she felt a distinction. This was a pattern she had lived with, a pattern she had felt. Jewel-bright glowing colors shaped essence and personality in a way she could not describe, could only feel.

She stepped forward, hand out to touch that section of wall, to understand what drew her to the desert tortoise that was also a storm cloud over purple cliffs.

Someone put a brush into her outstretched hand. The strange woman's voice said, "Now is your time to paint, Tiva."

There was no paint pot, no bark on which to mix colors, no fresh plaster. There was only the brush and the wall, and clear space beside or above or within Yongosona's tortoise.

Tiva set brush to wall, drew a long curve that followed the curve of the tortoise shell but was separate, distinct. It was the same clear summer-sky blue that crushed gembugs made. She filled her lungs with the odor of sandrose leaves and sun-heated sand, felt the tingle of thunder weather far away, and painted a brilliant zigzag descending from the storm clouds.

Then blue and red swirls—her dancing skirt at the spring gatherings—and the brilliant yellow taste of ceremonial corn cakes. Here her mother chanting as she ground corn, and there her brother's giggle. Ochre in all its shades—brown through yellow to red—built into the orphaned pup she was raising, a shaggy-coated dog herding sheep away from a cliff edge.

The peach tree, the branch she had drawn in charcoal on the wall of another cave, grew spine tree fruit and chicken eggs, then swirled into feather ferns that grew in sheltered places along the Sikanvahu River.

She sank to the cave floor exhausted, the brush lost somewhere under her skirts as she collapsed. She had not finished her painting—but how could she? She herself was barely begun. There were even places to fill in Yongosona's painting—her long life was not yet complete, and her painting, now joined with Tiva's, was vibrant yet.

"Who are you?" A whisper filled the cave, sourceless.

"I am. . . ." Tiva? A painter? Or something more? "I am everything I have ever seen or felt or thought or smelled or heard. I am sandrats in spine trees and gembugs they crack between their teeth. I am thunder and flood. . . ." There was more, but no words for the storm of perception.

"Does that answer your question?" She could not see the woman whose voice filled the cavern with warmth.

Tiva did not have to speak. Her soul, its walls thinned by understanding, communed with painters who had known her village in generations past. There had to be that understanding, and it could not be taught. She had won through.

☥❦☤

W hen Tiva sat up, she lay, arm across her basket, at the base of the path up to Ayantavi. Trembling, she pushed herself to her feet and settled the basket on her back. Had what she just felt, seen, done—had it been real? How could she paint with a brush that had no paint?

Whatever it had been, real or a vision from a god, it had changed her. She did not doubt, now, that she could paint. *She could paint!* Whether for Soul Walls or not, the painting had sunk beneath her skin, as much a part of her as her bones. The warmth of that knowledge buoyed her as she started up the path.

Sun rays shot from beneath storm clouds on the horizon, bathing Ayantavi in pink-gold light. Tiva jogged along the plateau to Yongosona's home, the basket on her back no burden. Yongosona looked up from where she sat grinding pigments, the light erasing years, bringing back her youth.

"There was a storm," Yongosona stated.

"Yes. A flash flood in Dry Gorge." Tiva took the basket from her back and held it out to Yongosona.

"You remembered the warnings."

Tiva acknowledged that with a brief motion of her head, and Yongosona took the basket. She opened the bag, sifted its contents through her fingers. "Much dirt."

"I'll sift the insects out."

Yongosona set the basket aside. "Sit." Tiva dropped to the mat beside her. "Tomorrow, we finish Chumana's Soul Wall. And the next Wall—I think it will be Honovi's—*you* will paint."

Tiva had wanted this since her eighth summer, when she came to Yongosona. She should be excited. But the knowledge achieved in the cavern under the mesa filled her, radiating from her body like the last golden rays of sunlight. "I must learn her soul."

"Yes, you must."

The sun set behind Red Cliff, and thunder rumbled, muted by distance.

LITTLE RED

by Melissa Mead

Learning either sword fighting or sorcery takes a great deal of time (measured in years, if not decades) and effort, so even if a girl has the ability to do either, she's still going to have to make a choice of which path to take. This can be much more difficult that it seems—especially if her choice isn't the one her family wants her to make.

Melissa Mead's stories have appeared in *Sword & Sorceress XXIII, Aberrant Dreams, NewMyths.com*, and various other places. She lives in upstate New York with her wonderful husband and two cats. Her Web page is http://carpelibris.wordpress.com/melissa-mead.

There once was a girl who always wore a little red hood and cape, so everyone called her Little Red Riding Hood.

She would have preferred Red the Bloody Blade, but her mother wouldn't trust her with anything larger than a bread knife, and refused to give Red fighting lessons. Instead, once a week she sent Red off to her grandmother's to learn witchery.

"But Mother, sorcery is for old women! Old ugly women, who like pottering about with smelly leaves and bat guano. There is nothing glamorous about bat guano. You're turning me into a Crone, Mother! I'm much better suited to be a warrior. Bruno the Blacksmith said he'd give me lessons, and the Amazons are always hiring. You're ruining my career aspirations."

"Ethelberta Smith, we're fairy-tale peasants. We don't have career aspirations. Crone is a perfectly respectable occupation. Now take this basket of hearty, nourishing goodies to your grandmother. Don't even think about calling her an ugly crone, and please, try to learn something besides Introductory Candle Lighting."

When Red's mother used her given name, Red knew she'd better obey. She took the basket and set off through the woods.

Red knew that her mother and grandmother expected her to study magical plants along the way, but instead she practiced swordplay with the butter knife from the basket. Absorbed in her footwork, she paid no attention to the enormous wolf pacing beside her.

"Ahem. This is the part where you scream and flee in terror," said the wolf in a voice like a dog gnawing on a bone. "Oh . . . and it's also the part where you drop that basket."

Red whirled and pointed the knife at it. "Stand back! I know how to use this!"

It sniffed the end of the blunt utensil. "So do I. You Humans grease your bread with it. Bizarre habit. Do I smell sausage?"

"Yes, and you're not getting any of it. It's for my sweet, beloved and wise Granny, who lives just down that path."

"Please?" the wolf whined.

"No."

"Just one little link?"

"No."

"Half of one?"

"No. Shoo."

The wolf growled, showing startlingly white, sharp teeth. It bristled and charged—past Red, down the path toward

Granny's house. As soon as her heart restarted and she realized she was still alive, and not wolf kibble, Red charged after it.

ୡଓଽ୪ୗ

G ranny's door handle had wolf slobber on it. Not good. Red knocked on a non-slobbery part of the door.

"Who is it?" called a voice that sounded like a mastiff trying to sing soprano.

Red winced, but decided to play along for now. "It's Ethelberta, Granny!"

Long pause. "Who?"

"Ethelberta Smith! Your beloved granddaughter. You held me at my christening. You cleared up that misunderstanding with those porridge-eating bears last year. You raised me until I was three. That Ethelberta!"

Another pause. "Sorry, not ringing any bells."

"Red hood and cape? That you made for me?"

"Oh, THAT Ethelburger! My dear, sweet granddaughter. Of course. Come in, my darling child. You don't know how much I've missed you."

Red shouldered the door open, dreading a scene of bloody carnage. She'd never seen Granny do anything impressive like shoot lightning bolts at people, and she could never fight off a wolf.

The room looked pretty much like it always did: red-and-white checked cloth and a vase of flowers on the table, copper kettle hanging over the fire in the fireplace, the scent of Granny's latest potion hanging in the air. In the bedroom, the only things out of the ordinary were the flannel-nightgowned wolf in Granny's bed and a notable absence of Granny.

"You brought me sausage, you sweet child!" said the wolf. "I could just eat you up."

Red's heart was pounding. This could get ugly. She wished in vain for a sword, and tried to remember the spells that

Granny had taught her. None of them dealt with talking wolves in nightcaps. Paralysis required certain mushrooms—or a stout club and good aim, none of which Red had. Besides, the last time she'd had a lesson in mushrooms . . . well, thank goodness Granny knew her antidotes.

"What big eyes you have, Granny!" she exclaimed, stalling.

"The better to see you with, my dear." The wolf watched her, seeming amused.

Blindness! If the wolf couldn't see her, it couldn't eat her. But that took six ounces of crushed fireflies and a phoenix egg—way beyond any fairy-tale peasant's budget. Even Granny wouldn't have that on hand. "What big ears you have!"

"The better to hear you with." The wolf licked its chops.

Ears. Red listened. Granny's thatch-roofed cottage housed generations of skittering mice. A sudden influx of plump, spell-dazzled rodents should be enough to distract any sane predator.

Trying to look casual, Red approached the bed—and the wall—and started whistling a tune she'd learned from a boy across the river in Hamlin. Enthralled mice crept out onto the cottage floor, but the wolf didn't even glance at them.

"Why, what big teeth you have, Granny!" Red said, pointing at the mice and willing the wolf to take the hint.

It didn't. "The better to eat you with!" The wolf sprang. Red screamed and cast her Introductory Candle Lighting spell.

The wolf's tail burst into flame. It howled—and transformed into Granny, beating at the back of her nightgown.

"Ethelberta Smith, that was the most ham-handed mishandling of a crisis I've ever seen. Didn't you wonder how a wolf could talk, or why it was wearing my nightgown? A simple Perception spell . . . and did you never notice the Wolfsbane in the vase on the table?"

Red sat quietly under the tirade, the picture of chastised penitence. "But Granny," she said, "don't you always say "Any spell is the right one if everyone gets out alive in the end?"

Granny stopped in mid-scold, and sighed. "I do. Very well; get those mice out of here and get lunch ready while I fix this gown. Candle-lighting . . . you'll be the death of me yet, Ethelberta!"

"Oh, I hope not, Granny dear!" said Red earnestly. She busied herself with setting the table in order to hide her triumphant grin.

If she could manage a few more months of this "incompetence," Mother just might reconsider giving her those sword lessons after all.

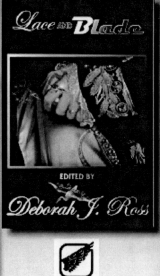

Norilana Books Proudly Presents...

TaLeKa

A New Dedicated Imprint

Showcasing the Works of **Tanith Lee**
and the Art of **John Kaiine**...

www.tanithlee.com

First title from the *Tales of the Flat Earth*

Night's Master by **Tanith Lee**
September 1, 2009

www.norilana.com/norilana-taleka.htm

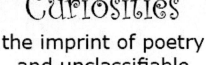

LaVergne, TN USA
17 August 2010

193647LV00004B/30/P

9 781607 620488